William Clark Russell

**An Ocean Free Lance**

A Novel

William Clark Russell

**An Ocean Free Lance**
*A Novel*

ISBN/EAN: 9783337032302

Printed in Europe, USA, Canada, Australia, Japan

Cover: Foto ©Andreas Hilbeck / pixelio.de

More available books at **www.hansebooks.com**

# A NOVEL

BY

## W. CLARK RUSSELL

Author of "The Wreck of the Grosvenor," "The Copsford Mystery,"
"My Danish Sweetheart," etc., etc.

NEW YORK
NEW AMSTERDAM BOOK COMPANY
156 FIFTH AVENUE
1896

# CONTENTS.

8 CONTENTS.

## CHAPTER X.

# LIST OF ILLUSTRATIONS.

# INTRODUCTORY.

FEW accounts of brilliant actions at sea exceed in interest those in which British privately armed vessels were concerned. The schooner *Tigress* was a well-known privateer, and the name of Shelvocke, who commanded her down to December, 1814, stood high for courage, humanity, and an exact conformity to the terms of his Government commission.

Only a portion of her cruise is related in these pages, for her chief officer's connection with her ceased when he took charge of the *Namur*, and his narrative of the beautiful vessel's exploits is interesting only so far as he was an eye-witness of them.

Privateering was abolished in 1856, by the Declaration of Paris, that is to say, abolished for Great Britain, which is all of that Declaration that need concern Englishmen. A singularly able treatise on this subject, entitled "Maritime Warfare," has been written by Mr. Thomas Gibson Bowles, who shows with such force of reasoning as no man who chooses to consider the subject carefully can resist, that in sanctioning the abolition of privateering, Great Britain, as the principal maritime power in the world, has directly weakened her State Navy, by depriving it of a valuable auxiliary, and by forfeiting, to quote Mr. Bowles's words, "one of the best schools for the formation of adventurous and daring sailors."

# AN OCEAN FREE LANCE.

## CHAPTER I.

### CAPTAIN SHELVOCKE.

It was on a day in the summer of the year 1812, that being completely, and I may say mercifully, recovered from a long and trying illness, the seeds of which had been planted in me by a fever taken in Bombay twelve months before, I left my lodgings near Charing Cross to call upon a firm of ship-owners whose offices were in the City. When I was near Temple Bar, I observed a man look me very full and eagerly in the face; our eyes met, and I seemed to know him; but my mind being full of business, I was walking on without giving him further attention, when he came after me, and stopped me by laying his hand on my shoulder.

"Madison!" cried he, "why, this is a real stroke of luck! Only a minute ago I'd have given any man ten pounds to tell me how I might find you. Where have you been lying hidden all these months; and where are you bound to now?"

"I am heartily glad to see you again, Captain Shelvocke," said I, shaking his hand cordially. "You'll forgive me, I hope, for not immediately making out the old lines under that big beard. You have not forsaken the old *Bombay Castle*, I hope, sir?"

"You want to know as much as I do," he answered, laughing, "and I see there's a yarn to be spun on both sides. But this pavement isn't the quarter-deck of a ship, Madison, and the cockneys know how to use their elbows. Are you in a hurry?"

"No, sir."

"Then come along with me," said he, passing his arm

through mine; and he led me across the road into a chop-house, full of bulkheaded boxes like the pews of a church, and a table in each box. It was hot in this place, for the ceiling was so low a short man might have touched it with his fingers; and the smell of cooked meat and the fumes of candles at the aftermost end, were the daylight was small, made the room like a cockpit in the tropics. Most of the boxes were occupied, but the place was quiet, the people talking low, and the attendants moving about leisurely. We seated ourselves in an empty box, and Shelvocke called for a couple of chops and a pint of Madeira. He then, with a peculiar smile, asked me if I had a ship.

"No, sir; but I am out on that very business."

"Have you been ill?" he inquired.

"Very ill indeed, but, thank God! I am sound enough now."

"I guessed by your hands that you had been on the sick-list," said he. "They are as thin as a poet's, and, flattery apart, your face is as tallowy as a Portuguee's. So you are going to look for a ship. As captain?"

I answered that if I was offered a captain's berth I certainly should not refuse it; but that I did not hope to get more than a mate's post this time. He looked me stead-fastly in the face, and leaning across the table and drop-ping his voice, said:

"It seems intended by this meeting that we should sail together. How would you relish the notion of being mate of a privateer under my command?"

"I should like nothing better," I answered quickly.

"By this proposal, Madison, I really intend a compli-ment. You and I are old shipmates, and know each other's calibre. Shall you ever forget our brush in the *Bombay Castle* with the French picaroon? The recollection of your behavior on that occasion brought you into my mind when this new command was given me, and I tell you frankly I should not have considered my complement complete had I been obliged to sail without you."

I thanked him for his good words.

"The mate I had intended to take is a smartish fellow," said he, "but no *fighter*—not a cur, but just a plain, sturdy merchantman. In a venture of this kind I must be well supported, and I mean to get a retiring pension out of it; I intend that the French and our old friend Jonathan shall endow me, Madison, and your share should set you up as a squire—a regular, landed, stiff-rumped Tory, my lad—with a seat in the House and strong views on the illegality of privateering."

He filled my glass, and we drank to each other. He was in high spirits, toward which his meeting with me had not a little contributed. When I had sailed with him in the *Bombay Castle* in 1809, he had worn shoulder-of-mutton whiskers; but he had since let his beard and mustache grow, and his face looked as much like a lion's as could very well be imagined of a human countenance. He was not handsome, though many persons admired the rugged strength and breadth of his massive features. His hair and beard were a dark red, his complexion brown with sunburn, his eyes small, gray, and extraordinarily keen, brilliant, and steadfast in their gaze; he stood a fraction over six feet high, and his limbs and shoulders were in perfect proportion with his stature. I knew him to be a fine seaman, a person of great resolution, and as brave as any man of that age; and the manner in which he had engaged the French picaroon of which he had spoken, his own ship having only sixty men and mounting four eighteen-pound carronades, while the enemy had a crew of one hundred and thirty desperate fellows and carried three timess our weight of metal, was an instance of daring and seamanship which will not readily be matched by examples drawn from actions in which merchantmen were engaged.

"Will you ask some questions first?" said he, "or shall we call it settled without palaver?"

"Settled without palaver!" I exclaimed. "I want no better chief than you, Captain Shelvocke."

"So!" said he, whipping out a pocket-book: "Mr. Julian Madison, first mate of the *Tigress*, pay (so many) pounds a month while at sea and the usual share in prizes."

He scratched this matter down, replaced the book, and we then turned to and ate our chops without further parley.

"Phew!" cried he; "this is too hot. There ought to be a room at the back yonder where a man can breathe the London air through a skylight, and take a whiff of tobacco."

He got up and went down the room and through a door into a small apartment. Some more wine was brought us, and Shelvocke drew a handful of cigars from his pocket, real Cuban leaf, and exquisitely aromatic. After he had asked me several questions about the voyages I had taken since I left the *Bombay Castle*, and the nature of my illness, and if I stood in need of money, he said that, in consequence of having lost three very valuable cargoes, which had been seized by French privateers, Mr. Wilson Hannay, the head of the firm of Hannay, Meadows & Son, of East India Avenue, had purchased a brand-new, extremely beautiful and powerful vessel of three hundred and twenty-three tons burden, and rigged her as a schooner, and armed her with some very heavy metal for a craft of her size. She was called the *Tigress*, and her lines had been laid for blockade-running, though it was believed that she had been built for the Dey of Algiers, and her scantling resembled a frigate's. It was expected that she would not only prove the fastest thing afloat, but one of the most weatherly.

"However," said Shelvocke, "you will be seeing her soon, and then you can judge for yourself. If I can only get out of her two-thirds of the speed her lines promise, Hannay shall admit that he never invested money more wisely than when he brought her."

"How many men do you carry?"

"Ninety; and there's room for a hundred and fifty. I have four mates—yourself, first; Silas Chestree, second; Buck Tapping, third; and Philip Peacock, fourth. Do you know any of these men?"

"No."

"They are all smart seamen, and have seen rough service. In work of this kind you want good navigators and plucky fellows for the prizes."

"When do you sail, sir?"

"On Monday next, from the West India Docks, stopping at Erith to take in our powder. There has been some delay over the letter of marque, for the Admiralty people are growing scrupulous, and the description of the vessel had to be altered, for Hannay meant at first to equip her with ten eighteens; but I prevailed upon him to substitute four forty-two pound carronades for close action, and a couple of heavy chasers. The whole adventure is the result of Hannay's rage over the loss of his ships. 'See here, Shelvocke,' said he, when he offered me the command of the *Tigress*, 'a letter of marque, you know, means reprisals, and my motive in equipping this vessel is that she may sink or blow up or capture as many French and Yankee merchantmen as she can overhaul. I don't want any man-of-war work done. Give your heels to the cruisers, and leave the forts to the admirals. I wish you to make the enemy's pocket smart; and I shall be as well pleased to hear of the vessels you have sunk or burnt as of the vessels you have brought in as prizes."

"Rather vindictive!" said, I laughing.

"Ay," he answered, with a twinkle in his eye; "but if the enemy's pocket is to smart it must be done by filling ours; and if we can see our way to enlarge the King's fleet by the addition of a sloop or two, we'll make the venture, Madison."

"Have you any particular cruising-ground in your mind, sir?"

"I shall hang about the Channel for a spell, and see what's to be got there. Some pickings ought to be found between Grisnez and Ushant. But the Bahama latitudes will be our later haunt, for the cotton ships bring a good bit of money." He then said that the tide would serve early on Monday morning, and that I need not be aboard before Sunday night.

The prospect of a cruise of this description pleased me greatly. My life had been passed in the merchant-service; and over and over again, when news of our brilliant successes at sea had reached me, I had groaned in spirit over the humdrum monotony of my seafaring experiences, the feeble chances they offered me of enriching myself or improving my position, and regretted that my father had not stuck to his original intention of entering me as a midshipman in the Navy instead of apprenticing me to a merchant captain.

Indeed, this was a period in the history of the Navy when merit and courage had chances such as had never before offered. In every direction officers were being promoted and decorated; prize-money was enriching hundreds, and laying the foundation of future fortunes; the Gazettes were choked with the records of brilliant deeds and the nation was filled with heroes. But these distinctions, as regards the sea, were limited to the Navy. Now and again, it is true, the master of a merchantman who had gallantly fought his ship against heavy odds would receive a purse of money or a piece of plate; but a great number of heroic exploits, which, had they been performed by naval officers, would have earned them the thanks of the country and have loaded them with civic gifts and courtly honors, were unnoticed, and the only satisfaction these brave men received was the applause of their own conscience.

On the other hand, if but little glory attached to the actions of privateers there was a great deal of money to be made by that kind of work, and the life included all the dash and romance of the naval service without its biting restraints. A privateersman owned only his captain as master. He fought for himself, but in fighting for himself he also fought for the British colors: and I am bold enough to say that not a little of the influence exercised by the "meteor flag" on the minds and nerves of the enemies of Great Britain was owing to the spirit and bravery of the English privateers of that age.

Shelvocke and I sat for an hour talking of our chances in the *Tigress,* and of the declaration of war against this country by the United States of America, the news of which had not long reached England. It was generally believed that there was more swagger than boldness in this declaration, and Congress were only courting a terrible punishment. But Shelvocke did not take this view.

"It's not fashionable," said he, "and it certainly, wouldn't be thought patriotic in an Englishman to speak a good word for the Yankees; but I am not going to be led away by prejudice. Mark what I say—the Americans will not be swallowed up quite so easily as we true Britons imagine. The way in which they turned us out of their country and beat our ships in the last war shows the sort of marrow they've got in their bones. To see a little cock, fresh and yellow from his shell, sparring up to, aye, and cornering a tough old rogue like John Bull is something to make one reflective. We shall be hearing 'Yankee Doodle' piped well to the east'ard of the Start before many weeks are over; and now that war is declared, I don't mind owning that I am thankful my estate is not in English bottoms."

He got up after thus expressing himself, and appointing an hour for me to meet him next morning at the offices in East India Avenue, he shook me heartily by the hand, and we parted.

2

# CHAPTER II.

I was much gratified by the eagerness with which Shelvocke had offered me a berth under him, and the pleasure my acceptance of it gave him. And so far as I was concerned, my meeting with him was extremely opportune, for, though I could still lay my hand on a little ready money, my illness had brought the locker low, and it was high time for me to be afloat. I had no wife, nor parents, nor relatives of any kind to give or make me a home in England, to link me to the land, nor to give significance to any sort of adventures I might have a mind to enter upon.

Being alone, I had leisure to think over my agreement with Shelvocke; and the longer I reflected upon it, the gayer grew the picture of the future. It would be a new life to me, full of dash, light, and activity. It was taking the whole ocean as a theatre for one's exploits. In imagination I felt and enjoyed the freedom of it. I pictured the chase, the rushing of white waters, the cloud of canvas soaring upon the horizon ahead, the flames and the thunder of guns, the rich capture, the dark nights, the crowd of determined men to command, the endless excitements of a roving commission and an ocean swarming with enemies' ships.

With fancies of this kind I amused myself for the rest of the day: and next morning, punctually to the hour of appointment, I presented myself at the offices of Hannay, Meadows & Son. Captain Shelvocke was waiting for me. He and Hannay were together in a private office, and I heard the sound of Hannay's voice before the door was opened.

This gentleman, who at that time was reckoned one of the wealthiest men in the city of London, and who filled several posts of honor and trust in connection with the city companies and the corporation, was a fat, red-faced man, with a great crop of perfectly white hair standing erect on his head, like the long grass in a field. He said he was glad to find me again in his employ—no doubt Shelvocke had been praising me, and I had not sailed in any ship owned by the firm since I quitted the *Bombay Castle*—but that he was afraid his conscience would trouble him for letting loose so bloodthirsty a man upon the French, much as he hated that people and eager as he was to have a hand in the destruction of their ships.

I answered that I hoped I should not be thought more bloodthirsty than I looked, and that I should not look more bloodthirsty than I was.

"But you like fighting," said he, "don't you?"

"I shall always be willing to fight when occasion requires, sir," I answered.

"No man can say more than that," exclaimed Shelvocke.

"When the occasion to fight *does* arise," said Hannay, twisting the great seals under his waistcoat irritably, "you will please to remember, Mr. Madison, that the owner of the *Tigress* has lost upward of forty-eight thousand pounds through the French. That's a grievance, I submit, Shelvocke, big enough to sharpen a cutlass upon. The French owe me forty-eight thousand pounds, and, by heaven, gentlemen, the *Tigress'* cannon-shot shall make them liquidate!"

"We'll do our best for you, Mr. Hannay," said Shelvocke. "And now that I have Madison, I'll say, and I am glad he hears me, that never since, privateering became a business, did any vessel go out of dock with a better company of men than the *Tigress* starts with."

"I'll do my share too, Shelvocke," exclaimed Hannay, walking up and down the room impetuously. "You have my orders to stint nothing. Whatever may make your ship formidable, buy! The small arms I left to you!"

"I'll warrant them, sir."

"I am still of opinion you err in not taking in a load of dismantling-shot. Wicked ideas are not always *bad* ideas, sir. Star-shot are a Yankee notion I should like to see aboard the *Tigress*. Your business is to cripple, whether you run or board, and star-shot will wreck a three-decker in twenty minutes if plied well."

"Mr. Hannay, I would as soon load my guns with broken bottles and tenpenny nails. If round-shot, and grape, and canister can't do our business, we must give up," exclaimed Shelvocke, with a little show of warmth.

Hannay looked at me as if he wished me to champion his views. But though I did not then know what star-shot were, I suspected a meanness in them, and held my peace.

"Well, Shelvocke," said the old gentleman, with a bland smile that I thought clever, seeing how quick he was with it, "you must e'en have your own way. But mark what I say—whatever may be thought of the *illegitimacy* of the Yankee's dismantling-shot, the British Navy will have to adopt sooner or later something that will wreck the spars of a ship more quickly than the missiles now in use. Can it be pretended that round and grape do half their work when we hear of ships coming out of engagements which have lasted for five and six hours with all their spars aloft? I think the invention of the dismantling-shot a monstrous clever thing. One of them will split a sail in halves, or sever one side of the standing rigging of a mast as though a knife were drawn across the shrouds. Will you tell me that round-shot do this?"

"Round-shot will do a deal of mischief, take my word, for it, Mr. Hannay," replied Shelvocke; and evidently wishing to cut short a distasteful discussion, he pulled out his watch, and exclaimed:

"Come, Madison, it is time to be off."

We shook hands with Mr. Hannay, and turned into Leadenhall Street.

"You would hardly suppose," said Shelvocke dryly, "that this advocate of a murderous invention is the founder and chairman of a Bible Society, that he has two sons in the Church, and that his friends quote him as a real example of benevolence, piety, and humanity. With all respect I would see him hanged before I'd use the shot he recommends. Do you know what they are like?"

"No."

"Imagine a dozen crowbars, each one about three feet

long, slung on a big iron ring, the spikes being kept together like a fagot of wood by bits of spun yarn, which are burnt by the discharge. That's one kind of dismantling-shot. Such things, no doubt, cut up the rigging of vessels, but I question if they do more injury to spars than round-shot. Their worst mischief lies among the men; they wound in the ghastliest way in the world. To use such shot is as bad, in my opinion, as poisoning an enemy's scuttlebutts. I am sorry that the Yankees, as an English-speaking people, should stoop to shin-kicking of this kind. With all Johnny Frenchman's faults, he is above-board; and when he *does* fight, he fights fair."

But though all this might be true enough, Shelvocke forgot in abusing the Yankees for employing what he considered, and what no doubt was, an unfair weapon, that the English had been willing to adopt a clockwork submarine engine that was designed to blow up the enemy's vessels with all hands aboard as they lay at anchor; though I admit that St. Vincent condemned the invention as inhuman, and predicted its failure. Nor in our wars have we scrupled to use fire-ships full of explosive material, and other infernal machines, the object of which was to destroy, without imperiling our own limbs, as much human life and property as such dastardly contrivances could come at. The truth is, we hated the Americans so bitterly in those days, that we never could find words sufficiently expressive of our detestation of even the tricks they had borrowed from our own methods of warfare. I do not defend any of the stratagems practised and the unfair weapons employed by the Yankees during their wars with this country: but I say that our condemnation of them comes very foolishly from us, who are accountable for more human lives destroyed by desperate and bloody inventions than any other nation on the face of the earth. As an instance, I knew a person who had sailed under Lord Cochrane, who assured me that he had often heard his lordship say he had a scheme by which he could decoy and kill a hundred thousand men, without risking a single life on our side. There never was, nor is there in this day, a braver officer than Cochrane; but will it be doubted that his scheme would have been submitted and adopted but for his unhappy quarrel with the Admiralty, by which the nation was deprived of the services of this brilliant, determined, and skilful seaman?

The West India Docks were full of ships, many of them Indiamen and South Traders, who, I was told, were loading as part of a great convoy that was to rendezvous at Torbay in the middle of August. The scene of the docks was very brilliant, for among the ships there was a great variety of build, and it was a sight to contrast the old Indiamen with their tall poops and overhanging quarter-galleries, their tops big enough to build a house in, their apple-shaped bows, and huge uncouth stems, and freeboards like the sides of a hill, with the modern long, low, piratical-looking vessels, many of which had been taken from the French and the models of which the English ship-builders were at last beginning to understand and imitate; while the whole surface of the sky over the docks was a mass of quivering color with the snake-like pulling of the long streamers from the mast-heads, and the flags and ensigns rippling at the peaks and the flag-staffs on the bowsprits and over the stern.

A man used to these peaceful times, or rather, I should say, to the change that has come over the spirit of the mer-cantile marine, would have been rather astonished by the formidable exhibition of guns aboard some of these homely traders, the shot piled round the hatches, the small-arms racks abaft the mainmast, and the resolute *fighting* cut of the crews at work upon the various vessels. After we had come to a certain place in the docks where we commanded a view of a large number of ships, Shelvocke grasped my arm and stopped me.

"Madison," said he, "you have a sharp eye. Look about you and tell me which vessel is the *Tigress.*"

There were several schooners in the docks, some of them large vessels, very smart and taut aloft, and most of them fairly answering to the description Shelvocke had given me of his ship. But I did not require to look about me long before hitting on my craft. We were five minutes' walk from her, but even at that distance she was instantly dis-tinguishable by a sailor as the loveliest vessel in the docks. She was lying alongside a high squab Indiaman, whose yards were braced up to allow the schooner to sit close; but the contrast was of little use to the *Tigress;* you needed to see her clear of all surroundings, alone upon the water, to do justice to her beautiful fabric.

"That should be your schooner, captain," said, I pointing to her.

"Yes, that's the *Tigress*. Is she not something to set a man's heart dancing?" he exclaimed, in a voice as impassioned as a lover's in speaking of his mistress, and forcing me to smile by the energy and intensity of it. "See," he said, drawing me a few paces forward and then stopping me afresh, "you catch her run here. Do you mark the swell of her side, the beauty of that faint inward curve from the water's edge to the rail of the bulwark? Observe how she tapers aft, until you might think it impossible that a gun could be trained through the stern-port. She has no channels to drag through the water, do you notice? Those chain-plates, with the dead-eyes coming inboard, strengthen the bulwarks, and are greasy things for a boarder's hands, while her beam gives a noble spread to the shrouds. But come along!" he cried, breaking into a laugh, and staring around him, "or they'll be taking me for some itinerant parson hired by Bonaparte to denounce the wickedness of fighting for one's country."

We walked to the schooner, and boarded her by scrambling over the Indiaman, whose decks were lumbered by a crowd of men swinging bales of goods into her capacious hold.

The *Tigress* was flush fore and aft, her main-hatchway small, and I never remember seeing such a roomy deck as hers. Her beam was twenty-seven feet, and her length a hundred and nine feet. She mounted a twenty-four-pounder on the forecastle, where there was plenty of room to work it. All her fining, indeed, was under water. Both the height and thickness of her bulwarks were unusual, for Shelvocke, six foot as he was, could only just see over the rail, and the gun-ports looked like embrasures in the walls of a castle. She carried six eighteen-pounders, three of a side, and four forty-two pound carronades, as well as the two twenty-four-pound chasers, making in all twelve guns. Her mainmast was eighty-four feet high, and the height from the deck to the topmast-head was very nearly a hundred and fifty feet; and as I glanced aloft at her magnificent spars, with the square-rig forward tapering into a little skysail-yard, and studding-sail boom-irons as high as her topgallant-yard, I had no trouble to guess the spacious folds of canvas she would be able to throw open to the wind when occasion required them.   Her hull was painted black, with a very narrow white streak running along the sides just under the gun-ports.   She sat low on the water, and would be lower yet when completely victualed and her crew aboard. But for her beam, her low freeboard would have threatened a wet ship in a seaway; but deep as she lay, her copper sheathing came a foot above the point of immersion, and the metal sparkled like new gold.

"What do you think of her?" asked Shelvocke, whose eyes had been fixed on my face while I noted these points.

"I think that for beauty and strength she's a wonder, sir," I answered, "and worthy to become a famous name."

"*That* we'll make her—at least among the mounseers!" he exclaimed, laughing.   "You can overhaul her below if you like, Mr. Madison," giving me the stiff *mister* on his own quarter-deck.   "I have to see a man on the *Palatine* lying yonder, but shall be aboard again presently."   And so saying, he went over the side.

The only man I had yet noticed on the schooner was an old sailor, who stumped up and down the starboard side of the forecastle with the regularity of a pendulum, occasion-ally pausing to squirt a quantity of tobacco-juice from his mouth over the bulwarks.   I walked to the companion, and went down the steps, noticing how the strength of the ves-sel's build was exhibited in the smallest detail, the brass handrail being as thick as a man's arm, and the scantling of the companion almost as stout as the bulwarks of a hun-dred-ton sloop.   On arriving at the bottom of the ladder, I found myself in a small cabin, lighted by a flat skylight over head.   The cabin was bulkheaded all around into berths, and against the partition dividing the after-cabin from the room used by the surgeon and the third and fourth mates, was a stand of muskets, cutlasses, and pikes, which gave a very grim and warlike look to the plain, dark-brown, and powerfully constructed interior.

A young man, who was reading at the table in the centre of the cabin, got up as I came down, and stared at me with an expression of surprise. He was as tall as Captain Shel-vocke, but for angularity and gauntness and general un-couthness I never saw his like; in short, he might have stood for the figure of the French musketeer in Hogarth's print of "Calais Gates." His immensely long legs when he was erect exactly resembled a pair of compasses clothed in ill-fitting trousers, and his monkey-jacket being unusually short, the length of his legs was proportionately exagger-ated. His ebony-colored hair was brushed down like a horse's tail, some inches below the collar of his coat; his dark, gleaming eyes were sunk deep in his head, and his capacious mouth appeared to extend the whole breadth of his jaws.

"Hallo, shipmate!" he exclaimed, in a hard, gruff voice, "where are you bound to? Your road home doesn't lie this way, does it?"

"Who the devil are you?" said I.

"You ask the question so civilly that I don't mind tell-ing you," he answered, with a grin that exposed a tremen-dous broadside of grinders. "I'm the second mate of this vessel; and if you've got any business to transact, please to let us hear of it."

"Then your name is Mr. Silas Chestree?" said I.

"At your service," he replied, making as if he would sit.

"My name is Mr. Julian Madison," said I; "and when I tell you I am chief mate of the *Tigress*, perhaps you'll be good enough to use me with a little civility."

"Chief mate! I'm very sorry, sir," he exclaimed, pull-ing off his hat and throwing it on the table. "It was im-possible for me to guess who you were, sir. I understood from Captain Shelvocke that Mr. Hollings was to be chief mate."

"Captain Shelvocke has done me the honor to appoint me in the room of Mr. Hollings," said I. "However, you are not to blame, Mr. Chestree, as I should have introduced myself to you at once. As it is to be shoulder to shoulder with us all, we'll shake hands."

He squeezed my fingers with a grip that made them almost bloodless, and seemed to think himself very fortu-nate that I should overlook his rudeness so quickly and easily.

Accompanied by this officer, I took advantage of Shelvocke's absence to thoroughly inspect the vessel, noting every point for my own satisfaction, and with the intention of indicating any weakness I might come across. Mr. Chestree told me that all the work had been done by the dockyard people, and that the crew were coming aboard on Saturday. He said Captain Shelvocke had found no difficulty in obtaining a crew; indeed, upward of two hundred men had offered, on hearing that the vessel that wanted seamen was the *Tigress,* and that the pick of them, every man being a native of Great Britain, had been selected, and that there were not above five boys among the whole lot of them. The more critically I inspected the schooner, the more she pleased me. Every improvement that had been suggested by the long maritime wars in which England had been engaged was adopted. The only doubt I had was whether she was not too heavily armed for speed, although I could not question the value of the long guns in the event of being chased by the large frigates and line-of-battle ships which the French had launched broadcast upon the seas.

In about an hour's time, Captain Shelvocke came aboard again, and took me into his cabin, where we had a long talk over the schooner and her equipment, and the plans he had in his mind. He was very sanguine, and believed that he should be able to achieve any end he designed with such a vessel as the *Tigress* under him. He said that he meant to have a very strict discipline maintained, and that he should look to me to help him to get as good a character for the schooner as any that was owned by the best-managed ships of war in the English service.

"There is no denying," said he, "that privateering has got to be thought a kind of legalized piracy, and the notion is not unjust. But I don't intend to let the *Tigress* get a reputation of that kind. We'll capture what we can, but we'll capture honestly, and earn our money as gentlemen. Our rules must be tenderness to women, kind treatment to prisoners, and no act that shall subject my letter of marque to revocation."

He produced his commission as he said this, and ran his eye over it, making comments as he went along.

"It's a *carte blanche*, Madison," said he. "In consequence of the insults and provocations his Britannic Majesty has experienced from the Government of France, he has ordered that general reprisals be granted against the goods, ships, and subjects of that nation."

"And small blame to him for that, sir," said I. "The French luggers would provoke the Archbishop of Canterbury into turning privateersman."

"Especially if his grace happened to be a ship-owner. So," continued he, looking at his commission, "in consequence of these insults and provocations, his Majesty has thought proper to permit Robert Shelvocke to equip, furnish, and victual a schooner called the *Tigress*, and to authorize him by force of arms to play the devil among the merchantmen owned by the enemies of his Majesty the King of Great Britain and Ireland, which the said Robert Shelvocke, being a loyal Briton, undertakes to do to the utmost of his ability, as much for the honor and glory of his country as for the filling of his own and the pockets of the people who are associated with him. So there you have the substance of a letter of marque," said he, returning the document to his pocket-book, "which, deprived of parliamentary language, means, Seize what you can, and what you can't pocket, destroy."

Laughing as he said this, he got up, and calling to Chestree, gave him some instructions; and after keeping me waiting on deck while he wrote a letter in his cabin, we left the schooner and made our way out of the Docks.

# CHAPTER III.

THE crew joined on Saturday, and when I came aboard on the following evening I learned that not a single man was missing. The decks forward were filled with seamen when I arrived, and their sweethearts and wives having been allowed to spend the evening with them, the crowd was a dense one. Here was a bushy-whiskered sailor nursing his little child, coddling and tossing it, while his wife hung over his back, silently crying; yonder a pretty girl was exhorting her sweetheart with all manner of passionate gestures: husbands and wives sat together talking earnestly. The whole scene was a remarkable picture, with the varied costumes of the men and women and children contrasting with the sand-white decks, the rows of sullen guns, the wand-like masts shooting into the blue sky, the gleam of the red evening sunlight in the metal work, the ships moored ahead and astern of us, their shadows hanging in the waters as though they reposed upon a bed of looking-glass, and their interlaced rigging soaring like cobwebs into the heavens.

Shelvocke had told me he would not join the schooner until early on Monday morning, as he was to spend Sunday evening with Mr. Hannay. I went below to put my berth to rights, and found the square box allotted to me as convenient and comfortable as I had a right to expect in a vessel of the tonnage of the *Tigress*. There was no room to swing a hammock, but my legs were not too long for the bunk, or sleeping-shelf, and a sailor has no right to ask for more.

When I went on deck again I found the three mates aft, and joined them. Mr. Buck Tapping, the third officer, was a square, very powerfully built young man, with a face like a prize-fighter's, long muscular arms, and short legs. He had a scar across his left cheek, which he told me he had received in a struggle with a fleet of Malay pirates. There was a remarkable expression of audacity in his eyes. The fourth mate, Mr. Peacock, on the other hand, looked almost effeminate with his slender build, small white fingers, and smooth, thin, handsome face. His teeth were beautifully white and even, his eyes large, dark, and melancholy, his hair a rich auburn. He looked more like a poet than a sailor, and the last man I should have thought fit for privateering. He interested me immediately. I asked him how long he had been to sea?

"Since I was ten years old, sir," he answered, with his sweet smile.

"And pray how old are you now, Mr. Peacock?"

"Nineteen, sir."

"Why, you have been to sea almost as long as I have!" I exclaimed. "The sun seems to have used you kindly," referring to his delicate complexion.

Yet Chestree afterward informed me that this same youth, girlish as he looked, had performed as gallant an action as any on record; he had been apprentice on board an Indiaman that was attacked by a heavily armed French sloop off the south coast of Ceylon. The yard-arms of the two vessels got locked. Three times the crew of the Indiaman endeavored to board the enemy, and were repulsed. At last little Peacock, shouting out for followers, sprang aloft, ran along the main-topsail-yard of his own ship, and, with half a dozen men behind him, gained the fore-topsail-yard of the sloop, drove a crowd of small-arms men out of the fore-top, and reached the enemy's deck unperceived amid the smoke. Their presence terrified the Frenchmen, a number of whom ran below: the crew of the Indiaman boarded in the confusion, and while the seamen of the two ships fought like devils on the deck of the sloop, Peacock went aloft and cut away the colors, on seeing which the crew of the sloop supposed their captain had struck and threw down their arms.

Glancing from the officers to the men, it seemed to me quite reasonable that Shelvocke should boast of his complement. Of course an eye used to the uniformity of the dress of men-of-war's men could have wished for less diversity of

costume among the men of the *Tigress*. But no private
owner could afford to give clothes as well as wages. Still,
as I said to Chestree, the *Tigress* would have been the better
for the finishing touch of a uniform dress among the crew;
for, though the motley costumes did not in the least damage
the fine appearance of the men, yet to see some in red shirts,
others in blue shirts, others again in jackets and waistcoats,
some wearing fishermen's caps, some high hats, and some
sou'westers, took away that sense of orderliness, discipline,
and regularity which, of themselves, the white decks, the
heavy guns, the exquisite trim of the gear aloft suggested,
and even gave the schooner a piratical air.

"But they'll look all one, sir," said Chestree to me,
"when they come to strip for an engagement."

Captain Shelvocke came aboard next morning a little after
eight o'clock, and the tide serving, we hauled out of the
Docks, and dropped down to Erith, where we brought up
and took in our powder.

It was a very bright, hot day, with a small breeze from
the northwest. A whole crowd of people stood looking at
us from the shore, and I noticed the crews of the vessels
which passed up or down as we lay at anchor point to us,
and by many gestures express the admiration that the beautiful fabric of the schooner excited in them. The powder
was all aboard and stowed by half-past eleven, when the
capstan was manned, the anchor lifted, and, with flowing
sheets and all her fore-and-aft canvas set, the *Tigress* went
smoothly over the surface of the Thames, the water of which
hereabouts was like molten silver, dazzling with the play of
sunlight upon it, and scarcely blurred by the breeze.

Every man of us knew that this was the schooner's first
run, and that her pace remained to be proved: and the men's
eyes were constantly aloft, or over the side, or upon the
land, to see how fast it slipped by.

The tide was beginning to ebb, but it was scarcely worth
noticing, though what little trickle there was favored us.
Had the schooner been a mere trader, no one would have
troubled himself to think of her pace with such a languid
air as was now stirring overhead; but, for privateering, the
best vessels are those which sail fastest with the least wind,
as any man knows who has chased a cloud of flying kites,

or who has been within range of the guns of a big enemy with not enough air to chill the skin of a moistened finger; and we were as anxious to discover the *Tigress'* slipping powers in little better than a calm, as we should have been to judge her capacity of forereaching and weathering in a gale of wind.

"There is no air down here," said Shelvocke, joining me at the gangway, "and the tide is certainly not yet running a quarter of a knot. Yet look at the shore! It is going past quicker than a man can run. We shall be opening Gravesend in twenty minutes."

"Shall I heave the log, sir?"

"Why, yes, Mr. Madison. It will give us some idea of the speed."

The log was hove by the third officer, who reported four and a half knots.

"There must be more wind than we think," said Shelvocke, looking both astonished and delighted, "or else the tide strengthens. Get the square canvas on her, and try her with that."

A number of men sprang into the foreshrouds.

"Stand by to sheet home! Overhaul your clewlines!"

In less than a couple of minutes all three sails were loosed, the sheets and halliards manned, and the canvas set. The men worked without noise, and to the piping of a boatswain's mate. Nothing was ever more smartly rushed aboard a man-of-war.

"Get the squaresail on her, Mr. Madison, and let her have all three studding-sails!" sung out Shelvocke.

Though we should not be able to carry these last sails long, for a bend of the river would bring them to leeward presently, yet the experiment of setting them was worth the trouble, and in a few moments the polished surface of the water reflected the brilliance of the shining cotton-white cloths, cut to perfection, and depending in graceful forms many feet beyond the vessel's side. The square-sail was an enormous stretch of canvas, big enough to hold a gale of wind. These extra cloths increased the speed to six knots.

"I think I told you," said Shelvocke to me, "that the *Tigress* would prove to be the fastest thing afloat. I call this a real miracle. Look at that big cutter yonder. We are approaching her as though she were a buoy."

He pointed to a large vessel a little on our starboard bow that we were overhauling as though she were stationary. She was a Margate hoy, a lumping sloop, with a deck-load of passengers between her rails. We had our gun-ports raised, and no doubt made a formidable as well as a noble show with the tompions choking the iron throats of the grinning guns, and the snow-white mountain of canvas topping the low, long, black, beautifully moulded hull. The people on the hoy crowded her side to have a look at us, and her skipper clambered on to the after rail and stared at us with his mouth open, amazed, as he well might be, at the way in which we were passing him, and looked up at our canvas, and then around him, as though endeavoring to find out where the wind that propelled us came from.

I have seen a good many vessels of all sorts and sizes in my time, from the Frenchman's four-decker to the Algerine felucca, and it is not therefore easy to guess why the picture of that Margate hoy should have printed itself strongly enough on my mind to last all these years. Yet I see her now in fancy as clearly as I saw her then in reality. Perhaps the contrast between the mission of these peaceful holiday seekers and our own bloody and destructive errand may have emphasized the little hooker to my imagination. There was such fat and placid contentment in the line of faces that crowded her side as was extremely pleasant to behold. There was the sound of a flute aboard, and there were children dancing in the bows, and most of the people were eating their dinners out of paper bags, munching like ruminant animals as they looked at us. It was a picture of old-fashioned life that has quite vanished. The hoy was a chubby boat, rather slatternly rigged, with a big jack on a flag-post over her stern. Her image was beautifully reflected in the water under her, with the row of gleaming faces over her rail. Her skipper called out to know where we were going, and Shelvocke answered "To blow up a few Frenchmen," whereat the men cheered and waved their hats, and the women kissed their hands to us and fluttered their pocket-handkerchiefs.

We slipped by her as swiftly and silently as a shark glides

along the side of a ship becalmed on the equator, and presently opened the merry little town of Gravesend, with its windows sparkling in the sunshine, and the outline of the green lands beyond waving like a serpent in the hot and steamy air.

I had some fear that the wind would fail us, in which case we should have been forced to bring up; but quite unexpectedly it breezed up across the flat Essex lands, and the water was all awobble with it. There was a very handsome thirty-eight-gun frigate, of French extraction, as any man might have known by the curl of the bows and the florid decorations of her quarter-galleries, and the lavish carving upon her stern, lying abreast of Gravesend; and near her were a couple of East Indiamen, newly arrived, with the rust of their long voyage upon their sides, and their canvas very clumsily stowed. The effect our vessel produced was exhibited in the rush of the crews of these ships to look at us as we went by. We were to windward of them, so that, from their point of view, the *Tigress* showed to the utmost advantage. The bend of the river had brought the wind right abeam, and with enough inclination of her masts to prove that she was in earnest, the schooner was ripping up the lustrous water with her stem as a sharp knife divides a length of satin. Every sail was full and round, the studding-sails tearing at the booms as though they were clouds seeking to blow away into the liquid blue heavens. She raised no foam, but amid the humming of the summer wind sweeping under the foot of the huge mainsail, one could hear the soft singing of swiftly passing waters, like the beating on musical glasses heard at a distance, or the clanging of a bell mingling with the rustling of leaves. The vessels at anchor went whirling past us, coming stem on, and then presenting their starboard broadsides as we swept forward. We seemed to keep place with the very shadows of the clouds upon the land. It is true that the *Tigress* had now every possible advantage: perfectly smooth water, a steady breeze, and every sail set with the exception of her skysail: still her qualities both in a light air and in a pleasant breeze had been tested: and that she had marvellously fine keen heels was proved to the satisfaction of every man aboard of her.

Indeed there was not one of the crew but understood the

3

significance of these tastes, seeing the perilous fun her captain was likely to poke her into; and that not only our fortune, but our lives also, must often depend on her running
powers. And the beautiful schooner had already won the
hearts of her men. I could see some of them hanging over
her bows, and slapping their thighs as they watched the
gleaming swirl of water spreading out from her stem, until
it was three fathoms distant by the time it was on the quarter, while others pointed out the trim and cut of the canvas
and the stay of her long masts, and others looked at the land
that was drawing away on either bow, and commented in
audible tones upon the rapidity with which one familiar
place after another opened and slid abeam, and went away
out of sight upon the broadening waters astern.

A little after six we were abreast of Sheerness, and
another hour of this sailing would put the waters of the
English Channel under our forefoot. The wind had veered
due north, and was blowing a gay breeze. The square canvas had been furled, and the *Tigress* was beginning to feel
the faint swell running into the mouth of the river from the
wider ocean beyond, and to tumble a small surface of foam
from her bows, as she ran over the light undulations. It
was a glorious evening, the land a dim, delicate green away
on the starboard hand, and the sun going down over our
stern, filling the water all that way with a strong yellow
light, while to the left the sea stretched in a tremulous dark-
blue surface, flaked with little spurts of foam. There was
a small cutter a couple of miles to leeward, like a snow-flake
on the sea, with English colors hoisted, but she was the only
vessel in sight.

I went below to get a cup of tea, leaving the captain and
Mr. Tapping on deck. I found Chestree talking to young
Peacock, whom he had called into the cabin, and the second
mate asked me if I had heard where we were going to cruise.
I answered that I believed we should hang about the Channel for some days, but that Captain Shelvocke had not fully
opened his mind to me on the subject.

"I hope he will give us some cutting-out job, sir," said
Peacock, his soft girlish smile and the white hand he raised
to push back the soft auburn hair from his forehead making
his wish sound extremely odd. "And one would like the

*Tigress*, before she turns trader—which I suppose, when peace is declared, will be her vulgar destiny—to capture a French seventy-four——"

"A French what?" shouted Chestree, opening his great mouth.

"A French seventy-four, I said," repeated the handsome young fellow, in a melodious voice, and looking at me with his dark, melancholy eyes. "There ought to be no difficulty in capturing the largest national ship afloat."

Here Chestree was interrupting.

"Pray let Peacock have his say, Chestree," said I.

"Frenchmen fight well with their guns, sir, and usually give a fair account of an English crew at a point-blank distance, all things considered. But there are no people in the world among whom a panic is more easily excited. They come into action with an English vessel *prepared* to be beaten. The secret of thrashing a big crew of Frenchmen by a small crew of Englishmen is to give the mounseers a big fright, sir."

He saw me laughing, and stopped, blushing to the roots of his hair.

"Pray continue, Mr. Peacock," said I, recovering my gravity.

"It was the idea of the captain of the last ship I was in," said he, glancing at Chestree to make sure that he was listening seriously, "that among every small crew there should be three or four men selected on account of their disagreeable voices."

"Hang me if ever I heard of such a thing!" exclaimed Chestree, looking with a kind of admiration at the boy.

"His notion was to dress these fellows like Frenchmen, and after the action had commenced and the English had got their ship into a position to board, the Frenchified Britons were to drop into the water and swim round to the unprotected side of the enemy, scramble into her, and get among the crew, who, in the confusion, would suppose them some of their own people who had fallen overboard. Once on the enemy's decks, it would be the business of these fellows to raise false alarms, and create a panic with their horrible cries."

"Ay, ay," said Chestree, "all that sounds very well in

talk, but to make any use of your transmogrified Britons would require what the Germans call a neat conjunction of circumstances. And pray how are your fellows going to scramble up the sides of a three-decker? Answer me that, my fine fellow."

"How? with their hands. They *must* get up, sir!" exclaimed Peacock, with a flushed face.

"But suppose they *can't?*" persisted Chestree.

"Why, then," said I, "the ruse must fail, of course. But even should it succeed once in ten times, I should consider it by no means a bad idea."

"It was twice tried by the same captain," said Peacock, "and was each time successful."

"Were you there to see?" quoth Chestree.

"No, sir, but I'll answer for its efficacy. The first time two fellows got aboard the Frenchman dripping wet, and one of them shouted out, 'The captain's surrendered! the ship's on fire! lay down your arms!'"

"What, in French?" said I.

"Yes, sir. And they *did* lay down their arms. The second time was not immediately successful, for the man was shot in the act of grasping the flag-halliards. But half the crew believed the alarm given was true, and a good many of them jumped overboard, and the English got possession easily."

"There goes the bos'un's pipe for all hands!" exclaimed Chestree, jumping up and unfolding his long body as he soared out of his chair, like a boa-constrictor lifting its head.

The clear whistle came shrilly down through the open skylight, and we all ran on deck. The sun was near his setting, and the water astern of us lay like a sheet of sparkling gold under the ardent light. The land to leeward, shelving away down to Shelness Point, was just a mere greenish film, and stretching out upon our port bow was the horizon of the North Sea. The breeze had moderated again, and the schooner, with a slight inclination of her masts, was running as noiselessly as the shadow of a cloud over the long-drawn tender undulations of the water, that in places was shifting its blue into dark green, while the sea in the east, toward which we headed, was a dark violet, and hazy where it met the sky.

The whole of the ship's company had assembled on the main deck, and I had now an opportunity of judging the full strength and appearance of the crew.   There were ninety men in all, not counting officers, and a determined, hearty set of fellows they looked.   They filled the deck from abaft the foremast, and presented a perfect bulwark of broad chests and whiskered faces.   The suggestion of their physical qualities was prodigiously helped by the rows of long guns which flanked them on either hand; and as they stood in the setting sunshine, the shadows of the delicate rigging lacing their figures and lying in slender bars upon the white decks, while the mold of the vessel was beautifully defined by the black line of the bulwarks against the darkening surface of the waters, and the tapering bows, terminating in the long bowsprit and jibboom, that arched out like a wand over the deep, as though a magician stood in the head of the schooner and pointed the way, from which the jibs soared in rounded curves—methought I had never witnessed a more picturesque scene, nor one fitter to brighten a man's eye and set his heart dancing.

Shelvocke threw the end of his cigar overboard, and, coming forward. got upon the flag-locker that stood lashed in front of the skylight, in order that he might see over the heads of the men in the van of the crowd.   Everybody was as quiet as death, and there was not a sound aloft, for the wind held the sails as steady as though they had been carved in marble, and the only audible noise was the cool tinkling of water under the bows.

"My lads," said Shelvocke, looking a fine imposing man, as he stood erect, and extending his right hand, and speaking in a voice the subdued power of which made me guess what its full force would be, "I have called you aft, not to listen to a speech —for I'm a plain sailor without the gift of the gab—nor do I mean to tell you what your duty is, for that, I take it, you know, but merely to hear what my plans are.   My purpose is to do as much mischief as I can to the enemy's merchant-ships, and to fill our pockets with the fruits of their industry, as they have filled theirs at the expense of ours.   We have the Yankees as well as the French to work upon, and we must hope for some decent pickings, men.   At the same time it is not my intention to lead you into needless perils. Our business is not to engage Government vessels, but to capture cargoes. But should I ever think it necessary for the honor of the glorious flag under which we sail, to show the enemy that we are as little afraid of his ships of war as we are of his merchantmen, I shall hope to be nobly supported by you. It may be our luck, sometime or other to restore to privateering a little of the credit that belonged to it before English seamen took their notions from costa-gardas and picaroons. Anyway, we shall always endeavor to act like Englishmen, and though we are not allowed to carry a pennant at the mast-head, the smartness and the discipline aboard our little *Tigress* shall make her an example for ships whose quarter-decks sparkle with epaulets."

This simple, but, as I thought, judicious harangue raised a cheer; the crew were then divided into watches, and the starboard watch went below. I now saw that the routine to be observed was precisely the same as that of the merchant service. This, on the whole, was a wise plan, since every man aboard, from the captain to the youngest boy, had been bred in trading-vessels, and would work more easily in the customs he was used to, than in a system borrowed from the Navy. I therefore found myself at the head of the port watch, with Tapping as my sub; while Chestree and Peacock took the starboard, or captain's watch.

It was a little after eight o'clock, the night as clear as silver with the moon, in whose white light the shadows of the rigging on the deck looked like drawings in India-ink on marble. We were abreast of the North Foreland, heading so as to fetch the Goodwin Sands to the eastward. The breeze was blowing very languidly, and what there was of it was over the stern. On the starboard hand the Kentish cliffs hung pallid and beetling on the sea-line.

The watch on deck were grouped about the forward guns, and the men on the lookout paced the forecastle with the regularity of machines. One would have thought that the *Tigress* had been six months at sea, so *settled* was the look of everything, so completely had the men adjusted themselves to the new craft. Yet it seemed strange to me, who was used to big Indiamen, to feel that here we were sailing along without a destination. The moonlight flooding the sea in the south gave us a wide range of horizon, but nothing was in sight, nor was it very likely that we should meet with anything good for our account hereabouts.

We held on in this way for about an hour until we had brought the north end of the Goodwins abeam of us, and there lay these deadly sands running in a dark line athwart the reflection of the moonlight, and the water so quiet that not the merest purring or breaking ripples reached the ear. Shelvocke, an inveterate smoker, was puffing at a cigar near the tiller, and presently he called me to him.

"After what we have seen of the schooner's behavior in the river to-day," said he, "and the way in which she slides now, with no more wind aloft than a lady's fan would raise, I think that we may have confidence enough in her heels to stand in to the French shore. Even the capture of a coaster would hearten the men, and at all events anything French (unless it be the privateers) that swims without consort is pretty sure to keep the forts close aboard."

"As we go we head dead for the coast below Dunkirk, sir."

"Ay, it is a pity the moon isn't astern of us. She smothers everything in the south, and shows us up against the water in the north. But this is beautiful weather, Mr. Madison. I never tasted a softer air, and the discharge of meteors might make a man think he is in the Malacca Straits. Those guns give the decks a solemn look, don't they? But yonder's the boy I pin my faith to," said he, pointing to the twenty-four pounder.

"No vessel sighting us would believe that a vessel of our tonnage carried such metal."

"No. I don't say we are not overweighted, but a gale of wind will have to prove that. If I discover that we have too much iron top-hamper I shall drop a couple of the eighteens, and two of the carronades may follow if the necessity arises. But I will stick to my long Toms. I'd rather mount a couple of heavy guns than a whole broadside of the pea-shooters which the Admiralty are furnishing to their small craft. I haven't a word to say against carronades for close action, but what use can a man make of pieces which will not carry much further than a boy can sling a stone?"

I was about to make some answer, when I thought I saw a flash of light down in the west of south, that dyed that part of the horizon with a pale blue glare.

"Was that lightning or a gun?" I exclaimed.

"Where away?" he asked quickly.

I pointed over the line of sand that barred the silver water. He peered, and we both listened. No report followed, but in a few moments there was another sharp glare.

"There's a flash of guns in the south'ard, sir!" sung out one of the men on the lookout.

Presently we saw another faint flash; and I thought, but I could not be sure, that I heard the rumble of an explosion.

"Put your helm up, and let her go off a bit," said Shelvocke to the fellow who was steering. "Keep her at south half west. So, Mr. Madison, get the fore and after sheets eased off, and loose the square canvas."

This, with the topsail, jib, and topmast studding-sail, increased our progress; but the night was so still, and the movements of the schooner so quiet, that, as she rose and sank upon the gentle swell that tenderly swung along the bosom of the water out of the northeast, one would never have imagined that she was making headway, until, by looking over the side, one saw the bubbles in the moonlight slipping past, and heard the delicate churning of the water under the counter.

We kept a bright lookout, but no more flashes were seen. This cessation convinced me that the glare had been produced by guns, for had it been lightning there would have been more of it. By this time the north end of the Goodwins was well on the starboard quarter, and the line of sands running away at an angle from our jibboom. By order of the captain I went forward with a glass, and climbed as high as the fore-topgallant-yard, from which point I searched the sea ahead; but the moonlight flung a haze that confused its own brilliance; and though a great space of water was lighted up, it was like looking at a sheet of dull illuminated silver.

I remained aloft for about ten minutes, gazing intently at the point where we had seen the flashes, and then descended, noticing, as I did so, the green phosphorescent line that was vivid at intervals round the sides of the vessel as she lifted and sank, and the showers of dew occasionally falling from the sails, which were dark with the damp, and doing their work the better for the moisture. I returned aft, and reported that nothing was to be seen.

"Send a hand on to the topsail-yard," exclaimed Shelvocke. "Something has occurred in the southa'rd, and we must mind what we are about."

I passed the word along, and a man jumped into the fore-shrouds. Three-quarters of an hour passed, and for the third time I hailed the lookout man to know if he saw anything.

"No, sir; there's nothing in sight," was the answer.

"It was perhaps only sheet-lightning, after all," said Shelvocke; but I thought otherwise.

We paced the deck together for some time, and he then dived below for a glass of grog. The moon, by veering to the westward, had brought her light on the starboard bow; the sky was so clear, that down upon the very water-line the stars were burning like fire-flies. Mr. Tapping was walking up and down the lee-side of the deck, when he suddenly stopped, and in the haze of light that came from the cabin through the skylight I saw him put his hands to both ears, and stand in an eager listening posture. I watched him. Presently he turned and said:

"Did you hear anything just now?"

"Nothing," I answered.

"I fancied I heard a sound like a man's voice hallooing," said he.

I crossed over to his side of the deck, and we both listened. The men forward were as mute as statues; the footfalls of the hands on the lookout were as soft as though they trod in their socks, only now and again the stillness was broken by the creak of a block or the moan of water alongside. The deck, save in the bows of the vessel where the lookout men were moving, was like a painted picture in the moonshine; the motionless shadows of the men, like carvings in jet, branched from their feet; aloft the canvas was sleeping, save when now and again the swell shook a fold of sail against the rigging, and the large yellow stars looked steadily down through the tracery of ropes.

"I hear nothing," said I.

"It wasn't my fancy either!" exclaimed Tapping, looking like an immense bull-frog, with his rounded legs, long arms, and immensely square body in the white, deceptive light. "It sounded like a human cry. I'm not often deceived. I've got ears that will hear through a brick wall, sir."

Shelvocke came on deck again; and seeing Tapping and me standing in an attitude of listening, he stepped up to us and asked what the matter was. I told him that Tapping believed he had heard a cry.

"What sort of a cry, Mr. Tapping?" inquired Shelvocke.

"A human cry coming out of the sea, sir," responded Tapping poetically.

"The plot thickens," said Shelvocke. "Damme, the night seems full of mysteries. Heard you anything, Mr. Madison?"

"No, sir; though here have I been listening for some minutes."

I had scarcely shut my mouth, when Tapping cried out triumphantly, "There, captain. Mr. Madison, I wasn't mistaken, sir."

Indeed he was not, for both Shelvocke and I had distinctly heard a thin, reedy cry, more like the imitation by a ventriloquist of a remote voice than a real sound—a faint, unearthly "Hillo," coming it was impossible to say from where.

"There's some one hailing us, sir," shouted a voice forward.

"Topsail-yard, there!" called Shelvocke; "do you see any sign of a boat about?"

"No, sir."

"Search the sea to leeward. Look brightly around you." And after a pause, "Well?"

"I don't see anything, sir, either to windward or to leeward," answered the man.

"That is extraordinary too!" exclaimed Shelvocke. "Here, Mr. Tapping, take the glass and jump aloft and give me your report."

As Tapping went up the main-shrouds the hail was repeated. It was a most distressful cry, a little more distinct this time.

"A sail on the weather-bow!" shouted the man from the topsail-yard.

"Ay, ay, there she is, sure enough," said Shelvocke, in a low voice, extending his hand.

"I think there are two of them, sir!" sung out the man.

I looked, and could just distinguish a smudge upon the horizon. That we had not seen it before was owing to the haze of the moonlight catching the vessel laterally, so as to fling upon her just enough radiance to render her invisible upon the silvered sky in that quarter. But the haze had left her, and veered to the westward, and there was the vessel, a mere smirch indeed, but distinct enough.

I ran below for a second telescope, and handed it to Shelvocke. He took a long look, and exclaimed:

"The man is right—there *are* two of them!" and gave me the glass, the magnifying power of which was considerable; but so vague and deceptive was the light down in the southeast, where the vessels lay, that the lenses merely resolved the one smirch that was visible to the naked eye into two dark blotches upon the sea, both close together; but no idea could be formed of the rig or size of the distant craft. While I was working away with the glass, the plaintive shout we had before heard arose clear in the air, and it was no longer possible to mistake either the character or the direction of it.

"There is a man overboard somewhere near us!" sung out one of the men forward.

"Ay, ay; keep a sharp lookout for him," answered Shelvocke. "Mr. Madison, call some hands aft to stand by the peak halliards and braces. Get your gaff-foresail brailed up, and swing the fore-yards. Some hands aft here, ready to man and lower away the cutter."

These orders were repeated by me, and executed quietly and quickly. The helm was put down and the schooner lay with her head close to the light air, her way arrested by her yards being aback, and a whole crowd of seamen were on her starboard bulwarks looking around upon the surface of the dark water for the man that had hailed us, for we had now brought the moon right astern, and the sea was as black as ebony for half a mile away from the schooner's side to the north and east, though it changed to a pallid hue from that point, growing a more defined gray, until it became an ash-colored line against the liquid, dark sky, just as a fog with a light burning in it gradually brightens toward the illuminated centre.

We all stood listening. Over and over again I thought I saw a dark object in the water, but it was only a deception of the shadows swayed by the undulation of the swell. From time to time exclamations broke from the men: "There he is!" "Look yonder, mate! close against that star there!" and so forth, but these cries were always followed by a gruff "No, no!"

Not having heard his hail for some minutes, most of us believed that the man had sunk, for the last time he had sung out it was certain that he was close enough to enable us to see a boat or a spar, or, in short, anything bigger than a human head, and I had no doubt that he had fallen overboard from one of the vessels away in the gloom, and that his strength had at last failed him, when, to the astonishment of everybody, his lusty shout was heard close aboard.

"Lower away a boat, for God's sake, good people, and pick me up! You'll be ahead of me in a minute!"

This appeal, in good English, made some of the men laugh. Tapping sprang into the cutter, and the boat was lowered.

"Pull gently, and mind how you go," shouted Shelvocke, "or you'll run over him. He's not far off!"

The water flashed up under the oars, and a few strokes carried the boat a dozen fathoms away. I saw Tapping in the stern-sheets, and a hand in the bows, standing up and peering around them. The men pulled another stroke. We then heard voices and a splash, and presently the grind of thole-pins as the boat came toward us.

"Have you got him?" cried Shelvocke.

"Yes, sir," answered Tapping.

"Let him lie where he is. We'll hoist him in with the boat," said Shelvocke, on which the boat came alongside, the crew jumped aboard, and the falls being manned, the cutter soared out of the water as though a giant forked her up through the sea on the end of a pike.

"Get all plain sail made again, Mr. Tapping," said I. "Haul round those yards forward."

I went up to the captain, who waited while the stranger in the cutter uncoiled himself, and asked him how we should head.

"As we go, for the present," he answered. "Keep your eyes on those vessels yonder. We shall be able to see more of them as the moon draws to the westward."

I ogled the craft again through the glass, but they were nothing more than a couple of blotches, and I rather fancied by the look of them that they were drawing away from us. I put down the glass, and walked aft, where Shelvocke was speaking to the man we had picked up. He was a hulking fellow, with a great cork-jacket under his armpits, which made him look like a turtle mounted on a pair of human shanks. The moonlight sparkled in a pool of water under his feet, and in the drops hanging from his hawk's-bill nose and well-thatched eyebrows. His face in the light was as white as the planks under him, and with the bloated appearance of his body, that reduced his legs in comparison to the thickness of a couple of capstan-bars, and the odd manner in which his arms overhung the top of the cork-jacket, he looked a very alarming object, and a proper sight for a painter in search of a study for a nautical ghost. However, he was perfectly fresh, and gazed around him coolly, and when the steward handed him a rummer of grog that had been brought by order of the captain, he drank to us with a pleasant nod, and said that he would take another drop when he had dried his clothes.

"You shall go and dry your clothes at once," said Shelvocke, laughing at the fellow's *sang-froid;* "but perhaps you will tell me first what those vessels are yonder?"

"One's a French armed lugger, and t'other's an English cutter of sixty ton," answered the man.

"Do you know how many guns the Frenchman carries?"

"I don't, sir; I took no notice of that; but she's full of men."

On this Shelvocke told the steward to take the man below, and give him a shift of clothes; then, jumping on a gun-carriage, he took another long squint at the vessels, which we had now brought a couple of points on the lee bow.

"We'll have the story presently, Madison," said he;

"but if the flashes we saw came from the guns of those craft, the cutter must have proved an easy capture. I shall attack the lugger—she will serve as practise for the men."

"She appears to have the cutter in tow, sir," said I, with my eye at the glass, "and to judge by the manner in which they are creeping away, they are using their sweeps. However, *we* are not stationary," I added, looking down into the water, and observing the long threads breaking away from the schooner's bows, and rippling out of the darkness into lines of silver as they went astern athwart the moon. Yet the breeze was very faint, and our fore-and-aft canvas hung up and down without further movement than such as was from time to time communicated by the soft swaying of the schooner over the delicate swell.

Presently Tapping came up to the captain.

"The steward reports the man ready to see you, sir."

"Let him come aft."

The man, who in his dry attire proved to be a more comely object than I had imagined, approached Shelvocke, who stood with me near the skylight, the haze from him enabled us to have a good sight of the stranger. There was something of the fisherman's trot in his gait as he came along the deck, and he had stowed away a large junk of tobacco in his cheek that threw the skin into a knob, behind which fell a short slant of lank black whisker. His eyes were dark, quick, and gleaming, and there was a set, resolute expression in the whole face of the man that persuaded me his bread was not earned in peaceful pursuits.

"Well, my man, how are you after your bath?"

"Right enough, sir, thank'ee. A cork jacket ben't like swimming, though. I reckon I lay in the water more than an hour."

"What do you know about those vessels yonder?"

"Why, you see, I happen to be one of the crew of the cutter. We were heading to fetch the Nor'-sands-head, when the lugger hove in sight, coming right down upon us. I don't know how it was that none of us took no notice of her until she was a couple of miles off. Anyway, we thought we'd stop to see what she meant to do, but as she drew near, rattling down upon us under her sweeps as though she carried a stiff breeze astern, we saw that she was a sight too big for us, and crowded with men. So we up helm, and tried to edge away, but there was no wind, and as we only carried twenty men, our captain sung out that it would be useless to fight him. He hailed us as he came along, and we answered that we were English, on which he let drive three guns, though, after he had fired the first shot, our skipper called out to say he had surrendered. I never waited to see what happened after this, but laying hold of a cork jacket I strapped myself up in it and dropped overboard, preferring to take my chances of drowning to starving in a French prison. That's just the story, gentlemen," said the fellow, shifting the quid of tobacco from one cheek to the other with his tongue.

"What's the name of the cutter?" asked Shelvocke.

"The *Happy-go-Lucky*, sir."

"What is she—a trader?"

The man hung in the wind so long that I thought he did not mean to answer the question. At last he exclaimed with great vehemence, "Capt'n, I'll not tell 'ee a lie. False speaking 'll sarve no end, and this ben't a king's ship neither. The *Happy-go-Lucky's* in the contraband line, a smuggler they calls her; and so you have it, gentlemen."

"Pooh! pooh!" said Shelvocke, "we must recapture the *Happy-go-Lucky* and put you aboard again. That will do. If you want some supper the steward will provide you."

The man went forward and Shelvocke gave a low whistle, looking around the silent sea that lay without a tremor under the wide space of moonlight. There was indeed scarcely any air to be felt now; the stars hung their reflection in the water without a blur, and the moonshine made the horizon so misty that one would have thought a fog was wreathed around the circle. It was only by straining the sight that I could obtain a glimpse of the vessels ahead.

"If this lasts, Master Frenchman will get away from us," said Shelvocke. "But it cannot be helped."

"Is it worth while to out boats after him, sir?"

"No, the recapture is no great matter, and the job is certainly not worth tiring the men over. Capturing these luggers is about as profitable as catching flies. They are the proper prey of the cruisers, but the *Tigress* wants larger and better-stocked holds than those boats carry. I suppose," he continued, laughing, "the *Happy-go-Lucky* was running for one of the gaps to the westward of the North Foreland. I am told that the cliffs thereabouts are honeycombed by the smugglers. It's reckoned a naughty trade, but upon my soul, I can't find it in me to denounce it. The revenue is so completely no man's property that you can't realize the notion of any one robbing it."

"Either the horizon gets thicker or Johnny Frog is drawing away fast, sir," said I; "I don't see him now."

"You're looking in the wrong place; there's one of them, at all events, yonder, like a bit of mother-o'pearl in the moonlight. Aye, and there's the other close to her. I knew their sails would be hove up when the moon got more to the westward."

He pointed into the south, where, sure enough, I saw the sails of the lugger glimmering like a waning star. The schooner had no steerage-way, and I had been deceived in the situation of the Frenchman by the *Tigress'* head having fallen off.

Shelvocke went below and I paced the deck alone, while Tapping flitted about the gangway like a spectre, snuffing about for the wind, and in various demonstrative ways exhibiting his disgust at the calm. This time last night we were lying snug in dock, with the hum of the distant metropolis in the air; and now here we were with the sea all around us, an enemy in sight, and a certainty of burning powder should a breeze spring up. But these quick transitions are the very spirit of a sailor's life; and of privateering the peculiar fascination lies in the rapidity of the changes of scene it opens up, the suddenness of the dangers and escapes, and the permanent and delightful sense of expectation it raises in a man.

Keeping my eyes pretty constantly fixed on the pale shadow in the southeast, I did at last clearly perceive that it was receding from us fast, and soon after six bells neither I nor Tapping nor the lookout men could discern the least sign of the vessels. Not more, however, than a quarter of an hour elapsed after we lost sight of them, when the water in the direction in which they had vanished grew sharp and black under the stars.

"I think there is some wind coming from yonder," I exclaimed to the third mate. "If so, we shall be able to hook our Frenchman cleverly, for it is dead on end for him."

Tapping sprang on to one of the guns.

"Ay, there's the wind, sir!" he shouted. "It's ruling a dark line as it comes; I see it breaking up the starlight, sir!"

It was a strong puff, and it breezed down upon us rapidly. I ordered the square canvas to be furled, and by the time the men were aloft the wind was all about us and the schooner lying down to it, every sail as flat as a pancake; the water squirting up under the bows and flashing white with threads of green fire alongside and far away astern. At the first coming of the breeze the captain arrived on deck.

"We have our friend now, I think," said he quietly; "and he is welcome to the weather-gauge with the wind dead off the French coast. See all clear, Mr. Madison, and have the lanterns lighted; but let them be hidden, for Johnny may not have yet smelt us, and we'll have the benefit of his doubts."

The boatswain's pipe rang clear and shrill upon the wind that was now humming a pretty tune aloft, and scurrying away with a booming note from under the foot of the huge mainsail. The men responded to this their first call to quarters with a smartness that delighted Shelvocke. In a few minutes they were all at stations, tompions out, boxes of canister and grape at the carronades, and a grummet of round-shot at every gun. There was, as might have been expected, some little confusion at first, but a few orders set everything to rights; and there they stood, ninety of them, ready for whatever might come, while the *Tigress* snored along, apparently defying the influence of the light swell, and the water crackling away to leeward like underbrush on fire and blowing up in white smoke, as though the stem of the schooner was a torch and her passage through gunpowder.

A few large clouds came sailing up with this wind, look-

4

ing like big sheets of wadding as they neared the moon; but as she ducked to them and hid her light, the horizon, strangely enough, grew clear: and in one of these intervals, when the cloud-shadows covered the sea and the water-line lay sharp against the stars like a ruling in India-ink, we spied the glimmering vessels, like bits of wool, to windward, about three points on the port-bow.

This was about a quarter of an hour after the breeze had started us. The excitement now began to grow lively. Here was the *Tigress*, jammed close up to the wind, not only overhauling, but weathering upon the two vessels, both of which, we might be sure, were fast boats; indeed, we had the evidence of the man we had picked up that the smuggler was "built for walking away, and that there was nothing on the coast, that could touch her," which I thought probable enough, seeing that one of the conditions of success in contraband traffic is speed in sailing; while, on the other hand, the French privateer luggers were famous the world over for the beauty of their bottoms, the strength of their fabrics, and the nimbleness of their heels. So if nothing more came of this chase, yet as a specimen of what the *Tigress* could do with her main-boom almost amidships and the weather-leech of the flying jib trembling like the fly of a flag, the adventure was worth the attempt.

Shelvocke and I kept our glasses pointed at the vessels. I expected every moment to see them go about, as the Frenchman stood a poor chance on this board. He was fast opening the cape to the westward of Calais, and once clear of that, we should have the Channel as far as Barfleur clear to run him down in.

"Can you make out the cutter, Mr. Madison?" said Shelvocke.

"Yes, sir; the sternmost one is she," I replied, for she looked the smaller of the two.

"Ay, you are right: but surely the lugger hasn't got the cutter's tow-rope aboard still!"

I watched them for some minutes, and then called out:

"There's some manœuvring going on between them, sir. They have closed."

"Steady!" shouted Shelvocke to the helmsman. "How does she go?"

"She breaks off, sir."

"Good! 'Bout ship, Mr. Madison. Smartly, now! a short board will clap us between Johnny and his home!"

The helm was put down, the canvas thundered as the schooner shot into the wind, and in a minute she was on the starboard tack biting fiercely into the short black running seas with lines of foam trailing down her stem, like the salival froth dropping from the jaws of a bloodhound on the scent, and ratching swiftly to the eastward.

"Ha!" I exclaimed, "I thought they were up to some game, sir. See, they have set fire to the cutter, and yonder goes the lugger on the same tack as ourselves."

All that could be distinguished for some minutes was a little spark on the water in the direction where we had last seen the cutter. It grew brighter and larger, and a line of black smoke went blowing low over the tossing and tremulous tract of moonlit sea. In a quarter of an hour the little vessel was blazing freely, casting a small circumference of red light upon the air, and staining the water a blood-red under her hull.

Hearing a commotion among a group of men stationed at one of the guns forward, I called to know what was the matter.

"Please your honor," replied a voice, "it's the smuggling cove cursing the Frenchman for burning his wessel. He says all his clothes and wallybles is aboard, and two-an'-forty pound in money."

I caught a glimpse of the poor fellow shaking his long arm over the bulwark and quivering about on his legs, but took no further notice. Meanwhile the lugger was stretching to windward, apparently sailing very fast, though with every foot of the road we measured we drew nearer to her. Indeed, now that we had a fast chase on the weather bow, we could estimate the *Tigress'* powers of weathering accurately. With spars erect, she walked to windward as though she were being warped that way. I had expected much of her, but not so much as she was giving us. Only a sailor can sympathize with the strong feeling of delight and pride that fired me when, looking forward, I felt the wind blowing through my teeth as though it rattled clean over the bowsprit, and then glancing astern, I marked the schooner's wake running away into the pale haze of moon-light as straight as a mill-race speeds from the foaming wheel.  By the lugger's having set fire to the cutter, it was plain that she had taken us for an enemy, and that, true to the Frenchman's marine policy, her business was to es-cape.  So far as the wind was concerned, she was in as bad a plight as she could well suffer from, if she was afraid of us and wanted the shelter of her own coast, for the wind was blowing dead along the course she would have liked to make.

The clouds were now tumbling up out of the sea, and slanting athwart the stars pretty thickly, and the water was full of shadows, amid which the moonshine fell down in lines like slender cascades of molten silver, touching the black troubled surface here and there with points of bril-liance as sparkling as the flash of diamonds, while the breaking waves glittered like the star-dust in the sky, as their foam crossed the path of these beams; but down in the west the smuggler cutter was making a great blaze, and resembled a solid ball of fire on the tumbling surges.  Fore and aft there was a grim silence in the schooner, nothing to be heard but the swarming of the passing water and the confused harping of the wind among the iron-stiff weather standing rigging.

A long twenty minutes went by, at the end of which time the lugger loomed larger, not above a point on the weather-bow.

"Round she goes again, sir!"  I shouted out, seeing the shadow of the sails of the Frenchman fine as he slued upon his heels.

"Ready about ship!" sung out Shelvocke, in a voice that seemed to ring across the sea.  "Stand by to fire the bow-chaser as she goes round."

There was a short pause as the helm was jammed over to leeward, and then, while the canvas rattled overhead as though, like an angry dog, the wind had seized the sails in its teeth and was furiously shaking them, and while the schooner chopped up and down upon the rising seas, which poured in foam against her bows; and while every block rattled like a gigantic dice-box to the jerking of the swing-ing booms and sheets, a broad glare of light flashed upon the darkness, throwing up the figures of the men as they stood around the guns, and every spar and rope and the seams of the deck, like a colored picture flung for an instant by a powerful red light upon a black cloth, followed by a heavy explosion, while the smoke of the gun whirled away to leeward and gleamed like a torn silk veil as it sped across the sea.

This was the first gun ever fired aboard the *Tigress*, and the report of it was followed by a loud cheer from the men. In a few moments the sails were trimmed, and the schooner was on the port-tack, having doubled upon the chase like a hound upon a fox.

"They'll guess our metal by that ball if it dropped any where near them," said Shelvocke to me; "and if so, I hope they'll give up trying to dodge us."

"There she speaks, sir!" I exclaimed, as a spark winked at the stern of the lugger; but wherever the shot fell, it did not drop within our ken. In a few minutes we yawed, and gave her another dose from the bow-gun, and then a third, as fast as the men could load. It was too dark, and she was too far off for us to see if our shot struck her; but though there could be no doubt that she was within range of the long twenty-four, Shelvocke stopped firing at her after the third discharge. In truth, we were coming up with her fast, and with a little patience we should be able to give her a broadside, for, in petty work of this kind, it is best to save powder until you can make it do what you want.

The lugger had only fired once; she held on in silence and darkness—the foam in a heap to leeward of her, and the stars whirling over her mast-heads as she reeled under the beam swell. By this time we had weathered on her so effectually as to have her dead on a line with our jibboom.

Suddenly Shelvocke sang out for the starboard guns to give her a broadside.

"Aim low! I had rather the balls should go under than over her," he exclaimed, and, with a motion of the hand, directed the helm to be put down. As the schooner came up in the wind, the whole five guns were let fly at the lugger; the blaze of light striking the eye used to the darkness was blinding, and the explosion was like half a dozen thunderbolts falling upon the deck. Still the lugger held on without swerving a hair's breadth out of her course, and apparently no more injured than had we blown through a pea-shooter at her.

"That is what the lawyers call contumacy," said Shelvocke, peering at the Frenchman through a glass. "It's quite certain that we haven't winged her. Can she be within range, Madison? This light is so confoundedly deceptive, that she might be two or five miles off."

"Nearer two than five, sir. I don't quite see through her moves. It doesn't look as if she meant to fight us. Perhaps she hopes to run us within sight of one of her cruisers."

"Try her with another shot from the forecastle."

The order was given, the schooner luffed, and the gun fired. We looked to see the effect of this shot; but if any mischief had been done, it was not indicated by the vessel's movements. All this while the wind had been gradually freshening, and was now blowing a strong breeze with a windy-looking sky, and a waning moon in the west that stooped among the clouds like an ill-balanced paper kite. The *Tigress* had now as much canvas on her as she could bear. She lay over until the water was almost level with her lee gun-ports: the sea was a whole smother of foam around her; the spray flashed in smoke over her forecastle, and, when the moonlight streamed upon the canvas, you could have seen the standing jib dark, half-way up it, with the saturation of the flying water. On the other hand, the Frenchman was as stiff as a church, albeit she carried an enormous press of canvas proportionally out and away greater than we were pelting under.

I was mentally reckoning how long it would take us to get alongside of her, when, to the great astonishment of everybody who was watching, she put her helm up and went swirling away to leeward, dead before the wind, with her lugs boomed out on either side. Our puzzlement was supreme. It seemed as mad a thing as the Frenchman could be guilty of. He was not only running away from his own coast, but he was bringing the southern limb of the Goodwin Sands dead under his stern; and unless he presently hauled his wind so as to make a more westerly course, he must inevitably run ashore. However, one must fain go where the devil drives. The helm of the schooner was put up, the sheets eased off, and hands sent aloft to loose the square canvas.

Blowing now as it was right over our stern, the wind appeared to have calmed amazingly; but soon it grew apparent that in scudding the lugger was more than our match. Half our sails were becalmed, the gaff foresail useless, and even the mainsail gave but little help; whereas the Frenchman, by booming out his lugs, made every cloth serviceable, and we saw him skimming away in the gloom ahead of us like a huge sea-bird swept over the surges by its expanded wings. Still, he had hooked himself dead under our lee, with our broadside to windward, and the Goodwin Sands to leeward of him. In this posture it was impossible for him to escape us, and so none of us took it much to heart that he improved his distance, or that the *Tigress* lagged a little, seeing the schooner never yet was built that proved herself a fast ship with the wind dead astern of her.

We bowled along in this way, keeping a bright lookout all around us, for this was a wind to give activity to the enemy's cruisers, and any moment might show us the canvas of a big ship. Eight bells, midnight, were struck, and as the last bell was echoing, I dropped the glass I was holding to my eye as I hung over the starboard bulwarks to get a clear view of the lugger that was glimmering upon the darkness a long way ahead, with the reddish moon shining close down upon the sea to the right of her, and said to Shelvocke that the chase seemed to be growing smaller and smaller; that not long ago I could distinctly make out her black hull, but that it was now indistinguishable.

"Surely," said I, "she can't be forging ahead so fast as all that, sir."

He took the glass from me, and had a long squint at her.

"Why, as you say, Mr. Madison, she does appear to have grown remarkably small on a sudden. I don't see anything of her hull at all now. And has she any notion where she's bound to, I wonder?" He paused and counted upon his fingers. "Send a hand on to the topgallant-yard," he exclaimed. "The sands can't be more than a couple of miles distant by the look of that light down there. Bid him keep a sharp lookout for breakers. We must mind that that fellow does not lead us into a mess."

A man went aloft, and I waited to hear if he had any thing to report, but no hail came from him. I walked aft to look at the compass, and was standing there with my eyes fixed on the card, and feeling rather fretful over this prolonged chase, and thinking of the small amount of glory and still smaller amount of profit we, as privateersmen, should get out of the capture of this lugger, and doubting whether we had not done better to jog quietly down Channel, reserving our powder and our heels for a wholesome cargo and daylight, instead of dodging about after a nimble and subtle chase under the perplexing moonlight, when Peacock sung out in his soft flute-like voice from the waist:

"They're burning a blue light aboard the Frenchman, sir!"

I sprang to the side to look, and there sure enough was the lugger illuminated by the blue fire, and looking as though she had been revealed by a flash of lightning, the outline of her sails clearly marked, and the whole square form of her pulsating in the fluctuating light, like the glow of phosphorus rubbed on the wall of a dark chamber; while at quick intervals she fired guns, sometimes two at a time, the white flames, as they spurted from her sides, contrasting with really grand effect with the ghastly radiance of the blue fire and the black surface of the water and the masses of clouds pouring over the now moonless sky.

"Those are clearly distress-signals!" exclaimed Shelvocke, who stood close beside me. "Surely she cannot have taken the ground. Hail the topgallant-yard, and see if the lookout man makes broken water in the neighborhood of the lugger."

But the answer was that the sea looked clear enough all that way.

"The lugger has hauled the wind, sir!" shouted Chestree, with his eye to the glass. "She is standing to the norrard—no! she is slueing right up into the wind!"

She was now firing to right and left, as though she were pouring broadsides into an enemy on either side of her.

"Get the square canvas clewed up, Mr. Madison—brail up the foresail—shorten sail fore and aft, and let her drive down easily. I must see where we are;" and while Shelvocke dived below to have a look at the chart, I half stripped the schooner of her canvas and set the lead going. The soundings gave us eighteen and twenty fathoms of water; besides, the tumble of the sands was not yet in sight, and all hereabouts was a fair-way channel, so we might be sure the lugger was not ashore. Was there anything wrong aboard of her? or were her distress-signals merely meant as a ruse to bring us alongside, unsuspicious of the reception she would give us?

Suddenly her blue lights went out and she ceased firing. At this moment Shelvocke came on deck.

"The chart gives six and seven fathoms almost alongside the sands," said he. "Where is the lugger?"

"Yonder," I answered, indicating the spot where I had seen her a minute before.

He looked, and then asked me for the glass. He looked again.

"I don't see her," said he. "Try you."

I levelled the glass, but there were no signs of the lugger where I expected to find her.

"How's her head?" I called out, thinking that the wind had veered, and brought the chase into other bearings.

"West by north, sir," came the answer from the helm, and this was the course we had been steering since the lugger ran off before the wind.

"Very odd," said I, sweeping the sea to right and left of the schooner's bows. "I can see nothing of her. Forward there! can you make out the chase?"

"No, sir; she's gone down, I think," was the reply after a lengthy pause.

"Then some of our shot must have told," exclaimed Shelvocke. "They did not burn their blue light and fire their guns for nothing. No doubt they took the crew of the cutter aboard before setting fire to her. For God's sake, go forward, Mr. Madison!" he added, apparently greatly agitated, "and look about you for any of her people in the water."

I made my way along the main deck that was thronged

with the men still at quarters, and reached the forecastle. The sea, away on the port-bow, was a coal-black line against the sky that was yet pallid with the reflection of the moon, though she had been sunk below the horizon some time, and all to the north the stars were burning brilliantly enough to define any shadow leaning against them. Had the lugger been afloat I must certainly have seen her.

"My lads," I exclaimed to the men on the lookout, "there can be no doubt the Frenchman has foundered. She had some of our countrymen aboard. Keep your eyes upon the sea and your ears open, for we are close to the spot where she disappeared."

We hung over the bows, gazing earnestly at the water, that was streaked with the foam of breaking surges, and straining our ears for a human cry. The seas, however, were so short and confused, and the showering of the spray so heavy as it was blown off the heads of the waves that the strongest swimmer battling among them would have been speedily overcome. We had drifted, according to my calculations, about a quarter of a mile beyond the spot where the Frenchman had foundered, when the man on the top-gallant-yard reported breakers ahead on the starboard bow. As these would be the Goodwin Sands, the helm was put over and the schooner hove to, and lanterns slung over her sides, and in this manner we lay for half an hour, every soul aboard of us eagerly searching the surrounding water.

But it was all to no purpose. Our shot had evidently knocked a hole in the lugger that let in water more quickly than her crew could pump it out. She had sunk, and not a vestige of her nor her people was to be seen, though ninety pairs of eyes hung over the bulwarks of the *Tigress*, and the lanterns flung a lustre that made the surface of the water clear for a dozen fathoms away.

I went aft and reported to the captain that none of the crew of the lugger was to be seen.

"It's a bad job," he exclaimed. "Those luggers are usually as full of men as a hive is of bees, and I should be sorry to guess how many human souls have gone to their account this night. Worst of all, they had the crew of the cutter aboard, and we have destroyed our own countrymen. Yet it could not be helped! so let the hands trim sail now,

Mr. Madison, and send the port watch below.    The first exploit of· the *Tigress* has not been a brilliant one, but it has
proved abominably murderous."

And more affected than I should have believed possible
in a man of his resolution and experience, he quitted the
deck.

# CHAPTER IV.

## THE ACTION WITH THE CORVETTE.

THE watch having been called, I went below tired out, and throwing myself into my bunk, fell into a sound sleep in a few minutes. I was aroused at four o'clock, and went on deck, and found the dawn bright in the east, and the schooner, under easy canvas, hugging the wind and heading west-southwest. Indeed, the wind had chopped around, and was blowing off the English coast, the nearest point of which was Dungeness, though not only was there no land in view, but the weather was so thick that the horizon lay at a distance of not more than two miles around us.

I had hoped that when the morning broke the haze would lift; but when the sun rose and hung over the sea-line like the bottom of a newly scoured copper kettle, the fog came down as thick as a feather-bed, and blew in steam across the deck. It was all a blank to within three ship's lengths ahead of us. The green seas came curling and foaming out of the fog to windward, but you could not see one inch beyond the point at which their forms grew defined, and they went combing in curves as polished as oil to leeward, vanishing instantly when they came in contact with the fog-curtain.

The breeze was warm, but the damp made it uncomfortable. The decks were so slippery that it was not easy to keep one's footing. The moisture fell in showers from the rigging, and drops of water formed at the brim of my hat as fast as I could shake them off.

At four bells the watch turned out to wash down. There were so many men to perform this job that it was soon over, and the decks being cleared up and the rigging coiled down, the schooner took a more comfortable air; but the fog remained unpleasantly dense, and sometimes settled down so thick, that the inner jib was not to be seen from the binnacle. Fortunately we had plenty of sea-room, for the French coast that edged away to the southward gave us a broad stretch of water to leeward, we were clear of the Ridge, and had good soundings for leagues. ·

But fogs of this nature were tolerably fruitful of disagreeable surprises; at any moment an enemy's hooker might ooze out of the thickness and be aboard of us. I therefore took care to see everything clear, and stationed some experienced hands as lookout men, keeping my own "weather eye lifting," as we say at sea, and enjoining Tapping to follow my example. Indeed, the man we had picked up on the previous night had told Shelvocke that his cutter had been chased during the afternoon by a large French corvette, who, finding that she could not overhaul the little smuggling craft in the light wind then prevailing, put her helm up, and apparently returned to her cruising ground, which the man believed to be between Calais and Lornel Point. We had no particular wish to come across this Frenchman, who was described as mounting very heavy batteries and a great deal too big for us to handle; but if our smuggler was right, she was undoubtedly somewhere in the neighborhood, and it would be no great joke for the fog suddenly to clear and expose the beauty lying close enough to deliver a broadside before we could give the schooner canvas enough to get away.

Shortly before eight bells Shelvocke came on deck, and seeing how matters stood, and that the breeze was dropping, the order was passed along for the men to keep silence, also for no bells to be struck, and for the leadsman to speak his report in a low tone to a hand stationed by his side for the purpose of bringing his messages aft to the officer in charge. In addition to this, the foresail was securely brailed up and the staysail and inner jib hauled down to silence their flapping; and the schooner, under her mainsail and standing-jib, glided slowly up and down over the breathing swell, as silent as a dead-house, and amid a fog as impenetrable as a blanket.

At eight o'clock I went below to breakfast, the *Tigress* being in charge of Tapping.

I have a lively recollection of our mess table aboard this privateer. Shelvocke was a *bon vivant ;* he had a liberal owner in Hannay; moreover his experience in victualling vessels for rich East India passengers was large, so that few men knew better how to furnish a table than he. We sat down to a breakfast fit to place before a prince.

"And if there is anything wanting," said Shelvocke with his fine smile, "Monsieur Crapeau shall supply it. He is a distinguished cook, and understands the secrets of digestion. And why should not we be well served, Madison? As well feed the inmate of a palace on hard salt junk and give majesty to drink of rancid water, as ill-provision the commander and officers of such a glorious little hooker as the *Tigress.*"

"These be noble sentiments, captain," said I.

"Yet historians say that the reason why the ancient Romans were licked by the northern savages was because they were too fond of roast peacock and the juice of the vine," observed Chestree.

"True, Mr. Chestree; but we are not ancient Romans, sir," replied Shelvocke, apparently surprised that a man like Chestree should know anything about the ancient Romans, "nor have we savages to fight with. Mr. Madison there is no blunder more deplorably stupid than the notion that well-fed—mind, I don't say over-fed—men won't do their work properly. Yet men of the type of the late Lord Howe—buckramed Britons with a yard of marlinespike down their backs—will tell you that good officers are only to be got by rearing young fellows on coarse food. I remember the first lieutenant of the *Latona* —that was one of the Channel fleet under Howe in the action of the first of June—telling me that the old admiral was always worrying the people about him with his opinions on eating, and that he would say that were he to found a state and organize a fleet, one of his articles should provide that no officer of what rank soever should consume better food than the cube of salt horse and the occasional dram of rum which are supposed to form fo'ksle provender at sea. Yet old Howe was never tired of stuffing himself with roast pig, and I have heard that he would swill port wine until the Dutch spirit he got from his mother was all on fire, and then he would talk of Anson, whom I believe he sailed with when a youth, as a person whose memory deserved his patronage."

"But surely Howe was a great admiral, sir?" said I.

"A great *what!*" shouted Shelvocke. "Why, it was the king who made him a man. What had Howe, down to '94, to do with his own advancement? If he only took a trip as far as the Soundings his Majesty sent him a letter, told him he was a fine fellow, and the glory of his country, and begged his respects to madam and the little Howes. If it hadn't been for Jervis, Howe, in my opinion, never would have beat the French in '94. The honor done that man—merely because his mother was the daughter of some old Hanoverian baron who had been master of the horse to George I.—will be thought one of the most sickening things in history when the magnifying glass of prejudice is crushed under the wheel of time, when the dwarf is dismounted from the shoulders of that short-lived giant called Faction."

I could not help smiling at Shelvocke's warmth, for Howe had been dead thirteen years, and St. Vincent and Nelson had so eclipsed his achievements that his name was seldom upon the public tongue. But I afterward learned that Howe was one of Shelvocke's cherished aversions, and that nothing fired him more quickly than to praise the earl as a good seaman.

"This fog is very bothersome," said I, willing to change a stupid subject, and glancing up at the skylight that lay like squares of smoked glass over the cabin. "I don't remember anything like this in summer, sir."

"It is rather a nuisance for us privateersmen that our ships of war should be blockading the French ports all round," exclaimed Shelvocke, lying back in his chair with a thoughtful frown. "Our cruisers whiten the offing from Boulogne to La Rochelle, and round to the Mediterranean as high as the Gulf of Lyons. I doubt if we can hope for much beyond recaptures. I am in favor of the high seas, clear of ports and forts and lee shores; though I am unwilling to leave the Channel without laying the foundations of a banking account. We are missing booty in my opinion, Madison, by not stretching across the Atlantic and endeavoring to intercept some of the homeward-bound

American traders. But Hannay believes in the English Channel, and I suppose I must give his prejudices a chance. Mr. Chestree, step on deck and see how the weather looks."

The second mate left the cabin, and returned after an absence of a few minutes. "It's as thick as mud, sir, and there's very little wind, and there's no appearance of it clearing." He went on deck again, and after Shelvocke and I had hung over the chart a few minutes we followed him.

It was my watch below, but I had no mind to turn in. The fog was irritating and burdensome; I considered it my duty to be on the alert, albeit the schooner was in good trustworthy hands with Chestree on deck; and moreover the smuggler's tale of the big French ship cruising in this neighborhood gave every man a reason why his eyes and ears should remain open.

Although there was very little wind, the fog blew athwart the deck in horizontal lines; it was as white as steam, but not the more penetrable for that; sometimes it would open a little in folds and disclose the water for about a cable's length from the side of the vessel lying as white as though it were full of chalk sediment, and not a blur upon it, though there was a small ground-swell upon which the schooner rose and sank sluggishly, but quite noiselessly, as everything had been hauled taut aloft and the sheets flattened in to prevent the canvas from shaking. For the most part, however, the fog hung around and over us in a curtain, sometimes so dense that the men forward could not be seen, while the masts shot up and disappeared in it as if they had been sawn short off at the point where they vanished.

Seeing the surgeon smoking a pipe just abaft the galley, I went over and joined him. He had served in a man-of-war, and was a rather coarse-looking person, but he was reputed a very skilful hand, and possessed of more humanity than was commonly to be found among the ship-surgeons of that day. I always thought of "Roderick Random" when I looked at him, for he came very near to the marine medicos of that novel, with his red hair, broken nose, and dirty linen. I spoke to him about the illness I had lately recovered from, and we then drifted into other subjects, and I was rather surprised to find how well he talked. He told me that he was master of four languages, and that it was more on account of his fluency in this respect than because of his professional knowledge that Shelvocke had chosen him out of three or four dozens of applicants for the berth, as it was thought that his capacity of pronouncing these languages skilfully enough to deceive the ear of foreigners might prove of use in strategic measures.

"I think so too," said I, "and heartily wish I had your gift of tongues, Mr. Corney," for that was his name.

"How it may be with privateering I don't know," said he; "but for the British navy I contend that no captain ought to be allowed to take charge of a ship of war without being able to converse with tolerable fluency in at least two languages—say, French and Spanish. Last year an English ten-gun brig was surprised and fired into at night by a large French vessel, whose first broadside made a perfect shambles of her deck. The Englishman wore, and under cover of the darkness gave his big enemy the slip; but a few hours later another large Frenchman came down upon him, and ranging alongside, hailed to know who he was. The captain was about to answer, when the second lieutenant sung out in pure Sicilian that they were the brig *Manfredonia*, of and from Palermo, bound to Rio Para, on which the Frenchman braced his yards round, and left them. The captain reprimanded the lieutenant for answering the Frenchman's hail without leave, and in consequence the lieutenant demanded a court-martial on his own conduct; and the captain was obliged to admit in court that had it not been for the prompt answer of the officer that had completely deceived the Frenchman the brig must have been taken, as half his men were killed or wounded."

"A very good illustration in favor of your argument, Mr. Corney," said I; "and I have no doubt that many a small, disabled English vessel might have given the enemy the slip, had she been commanded by a linguist like your second lieutenant. But I say, when is this fog going to clear? it is enough to choke a man."

And truly it was more ponderous at that moment than at any previous time; the helmsman was a mere looming

5

shadow; although there was a brilliant sun shining over-head it produced no other effect upon the extraordinarily thick mist than to whiten it; the swell was fast subsiding, and the lines of fog, like trailing smoke, were barely driven by the languid draught of air that was moving from the north.

"Hark! what was that?" I exclaimed, holding the cigar I was raising to my mouth poised midway, as though I had been changed into stone.

"What did you hear?" whispered Corney, looking first into the fog on the right and then into the fog on the left of the schooner.

"Hush!" I muttered: "there is a vessel near us."

I went away to Shelvocke, who was sitting on a gun-carriage.

"Did you hear a noise like the creak of a block just this minute, sir?"

"Like the creak of a block? Where-away?" he exclaimed, jumping up.

"I cannot say where the sound came from, sir, but we may hear something more by listening."

I got on to a gun to give my ear a good hoist above the bulwarks, and hearkened with rapt attention, while Shelvocke, with his head inclined, stood like a war-horse with cocked ears, waiting. The men, observing our posture, watched us to know what the matter was. There was a perfect silence throughout the whole length of the vessel that was not a little impressive when one thought of the crowd of living beings that filled her. Now and again the water gurgled alongside, or the rudder faintly jarred, or a timber groaned; but these last sounds were barely audible, while aloft the canvas was quiet as a church-yard.

*On a sudden a cock crowed out in the fog.*

The noise, as I fancied, came from the starboard quarter, but Shelvocke bent his ears toward the starboard bow. Every man on deck had heard the crow, and a half-suppressed titter ran along. It was funny enough to hear the bird's voice sounding from the sea, and amid the dense fog, but the humor was made somewhat grim by the possibility that an enemy was close to us.

The moment Shelvocke heard the cock, he whispered to

" On a sudden a cock crowed out in the fog."
—*Page 66.*

me to see all clear and to have the men stationed; but they were strictly ordered not to speak above their breath, and they went to quarters in their bare feet.   This was one of the strangest, and certainly one of the most exciting, experiences I had encountered since I had been to sea.   Here we were at quarters, and lying all breathless, so to speak, in an impervious fog that hung in dense vaporous masses all around us, in close company with a ship that was not only utterly invisible, but whose very neighborhood could not be guessed, nor her nationality and character imagined.

Shelvocke stood groping along the fog with his eyes.   I went softly from one side of the deck to the other, frequently imagining I saw a dark outline looming amid the vaporous folds.   Presently we heard a sound like that of a coil of rope flung upon deck, and the rattle of shot or a chain.

"Where does it come from, Mr. Madison, think you?" whispered Shelvocke.   "I never knew anything more deceptive."

"She should be yonder if she's anywhere at all," I answered, pointing over the starboard quarter.

"I would to heaven it would clear, that we might obtain but one glimpse of her," said he.   "Were she as big again as we, and an enemy, I'd try my hand on her, and make capital out of this blanket.   Why do you stare?   Do you see anything?"

As he spoke, another cock-crow rose shrill and clear, and again a soft little titter ran along the decks of the schooner.

"I think I see a sort of darkness out yonder, sir," said I, pointing to the quarter in which all along I believed the vessel lying.

"Look a little way to the left of the stern of the cutter."

But as I said this the fog closed all round again as thick as the smoke from the batteries of a ninety, and Shelvocke shook his head.

"I see nothing," he answered, and went to the side and looked over; then returned to me.   "She has not an inch of way on her!" he exclaimed, and motioned with his hand to the leadsman, who was astride of the bulwarks just abaft the fore-rigging.

The fellow dropped the lead softly. I went to receive his report, and came back to tell Shelvocke the soundings made twenty-two fathoms.

Four bells were struck in the fog. The tone was marvellously clear, and so close as to make me start, and a moment after we heard a man's voice hailing some one aloft or forward on the vessel.

"What lingo was that?" exclaimed Shelvocke, eagerly.

"I only caught two words *'laissez! laissez!'* which I took to be French for 'drop it!'" I answered.

"Hush!" cried Shelvocke; and at that instant another voice called out loudly. This evidently came from aloft; it seemed to be up in the air, over our heads. Corney came creeping along the quarter-deck.

"They're French aboard that vessel," said he. "The man who first spoke said: *'Those English are too mean to grease their masts, and here's a fine spar rotting!'*"

Shelvocke smothered a laugh, but looked grave enough a moment after. He made no remark, but walked aft and stood looking over the taffrail. For some minutes we kept staring and listening, and I was beginning to think that it would end in the vessels drifting apart, and in our getting no sight of our neighbor if the fog did not lift before the night came, when all at once the fog thinned right abeam, as though a lane were opened in it by a passage of wind, and disclosed about a quarter of a mile of white water, with just a faint spangle of sunlight touching the further extremity of it. The folds of the fog rolling to the southward, this lane went with them, and when it reached the quarter, there, standing in the clear space of it, and about a pistol-shot away from the *Tigress*, was a large black ship of not less than six hundred tons, lying broadside on to us, with great channels which gave her rigging a tremendously wide spread, and immensely square lower yards. The fog came down as low as her tops, so that all her upper spars were hidden. She showed five guns for her broadside.

I sprang aft to take her bearings by the compass, and when I looked again she was gone.

But gone only to the eye, for now that they had seen us the ear could determine their whereabouts with laughable precision. It was evident that our sudden apparition had greatly alarmed her people; we heard a whole volley of orders thundered out in French; ropes were let go, blocks squealed, yards were sharply braced around. Indeed, the confusion was as sure a sign as the lingo that she was in French hands.

"A merchantman, and a fine one!" exclaimed Shelvocke. "Pass the word for Mr. Corney."

The surgeon was called, and came up from bel w.

"Mr. Corney, you speak French, I believe, in a way to deceive Frenchmen," said Shelvocke. "Will you please hail that vessel, and get them to tell you what they know of her?"

"What vessel, captain?" said Corney, staring into the fog.

"Why, the vessel you can *hear*, sir!"

"Ho, the ship ahoy!" shouted Corney, funnelling his hands and aiming his voice in the direction of the hullabaloo.

At this hail a silence fell upon the Frenchman, and a voice answered in French.

"What ship is that?" cried Corney.

"Who are you that inquire?" came back the reply.

"The French schooner *St. Brieux* from the north, bound to St. Nazaire," responded Corney promptly. "And you?"

There was no answer to this; instead, I heard a sound uncommonly like the traversing of carronade-slides, accompanied by more hauling and pulling and boxing about of the yards.

"Mind!" I sung out.    "They are making ready to give us a broadside, sir.  They evidently suspect us."

And sure enough, as I said this, the white mist flashed up all crimson, as though a mine had exploded close aboard, a heavy roar of artillery followed, and the sea was torn up by a shower of grape about twenty feet away from us.

"Let them have it, men!" shouted Shelvocke in a voice that must immediately have let the Frenchmen into the secret of the "*St. Brieux*"—"aim as I point, and high, to cripple her for us when the fog lifts.  How does she bear, Mr. Madison?"

"Northeast three-quarters east, sir."

He glanced at the compass and indicated the position of

the vessel by extending his hand. The guns were canted and fired. In all five pieces were discharged, and to judge by the crashing and splintering of timber and several sharp yells, the grape and round-shot had plumped faithfully home. Another broadside followed from the Frenchman, and again the iron sleet tore up the water wide of the mark. From the heavy, broad scattering of the missiles it was plain that they were fighting us with carronades, and it seemed by the explosions that the metal was of heavy calibre.

Our men, following the direction indicated by Shelvocke, fired again, and once more we heard the grape rattling and tearing along the invisible deck and the splintering and crashing of yards and masts aloft. If the fog was thick before, there remains no word to express the opacity of it now that the smoke of the cannon hung around us. Although, as I have said, the enemy lay within pistol-shot, the very flame-spouts of his last broadside had not glanced the least reflection on the solid body of smoke and vapor; the men stationed at our guns could scarcely see one another, and when we fired our third broadside they had nothing but the recollection of the spot indicated by the captain to go by, for they could not see him.

Five times the Frenchman fired at us, and the last time his grape sung close along the *port* side of the schooner, showing they were aware that their shot had taken no effect and that they had shifted their aim. A little more and this broadside would have raked us, for they fired with depressed muzzles, and their vessel was twice as high out of water as ours. As it was, not a single shot touched us; we had taken their bearings, but they had evidently *not taken ours*, and it was by omissions of this kind, apparently so inconsiderable, but in reality of the very first importance, that French naval officers lost most of the vessels entrusted to them by a country whose reverses at sea were only to be equalled by its disasters on land.

We were in the act of giving them a fourth broadside, when they hailed to say they had surrendered. Shelvocke immediately ordered the pinnace to be lowered and manned with twelve seamen, in charge of Mr. Tapping, with orders to take possession. The boat's crew were armed to the teeth, Shelvocke being apprehensive of treachery; and a small compass being sent down, and the vessel's bearings given, the pinnace shoved off, and was immediately swallowed up.

We awaited anxiously for Tapping's hail to announce his arrival, the men being still at quarters and the guns double-shotted, ready to bestow their terrible dose should the boat's crew meet with any resistance. But we had no fear that the third mate would overshoot his mark, as he had the bearings of the prize; and it was certain from the result of our broadsides, that the vessel had not drifted half her own length from the spot in which we had sighted her.

We remained waiting some time, I, for one, expecting every moment to hear pistol-shots and the clash of cutlasses, as I thought it extremely probable that the Frenchman had called for quarter as an excuse to get his boats out and tow away from the place in which we had nailed him, when, to our great relief, we heard a shout from Tapping.

"Hallo!" answered Shelvocke.

"It's all right, sir. She's a splendid ship. We've got the Frenchmen under hatches, and liberated the prisoners."

"What the name of the vessel?"

"The *Hanover*, bound from London to Jamaica. She was captured this morning at three o'clock by a French privateer, and has a prize-crew of fifteen men, who were taking her to Havre. There are forty of her crew and the master aboard."

"Is she much damaged?"

"Her foretopmast is in halves, sir, and the royal mast-head rests on the forecastle. Her lower standing rigging is a good deal cut up, but I can't see anything above her tops. She has three men killed and one slightly wounded."

"Very well, Mr. Tapping; while this fog holds, I shall fire a musket from time to time, which you will please answer. Let the liberated men turn to, and refit as well as they can."

This was the only instance that I can remember of a ship having been fought and taken in a fog. A fog is not like the blackness of night. A night must be supernaturally black indeed to prevent a man from obtaining some idea of an enemy's size and even his postures. The very guns he discharges reveal him; or there is a phosphorescent sparkle in the water to tell you where he lurks; or he makes a deeper shadow against the sky than the sky elsewhere holds. But a fog is like blinding a man. You hear a noise, but you cannot tell where it comes from. The flashes of the guns are invisible; and when you think you have the enemy under your muzzles, he has drifted athwart your bows or is lying dead on end astern of you.

It was extraordinary to think of our having a big recapture within hail of us, and yet out of sight; of our having fought a ship of which only a few of us had caught the merest glimpse. The fog remained as thick as a Cape Horn snow-storm until noon, during which time we kept on discharging muskets at intervals, which were regularly answered; so that each vessel was very exactly apprised of the other's distance if not position. Shelvocke was in high spirits, and ordered the steward to serve out an extra dram of rum to the men, who had exhibited a remarkable discipline in the silent and resolute manner in which they had gone to quarters, their stillness as they stood in groups, and in their determined bearing as they waited for the fog to discover their near neighbor, who, for all they then knew, might prove to be a French line of battle-ship.

Scarcely had the sun reached the meridian, when the fog began to thin down in the west. One could see it breaking up into masses like the clouds round the brow of a mountain, with glimpses of the sky shining amid the intervals, and the sparkling of the open waters while, astern of us, it was as thick as cream, and the ship invisible. We were all of us anxious to have a sight of the recapture, and every eye was turned aft, as the vapor thinned down upon the ship, revealing first her hull and next her courses, until presently her main-royal yard oozed out, and then the whole of her lay exposed; and a fine great ship she looked as she floated on the perfectly calm surface of the blue water about eighty fathoms away on our starboard quarter, with her tall, black sides, and the short muzzles of her guns projecting beyond the ports, and her immensely square yards mirrored with extraordinary precision in the transparent sheet of azure on which she reposed, while her

large black shape was thrown into strong relief by the solid
snow-white bodies of vapor which were slowly rolling and
settling away down in the east.

Tapping had turned up her people to refit during the
time they lay in the fog; they had jury-rigged her forward,
though there was enough hoist left in the stump of her
foretopmast to enable a double-reefed sail to be set; and on
the whole, they had made a very respectable figure of her
aloft, where most of our shot had flown, and left her in a
condition very well fit to sail across the short space of
water that lay between us and the English coast.

No sooner had the fog left the two vessels visible to each
other, than the ship's gig was lowered, and three men and
a stout old fellow got into her, and shoved off for the
*Tigress.* While the boat approached our vessel, I jumped
on to the bulwark, and had a long look around the horizon.
In the east, and stretching a considerable distance north
and south, the vapor still hung in heavy masses upon the
water, obscuring all that part of the deep down to within a
couple or three miles of us; but the sea was beautifully
blue and bright with the flash of sunlight on it, and for
leagues in the west it was clear, and not a sail in sight.
The atmosphere was breathless; the swell had entirely subsided, and the two vessels lay motionless, without so much
as a stir of their sails to waft a draught of air along the
deck, upon which the sun was beating fiercely, and already
softening the pitch between the planks, and distilling the
smell of paint from the schooner's side.

The *Hanover's* boat hooked on under the gangway and
the old fellow, who proved to be the skipper, stepped on
board. He immediately inquired for Captain Shelvocke,
and then ran to him with outstretched hands and fairly
embraced him, thanking him in broken tones for having
saved his ship and rescued him and his men from the horrors of a French prison. He was a fine, portly looking old
fellow, and had figged himself out for this visit, being
dressed in a blue swallow-tail, with a couple of brass buttons nearly as big as saucepan-lids under his shoulder-
blades, a fine frill, new silk stockings, big square-toed
shoes, heavily buckled, and a hat like Cobbett's.

He said he had left Gravesend at two o'clock on the preceding afternoon and had reached the Downs at ten o'clock at night, where, not liking the look of the weather, he had brought up within musket-shot of an English brig of war. At three o'clock in the morning he was in his cabin asleep, when he was aroused by a disturbance on deck, and on running up the companion, he found that his ship had been boarded by three boats full of men belonging to a French privateer that was lying hidden close under the South Foreland. Before the alarm could be raised, the hatches were closed, the cable cut, and the *Hanover* standing away to the southward under a press of canvas. It appeared, however, that though the English brig had no suspicion of anything being wrong aboard the *Hanover*, she sighted the privateer soon after the Frenchman's boats had returned to her, leaving a prize crew in the *Hanover*, and made all sail in pursuit. The captain added that he had left London bound to Stokes Bay, to make part of a small convoy that was to sail on the following Monday; he had a crew of forty men, and mounted twelve guns, and certainly hoped, by hugging the English coast, to have dished the French cruisers.

"But," said he, in a passion, "the audacity of those privateers is something shocking, sir. Their impudence is only to be equalled by their cowardice. They run like hares at the first alarm, and they rarely try their hand on any game that is likely to cost them so much as a black eye."

Shelvocke invited them below, but they had hardly reached the bottom of the companion steps when the quarter-deck was hailed by a fellow on the topsail-yard.

"There's a sail on the port quarter, sir, about a couple of points abaft the beam."

I looked, and sure enough there, about four and a half miles away from us, lay a large corvette, which the fog, as it fined away down, had unfolded, just as one lifts a curtain to disclose a scene, with the lustrous water on which she lay becalmed gleaming in her glossy sides, and her courses and topgallant-sails hanging in the bight of the leech-lines.

I went to the open skylight and gave the news to Shelvocke, who had just seated himself; but the instant he heard me, he jumped out of his chair as though a shell had exploded under him, and ran on deck, followed by the portly skipper of the *Hanover*, who arrived through the companion wheezing like an old hound after a run.

"One, two, three—*fifteen* gun-ports of a side, by jingo," I exclaimed, working at her with a glass. "As stout a twelve-hundred ship as was ever launched, sir!"

"Yes, fifteen gun-ports, and all furnished too," said Shelvocke; "and if the height of her lower masts and the narrowness of her topsail-yards, and the hollow cut of the foot of her sails don't speak her a Frenchman, let me be called a Dutchman. What say you, captain?" and he handed the glass to the *Hanover's* skipper.

The old fellow took a long steady stare, and then letting the glass drop from his eye, said:

"A Frenchman, sir—and a very ugly one, too."

Shelvocke glanced round the horizon.

"I see no signs of a breeze, Mr. Madison, so let the crew go to dinner. Mr. Peacock, jump aft and hoist French colors. I'll bother that chap. Carry the halliards forward that the bunting may show."

No sooner was the French flag drooping at our peak than a similar flag was run up to the mizzen-masthead of the corvette. In a few moments this was hauled down, and a private signal hoisted.

"Dip the flag, Mr. Peacock," sung out Shelvocke. "That will perplex them, Mr. Madison. They *may* take us for one of their own privateers becalmed with a prize."

Our flag was lowered half-way down, and then run up again. After a little they hauled down the private signal and hoisted the blood-red St. George's cross.

"No, no, my fine fellow, that won't do," exclaimed Shelvocke, laughing. "Mr. Peacock, belay the flag-halliards, and let them puzzle for a while over that guarantee of our honesty. Captain Jenkinson," addressing the skipper, "if yonder craft prove to be, as I am cocksure she is, a Frenchman, shall you and I fight her?"

"With pleasure," answered the hearty old chap, with a sharp gleam in his eye; "if she'll let us."

"You say you can muster forty men—you have thirteen

of my crew besides, whom I shall leave with you. What are your guns?"

"Eighteen-pound carronades."

"You have five of a side—any swivels?"

"Two."

"Why, you have men to fight them and to spare. What is the risk compared to the chances of success?" He took a few short turns, and slapping his leg vehemently, exclaimed: "We'll have her! we'll have her! Mr. Peacock, jump below and tell the steward to hurry forward the dinner. Captain Jenkinson, we'll settle our tactics over a piece of English beef."

Presently the steward came up to say that dinner was on the table, and I remained alone on deck to watch the movements of the corvette. All this time she had kept English colors hoisted, but shortly after Shelvocke had gone below she replaced the English with the French flag and at the same time sheeted home her topgallant sails and set all three royals. I construed this into a make-ready manœuvre, but whether done with the intention of drawing closer or hauling off when the wind came I could not guess. It was quite probable that she was deceived by the hull of our schooner, which had the true French lines, and the dogged way in which we kept her country's flag hoisted would also help to give her people confidence in us.

Our men, having eaten their dinner, came up in twos and threes at a time, and hung over the bulwarks watching her. So motionless was the air and so marvellously restful the surface of the water, that the *Hanover* and the *Tigress* remained almost precisely in the same posture in which the lifting of the fog had disclosed them.

Twenty minutes passed, and I was looking at the corvette through the glass, when I saw them lower a boat, and distinctly perceived the glitter of the uniform of the officer who entered her. I watched to see what this meant, and on observing that the boat was making for us I reported the circumstance to Shelvocke, who immediately came on deck. It was evident from the leisurely manner in which the boat came along that the officer had not been despatched to make a *tête-à-tête* inquiry. Several times the men rested on their oars while the officer stood up and scrutinized us with a glass. Each time he sat down the boat's crew gave way again, as though another few strokes of the oars would give them a better chance of observing us.

I heard our men forward chuckling over this amusingly reluctant approach when the boat was near enough for them to see her. Indeed, it reminded me of some cowardly though savage animal creeping toward one, ready to turn and fly at the first sound. Yet that boat upon the lustrous blue water and the shape of the heavy corvette beyond made a picture of uncommon beauty. The sea was just broken and blurred under the rise and fall of the oars as though they were dipped into a sheet of quicksilver, and the boat looked like one of those long-legged insects one sees on the surface of stagnant pools on summer evenings as she cautiously advanced with the oars rising and dropping; while the pale blue sea rose like glass to the black hull of the corvette, and terminated a short distance beyond the ship in a gleaming line that was barely distinguishable from the sky; for the fog had now melted out of the air, and the horizon was an unbroken circle.

The boat had got to within a mile and a quarter of us, and Shelvocke had sung out to the boatswain to pipe away the cutter's crew ready to chase her; when, for the tenth time, her men rested on their oars while the officer stood up and examined us. But on this occasion he appeared to have discovered as much as he wanted to find out; for in a moment he flung himself down, the boat's head was pulled round, and off they went back to their ship as hard as ever they could pelt.

"Give him a shot from the stern-chaser!" shouted Shelvocke. Haul down that flag and hoist English colors!"

The gun was pointed and fired, at the instant the English ensign was run up. The roar of the heavy piece of ordnance, amid the dead calm that then prevailed, seemed to shake the schooner down to her kelson. I watched the shot strike the water a long distance astern of the boat and go hopping after her like a pea along a polished table, tarnishing the sea where it struck it as a mirror is blurred by the passage of a damp finger, and flashing up white jets as it ricochetted. The eye lost sight of it after a certain distance, but though it did not hit the boat, it was a well-thrown shot.

"They have the truth now," said Shelvocke, with a glance at our ensign, the nationality of which was clearly displayed by the halliards being taken forward, so as to let the flag hang down like a table-cloth in a laundress's drying-ground. "Captain Jenkinson, I think you had best get aboard your ship and see all clear. We shall take advantage of the first slant of air, and I shall not be surprised if the fog be not presently followed by a breeze from the westward."

The old fellow immediately shook hands with Shelvocke, saying, as he went over the side, that we might count upon his supporting the schooner if the corvette only allowed him to bring his guns within range; and getting into his boat, shoved off, and was presently scrambling up the tall side of the *Hanover*.

"A regular Briton, all of the olden time," exclaimed Shelvocke, watching him as he gained the side of his ship, "as full of spunk as a terrier. But, Mr. Madison, you had better step below, and get something to eat while there is time."

I was not sorry for the chance, but did not stay at table above ten minutes. When I came on deck again, I found Shelvocke pacing up and down the quarter-deck with a cigar in his mouth, casting light glances around the sea from time to time, and constantly humming a soft tune.

The men hung about in the shadows of the sails and the bulwarks, with their breasts bare and their faces crimson. It was, indeed, as hot as ever I remember experiencing in any part of the world. If I stood still a moment I could feel the heat on the surface of the deck through the soles of my boots. A faint haze had gathered over the horizon, and hung in some places in grayish streaks like smoke, while here and there it resembled the outline of a coast. For all that, the air was amazingly transparent, and such was the refractive power of the light that the sea beyond the normal line of it was lifted up so as to form a mirage, which caused the corvette to appear close to us, though, as I have said, she was between four and five miles distant.

"What is the time, Mr. Madison?" asked Shelvocke.

"Hard upon two bells, sir."

"The wind is a long while coming, but after such an extraordinary fog as the one that has just left us, we must be prepared for wonders. I doubt if that fellow will show fight. I have arranged with Jenkinson to let him go if the wind comes northerly—that is, if he means to go—as I don't want to find France a lee shore with a half-masted ship like the *Hanover* in company. On the other hand, if the wind comes south, or east, or west, we'll fight him. My tactics will be to dismast him, for really I believe the *Tigress* will be able to post herself where she pleases, providing the right kind of wind blows. Anyway we must cripple him aloft if possible, so as to give the *Hanover* a chance of pounding him on one side, while we hammer him on the other."

"He won't come up to the scratch, sir. He will have guessed that the *Hanover* is a recapture, and depend upon it he knows that M. le Ministre will forgive his anxiety to preserve the corvette to the grand nation, when he reports that he was opposed to two British vessels, one of them of *trois mâts,* both heavily armed, and, of course, chokeful of men."

"Ay, especially the one of three masts," said Shelvocke with a laugh. "Well, Mr. Madison, it may prove as you say. Our business, I will not call it our duty, is to capture her if we can; and, as I have said, if the wind blows from any quarter but the north I will chase her if she runs, and if she offers fight will engage her, let the wind blow how it will."

He then repeated his conversation with Jenkinson, and explained the tactics agreed upon, should the vessels come into action. I was in the middle of an anecdote of an American privateer that had very cleverly fought an English sloop-ship by means of certain manœuvres which the reader would hardly thank me for particularizing, when, my eye being on the corvette, I noticed that she had set her foresail. I immediately called Shelvocke's attention to this, and suspecting the reason, I took the glass and sprang into the main rigging to make sure of it.

One look satisfied me; the water was dark all away

astern of the Frenchman, and a fresh breeze was coming down dead over her taffrail as she lay with her head to the northward and westward. On my reporting this, Shelvocke immediately passed the word along for the hands to be stationed and everything seen clear. Boarding nettings were triced up, the guns double-shotted, the primings carefully looked to, and all the usual warlike preparations made.

Owing to the sea being cast up by the refractive light behind the corvette, we could see the dark blue line of the wind ruffling the water astern of her when she herself lay motionless upon the placid lustrous-gray surface. We watched her anxiously. Would she keep her yards square and come down with the breeze upon us, or brace up and haul away on a bowline? In a few minutes the flag she carried at the mizzenmast head and the long pennant at the main blew out, her sails rounded, throwing off the shadows which filled them while they hung slack from the yards, like the moon dipping clear of a cloud, and resembling ivory hemispheres as they soared brilliant in the sunshine, one on top of the other. Indeed it was a beautiful sight to see her canvas fill, and the water all around a rich quivering blue, and the passage of the wind along the sea marked by a line as clear as the horizon against the sky.

"She steers as straight as a hair for us," said Shelvocke coolly; "and has more pluck than you think, Madison. She is a big pill for our small throats, but we'll try to swallow her all the same."

"Look, sir!" I exclaimed, almost bursting into a laugh, so strong upon me was the excitement of the moment.

As I spoke the corvette's jib-boom made a slow, majestical sweep, her yards were braced round, her main tack was boarded, and, giving us a whole-length view of herself, there was our heavy friend ratching dead to windward, and going away to the southward under every stitch of canvas she could carry. A regular groan broke from our crew, and a loud, derisive shout came ringing across the water from the *Hanover*.

"No matter, my lads!" exclaimed Shelvocke. "She'll have to go pretty nearly as far as Cherbourg to fetch her native shores if this wind holds, and I have no doubt, men,

she'll reach the nearest port she can come at safe enough—
*if we let her.*"

"We never will let her, sir!"—"Give the *Tigress* the
scent, and she'll know the road!"—"More prize-money for
the gals!"—"Hurrah, boys, here comes the breeze." And
plump it fell upon us while these cries broke from the
crew. The schooner's helm was put hard down, her after-
sails rattled her round, and like the wild and desperate
beast whose name she bore, she seemed to give a long-
plunge, settle herself for a bounding run, and in a minute
was tearing after the Frenchman.

It was a fine fresh breeze that blew now, with a promise
of more weight in it presently. The sea was all of a dance
at once, and blobs of foam like chips of white pine blew
about the merry, streaming waters. The *Hanover* took the
wind, and rounded to it handsomely, and there she was
astern of us, with a double-reefed fore-topsail, and staysail,
and jib set flying forward, and a tower of canvas behind.
I laughed when I looked at her, but I caught Shelvocke
watching her with an expression of great anxiety. A very
few minutes proved that the *Tigress* would leave the *Hanover* hull down long before the corvette fell within range
of our guns. Her round bows made a great hullabaloo in
the water, and she splashed and wobbled like a negro
bathing; but her rate of progress was very slow. Although her bowlines had been triced out to a regular sailors'
song, she appeared to be going free in comparison with the
close-sailing of the schooner; and although she had started
somewhat to windward of us, already in this short distance
of time she was well on our lee quarter. A dull sailer she
undoubtedly was at the best, but with her fore-topmast in
halves, she was simply nowhere at all; and it was immediately apparent, now that the corvette had hauled her
wind, that the *Hanover* could not possibly take part in the
tactics which had been concerted between her captain and
Shelvocke.

For the first and only time that I can remember Shelvocke appeared irresolute.

"Jenkinson ought to have told me she was a tub," he
exclaimed angrily. "I knew by her bows that she wasn't
a clipper; but, confound the man! who would have guessed

6

his hooker couldn't sail at all? Shall I order Tapping to carry the old sugar-box home or let him take his chance by following us?"

"You'll find the Frenchman will shorten sail and bear down upon us when he sees the *Hanover* going. Don't fancy I want to back out of the job, captain, if I ask whether you don't think a thirty-eight-gun ship, as I take that corvette to be, is not a trifle too big for us?"

"No!" he answered, passionately; "and were she twice as big, I would chase and fight her after my speech to the men. That's not the question. What am I to do with that old tea-wagon on our quarter yonder?"

"Send her adrift, sir. She'll be safer out of the road, and she is certainly of no use to us."

He immediately ordered Chestree to signal to the *Hanover* to make the best of her way at once to England. Old Jenkinson seemed annoyed by this order, to judge at least by his tardiness in executing it. I suggested to Shelvocke that, as he had practically reinstated Jenkinson in his old command, Tapping might have been prohibited from carrying out the injunction made by signal.

"More than likely," exclaimed Shelvocke, still in a passion. "But I'll soon show Jenkinson who's master. Molloy, throw a shot across the *Hanover's* forefoot."

The man who was stationed at the aftermost gun sighted the piece and fired. The hint sufficed: for when the smoke cleared away, we saw the *Hanover* in the act of going off before the wind, and in a few minutes there were hands aloft, rigging out the studding-sail booms.

Shelvocke paced the quarter-deck quickly, sometimes glancing at the Frenchman whom we were slowly weathering, though he was spanking along at a sharp pace, sometimes looking after the *Hanover*, whose stern was now at us, and who with her studding-sails appeared a whole hill of canvas on the smooth water.

Chestree came up and asked me if Captain Shelvocke meant to engage the corvette.

"It looks uncommonly like it," I answered, "considering that we are not sailing her for a wager."

"She's a big ship, Mr. Madison," said he, looking at her with his head askew as though he were wall-eyed.

"Yes, a trifle bigger than we are, Mr. Chestree."

"Pray the Lord her batteries prove carronades, Mr. Madison. How many men might she carry now, think you, sir?"

"Why, vessels of her class are usually crowded; and I think we may safely calculate on being opposed by three hundred and fifty men."

"And Tapping away with twelve of our crew!" said he, in a voice so like a groan, that Shelvocke, who was pacing the other side of the deck, stared hard at him.

"No doubt the task before us would be easier if she were smaller or we were bigger," I observed; "but then half the fun of fighting her would be lost."

And so saying, though not in heart one jot more comfortable than my friend Chestree, I went over to the weatherside to watch the enemy. She bore about two points before the beam: and in consequence of the superiority of a fore-and-aft over a square-rigged vessel in hugging the wind, we were lying up well for her, and every minute decreasing the space between us. She was not more than three and a half miles away; and even at that distance was as beautiful a sight as any man could wish to look on. Viewed through the glass, her people could be clearly distinguished upon her snow-white decks, which the pressure of the wind on her canvas inclined toward us sufficiently to enable me to see the breeches of her port-tier of main-deck guns. It is likely that she took us to be a larger vessel than we were; for our far-reaching mastheads and prodigious spread of clothes— the end of our main-boom when amidships seemed to go a whole ship's length over the taffrail!—made us an imposing object; but whether the sight of the retreating *Hanover* gave her courage, or whether she found that we were forereaching and weathering on her too fast to give her a chance, or whether she grew ashamed of running away from the vessel that might have made a long-boat for her, she presently clewed up her royals and fore and mizzen topgallant sails, and hauled up her courses, and, putting her helm to port, ran down to meet us.

I had been expecting this every minute; but the moment she altered her course, Shelvocke gave the order to put the schooner about. The *Tigress*, having brave way on her, ran into the wind to the tune of the boatswain's pipe, and before a man could have counted fifty she was standing to the eastward, with sails as flat as boards, and the men, as quiet as figureheads, massed along the decks.

This manœuvre seemed to capsize Johnny's theories. I suppose he could not guess what we would be at. He stood on for a few minutes, during which time Shelvocke watched him with gleaming eyes and as mocking a smile as ever I saw on a man's face; then he put his helm down.

Probably few landsmen, how ignorant soever of the sea, but knows that a square-rigged vessel does not go round on her heels to stays like a schooner. It seemed an age, in comparison with the nimbleness of the *Tigress*, before the corvette swung her foreyards; and when at last she was braced upon the starboard tack, we had made half a mile of weathering and were well on her lee-quarter. She had hardly got her yards trimmed when she let fly two guns at us, probably to test the range; but, whatever might have been the calibre of the pieces, nothing, so far as we were concerned, came of the experiment but the veil of cobweb-colored smoke that puffed up over her stern and blew down toward us along the sea.

We watched her setting the flying-kites she had clewed up, and when she had boarded her tacks and made herself comfortable, once more Shelvocke shouted out: "Hands about ship!" and amid the half-suppressed grins of the men, who heartily enjoyed the manner in which the captain was bothering the Frenchman, and who believed that behind this dodging lay a bold and clever scheme, the helm was again put down, and the *Tigress* headed on her former course.

It was the right kind of breeze for the schooner, fresh without much weight, and the sea smooth, and she went along like a sledge over a level plain of ice. This time Johnny was more alert. While our own ropes were coiling down, his sails were shaking, and as he gave us his stern, he favored us with another gun. The ball dropped a long way short, though I saw the flash of the foam where it fell.

"Look! look!" shouted Shelvocke suddenly. "She's missed stays! By heaven, they've got her in irons! Put your helm down—flow your head sheets—quick, men—so!

Make ready with your bow gun there, and aim at her spars. Don't fire before the order's given!"

The corvette was indeed in one of those unfortunate predicaments which, in ninety-nine cases in a hundred, are the result of bad seamanship. It happens sometimes, it is true, that, in a cross-sea, and under small canvas, a ship will come up into the wind, a short way, and fall off again with her helm hard down; but in smooth water, with a fine breeze blowing, and all plain sail set, missing stays can only be the consequence of culpable ignorance on the part of the captain or officer in charge, or an inattention on the part of the man at the helm serious enough to deserve the penalty of the yard-arm.

There lay the corvette all aback, the utmost confusion prevailing aboard; and we could only hope that the ignorance or neglect that had got her into this trouble would keep her in it until we had found our account. The *Tigress* was again on the starboard tack, heading up nobly for the enemy. Shelvocke watched her like a cat. Presently she squared her afteryards, and began to pay off slowly. As her broadside veered round to us, she let fly the whole of her main-deck guns. The iron shower tore up the sea at an equal distance between her and us, and buried itself.

"Ready there with the forecastle gun!" shouted Shelvocke. "Take good aim—fire!"

The explosion filled the forepart of the schooner with smoke, and for a few moments the corvette was hidden. Shelvocke sprang on to the weather-bulwarks, and craned himself over the side.

"Load again quickly, and let her have another dose!" he sung out, while I ran aft, ready for the manoeuvre I knew he would execute in a moment or two.

On the second shot being fired from our forecastle, the order was given to put the helm down, and as the schooner shot up into the wind, presenting her broadside to the enemy, who was wearing to come up on the port tack, we gave her five guns. They were discharged with splendid precision. As the white, sulphurous folds were swept off to leeward, I saw the corvette dead abeam of us about a mile to windward, with her mizzen-royal-mast gone, and her main topsail-yard on the cap, the halliards having been shot away. There were several large shot-holes in her fore topsail and mainsail, showing the accuracy with which our guns had been aimed.

We were now, however, in a position to receive *her* broadside, and in a moment it came. The whole side of the black hull flashed into a blinding blaze of light, and I held my breath, expecting to hear the crash of spars tumbling about our ears. One or two shrieks from our crew followed the discharge, and I saw a man stationed at one of the amidship guns spring a couple of feet in the air, and fall like an overturned statue. But aloft the only injury received was a large gape in the foresail and the cutting in halves of some of the running-rigging, the ends of which streamed away like serpents.

For some time the two vessels held on in grim silence. The corvette hugged the wind to preserve the weather-gage as we did to gain it; but she was no match for us either in weathering or forereaching. Although they had bent the topsail halliards afresh with great promptitude, yet even the short period during which this sail had been useless had given us a decided advantage. We were approaching each other fast, and why she did not ease her helm and give us another broadside at once I can only account for by believing that she reserved her powder in the hope of being able presently to transmogrify us by a single discharge. Anyway, she could judge of our strength accurately enough now, and, despite our sauciness, would reckon upon an easy capture.

"Luff!" suddenly shouted Shelvocke. "Fire, men, when your broadside bears."

We spun on our heels, giving the corvette a heavy dose as we rounded, and receiving from her in return a whole storm of canister and round-shot that wounded three of our men, one badly, nipped the fore-topmast just under the royal yard as clean as a handsaw would have done it, filled the foresail as full of holes as a piece of embroidery work, and knocked the gig into staves, which tumbled astern and went away as though an old cask had gone to pieces.

I noticed the moment we had got the schooner round that the wind had veered to the westward of south, which must have happened while we were in stays, so that when the vessel lay close her bowsprit pointed slightly to windward of the corvette's weather-quarter. This shift of wind necessitated a return to our former posture, and the helm was put up to let the *Tigress* wear, as by tacking we should have run aboard the Frenchman. His guns had raised such a smoke that it was impossible to know for some minutes what mischief we had done him; it was then seen that his mizzentopmast had been shot away, his starboard main standing lower rigging was trailing alongside, his jibboom was gone at the cap, and his jibs, ballooning in the water, held him as though he had been warped to a buoy.

Meanwhile we were edging away from him fast, and crawling to windward, some of the hands busy in doctoring the running gear and bending a new foresail, while we kept playing the enemy with round-shot from our long eighteens, which he made ineffectual efforts to return owing to his dismantled condition forward that prevented him from bringing his broadside to bear.

I will not deny that our luck so far had been extraordinarily great. His missing stays had, indeed, permitted us to do almost what we pleased. But, luck or no luck, the manner in which Shelvocke had handled the schooner was beyond praise, and such was the precision with which our men fired that every shot they launched at the clumsily worked corvette carried death and destruction with it.

The wind had now freshened into a strong working breeze, and the *Tigress* was tearing through the water as though she had had enough of this business, and wanted to get home. With our guns trained well aft we kept pegging away at the enemy, whose return fire was of the most capricious and wavering kind, while her bowsprit was black with men clearing the raffle forward.

At the distance of about a mile away from her we tacked, shortened sail, and there we lay snugly to windward, our people peppering her with the coolness of men practising on a target. The order had been given to aim low so as to hull her and shatter her rudder, and the spray flashed up under the balls that raced along as though shells were exploding under the surface of the water.

She had fallen off with her head to the northward, and they were answering our fire with great persistence with their stern-chasers, the shot of one of which crashed through the bulwark close to where I was standing, and filled the air with a whole shower of splinters, by which one of the best men in our crew lost his right eye. It was difficult to see what they were about; but a quarter of an hour after we had got the weather-gage of her they rounded their yards, braced up sharp on the starboard tack, and headed to the eastward. She kept her colors flying, and so soon as she presented her broadside she aimed a shower of grape at us, which, however, fell short, as in squaring away she had widened the distance between us to over a mile.

Suddenly some one sung out, "A sail on the lee quarter!" and looking that way I saw the canvas of what was apparently a large ship, gleaming like satin in the ardent blaze of the afternoon sun. The Frenchman had seen her as well as we, and, being a mile farther that way, could judge better than we what she was like; and his sudden eagerness to crowd away to the eastward looked very much as though he suspected the stranger was an Englishman.

"If we are not sharp," cried Shelvocke, rapping out an oath, his face dark with perspiration, and standing bare-headed, with his rough hair blowing over his lion-like fore-head, "we shall have burned our powder merely to make that corvette an easy prize for a king's ship."

"Unless yonder sail prove a national vessel," I said.

"We'll risk it!" he shouted. "Men, double-shot the long gun forward. Aim at her colors when I put the helm up—if you can bring that flag down she may not want to hoist it again."

The tiller was put to starboard, and the twenty-four-pounder fired.

"Now let fly your broadside as she comes to," and crash went the three after guns. I saw the white splinters glance from her side like bits of silver under the discharge an instant before she delivered another whole broadside at us. This time she had got some of her long guns to bear, and down came our mainsail along with the colors, and a whole shower of blocks and fragments of rope.

A dozen hands sprang aft. The throat and peak halliards were spliced, and with admirable smartness the great sail was hoisted again, along with the red flag streaming at the peak, a sight that raised a hurricane of cheers, in which I found myself joining until I was hoarse.

"Another broadside, my lads, to avenge that affront!" shouted Shelvocke; and again our guns belched forth their lightning and thunder, and the thick pall of smoke swept in an ugly cloud over the radiant blue waters.

"The ship to leeward has hoisted English colors—she is coming up fast—I can see her courses down to the tacks of them!" I cried, working away with the glass.

"We have shot away the Frenchman's colors!" sung out Chestree from the waist, where he stood with his face as grimy as a chimney-sweep's from the sweat and powder that covered it.

"She has hauled them down, sir!" cried a dozen voices.

"Not a bit of it!" shouted Shelvocke. "Let her have another broadside! She's not to be meat for our masters!" pointing with a passionate gesture to the ship to leeward, whose presence seemed to make him mad.

Amid a volley of cheers, the guns were again fired. We looked to see the effect. For some minutes the corvette had ceased firing, and heeling over to the breeze, she was stretching along the water with a line of foam along her, against which sparkled her bright copper, though the stately fabric aloft was in sad ruins, her sails full of holes, her mizzen-topmast gone, her high-pitched bowsprit looking like the stump of an amputated arm, and her colors vanished.

Hardly had the smoke of our last broadside cleared away, when two flags were run up to her main. They got foul when they had mounted a short distance, and were hauled down. In a few moments they were hoisted again, and when they were level with the maintop, they blew out and disclosed the English flag flying over the French colors. We stood looking on in perfect silence until the flags were mast-headed, and then such a roar broke from the men as I believe only British throats know how to deliver. I saw rough fellows stripped naked to the waist *blubber like children* as they shook hands with one another. On the news being taken below, where the surgeon was working like a horse, a man whose knee had been shattered by a grape-shot compelled the bearers of the news to carry him on deck, where, snatching a cutlass from the hand of

one of his mates, he brandished it over his head, and with
a half-suffocated cheer for Captain Shelvocke and the
*Tigress*, fainted dead away.

"It was worth the risk, was it not, Madison?" said Shelvocke, looking with a proud smile at the corvette, and
combing the sweat from his forehead with his hand.

"It was, sir," I answered promptly; "and I cordially
congratulate you on a remarkable victory."

"Which would have been won by us," said he, "not so
speedily perhaps, but in the end quite as surely, without
the presence of that big cruiser."

Meanwhile we were running down to the Frenchman,
who lay with his mainyards aback, a pitiful spectacle indeed, the significance of which was enormously increased
by the flags at the mast-head. As we drew near, we saw
that her hull was badly knocked about, especially in the
after-part, and her bulwarks abaft the mizzen-rigging were
full of holes, some of them as cleanly cut as if a chisel had
gouged them out. We rounded to about a quarter of a
mile to windward of her, and lowered a boat, into which I
got with ten men, and a few strokes of the oars took us
alongside.

On gaining the deck of the prize, I was received by a
man who proved to be the first lieutenant, whose resemblance to Bonaparte was so extraordinary, that I came to
a dead halt when I saw him. His very pose, as he stood
to receive me, was that of the First Consul: the head inclined forward, one arm reposing on the breast, and the
other hanging by his side.

"Monsieur," said he in French, with much grief not un-
mingled with dignity in his manner, "my captain being
dead, it is my melancholy duty to take his place, and to
yield possession of the *Diane* to her conquerors. It is the
fortune of war, monsieur;" and with a low bow he gave me
his sword.

I understood very well what he said, but my stock of
French was small, and what I knew I was reluctant to pronounce for fear of being laughed at. I asked him if he
spoke English.

"A leetel," said he with much such a grimace as a man
would make who had an unpleasant taste in his mouth,

"Then, monsieur," said I, "I should be glad to learn from your lips that your yielding to the privateer schooner *Tigress* was not occasioned by the presence of that ship yonder;" and I pointed to the British vessel to leeward, that had tacked, and was now heading to fetch us by a couple of boards, and that turned out to be a large two-decker.

"Sare," he replied with a slow smile, "ze *Diane* yields to *you*. "But," with a flourish of his hands, "had it not been for zat sheep zaire we should have continue ze fight."

And this was all I could get him to admit.

That the fight would have been protracted had the liner kept her sails out of sight I do not deny, and have always admitted in talking over the engagement; but that the corvette would *ultimately* have yielded to us I am quite confident; for having the weather-gage, being almost uninjured aloft, having marvellous sailing qualities, and being armed with guns which could have battered the enemy within a radius of two miles, the *Tigress* might have been backed to have knocked the *Diane* into a sheer hulk in less than another hour.

The survivors of her crew had been got below, and my men stood guard over the hatches; and, having a clear view of the deck, I beheld as ghastly a sight as the horrors of warfare ever furnished forth. The main-deck was strewn with carcasses: the scene reminded me of the description of the deck of the *Salvador*, after the action off Cape St. Vincent. In addition to the slaughter caused by our own guns, one of the main-deck carronades had burst, and killed twelve men who were stationed at or near it. It was enough to freeze the marrow in a man's bones to see the shattered human remains, the broad, dark scarlet pools in which the sunshine flashed, and the blood straining through the scupper-holes, and marking long dull-red lines down the ship's side, and crimsoning the green water where they touched it.

The corvette was more wrecked aloft than appeared at first sight: her main topmast was badly wounded, the after part of her main-top shot away, and to starboard her mainmast was supported by two shrouds only. I saw that if the wind freshened these spars must go, unless the canvas was handed and preventer backstays set up. I accordingly jumped on to the rail, and waved my hat to the *Tigress*, signifying that I wanted to speak her, on which her helm was put up and she stood toward us.

Surrounded as I was by the ghastly memorials of the conflict, it seemed scarcely a moment in which room could be found for admiring the beauty of the schooner: yet, so ennobled was she by her triumph, she did so plead to my admiration, that I could not remove my eyes from her as she swept down before the bright breeze, floating like a swan on the deep green waves, which ran along her ebony sides without lifting her, and revealing as they curled past, the vivid sheen of her metal sheathing, while the British cannon bristled under her high bulwarks, and her white sails, delicately shaded at the after-leeches, soared upon a sky whose ripe afternoon beauty made a superb background for one of the gracefulest fabrics which ever breasted the waters of the deep.

As I knew Shelvocke would sing out some inquiries, I put a few questions to my Napoleonic friend, who remained at my side, and whose utter dejection deprived me both of the will and the wish to send him below, though I believe it was my duty to have done so. In a few minutes the *Tigress* was within speaking range, whereupon she hauled up the clew of her mainsail, and ranged abreast of us with her sails shaking.

"*Tigress*, ahoy!" I shouted.

"Hallo!" answered Shelvocke, standing on the rail of the bulwark.

"You had better send some men aboard to fish and doctor the corvette's spars, sir, a few of which are badly wounded. We are terribly crippled aloft, and a gang of thirty men won't be too many to do what is wanted."

Shelvocke raised his hands to betoken that he heard me; and after a short interval, during which a boatswain's pipe sang like a bird on the schooner's forecastle, a couple of boats full of men shoved off.

While they approached, Shelvocke called to me to give him the particulars of the prize.

"She's the French thirty-eight-gun corvette *Diane*, Captain Eugene Tournelle," I answered, delivering my words through the hollows of my hands, and shouting at the top of my voice; for not only was the wind dead in my teeth, but overhead the sails were shaking like a thousand cocks flapping their wings for a crow, and the water washed noisily along the side of the motionless hull. "She mounts a few long eighteens and twenty-six sixty-four-pound carronades. It is believed that she has twenty-eight men killed, twelve of them by the bursting of a gun, among them her commander, and between thirty and forty wounded, including her second and third lieutenants. Her complement is three hundred and eight and she has seven English prisoners aboard, being a portion of the crew of H. B. M.'s cutter *Severn*, which she captured three days ago, with despatches, ten miles to the norrard of Cuxhaven."

Shelvocke again waved his hand, and got off the rail and went aft, where he stood looking over the taffrail at the two-decker, that had gone about and was lying up to fetch us under every stitch of sail that would draw.

I had now half the *Tigress'* crew aboard; and, with the help of the boatswain and carpenter, I started them on the various refitting jobs which the corvette immediately required. There were some shot-holes in her hull that wanted plugging, but none between wind and water, and the pumps gave us an almost dry hold. What needed most attention was the mainmast, that, on examination, was found to have received one of our twenty-four-pound shot about half a dozen feet below the top.

Our men were appalled by the sight of the dead upon the decks, and seemed glad enough to jump aloft to get away from the bodies. I inquired of the first lieutenant for the body of the captain, and was told that he had been carried below on receiving his wound, and that the corpse lay in the state-cabin. Shocking as the ship looked with the dead scattered about her decks, I could not glance my eye over her without pride and wonder. She was only a year old; and in spite of her having been ploughed into a shambles and so cut up in her rigging that, fore and aft, she was littered with rope's-ends, fragments of canvas, splinters, blocks, and such-like raffle, together with capsized tubs, muskets, pikes, and a whole ocean of different kinds of shot—enough hints yet survived to suggest the beautiful completeness she had exhibited before she came into action. Where her decks were not stained with blood or blackened with the grime of powder, they were as white as the paper on which this is printed. Her brass-work was so radiant that the eye was blinded by the sparkle of the sunshine in it; her guns were noble pieces of ordnance; her masts and yards, magnificent spars: the French love of embellishment had gone so far in her that even the coamings of her hatches were ornamented with graceful carvings; every rope lying in the chafe of another was carefully served; and the ends of most of her running rigging, instead of being "pointed" or "whipped" as with us, were fitted with small brass caps. There was a "cap of liberty" on the skylight, an object about seven inches long, made of wood and painted red, with a round tapering spear of brass, three and a half inches long, the lower half blackened, with a screw at the end, to fix it to the masthead—a genuine republican signal, which many French vessels in those days sent aloft when they went into action, but which, in the case of the *Diane*, had probably been overlooked amid the confusion when she missed stays.

The French lieutenant, who appeared crushed with his misfortunes, watched me as I ran my eyes over the corvette, and when our glance met, he said:

"A fine sheep, sare."

"Ay," I rejoined, "a vessel that does honor to the skill of your dock-yards."

"But she will fight ze battles of Great Bretagne now, monsieur," he exclaimed mournfully.

"It is the fortune of war, sir," I answered, repeating his own remark.

"What a prize for zat footy leetel sheep!" cried he, extending his hands with a passionate gesture of annoyance and astonishment as he looked at *Tigress.* "Your papaires vil make moch of this sare, no doubt."

"Still we would rather have risked another hour's fight with you than have seen these colors up there flying with that English ship in sight."

"Yes, I understan'," said he, with a shrug of the shoulders, and, raising his hat, he went below.

His wonder that the *Diane* should have fallen a prize to the schooner was quite reasonable. The result of the engagement I considered little short of a miracle when I con-

trasted the sizes of the two vessels, and considered the difference between the strength of the crews and the weight of
the metal.   If it had not been that the *Tigress'* fore-topmast was shot away under the royal yard, she would have
exhibited no visible injury whatever aloft, beyond the shot-
holes in her canvas.   Also we had suffered a very trifling
loss in men, and our hull was but little damaged, in consequence of the habit of the French gunners of elevating their
pieces so as to cripple their enemies's spars.   Comparing
the *Tigress'* condition with that of the *Diane's*, and bearing in mind the schooner's qualities, and Shelvocke's clever
handling of her, I began to sympathize with my captain's
chagrin when I looked over the corvette's lee quarter, and
watched the British two-decker edging up for us.   Argue
as we might, *her* presence would rob us of half the glory of
our conquest.   No one would credit that this thirty-eight-
gun corvette would have struck to a privateer of twelve
guns, had the British line-of-battle ship not hove in sight.
But it could not be helped, and I now waited impatiently
for the two-decker to come up to us, as it was evident that
Shelvocke meant to take instructions from her before he left
the ground.
   Strong as was the sense of pique in me, however, I could
not behold the majestic fabric drawing along the water without kindling emotions.   Her stately heights of canvas slanted
her about a couple of streaks, and she presented her weather
broadside as she swam forward, her long jibboom pointing,
like the spear of a Colossus, a few points to leeward of our
bow, and her prodigious stretch of cloths filling a broad
space of sky with canvas that glistened like snow on a
mountain-top.   Her double lines of guns grinned along the
white streaks, and the green and foamy surges toppling
against her huge side looked, by contrast with her bulk, no
more than the ripples of an inland lake.   Her long pennant
flashed like a line of fire against the deep azure, and, start-
ing from that great altitude, the eye ran down a succession
of widening sails and spars of black rope, and the exquisite
lace-work of the thin, running-gear.   Her forecastle rail
was dotted with seamen dressed in white, and figures could
be seen in her tops, while here and there in a window
glanced back the play of the luminous water, and a small

bed of foam hung like a heap of snow at her stem, and twinkled frostily along the gold-bronze metal armor that sheathed her bottom.

She proved to be His Britannic Majesty's ship *Endymion*, and as she floated into a position abeam of us she clewed up her light sails and courses and backed her fore-yards all simultaneously, as though the whole operation had been performed by pulling a lever, as the motion of a crank sets a hundred dolls dancing in a breath. No sooner was she at rest than a boat was lowered from the *Tigress*, into which jumped Shelvocke, and pulled away to the seventy-four.

All this time the weather remained magnificent, with a soft, fresh wind blowing out of the south, and here and there a wool-white cloud speeding across the liquid blue like a puff of steam. I have often thought that the three vessels, as, they lay abreast, made as striking an after-battle picture as any which the records of single actions could supply. The presence of the line-of-battle ship with her sky-searching masts and enormous breadth of yards, on which a man looked no bigger than a fly, and the superb completeness of her trim aloft, and the sparkle of epaulets at the gangway, and the color of the uniforms of the marines, and of a number of soldiers which she had on board, lent such an emphasis to the maimed, blood-stained, and crippled corvette, whose spars were dotted with our men at work on the difficult and perilous job of refitting, as she would hardly have taken from the neighborhood of the *Tigress* only.

In truth, I was glad to look anywhere but on the deck of the prize where the dead lay. It was evidently the broadside we had given her when she missed stays and while we were tacking under her quarter that had done most execution; and considering the small quantity of powder that had been burnt in this action, the condition of the *Diane's* spars and rigging and the sieve-like appearance of her after-bulwarks illustrated in a manner that struck me forcibly the extraordinary precision with which our guns had been pointed.

Just as the boat containing Shelvocke passed under the stern of the *Endymion*, the lieutenant of the corvette came up out of the cabin and stood for some moments with his hand resting on the companion, looking at the big ship.

He glanced round at me and broke from his reverie with an apologetic smile.

"We have built some fine ships for your service, monsieur," said he in French. "That vessel was our *Renommée*, and once carried the flag of Admiral Villebert."

I replied in English that our Government was quite willing to leave France in possession of her fleets, providing she would use them for the preservation of her own trade instead of the destruction of the trade of other nations. "We have in our country," said I, "a place called Hartwell, where there lives a country gentleman known by the name of Monsieur. You have doubtless heard of him, sir. He may not be able to gain your ships, but if you will call him to Paris he'll show you how to keep what you have."

"*Sot! animal! fainéant!*" said he, grinding out the words between his teeth and turning away with an expression of bitter indignation after having bestowed upon me a frown so Bonapartesque (if I may use such a word) that the resemblance was enough to make a man a laugh outright. Whether these flattering epithets were meant for me or "Monsieur" I did not know, and to be plain I did not care. I never thought much of a Frenchman's rage. Perhaps I should have spared the observation that annoyed him; but it was almost impossible to look at him without irritation, he was so deucedly like the Corsican bully. However, I was sorry for the poor fellow's situation, and recognized the claim he had upon my utmost civility; so mustering up the blandest smile at my command, I begged his pardon if I had said anything to offend him, and changed the subject by asking him how his ship had managed to miss stays?

He gave me the technical reasons, but as he did not know the English equivalents, and as I could not understand the French professional terms, he left me as wise as I was at the beginning. Had he said they had jammed her up in the wind, and stopped her way before they put the helm down, he would have given the right explanation. But he talked of *le vent* and *le gouvernail* and the *démoralisation* of the *timmonier*, so far as I could follow him, and made a long scientific yarn out of an incident which was to be explained by two words, "Bad seamanship."

The English prisoners had been liberated on our coming

7

aboard, and had been sent aloft along with the *Tigress'* men to help doctor the spars and rigging. Some of them, as well as a portion of my own men, having finished the jobs allotted to them, came down, and I ordered them to range the dead bodies decorously and cover them with a spare sail until orders for their disposal should have been received. I imagined the fellows would not like the task; the *Tigresses* certainly went about it reluctantly, and from some of the ghastlier things they hung back with such disordered countenances that I had scarcely the heart to urge them on. But the men out of the captured cutter had no compunction. Their treatment of the dead was grossly indecent and revolting. Every insult that it was possible for them to offer, they heaped upon the remains of their dead enemies, and from time to time one or the other of them would make some remark which invariably produced a shout of laughter from his inhuman companions.

"What are you about?" I shouted, horrified by the rascals' behavior, and enraged that the French lieutenant should witness such conduct in British seamen. "Why, the South Sea cannibals would set you an example in decency, you brutes! Treat those bodies respectfully, do you hear? or I'll send such a report to the captain of that ship yonder as will earn you the best lashing that ever you got in your lives."

"Please your honor," answered one of them, pointing to a body, "this here cove kicked me on the shins yesterday for axing him for a chew of tobacco."

"And they thought nothen of calling our King a cochong, sir!" bawled another.

"I don't care about that," said I. "Handle those bodies respectfully, or I'll have you stretched until you're thin enough to crawl aboard through a scupper-hole."

I watched them sharply, thinking that, as men in receipt of King's pay, they might dispute the authority of a privateersman, in which case I should have set my own men upon them; but they took fright at my threatening to report them, and one of them looking over the bulwarks and seeing a boat pulling toward us from the *Endymion*, they went to work as soberly as monks, and in a few minutes the dead were hidden, though in the waist and forward there was blood upon almost everything the eye rested on.

The French lieutenant went below when he saw the *Endymion's* boat; and observing Shelvocke and an officer in her, I sung out for the side to be manned. The foam flashed up in smoke under the boat's bows as she advanced, swept along by twelve oars which dropped and rose with beautiful precision, while beyond her floated the huge two-decker, as motionless as a tower upon the water, and the reflection of the lustrous waves trembling in her sides as you may see the sunlight gleam in the well-curried hide of a horse.

The moment Shelvocke gained the deck he shook me by the hand and thanked me for my assistance in the engagement that had made this noble ship prize to the *Tigress*. His manner was more gratifying than his words. The officer who accompanied him, making me a bow, said that he considered the achievement of the schooner truly remarkable, "and I only regret," said he, "she is not a King's ship, that her commander and officers might obtain the reward which their courage merits."

All this was very nice, and I think that we had some right to feel proud when we saw the officer looking around at the vessel, and at her heavy batteries, and her powerful scantling and the wreckage aloft; and then at the *Tigress*, the audacious little instrument of this new disaster to poor Johnny Frenchman, lying to windward, slightly lifting to the green waters which played round her stationary hull, with nothing missing aloft but her royal and sky-sail yards, and her white canvas filling and shivering as she fell off and came to under the action of the helm.

It had been arranged aboard the liner that the prisoners were to remain in the prize, that I was to take charge of her to Portsmouth with such of the crew of the *Tigress* as were on board, and that, as in consequence of the division of the schooner's crew, neither she nor the corvette would be in a position to engage any enemy's ship that might come upon the scene, the *Endymion* would convoy us to Portsmouth. Having therefore given me the instructions I required, Shelvocke returned to the schooner and the officer to the *Endymion;* and on the latter firing a gun, we sheeted home the fore and main topsails and under as much canvas as we dared carry stood after the two-decker, with the *Tigress* on our weather quarter.

So terminated the action with the corvette, which, I need hardly say, we brought safely into Portsmouth, along with the *Hanover*, whom we overhauled at daybreak next morning. The *Diane* was purchased by the English Government, and taken into the Navy under the name of the *Diana*. She was wrecked off the Isle d'Oléron only seven months after she had refitted, and one hundred and twelve persons perished with her.

Several accounts of the engagement appeared in the newspapers of the time; but though the pluck of the *Tigress* was warmly praised, it was also said that the corvette had been hurried into striking by the *Endymion's* heaving in sight, and thus robbed the bullion of its lustre, though it left the metal good gold all the same. We remained at Portsmouth twelve days, during which time the *Tigress* was visited by several hundreds of persons, so lively was the interest her exploit had raised. Among these visitors was Sir James, afterward Lord de Saumarez, the hero of Algesiras, one of the bravest and certainly one of the most neglected men of that age, whose share in Aboukir was only second to that of Nelson, and who was rewarded by Evan Nepean's *private applause*, when men for smaller deeds were being raised to the peerage, and getting the thanks of Parliament. Shelvocke was in London at the time, and I had the honor of receiving this brave and Christian gentleman, and relating to him the story of the action with the Frenchman. He said to me as he went over the side: "I have always had a dislike to privateering as a business in which more evil is done than any government ought to sanction. Merchantmen have no right to fight unless in their own defense. But after hearing your story, and observing the discipline and beauty of this vessel, I shall hereafter think of privateering with indulgence."

When I repeated this to Shelvocke, he said it was the best bit of praise he had yet received.

# CHAPTER V.

THE triumphs of the *Tigress*, won within twenty-four
hours after her departure from the West India Docks, and
Shelvocke's clever and audacious handling of her, had given
wonderful confidence and enthusiasm to the men, who not
only knew the qualities of the vessel, but their power to
fight an enemy three times the *Tigress'* size; and when the
schooner, thoroughly refitted, and with her full complement
of men aboard, set sail from Portsmouth, there was not a
crew afloat upon the seas at that time more resolute, hearty,
and united than the ninety brave fellows who swung their
hammocks in the 'tween-decks of Hannay's beautiful
privateer.

I never felt the gladness and independence of our life of
licensed freebooting more keenly than on this day as I stood
on the *Tigress'* quarter-deck looking at the distant green-
crowned heights of the Isle of Wight, with Nettleston
Point drawing out to Bainbridge, and receding into San-
down Bay, where the coast-line melted into a film of blue
cloud, with a line of lustrous white between it and the
throbbing waters of the horizon, while the broad English
Channel opened into an interminable reach of gleaming sea
over our bows.

The wind was off the shore, and we went along leisurely,
with the main-boom well over the quarter, and the huge
squaresail softly lifting, and the water creaming past us;
when, Donnose being a pale blue blob no bigger than a pea
astern of us, a sail hove in sight that, on nearing, proved to
be a small armed English cutter, having in tow a large
French schooner, cut in pieces aloft. It was as odd a sight
as ever I saw, and the men stood laughing at it until the tears
hopped down their iron visages; for the cutter was certainly

not more than five-and-thirty tons, and looked deplorably ragged and dirty; whereas the hulk, for she was a schooner no longer, having only her lower masts sticking out of her deck like two immense pumps, was considerably over a hundred tons, with four guns of a side, and a big brass swivel on the forecastle; so that, as they crept along the sea, they resembled an ant hauling a caterpillar into its nest, or a puppy with the carcass of a sheep made fast to its tail.

We ran down for a near view, and on hailing the cutter, a midshipman about the size of a common monkey got upon the rail, and asked what we wanted.

"Are you in charge?" inquired Shelvocke.

"Certainly I am," answered the middy, in a haughty drawl, thrusting his hands into his pockets.

"You appear to have a lumping prize astern of you," said Shelvocke, preserving his gravity with an effort.

"Yes; but, you see, we've dismasted her, though not before they killed all the cutters' officers but me."

"Where are your prisoners?"

"Most of 'em overboard, but there are thirty of them in the hulk; and if you were going my way, I'd ask you to lend me a couple of those fat, grinning hands of yours to *sit upon* the prize's fore-hatch, as I can only muster seven men, five of whom are wanted to work the cutter, so that there are only two to guard the hulk's hatches; and they're so reduced in flesh by feeding on Admiralty stores, that if the Frenchmen were only to combine their lungs and fetch a heavy breath, I'll be hanged if they wouldn't blow my men overboard like chaff!" and the little fellow laughed so uproariously that he lost his balance and toppled backward on the deck, though he was up again in a moment.

"We'll convoy you in if you like," sung out Shelvocke.

"No, thanks; we've managed without you so far, and we'll risk what remains. I say," he shrieked through his hands, for we were fast widening our distance, "how far are we off the Isle of Wight?"

"St. Catherine's point bears about fourteen miles N. W. by W."

The plucky little creature flourished his hat and dropped on to the deck, where, the bulwarks being taller than he, we lost sight of him. Aboard the hulk we could only see two

men, armed with cutlasses and muskets, standing at the
fore-hatch, and a boy steering. Whether there were really
thirty prisoners below, it was impossible to say; but that
the prize was a genuine capture, and won by a desperate
fight, was proved not only by the smallness of the number
of the cutter's people, but by the manner in which she was
cut up aloft and by the shots in her hull and the splintered
condition of her bulwarks and stern.

"Smite my timbers, Bill, if ever I see the like of that!"
I heard one of our boatswain's mates exclaim as he looked
after the cutter; "no wonder old Wooden Shoes funks us
when newly weaned British babbies go forth and capture
his vessels."

Although Shelvocke did not want to insult the little chap
by keeping near him, he shortened sail and hauled to the
westward, and so held the cutter and her prize in sight
until shortly after one o'clock, when the cutter having tacked, we sighted a sloop-of-war, apparently fresh
from Spithead, coming down toward the two vessels, on
which, as we knew she would give the midshipman all the
help he required, we made sail, and stood for the French
coast.

We dined this day at two o'clock, and Peacock was invited to join. So four of us sat down, while Tapping
stumped the hot deck overhead. It was cool enough, however, in the little cabin; for the mild wind blew in a pleasant draught down the open skylight, through which you
could see the immense mainsail stretching in a whole ocean
of white canvas against the sky, while the long withe-like
topmast, that terminated at a height of a hundred and
forty feet from the cabin-floor, seemed, like a pencil in the
hand of a giant, to be making a scroll of the face of the
heavens, as the gentle motion of the vessel swept the point
of the tall spar here and there.

I ate my dinner thankfully, for I was as hungry as a wolf,
while Chestree let his plate grow cold over some long yarn
of a cutting-out expedition he had picked up from a third
lieutenant whom he had met at Portsmouth. On my ear it
was a story that fell flat enough; but Peacock attended,
with his handsome eyes gleaming like the optics of a Spanish woman when listening to the man she loves, and his

delicate cheeks glowed with as pretty a damask as ever the eloquent blood wrought in the human face.

I caught Shelvocke—when he thought himself unperceived —watching the lad with great admiration, and another expression which I cannot very well define: it was such a mixture of melancholy and pleasure, half-wistful, half- reluctant, as though memory were working in against the will; but in all which I should have found nothing to marvel at, seeing that the youth had one of the most beautiful faces I ever beheld out of the canvas of some of the Italian masters, not to mention his melodious voice and an indescribably delightful gentleness of manner mingled with a sound element of manliness, had not the skipper suddenly caught me with my eyes fixed on him, whereupon the pensive expression went out of his face with an abruptness that had it been acted would have been thought as fine a thing as Kemble's transition from softness to scorn in *Hamlet;* and for some moments he was as cold and stern as ever I remember seeing him when preparing his vessel to engage.

However he presently thawed, and asked me to take wine with him.

"You remember the French lugger we chased, Madison?" said he—"she that burned the little *Happy-go-Lucky?* I have often been bothered to think what she could have meant by booming out her lugs and running dead for the Goodwins. My idea was that they meant to run her aground and set fire to her and drag their boats over the sand into the waters beyond and escape in that way. But a pilot whom I met in London, and to whom I told the story, said that this was an old trick of Johnny's—that what they were really trying for was a swatchway about a mile to the east of the South Sand Head. They could have floated over by dropping their guns and stores overboard, and had they managed it they would have escaped. Their dodges are a proper study, and I live and learn."

"Strange that the French, who are so fond of dancing that a lump of sugar in a glass of water will set them capering, don't like our English *balls*," said Chestree, grinning with his capacious mouth over his vile pun.

"By the way, Chestree, talking of balls, you were rather

against our engaging the *Diane*, weren't you, eh?" exclaimed Shelvocke.

"Yes, sir, I was—I considered she was too big for us, sir," answered Chestree candidly.

"Nothing is too big for us," said Shelvocke shortly.

"No, not to look at, sir—but to fight! One Englishman is equal to ten Frenchmen, I'll allow—but when you come to double that number——"

"Pooh, pooh!" interrupted Shelvocke, "never talk of counting your enemies, man. Had you begun to *compute* when you were third of the *Syria*, and headed the boarders who cleared the decks of *Le Phœnix*, where would you be now? Why, the French worms would be polishing your bones, man, wouldn't they? Never trouble yourself to *think* when once fighting becomes necessary. That's the principle of that magnificent fellow Cochrane, who is the noblest Roman of us all since Nelson's death. Lord Gambier, poor old thing, *thought*, you may remember, and you now what came of it. Madison, this is no oblique denunciation of you, though I believe you were of Chestree's mind."

"I was," I answered, and was beginning to state my reasons when he interrupted me.

"Come, gentlemen, pass the wine along. Whatever people may be pleased to say concerning the audacity of the *Tigress'* commander, my resolution would have made but a ridiculous figure of me had I not officers not only equal to that occasion, but superior to any occasion my temerity is likely to bring about. Gentlemen, I give you the health of Bonaparte. May he long continue to build vessels for us to take!"

"I couple with the health of Bonaparte that of my namesake, the President of the United States of America," said I, emptying my glass.

"Hush!" said Shelvocke; "before we toast him let us be sure that we can thrash him."

"Do you think there is any doubt of that, sir?" inquired Peacock, in that sweet voice of his, which I never could hear pronouncing warlike language without smiling.

"I do, Mr. Peacock, indeed. I would not own as much just now at a Mansion House dinner, for instance, nor whisper it within a league of St. James's. But so surely as I sit at the head of this table—which, by the way, and as I have all along thought, would be the better for another six inches of beam, seeing that it has to accommodate Chestree's shanks for a cruise which I hope may last for months —so surely, gentlemen, will the Yankee captains give their fellow-republicans an account of King George's cruisers that shall make some of us hang our heads. Mark well what I say, as among my other ambitions I wish to shine as a prophet. There will be a heap of horrible lies told; but from the ashes of Yankee fiction the future American historian of this unfortunate war of ours with beings who speak our tongue, and who, at heart, are pretty nearly as proud of us as we are of ourselves, will rake us up some gems of truth to decorate the page that remains to be filled."

"They would make a great man of you were you to go among them," said I.

"Come, Madison, don't let prejudice blind you," he exclaimed good-naturedly. "I like the Yankees as little as you. I will admit that their bad qualities are more numerous than our united fingers and thumbs. But give them time, man. When you were a little fellow, I'll warrant you stole mammy's sugar, and robbed old Ox's orchard, and went a bird-nesting. But such matters are not going to earn the conviction of your manhood. Give the Yankees time, I say; and while you denounce what is bad in them, admire the genius of a people who are quickly rearing a magnificent empire t'other side of the water, and who have in a superlative degree the admirable virtues of perseverance, courage, patience, and—yes, *and* — patriotism, whether you call them rebels or not."

"Do you know, sir, I think we are going to have dirty weather," said the prosaic-minded Chestree, shoving in his oar without the least intention of being rude; the poor fellow had been staring up the skylight while the skipper was sporting his periods, until he was so engrossed with the look of the sky as to sing out without reflection.

"Thanks, Chestree, for saving me the trouble of *perorating*," replied Shelvocke, laughing: and rising, he led the way out of the cabin.

Thre was some shrewdness in Chestree's perception, for though the sky was blue enough to have made a landsman in love with it, with a bank of rich white clouds down in the east, and a few lines of vapor overhead, in the pearly margins of which the sun had painted a dozen languid tints like the colors of a fading rainbow, there was a haziness about the azure, a blearedness resembling the film on a sick man's eyes, that betokened a change of weather. The breeze was steady, well on the starboard quarter as we headed west-by-south, with nothing but the gleaming heaving sea around us.

I asked Shelvocke if he had any special cruising-ground in his mind.

"None whatever," said he. "As we go we shall raise Cape Levi by holding on, and we may find something to serve us creeping out of Cherbourg. We can only grope and hope—that's the privateer's article of faith. I asked everybody I met both in Portsmouth and in London for news of a convoy, but could get no information."

"I think you were right when you said that the West Indies are our true latitudes. There are too many brooms sweeping this Channel to leave any good findings, unless, indeed, we confine our hopes to the enemy's Government ships."

"That's just it," he exclaimed: "whereas in the western Atlantic we are not only pretty sure of Frenchmen, but of Yankees also. However, we may get an oyster or two off the coast of France, by jogging along it, and should Ushant come abeam without anything turning up, we'll head into the big waters, Mr. Madison."

"What think you of the weather, captain?"

"Why, I think we shall have a black night: but there's no appearance of wind."

"We have tested the *Tigress* in calms and fresh breezes," said I; "and I want to see her in a gale of wind."

"Time enough! time enough!" said he, pulling out a cigar and walking aft, where he stood near the binnacle watching the vessel, and throwing keen looks around the sea.

As the afternoon wore away the blue of the sky grew thicker, and though every cloud had vanished, yet an indefinable smoky sort of veil, through which the blue was apparent, but pale and sickly, appeared to be drawing up all around the horizon, while the sun in the west shone with intense heat, though with a dull, reddish, subdued light; and the orb itself, that was not so brilliant but that the eye could rest upon it for some moments, had a remarkably clean and well-defined edge, like that of the rising moon on a hot August night.

It was melancholy to look around upon the sea, and mark the desolation of waters which in time of peace swarmed with vessels trading to all parts of the world. In spite of Howe (begging Shelvocke's pardon) and St. Vincent and Nelson, and a multitude of magnificent feats of valor performed by single ships, the Danes in the North Sea, and the French in the Channel and away south past the Mediterranean, were disputing every foot of the sea with us, and our naval supremacy was being recovered not only at a prodigious cost of human lives, but by the loss of millions to British merchants. Few trading vessels durst venture on a voyage alone, and for days and days the only sort of craft to be met in the Channel were the Government ships of England and France, and privately armed vessels like our schooner, with here and there a few fishing-boats or a coasting sloop creeping cautiously along, close in-shore. It was perhaps the dull and loaded look of the sky, and the oppressive redness of the sunlight and the muddy green of the sea, that lent, to my imagination, a peculiarly mournful impressiveness to the blank waters around me. They gave me a notion of the horrors of war, more startling and affecting than is got from the butcheries of a battle-field or the carnage on a ship's decks. It was like viewing the once populous and brightly colored thoroughfare of a town that has been laid waste by a siege, with the roofless and ruined houses yawning in grim silence, and no sound of life but now and again the clank of a musket grounded on an echoing pavement.

I went below at four bells in the first dog watch to lie down; and on coming on deck again at eight o'clock, I found the sun setting and the wind gone round to the east. I never beheld a scene of gloomier grandeur in British latitudes. The whole of the western sea-line was buttressed by masses upon masses of ponderous clouds, resembling gigantic fortifications, with the forms of castles, and moles, and towers, and walls, sufficiently well-defined to make the illusion extraordinary. They rested upon a sea of cochineal that emitted no radiance, but stood like a surface of blood under the sun, whose flashing was dulled by the indefinable pall of murky haze that overhung the whole of the heavens; but the upper extremities of the clouds, being near the sun, glowed like red-hot iron, while streaks of purple and orange shot the surface of the vaporous masses whose centres were round, and of a darkish cream-color, like the distended sails of a ship in moonlight.

Meanwhile out of the east, wherein lay the delicate pink reflection of the sunset, a fresh wind was whistling and striking one's lips with a salt and tart flavor, from the whipping of the foaming surface of the water. The schooner was tearing through it at a great rate, though under her mainsail and jib only, with the muzzles of her starboard tier of guns almost level with the flashing froth that whirled away alongside, and with the spray smoking over her forecastle and cooling her decks as far aft as the gangway. Had this wind been blowing out of the bank of clouds in the west I should have calculated on its freshening into a gale; as it was, the most inexpert reader of weather-signs might have guessed it would drop soon, or rattle round to the west.

Hardly had the sun vanished, and while its rays were forking, like a glory round the head of a saint, out of the clouds, gilding our topmasts with fiery lines and turning our upper rigging into gold wire, while all below was in evening gloom, when a lookout man who was stationed aloft reported a sail on the weather bow. We sprang for our glasses, but nothing was to be seen from the deck. I ran forward and trotted aloft to have a view of the stranger before the shadows deepened, and from the foretopsail yard could just catch a glimpse of the spars and canvas of a brig, hove to with her head to the eastward and her foretopsail to the mast. Believing that she would not be alone, I shinned on to the royal yard, and from this immense elevation searched the sea, but the brig was all that I could discover. Before I reached the deck the sea lay darkling, and of the gorgeous sunset nothing survived but a dull reddish flush lingering over the brow of the clouds.

Shelvocke asked me how far I reckoned the brig to be off, and I answered about thirteen miles. He walked hurriedly to the compass and then looked over the side, and presently ordered the foresail and main-topmast staysail to be set. These were large sails, and under them one could feel the *Tigress* tearing up the water, and the parted seas as they raced along her sides hummed like the continuous roll on a drum.

Darkness in these parallels, however, never closely follows sunset, even with a cloudy sky; for some time after the hectic tinge had faded out of the west there remained a sort of sallow gray light in the air, that enabled the eye to determine the boundary-line of the deep; and before complete darkness settled down we had risen the brig so as to render her visible from the deck, though even with the glass we could form no just notion of her size and character, the only certain thing about her being that she still lay hove to, as though she waited for a boat, or expected some craft to heave in sight.

When the night at last really closed round, it was as dark as a pocket, to use Jack's phrase. And, as most of us had expected, the wind failed us, not suddenly, but with a sober fining down, graduating into softness as though through the operation of some mechanical contrivance, until from a fresh strong breeze nothing but a languid current of air was perceptible; and even this presently ceased, and then we lay in a breathless calm, the schooner rolling quietly to the little swell which the wind had left behind, and her sails rattling against the rigging in sounds so like musket reports as to frequently cause me to start and look around, with the darkness so dense that from the skylight the figure of the man at the tiller was invisible, and a ponderously black sky overhead that seemed to touch our mastheads. Here and there a gleam of light raised a luminous mist along the obscured decks, from the main-hatch, from the galley, and from the skylight over the cabin; and as the figures of the men passed through these illuminated spaces it was strange to witness the apparition of their rugged forms with their eyes glittering and their breasts exposed, and their muscular arms hanging bare: and then to completely lose sight of them as they stepped away from the sphere of light into the darkness.

Shelvocke called my name, and I went up to him, guided by the glowing tip of his cigar.

"I don't ask if you can see any sign of the brig," said he, speaking in a low tone, for the influence of this oppressive darkness insensibly subdued one's voice into a whisper; "but how far do you reckon she was distant when the wind dropped?"

"I have been calculating, sir, and I should say the schooner is within a mile of her."

"That should be about it—our reckoning tallies. Pass the word forward to hide all lights, and get a tarpaulin stretched over this skylight."

These orders were obeyed, and in a few minutes the vessel was wrapped in blackness. I returned to Shelvocke.

"It's enough to stifle a man," said he. "I never remembered a darker night. I'm waiting for a flash of lightning to give us some rain and relieve this over-stuffed sky."

"I have stationed a couple of men forward and two at the gangways, with sharp instructions to keep their ears open. The brig *may* prove a friend, sir, but I am always suspicious of short yards and great hoist of topsail," said I.

He seemed to pay no attention to this, but after puffing strongly at his cigar he sung out to Tapping.

"Yes, sir," responded the third mate, who stood somewhere forward of the mainmast.

"Call some hands aft to get this mainsail in. Let go the staysail halliards, and get both jibs stowed. Let the men keep silence."

"Ay, ay, sir."

"This is the business of the fog over again," said I.

"Why, yes, in one sense; only there is no sulphur in fogs, Mr. Madison; and when I think of lightning, I think of my powder magazine," he replied.

The men came along the deck as softly as cats, although they had to grope their way. Presently the canvas was taken in, and this quieted the schooner, though the foresail gave a short slap sometimes when the vessel rolled and the shrouds complained. Shelvocke stood sucking at his cigar in silence, and I was leaving him to go forward, when he said:

"Get the nettings triced up, and pass the word along for

the watch below to keep wide awake ready for a call to quarters; also, clap a round of grape over the round-shot in the
chasers, and send the carpenter aft."

These orders were promptly executed, and when I joined
Shelvocke again he was talking to the carpenter.

"It can easily be managed," he was saying, evidently com-
bating some difficulty Mr. Chips had interposed, "by lashing, or nailing—but they had better be lashed, as I want no
hammering—some half-inch stuff at each side of the cask,
and that will keep the bunghole uppermost. See that your
light is securely fitted, and get a jewel block made fast to
the extreme end of the main-boom, and another to the end
of the flying jibboom, with lines ready rove, so that when
the cask is overboard, it can be hauled away to the length of
those booms from the vessel's bow or stern. Do you
understand me?"

"Yes, sir."

"Then get about it at once. There is no harm in making
ready," he continued, addressing me. "Hark! what is
that?"

"Rain," I replied, as a drop, heavy and warm as a gout
of blood, splashed on my nose.

Only a few drops fell, and all was silent gain. It was
oppressively hot, and going below to get a sou'west cap to
protect me against the rain that I expected every moment
to open upon us, I found the cabin suffocatingly close, and
came on deck again bathed in perspiration.

I went aft to look at the compass, the candle in which
gave the only spot of light to the black air throughout the
ship, and found that the schooner had drifted with her head
to the northward, so as to bring that part of the sea where
the brig was lying when we last saw her, almost directly
astern of us. I put my head over the taffrail and listened
and strained my eyes against the gloom; but nothing dis-
turbed the breathless silence save the gurgle of the eddying
water about the rudder, and the faint flapping of canvas
forward.

I held my watch to the binnacle and noticed that it was
past ten. Shelvocke's position was beaconed by his cigar,
otherwise I had not known whether he was on deck or
below.

"Is that you, Madison?" said he, as I approached him.

"Yes, sir."

"Anybody wanting to know what highly wrought suspense or expectation is," said he, "should be with us here. It is not over-cheerful to be becalmed on a pitch-black night within hail of a vessel whose character you do not know, and whose boats may be under your channels while you are wondering whether she has seen you. To complete a situation of that kind, you only want a sooty sky, choke full of electricity, resting its ponderous burden of thunderbolts upon your mastheads, and likely at any moment to burst asunder and let fall an ocean of flame upon you."

"I expect we shall have it when it *does* come," I answered, wiping from my face the perspiration that gathered again the moment I removed my handkerchief. "It's a *leetle* too warm, I take it, sir, for people whose lungs are not diseased. Look yonder! there's the first composant I have seen this cruise."

A ball of very delicate blue fire, that sometimes looked green, was poised in the air as high as the topsail yardarm, upon the point of which it no doubt hovered; though, as the spars were invisible, the luminous thing seemed to be afloat in the void, and hanging like a star. It produced a curious effect, for with a very small effort of imagination the eye was easily cheated into believing it a prodigious distance off, and that the heavens, having extinguished the familiar luminaries, had given birth to a new species of orb. It emitted a greenish mist for the space of a yard around it, and its reflection in the water was like an illuminated jellyfish shining a long way down. It shifted its position presently, and went as high as the skysail yardarm, then vanished; but in a few minutes it reappeared on the forestay, where it shone like a gigantic glow-worm, and faintly lighted up the figures of some men who stood in a group near the starboard cathead looking at it. It then floated out to the end of the flying jibboom, and after swinging to and fro like a bubble on a pipe-stem, it disappeared.

Scarcely had it vanished, when a whole galaxy of similar lights was kindled all over the schooner's spars and rigging, and the water around swarmed with their reflection. One of them hovered over the breech of the gun near which Shel-

8

vocke and I were standing, and we could see each other's face, looking as green as a spring leaf, distinctly. They went out one by one, apparently being extinguished the moment they were disconnected from the iron and woodwork of the vessel, and all was black as pitch again.

Suddenly a voice forward called out a question sharply and hurriedly. Some one midway between us and the speaker cried, "Hush! listen, can't you?" Immediately after, Tapping pronounced my name.

"Hillo!" I answered, looking in the direction whence his voice proceeded.

"Will you please step aft, sir? I fancied I heard the dip of oars just now."

Shelvocke and I went to the taffrail, where we found Tapping. We all three listened, and in a few seconds heard the dripping sound made by muffled oars when lifted out of the water.

"I expected this; though, if they be Frenchmen, it's unlike them! exclaimed Shelvocke, softly. "Mr. Tapping, go and send Mr. Corney and the carpenter aft. Bear a hand, men," addressing the fellows who stood grouped around the stern-chaser, "be careful not to fire until the order is given, and then take sure aim. Point your gun deliberately. You will have no excuse to miss the mark, for you shall have a light to guide you."

Corney and the carpenter came aft together. During Tapping's absence the sound of approaching oars was quite audible, though they were evidently worked with extreme caution, and the boats moved slowly.

"Carpenter," said Shelvocke, speaking hurriedly, "the barrel must be dropped astern, for the boats are yonder. Make ready to sling it overboard, and be cautious not to dowse the light in hauling on the line. Is that you, Corney?"

"Yes, sir."

"There are one or more boats astern. Be good enough to hail them in French and represent us as Frenchmen."

"Ho, the boat ahoy!" shouted Corney, with a real Gallican shriek.

No answer, and the sound of the dipping oars ceased.

"If you don't answer we will fire into you!" rapped out

Corney, rattling his r's with a throaty richness that would have baffled old Villeneuve himself.

"What vessel is that?" sung out a gruff voice in French, apparently not more than a cable's length astern.

"The *Jean d'Acre*, Volberg, capitaine du vaisseau, bound to Cherbourg, from the East," answered Corney promptly.

On this there was a hail as from one boat to another, and the buzz of a dozen voices all speaking together.

"That shindy convicts them!" whispered Shelvocke to me. "Only Frenchmen talk all at once like that. Mr. Corney, ask them what they want."

But owing to their jabbering like a lot of Boulogne fish-wives disputing, they probably did not hear the question, for no answer was returned. Their nationality, however, was unmistakable.

"Carpenter, get your blaze afloat smartly!" exclaimed Shelvocke. "Men, take aim at the largest of the boats you can cover, or the nearest that you can see."

While he spoke, the carpenter had fired a blue-light, fixed in the bung of a small cask, to the sides of which a couple of short pieces of plank had been affixed to serve as out-riggers. The apparatus was cautiously but quickly lowered over the side, and towed, by means of a line rove through a block at the end of the main-boom, astern, where it glanced out a broad circumference of ghastly illumination, within the further sphere of which we saw three large boats, which lay in solid black shapes upon the blue sheet of water, each boat full of men armed to the teeth, their weapons in the unearthly light appearing as if scored with lines of burning brimstone, while beyond the ghastly luminous cir-cle the sea stretched away into ebony blackness. The motionless boats, looking like centipedes, with their oars fork-ing out on either side; the pale blue outlines of their crowded crews, resembling sketches done in phosphorus; the quiver-ing reflection of the boats in the fearful, death-like hue of the water; and the pitchy, oppressive, imponderable black-ness drooping its electric and breathless folds all around, formed an impressive and wonderful scene.

"Quick, men!" shouted Shelvocke. "Fire while the light holds! Take the nearest boat—she is the biggest!"

The Frenchmen saw the trick, and with a yell all three

crews buckled to their starboard oars, which they were in the act of raising to pull their boats' heads round, when Shelvocke gave the order to fire. The flash of the gun paled the blue light as a sunbeam a candle, and the roar of the explosion was immediately followed by a crash and a perfect hurricane of shrieks, proving fearfully how our shot had told. At the same moment, and as if in rebuke of our presumption in mimicking the tremendous artillery of the skies, the blackness overhead was rent asunder by an astounding flash of sunbright lightning that revealed the whole surface of the sea, down to the nethermost circle of it, in the midst of which, and about three-quarters of a mile distant, lay a large brig, while *two boats only* were making for her, under furiously brandished oars.

The lightning was followed by a crash of thunder directly overhead. The concussion shook the schooner as though she had thumped upon a rock. The ear-splitting bellow was so confounding that, by the next glare of lightning, which followed the thunder after an interval of only a few seconds, I beheld the men standing motionless, like petrified figures. And then down came the rain, in a whole sheet, mingled with hail that boomed upon the hollow deck like a gale of wind through a line-of-battle ship's rigging. In an instant we were awash, and the water pouring in cascades out of the scupper-holes, and the sea around us flashing up in froth under the heavy discharge, while the lightning played in tongues and lances from the clouds, whose huge masses, lying in layer upon layer, were revealed by every flash, and the thunder roared continuously.

The storm had indeed burst with a vengeance. It was right overhead, and fiercer lightning and louder thunder I never saw nor heard out of tropical latitudes. It was evident that the Frenchmen had not stopped to succor their shipmates whose boat had been knocked to pieces by our shot, nor would it have been reasonable for us to send help, as, the play of the lightning being incessant, our boat would have been exposed to the guns of the brig, whose people, we might be sure, would not recognize in our humanity any claim upon their forbearance. All that could be done, therefore, was to direct a lookout to be kept around the schooner for swimmers.

The rain and hail fell perpendicularly with such weight that it was difficult to stand upright under the discharge; it poured down my back so as to completely fill out my shirt with water down to the waist-band, and I felt as though buttoned up in one of those skins which the Arabs carry water in, in their journeys along the African coast. Moreover, not only was the continuous cannonading of the thunder in the last degree bewildering, but the sight was rendered temporarily useless by the quick alternations between the dazzling blue flashes and the stone-blind darkness. However, I made shift to watch the brig, and presently noticed the boats reach her. On a sudden, the hoarse and rushing sound of the rain ceased, and though the lightning continued to flash with extraordinary fierceness, it was evident, from the increasing intervals between the flash and the thunder-shock, that the worst of the storm was settling away to the north.

All at once a voice hailed the schooner alongside: a lantern was slung over, and a man in the last stage of exhaustion was seen clinging to one of the main chain-plates. A bowline was lowered, into which he dropped his arms and was hoisted over the bulwarks. He proved to be a French soldier, probably of the *infanterie légère*, dressed in a single-breasted coat, the collar of which was a bright scarlet, and coarse worsted epaulets and blue trousers. How he had managed to swim the distance from where the boat had sunk to the schooner, seeing that he had a musket slung over his shoulder and a great pistol stuck in the belt round the waist, was an utter mystery to me. On gaining the deck he fell down in a heap, and was immediately carried below, where, in about ten minutes, he was sufficiently recovered to answer Corney's questions, who ascertained that the brig was the national vessel *La Patrie*, pierced for fourteen guns, and mounting six long nine-pounders and one twenty-four-pound brass pivot. She had left Brest four days before as consort to a frigate that had signalled to her to heave to while she chased a suspicious-looking sail that was seen early in the morning standing to the westward. The brig's people, on sighting us before dusk, had taken us for an English trader which a lugger they had fallen in with on the previous night had reported was to pass down the Channel, bound for Lisbon, with a valuable freight; and her boats had therefore been ordered out to attack us. The *La Patrie* had a draft of eighty troops of the line aboard, besides a crew of one hundred and thirty seamen, making in all two hundred and ten souls, some of whom were priests. Of her people sixty were in the boats, half of whom were soldiers.

This information was hurriedly communicated to Shelvocke.

"Sixty in the boats," said he musingly, looking at the vessel which the lightning continued to exhibit with perfect clearness: "divide sixty by three, leaves twenty who have been knocked out of time, and gives the brig one hundred and ninety men. If I flew a pennant I would risk it for the sake of promotion; but I must not needlessly expose my men, for if the brig should serve one of our boats as we served——"

He was silenced by a bright glare aboard the Frenchman, and a ball flashed up the water just astern of us. The lightning was playing in the north, but the thunder rolled with a subdued note, and the rain had entirely ceased. There was promise of improving weather in the west, but the gloom was still intense. The schooner had swung so as to present her starboard quarter to the brig, but the lightning revealed the enemy lying with her stern directly at us; and it was evident from the character of the shot and the sound of the explosion, that she had trained a long nine-pounder through her after-port.

Hardly had the report of the brig's gun faded upon the ear when a sharply uttered order from Shelvocke filled the deck of the schooner with the glare of battle-lanterns. The crew stood at quarters waiting for the word of command, but I saw by Shelvocke taking up his position at the binnacle that he waited for the *Tigress* to swing her broadside to the Frenchman, who meantime kept blazing away at us with his one gun as fast as he could load; he had elevated the piece, and the balls whistled through our rigging and struck the water a long distance ahead of us. It was impossible to see what mischief they did; sometimes a rope's end would fall on the deck, sometimes a block, once there was a small crash of splintered wood aloft, but nothing heavy fell.

"Have you her bearings, men?" rang out Shelvocke's voice.

"Ay, ay, sir!"

"Wait for the next flash to point—aim low, as I always tell you. . . . Now you have her—fire!"

Heaven preserve us! if ever a vessel was raked that brig was. She was within point-blank range of the carronades, and the aim of the men was exact. But by this time she too had canted sufficiently to enable her to bring her broadside guns to bear, and I believe she had traversed the guns from the idle side to the empty ports opposed to us, with a view to frightening us by an exhibition of metal, for she flashed into a whole sheet of flame, and we could hear portions of the iron hail tearing up the sea fathoms away from us, though some of the shots hulled us, as any man could have told by the quivering of the schooner.

She exchanged four broadsides with us, but our fifth was not answered. The lightning had ceased, and there was a pallid gray dawning upon the western sky. We could not see the brig, but the compass-bearings told us that the *Tigress* had swung bow on to her; on ascertaining which I sprang into the waist and ordered the forecastle gun to be double-shotted and fired.

The Frenchman remained silent.

I mounted the bulwark to see if I could distinguish her, and when I lifted my head above the bulwark I felt a draught of wind.

"I expect she is leaving us, sir. She will have had the first of the breeze!" I shouted.

"After her, then," echoed Shelvocke. "All hands make sail! smartly, boys! we'll give the newspaper men another job!"

A dozen of the crew bounded over to the main throat and peak halliards. "With a will, bully boys!" bawled one of them, when—crack! the whole group lay sprawling on their backs, with the halliards writhing among them. The gear had been severed with a shot, and the troublesome business of reeving fresh halliards had to be performed. This was not the only wound our rigging had received. The jib-halliards were cut in halves, the gaff-topsail sheet was on deck, and a couple of backstays were trailing overboard.

However, all available canvas was set, the helm put down, and under a freshening breeze the *Tigress* stretched along the course which Shelvocke with instinctive accuracy guessed the brig to be heading. Trifling repairs such as we needed are soon executed, even on the blackest night, when you have ninety men to do the work; our lanterns illuminated the decks, and in less than ten minutes we were under a press of sail heading due south, and in chase of a bright light that was leading about a mile and a half ahead. This light had sprung up suddenly, and its appearance was reported to us by a hail from one of the lookout men.

"Those Frenchmen call us barbarous!" exclaimed Shelvocke laughing, after answering the hail, "and found their notions of us on the belief that we don't read any nation's history but our own. They may be right; but they forget that there is enough of the history of the world in the history of England to make any student of our story learned enough for all practical purposes. There's a preface for a simple observation, Madison! Do you see that light? Now what imbeciles they must be to hope to trick us by such an old stratagem!"

"Why, yes, sir; anybody may see through that trick."

"Forward there!" he shouted. "Fire the bow-gun at that light. Elevate your piece, or you'll bury the shot."

The report followed within a few seconds of the command. The chase kept silence.

"I have a noble crew, a splendid set of men, Madison!" exclaimed Shelvocke, in a voice rich with enthusiasm. "I would to heaven you and I wore epaulets, and that my men took King's pay. We'd make a name with such a body of seamen under our command."

But recollecting the disaffection that was at that time notorious among the crews of many of His Majesty's ships, and the difficulty that attended the procural of men to fill out the complements of vessels of war, I was inclined to doubt whether King's pay would have inspired the *Tigresses* with the zealous unanimity that was one of their best characteristics.

"Give them another dose!" he sung out. "Ply them while that light shines."

The gun was fired again a moment after the light disappeared.

"The idiots!" muttered Shelvocke. "Now, Madison, mark them!"

The wind had freshened into a strong breeze. All away down in the west the sky had cleared, and here and there a watery star was tremulously glowing among rifts in the heavy clouds which solemnly journeyed across the dark heavens. The sea under the increasing wind was breaking into spaces of foam, and the roaring noise at the bows of the schooner, and the gleam of the belt of froth scurrying within the reach of a man's arm along the lee side, and the hooting up aloft, and the fierce patter of spray, like the discharge of small firearms upon the forecastle, indicated the speed of the *Tigress,* and the pressure of canvas that was rushing her.

A minute after the light ahead had vanished, it reappeared. Shelvocke sprang to the compass; he took a sharp look at the card, and shouted:

"Put your helm up! Ease away your sheets fore and aft. Fore-topsail-yard, there!"

The man stationed on that yard answered.

"Look brightly about you, and report the brig the moment you see her."

"Ay, ay, sir!"

The men appeared astonished to find the schooner leaving the light, which they did not doubt was aboard the enemy. It was right ahead just now, and now it was almost astern. I saw them looking over the bulwarks at it, and heard them talking; but Shelvocke appeared not only blind, but deaf, too.

Presently he sung out:

"Mr. Madison, let the watch be called. A stern chase is a long chase, and even a Frenchman knows a schooner's weakness."

As he spoke, eight bells were struck, by which I had the pleasure to find that it was my turn to stay on deck for the next four hours. However, I had had no supper, and was wet through, and so, desiring Chestree to keep my lookout for a short spell, I went below, where, after shifting my clothes, I demolished nearly the whole of a remarkably tender and well-flavored piece of hung beef, which, with a caulker of cold brandy grog, restored my good humor.

I left Shelvocke, who had come below as wet and hungry as myself, at the table, and went on deck and found the weather clearing fast, but the wind increasing, and the schooner beginning to courtesy to the surges which ran under her. She was heading so as to hit the French coast between Havre and Fécamp), but on an errand that had become intelligible enough, now that we could see about us; for almost the first object I beheld after leaving the cabin was the shadow of the brig right ahead of us, a large square blot which the telescope resolved into a whole cloud of canvas.

I put my head into the skylight and gave the news to Shelvocke, who presently arrived. He examined the chase in silence for some moments—I should say a whole minute —and then exclaimed:

"She is undoubtedly within range of the bow-gun, Mr. Madison, should not you think?"

"A ball would have all its work to reach her, sir."

"Well, as I look again, you may be right. But even were she within range, it is not our policy to signalize any friends of hers hovering in the neighborhood, by blazing away with one gun, when, with a little patience, we shall be able to bring our broadside to bear."

"I agree with you, captain; here is the Calvados Gulf under our bows, and there are batteries enough along the coast from Barfleur to Antifer to inspire the French cruisers in these waters with unusual pluck."

"I say," he remarked, laughing, "the brig's people will think us the very devil when they look astern and find us sticking to their skirts. But did they really suppose they could amuse and throw us off the scent by dropping a lantern in a tub overboard, and squaring away to the east'ard? I should like to know how many times that trick has been tried in the last fifty years, and how often it has succeeded. I *knew* she must try for Dieppe or some more southerly port, and I was right, you see. Do you think we gain on her?"

"I do not, sir. If anything she is leaving us. By the

lumping shadow she makes she appears to have stunsails alow and aloft."

The enemy had manœuvred so as to bring the breeze into the quarter that gave the *Tigress* her poorest chance of sailing.

Every cloth on the schooner that would hold wind was exposed, but it was all of no use; we could not shorten our distance from the chase, and though she remained well in sight over our bows, she had edged a long distance out of gunshot.

Shelvocke's obstinate spirit was aroused. When he perceived that he did not gain on the enemy, he turned the men up to get the studding-sails upon the schooner, but in the midst of the work the topgallant studding-sail boom snapped short off at the iron, and the sail blew away like a puff of smoke. In truth, the wind was fast freshening into a moderate gale that had put every vestige of the ponderous thunder-clouds to flight, and replaced them with lines of light scud that blew like sheets of muslin across the stars. Had we been beating, there was wind enough to have reefed our sails; but being astern, its force was sensibly diminished by the speed with which the *Tigress* drove before it. Under this increased pressure the schooner ran fiercely, heaping the water up in froth above the hawse-holes, and raising a tall sea on each quarter; and that the brig maintained and even improved her distance from us proved her the possessor of qualities that would not only test the capacity of the *Tigress* but harass the obstinacy of Shelvocke, as well as challenge his seamanship.

Suddenly the Frenchman hauled his wind about four points, keeping all his studding-sails aloft. The inclination of the shadowy outline of the vessel was at least forty degrees under the lateral pressure of the heavy wind, and her swinging boom soared up from her side like a bowsprit. Finding that she could beat us in scudding, she was going to try us with her tacks aboard, her people evidently having confidence in her heels, and eager to reach their own coast by the shortest cut.

The instant she shifted her helm we altered ours; but scarcely had we got the wind abeam when crack! the jib-sheet parted, and before the down-haul could be manned, the sail had flogged itself into rags.  I watched our spars anxiously.  It was impossible to know how the shot of the brig had told; one crash of splintering wood had certainly followed the discharge of a gun, and I waited to know what spar had been wounded by seeing it go overboard.  But nothing gave, though our press of sail was enormous; indeed I never before in all my life saw any vessel so driven as the *Tigress* was now: the lee rail of the high bulwarks was almost flush with the seething foam; standing on the deck was like being on a steep hill-side: she did not rise to the seas, but cut clean through them, shipping whole oceans of water, which came rushing aft as high as a man's knees along the lee-scuppers.  She took four men to steer her, and I saw the binnacle-light shine in their sweating faces, and watched them tearing off their coats and loosening the collars of their shirts, and baring the arms to the shoulder.  The booming and bellowing overhead was deafening, and powerful as was Shelvocke's voice he had to send Tapping for his speaking-trumpet before he ventured to deliver an order.

At this moment the scene was one of wild beauty: the schooner almost on her beam-ends hurling through a whole acre of snow-white foam, the dark and frothing waters tossing wildly to windward; above us a sky full of bright stars and flying scud, and ahead the leaning shape of the brig as steady as the schooner under the sweeping gale, and leaving astern of her a wide, white creaming wake whose seething extremity seemed to meet the very stem of the *Tigress*.

But the square-rigged vessel never yet was built that could dispute the lead with Hannay's privateer under these conditions.  The brig was every moment looming larger and larger as we gained upon her.

"Make ready the bow-gun!" shouted Shelvocke through his trumpet.  "Let her go off a point"—and when this was done—"fire!"

The flame flashed out of the head of the schooner, and a smother of smoke fled down upon the water; but simultaneously with the explosion, the brig put her helm up, squared away her yards, and in about ten minutes' time had forged out of gunshot distance again.

This was very irritating, but, as Shelvocke had said on a previous occasion, it could not be helped. We held on steadily; and shortly after the dawn had broken in the east, I went below to look at the chart, and found that if this strong wind held, we should in all probability make the French coast a little to the north of Cape Antifer by seven o'clock. I had been up all night, and was tired out, and the sound of ship's bell was never more grateful to my ears than the eight strokes which indicated four o'clock, and changed the watch. Before I left the deck the sun had risen, and the sky all away on the port-bow was a vast sheet of frosted, rosy-tipped silver, and in the west and south a bright light blue, and the sea a streaming, running, throbbing, and foaming tract of waters, with a strong wind sweeping noisily across it, and vacant as a desert save in the point toward which the jibboom of the *Tigress* arched, where there shone a white form no bigger than a man's hand, but which the telescope proved to be the French brig, that had widened her distance to between four and five miles, and whose hull, under the broad and tall space of canvas she exhibited, was like a car under a Lussac balloon; and one could almost have imagined that the whole thing would soar into the air and be blown away into the silver sky, so delicate and lily-like and aerial did the fabric look upon the leagues of sea which poured their boiling surges toward the rising sun.

I went to my cabin and turned in and fell asleep, and had slept two hours, and was dreaming of being grasped by the throat by a huge French grenadier, whose immense pistol (the cold muzzle of which, by the way, I distinctly felt like the snout of a dog against my right temple) threatened a most murderous *coup de grâce*, when I was aroused by young Peacock putting his hand on my shoulder. I opened my eyes.

"The crew have been called to quarters, sir. We have hove up the French coast, and I think Captain Shelvocke means to give us some fun, sir," shouted the youth, and immediately ran on deck.

I was there almost as soon as he, and found the crew tumbling up out of the hatchways, and some of the watch hauling down the studding-sails, and others handing the square canvas, while the schooner, with the wind a point before the beam, into which quarter it had veered within the last five minutes, was racing along at a speed that made every bone of her tremble as though she must go to pieces like a pack of cards. Right ahead loomed the pale chalk cliffs and green summits of Cape Antifer, with the land on either side shelving away south and east until only little blobs of hazy film trembled upon the white reflective line about the dark waters of the horizon.

The brig lay broad in view upon our lee bow, having braced up to meet the shift of wind, and her hull almost buried in the veil of foam she tore up. She had evidently been trying for Fécamp and the Criquebœuf batteries, but probably fearing that the wind would haul further to the eastward, was hoping to get the land aboard, so as to bring up and fight us under the shelter of a fort to windward of Cape Antifer.

"Ay, but fighting, I am afraid, is the last infirmity of those noble minds," said Shelvocke, to whom I had put the above probability, speaking with bitter contempt, and looking harassed and weary, though he had managed to snatch an hour's sleep while I was below.

We soon began to close the chase, now that we had the wind abeam, and I had a good look at her through the glass.

She was a handsome vessel, probably fifty tons bigger than the *Tigress*, with a gayly decorated stern, and a broad white streak along her sides, out of which forked the muzzles of her guns. She had large square tops painted black, wide channels, and sat low on the water, and was apparently a very powerful boat. Whatever mischief we had done her aloft was repaired, nor could we suppose, having regard to the tremendous press of canvas she carried, that we had wounded her spars. If she had suffered at all, it was in the hull, but to what extent, as the sequel will show, we were not able to ascertain.

Suddenly she hoisted French colors, and fired a gun at us, probably to alarm the lookouts on the heights, for her people must have been perfectly well aware that we were out of range.

"Answer that challenge, Mr. Peacock!" called out Captain Shelvocke. "Hoist the ensign!"

Having said which, he jumped on to one of the guns, and stood with his arm round a backstay, watching the chase with an expression of extraordinary eagerness.

Most chases are mere lotteries, for the issue of a pursuit at sea can seldom be calculated on. Shelvocke's hope in following the brig had evidently lay in a shift of wind, or in being able to get within range, and to cripple her so as to oblige her to make a stand and fight. The natural obstinacy of his nature, moreover, was not a little inflamed by the attempt that had been made to board us, and they had failed entirely because of the vigilance of the lookout we had kept and his sagacious suspicions that something of the kind would be ventured.

The sight of the towering French cliff now lent a new significance to the pursuit. This was the first time the *Tigress* had been in sight of the enemy's coast, and one thought of the wrongs done to humanity by the inhabitants of that soil, of their hatred of England, of the scores of one's fellow-countrymen languishing in its jails. Indeed no words can express the bitter feelings excited by those lofty heights of chalk clad with verdure that gleamed like silk in the sun. The faces of our seamen darkened under the moods which the sight of the French shore aroused. The children of the Englishmen of this period will never be able to gauge the hatred of the French that fired the hearts of their fathers, and made them the most deadly and disastrous enemies the arms of France ever encountered. I noticed some of our men, after they had looked a while at the shore, feel the edge of their cutlasses and slap the breeches of the guns with gestures of uncontrollable excitement. No quarter-deck speech ever awakened such deep and eager passions as were excited in our men by that line of coast, growing whiter and taller and greener as we raced after the brig, with the water flying in sheets over the forecastle, and the air all around filled with the roaring of canvas.

The brig continued to fire at us, though her balls dropped a long way short, but Shelvocke took no notice of this. It was plainly her intention to seek the shelter of a fort that protected the entrance of a small bay at the base of a very noble green and fertile valley, whose rich, deep verdancy beautifully contrasted with the dazzling white of the chalk cliffs, and it remained to be seen whether she would be able to reach that shelter before we could get between her and the land.

The eyes of every man and boy in the schooner stared forward at the brig, and it was strange to behold the set, lowering expressions on their faces: how some stood with their rugged, naked arms locked upon their breasts, and some leaning with their hands upon the guns, and some crouching like leashed hounds to gaze through the wind-ward ports, and all of them preserving a dead stillness; for the end of this long pursuit was at hand. It was a matter of time only whether we should get to leeward of the Frenchman. If she reached the protection of the fort, Shelvocke was the man to cut her out; if we passed her, and separated her from the land, we were sure of a hot action. In either case warm work was certain, and it was being led up to by as exciting a chase as ever took place on broad waters.

All this while she kept hammering at us with a couple of long eighteens, which they had trained through her after-ports, and at every discharge the shot flashed up the spray nearer and nearer. As she was now certainly within range of our bow-gun, Shelvocke gave the order to peg away at her in return; but owing to the lively motion of the schooner I could not swear that we did her any mischief. No sooner did we begin to fire than the fort opened, by way, I suppose, of encouraging the brig. To judge by the volumes of smoke that went pouring away toward the giant head-land, this shore-battery mounted heavy metal; the boom of the ordnance struck the ear with a ponderous note that sounded high above the yelling of the wind and the roaring of the passing waters. In ten minutes from this time the brig was not a mile ahead, and her shot were flying over us.

"I fear we shan't be able to round her, sir," said I to Shelvocke, who still stood on the gun, steadying himself with the backstay. "Would it be worth while to luff and give her a broadside?"

"They'll be in a mess in a moment or two if they don't mind their eye," he replied. "I see something that looks uncommonly like broken water a little ahead of them, and they're steering for the thick of it. How far off is that . coast, think you?"

" Four miles, sir."

" Just see what soundings the chart gives, Madison."

I ran below, overhauled the chart, and returned.

" Fourteen to eight close in shore, sir, but there's a shoal with twelve feet at high-water mark, that bears W. N. W. from the fort."

He made no answer, but kept his eyes steadily fixed on the brig. Now and again I could see the water spirt up under the discharge from the fort, well to windward of the brig, which the shot were more likely to hit than ourselves; but the leaping and glancing of the foam under the strong wind made the surface of the water extremely confusing.

I levelled the glass at the battery that was situated on the left of the bay, and that stood out in bold relief against the deep green of the valley and the paler verdure of the further inclines. It mounted six guns, three pointing seaward to the north, and the others covering the mouth of the bay; they were being fired one after another, and through the telescope I could see the red tongues of flame flash out, and the white, dense clouds of smoke go sluggishly to leeward, with a glimpse of figures moving on the outer walls and the sparkle of small arms and military accoutrements.

There were a couple of small coasting sloops at anchor in the bay, pitching and tossing consumedly on the troubled waters; the glitter of the high surf was visible all along the coast, but with the exception of a small cluster of huts upon the slope a long way behind the fort and on the confines of the valley, I could perceive no sign of human habitation; nor, away from the fort, was there any living creature to be seen.

I was ogling the enemy's territory with active curiosity, when a cry from Shelvocke made me dash down the glass and spring to his side.

" Hard aport! in with that foresail! let go the jib-halliards!" he pealed through his trumpet: and as the schooner plunged round into the wind, chopping the heavy seas which ran to meet her, and with the canvas so furiously shaking overhead that the shrouds and backstays rattled like the

9

contents of a china warehouse to a passing van, he shouted:
"Steady! bear a hand, men! keep your stations at the
port-guns—you have her under your muzzles—now you
may physic her!"

And while thirty of the crew were brailing in, and clew-
ing up, and stripping the schooner of half her canvas, our
port broadside was fired, raising, what with the slatting of
the sails, and the stamping of the men, and the flinging
down of coils of rope, and the splashing of water, and
groaning of timbers, and hooting of the wind, such a hullabaloo as would have set an inexperienced hand calling upon
heaven to have mercy upon his soul.

The moment I could find time to look about me I saw
the reason of this sudden change in our movements.   Just
as Shelvocke had hoped or predicted, the brig's people had
run the unfortunate craft ashore on the shoal whose existence had been observed by our captain's keen eye when two
miles away from it.   The vessel lay on her port broadside;
the thumping blow she had dealt herself had carried away
both topmasts, and as she had a press of sail at the time—
royals, studding-sails every cloth, indeed that she could
stretch—she presented one of the most perfect images of
confusion the imagination could picture forth.

Her masts, however, did not go until after we had given
her our broadside, and when Shelvocke saw her deplorable
condition, the word was passed to cease firing.   They continued blazing at us from the fort, but whether because we
were just out of range or because they guessed our humane
motive in not playing on the brig, they presently stopped
their cannonading, and their attention, as well as ours, was
fixed on the hapless chase.

Very fortunately for her people she had fallen over so as
to expose her higher side to the sea; had she slanted her
decks to the surges which broke against and burst in smoke
over her, she would have gone to pieces in ten minutes.
The speed with which she was travelling at the time she
struck had run her high on the ridge: she lay with two-
thirds of her copper exposed and glowing like a furnace in
the sun, her bow hove high, and her wrecked spars and
sails tossing and beating and looking like a mass of tangled
seaweed alongside of her.

There was a whole swarm of people gathered aft, and apparently utterly helpless, and another equally helpless crowd in the bows. They made no effort to help themselves, nor was there any appearance of a rescue from the shore. Shelvocke beckoned me to him.

"Madison," said he "those people must be rescued, and by us; not only for the sake of our common humanity, but for the sake of our reputation as generous enemies. I select you for this task, as I should for any job requiring nerve and judgment."

I immediately sung out to the boatswain to pipe the crew of the first cutter away. This was a large, powerful boat, pulling twelve oars. A flag of truce was thrown into her and fixed in the bows, and as we shoved off a gun was fired to windward, and a white flag hoisted at the main, which a few moments after was answered by a white flag at the battery ashore.

The water was even more lively than I had supposed it. At one moment the boat would be thrown up to the summit of a roaring sea, whose boiling crest foamed above the gunwales and covered the knees of the men and the floor with hissing spume, that crackled like pods of seaweed under the tread, and we seemed to look down, as from a hill-top, upon the surrounding plain of waters, where in one place lay the beautiful schooner bowing to the surges like a noble steed, whose curved neck and pawing forefoot betoken his eagerness to be gone, and where in another place lay the dismantled and motionless brig over which the sea was tossing a haze of spray, while her hinderpart was black with human figures watching us; and then in another moment down we would sink between two walls of bottle-green water, in whose translucent depths one now and again could catch fleeting glimpses of a fragment of marine vegetable torn from its sandy soil, or the horn-like yellow of an immense jelly-fish, or a five-finger washed from its home among the rocks, while not a breath of air reached us to cool our cheeks, though the spray flew over our heads in wreaths and clusters like masses of snow.

There was but one way of boarding the brig, and that was on the lee bow, the raffle that was overboard being chiefly on the port quarter. The poor creatures raised a quivering sort of cheer when we were near enough to hear them; they guessed our errand, and really our country had furnished them with some substantial grounds for believing in the humanity of English sailors.

I steered the boat to leeward and made signs to the people on the forecastle to coil down a rope ready to pitch to us; and when we had the rope's end aboard, the boat was hauled cautiously toward the wreck. The hull of the brig acted like a breakwater, and the sea was tolerably smooth under the lee of her, though the moment we got within the range of it we were drenched through with spray. She lay in about ten feet of water, and, watching our chance, ten of us jumped aboard, while the men left in charge of the boat veered out the line, and the cutter went clear of the wreckage, and lay rising and falling like a cork.

I never recall the scene of that brig's decks without feeling how beggarly words are as reflectors of facts. Benjamin West might have painted it, but even the artist could only show it as it appeared at one instant of time; the swift and endless changes of posture, the despairing expressions of face, the *throbbing* of colors supplied by a thousand passionate motions and gestures, could only be conveyed by as many pictures. And then the uproar! the lamentations, the imprecations, the supplications—tumbling inboard that vessel was like dropping into the infernal regions.

In the first place the vessel lay bilged at an angle of about fifty degrees. The shooting of the seas over her side filled the deck to leeward with water, and I was up to my armpits the moment I got aboard. The guns had fetched away and helped out the frightful mess of rigging, hencoops, hatchway-gratings, round-shot, pikes, muskets, splintered wood, and a hundred things besides, which choked the lee-scuppers. At least a dozen dead bodies lay floating or sunk in as many postures in the water that extended like a small lake from the main-hatch to the rail of the lee-bulwarks. At each end of the vessel there was collected a dense crowd of men—soldiers and sailors—indiscriminately mixed, and at least a score of priests. I scanned the mobs eagerly, and was glad to find no women.

I own I was amazed to observe how helpless these creatures had been made by fear. There were two good boats hanging at the lee davits, and a cutter on chocks amidships, big enough to hold thirty persons. Yet no one had thought of getting these boats afloat.

Clinging with my hands, and shoving with my feet, like a dog on all-fours, I made shift to scramble clear of the water, and steadying myself with my heels against the coamings of the main hatch, I sung out in my native language to know if there was anybody aboard who could speak English. Two or three voices answered, and a priest (as white as wax) waved his hand to engage my attention.

"Do you speak English, sir?" I shouted.

"Yes, I speak," he replied, in a good accent.

"Then please order silence to be kept. You may say I shall make no effort to save them if they don't stop their shindy."

He hollowed his hands and delivered my message with a shriek like a woman's. It produced the effect I wanted; the people grew as silent as death, and nothing was to be heard but the thunder of the seas striking the brig, and the sharp artillery of the spray lashing the decks and the water beyond.

"Where is the captain?" I shouted.

The priest pointed to the water where the bodies lay with a gesture inexpressibly mournful and pathetic.

"Are there no officers aboard?"

The priest glanced behind him; there was a movement among a group of soldiers who stood wedged together and holding on to one another, and a very small man, not above five feet high, and looking more like a corpse than a living mortal, was unceremoniously thrust forward; but the moment the hands which propelled him let him go, he fell down, and would have rolled into the water in the scuppers, had not one of my men caught him.

This poor little creature, who appeared to have been badly wounded, proved to be the first lieutenant; but, as he was in a condition to be of no possible service, and as it was evident that the other officers were too much ashamed or too much alarmed to stand forward and offer to help, I resolved to waste no more time in questions, and telling my men to turn to smartly and cut away the wreckage that we might get the boats overboard, I requested the priest to order the French seamen to assist my crew, but at the same time to require the soldiers to remain where they were so that the sailors might not be hindered by crowding.

The sight of the *Tigresses* going to work on the laniards and gear with knives and cutlasses, hacking away, some of them with the water up to their throats, and laughing loudly as the seas came foaming down upon them, heartened the Frenchmen, who, giving a cheer for the brave English, fell to work like men. In ten minutes' time the wreckage was cut away and floating free of the brig. The gangway was then cleared, the boats lowered one after the other, and the soldiers, priests, and twenty seamen crowded into them.

Before the first boat shoved off, the priest who had acted as my interpreter stood up to ask whether they were to row for the schooner or the shore, probably expecting that I should claim them as prisoners; but when I said the shore, every man shouted *Vivent les Anglais!* The soldiers waved their hats, the sailors (out of compliment) huzzaed after our British fashion of cheering, and my poor priest seemed to bless me with his extended hands. It was a touching scene, and I was heartily glad to be an actor in it.

We had great trouble to get the big cutter out; happily the mainstay stood, and by clapping tackles on to it and the fore-yardarm, we managed to sway the boat out of her chocks and drop her overboard without accident. The remainder of the crew and soldiers were numerous enough to load her down to the gunwales. I saw that she would be too full to go safely through such a sea as was running, and therefore got our own cutter alongside, and stowed fourteen Frenchmen in her. This done, and having ascertained that nothing living was left aboard, I jumped down the main-hatch, and with a flint and steel set fire to the brig in three places, after which I got into the cutter, and with the French boat in company pulled away for the shore.

I do not believe the Frenchmen who were removed from the brig cared twopence about our burning her; indeed, the soldiers, as we shoved off, exhausted themselves in imprecations upon her, and again and again I burst into an uncontrollable fit of laughter over the extraordinary grimaces, the shrugs, the extravagant gesticulations of the people we had stowed away in our boat. They all spoke together, the opening of one man's mouth being the signal for all hands to burst out, and after a while the poor fellows actually began to *sing*, and were joined by the others in the boat astern of us, though the spray flew over us in sheets, and as we neared the bay the popple grew ugly enough to demand the closest vigilance.

On the road it occurred to me that we ought to have brought the body of the French captain with us, that he might be buried with honors; but when I turned to the Frenchmen, and in my broken way suggested that we should return before the fire laid hold of the brig, and that I would take the risk of procuring the corpse, they all to a man shook their heads and flourished their hands with an air of passionate contempt, and said—so far as I could gather from the rude *patois* they spoke—that their captain had proved himself a *fainéant*, a poor creature, and that his memory deserved no respect. They might have said the same thing of the other officers, naval as well as military (for I presume the soldiers had officers to look after them), all of whom had behaved like arrant cowards, neglecting their duty and hiding among the men when the brig was in danger, and skulking into the first boat that came alongside.

However, I had not much time allowed me to think over these matters, for the sea ran so high as we approached the land, and both cutters were so deeply laden, that there were moments when we were in real peril, and it was not until we had got the southern fork of the bay between us and the tossing surges that I drew an easy breath. Here, close in shore, the water was smooth, though opposite the tumble was rough enough to keep the two coasters dancing like circus-horses, and a heavy surf roared upon the white sand and flung a hundred sparkling rainbows upon the deep summer foliage that enriched the gradual slope down to within fifty feet of high-water mark.

The whole spot, indeed, was a perfect paradise, and any man would have thought himself upon a tropical coast, on viewing the deep cool forests of trees which backed the

bay, and spread a broad surface of lovely green over the
huge hollow in the cliffs which rose on either hand from
the margin of the water until they attained an elevation of
some hundreds of feet of shining chalk, upon whose summits lay the verdant plains of one of the most picturesque
of the French Departments, resembling at that distance an
endless carpet of embroidered green silk.

Immediately opposite the beach where the people were
landing from the boats which had first left the wreck was
the fort, built on a point of headland about sixty feet above
the sea; the white flag still blew from the tall pole in the
centre of it, and the outer wall was lined with soldiers
watching us.   Stumbling upon such a scene as this, set like
a gem on the breast of a towering range of cliff, was like
falling asleep in the middle of the sea, and dreaming of a
beautiful land.   The uniforms of the garrison at the fort,
mere spots of color upon the grim, coarse outer wall;   the
white flag streaming against the green of the outer slopes;
the dazzling white of the immensely high cliffs, stretching
far away into the sea;   the line of boiling surf that extended, like a pile of snow which had been swept off the
ocean, from the base of the cliffs as far as the eye could
reach, down to the northern curve of the bay;   the tumbling
waters blowing up in smoke upon the dancing greens and
whites of which the sloops were leaping, with the sunshine
flashing in their streaming sides, and kindling stars of
blinding brilliance in the glass upon their decks;   the shaggy
mass of green stretching for miles up the gigantic defile,
and the glittering silver of the circle of white sands, in the
southernmost corner of which were collected the crowd of
soldiers and sailors and priests who had scrambled ashore
out of the boats—formed such a scene of unfamiliar beauty,
that to this day it never comes before me without a disturbing sense of unreality.

I headed the cutter for the spot where the other boats
had grounded, and no sooner did her stem grate upon the
sand, than my Frenchmen toppled over the sides and
plunged up to their waists in the water, and splashed
ashore as fast as they could wade.   Immediately afterward,
the fourth boat grounded, and the haste of her people to
land was more diverting still, for they sprang all together,

and many of them tumbled on their noses under water, while their shakoes and hats floated away to sea in squadrons.

I had leisure now to cast my eye over the crowd, and noticed an officer dressed out in full puff, in a fine blue coat laced with silver, a cocked hat, glossy boots, white nankeens, and a long sparkling sword. He was a handsome old gentleman, silver-haired, with dark, shining eyes, and heavily thatched brows. He proved to be the commandant of the fort, but I did not know this until my priest—who, now that he was ashore, and safe, had gathered a healthy complexion, and whose gentle, pensive, intellectual cast of countenance made me in love for the nonce with the religion that could work so beautiful an expression in the human face—stepped forward, and raising his voice exclaimed in English :

"Sir, I am desired by Monsieur le Colonel," indicating the figged-out officer with a graceful gesture, "to express to you, in the name of the French nation, his gratitude to you and your noble seamen for your exertions in the cause of humanity. It was in your power, sir, to make us captives by taking us on board your ship; but you have chosen to complete your admirable mission, and to make it in all respects worthy of your great and courageous country, by giving us our liberty. · Sir, I thank you for myself, and for these my comrades."

And while I raised my hat to the colonel, whose cocked head-gear swept the ground as he returned my salutation, the priest repeated his speech to me in French for the edification of the people, who immediately murmured all manner of thanks, though I caught one little chap, who, I believe, was third lieutenant of the brig, scowling venomously at me between the elbows of a couple of tall seamen.

"Monsieur le Curé," said I, determined not to be outdone in politeness, "you will do me the favor to assure Monsieur le Colonel that it has given us great pleasure to be of use to you; and—speaking for myself—I may add, I am heartily sorry that the dreadful necessities of war should have brought about the melancholy disaster that has befallen you." He raised his hands and looked up to heaven. "Monsieur, I will not say *au revoir*, I do not want to meet any of you again until peace is declared between our two countries; I am glad to have been able to help you; and so, monsieur, I wish you heartily *adieu*."

The priest translated this to the crowd while we were shoving off, and as we pulled the boat's head round, they gave us a loud cheer. I again raised my hat, the men squared their elbows, and off we started for the schooner.

The brig was burning bravely on the shoal in spite of the spray that dashed over her, and dense volumes of smoke poured from her along the water, so that we had like to be smothered as we passed by; but this was a small matter compared to the risk we ran from her guns, and the chance of her blowing up before we should get well away from her. It is true that several of her cannons were under water, but I had noticed that some of her pieces were in a serviceable condition, and we really did not require more than one shot to sink us.

However, we got past without accident, though soon after the *Tigress* had sighted us and put her helm up to meet us, the mainmast and gear of the brig being in flames fell along the deck, and I had turned my head to look at the astonishing shower of sparks which fled in whole galaxies along the black line of smoke, when the powder caught, and the vessel blew up. We were to leeward of the wreck, and consequently got the full force of the noise, and I never would have believed that the explosion of a vessel of her size could have produced so tremendous a concussion. The whole scene all around, to a height of a hundred feet, was full of smoke and flame, of exploding hand-grenades and bombshells, of huge beams of glowing wood and fragments of blazing canvas, and a wonderful sight was the huge mainmast that darted upward on fire, like a flaming spear hurled from the hand of a giant, described a curve like the boomerangs mentioned by Cook, then rushed into the sea with the flames in the form of wings all around it, and smiting the foaming surface of a wave, vanished with a loud shrieking hiss, shooting midway its own length again into the air after a short interval, when it lay tossing upon the waters, a charred and blackened spar.

Scarcely had we brought the cutter alongside, and scrambled aboard the *Tigress*, when the white flag was hauled

down from the fort, and they opened fire upon us. I have
no doubt the destruction of the brig maddened the old commandant. As soon as the fort began, Shelvocke ordered
the flag of truce to be hauled down, and the English ensign hoisted at the peak; the hands were turned up to
make sail, and before a fourth round could be discharged
at us, the *Tigress*, untouched by the iron showers which
fell all around her, was stretching her noble form along the
flashing waters, and dwindling the fort into a thing no
bigger than a pea upon the green of the beautiful valley of
the Seine coast.

# CHAPTER VI.

## AN OLD FRIEND.

Had the *Tigress* been a King's ship we should have got some credit for this business. No particular heroism, it is true, had been exhibited, though that was not our fault, for the brig would not fight us; but we had destroyed a fine vessel, and this exploit quickly following our action with the corvette would, had we flown a pennant, have brought us some civil letters from the Admiralty, the honor of a gazetting, and better things still. But being only a private ship, the adventure yielded us neither glory, which we could have made shift to do without, nor profit, which was one of the things we wanted.

However, as Shelvocke said, in the speech he delivered to the men an hour after we had got away from the fort, he had chased the brig in the hope of capturing her, and he was perhaps sorrier than any man aboard that the pursuit had ended so unprofitably for his crew. Luckily, said he, the brig was not the only fish that swam in the sea; he meant to give the Channel another chance or two, as, so far, he had no reason to complain of his luck in these waters; but he should extend his field presently, and if a cruise in the West India latitudes did not tassel their pocket-handkerchiefs with dollars, it would not be for the want of laying the *Tigress* alongside rich ships.

We cruised for four days without anything particular happening. On the morning of the fifth day we were off the Casquets, a group of rocks to the westward of the clean and tidy little island of Alderney, and we were feeling our way toward the south, and indeed had worked as far as the Schole Bank, when a sail hove in sight right ahead, standing northeast by the compass, and closing the south horizon

to us; for no sooner had her topsails risen than we pronounced her a Frenchman.

This was disappointing, as Shelvocke had talked of looking along the coast as far as Granville, where we might
hope to have found some business waiting for us. However, the tower of canvas rising ahead advertised us of a
great hull underneath, and when we had lain to long enough
to see the whole of her (for Shelvocke was not the man to
turn tail until he knew what he was running away from)
the stranger discovered herself to be a ninety-four, her
sides swarming with gun-muzzles, and cannon bristling
from her poop, gangways, and forecastle.

I searched the horizon around her, suspecting her to be
the van of a squadron; but no other sail was in sight,
whence Shelvocke suggested that the Channel fleet having
put into Cawsand Bay (as had been reported to us by a
small English collier that we had spoken two days previously), this Frenchman had been detached to reconnoitre
the island of Guernsey, upon which fertile and pleasant
piece of vantage-ground Bonaparte had been casting a
languishing eye for some considerable time past.

There was a noble sailing-breeze blowing, and though the
monster astern, on sighting us, had braced up and triced
out her bowlines and headed for the weather-gage, neither
her presence or her movements gave us the least uneasiness.
Guernsey was within easy reach, and from Petit Bot Bay
to St. Peter's Point there was as much protection as we
should need. The schooner was put about, the English
ensign hoisted, and every stitch of fore-and-aft canvas set.
In a few minutes we found we could drop our friend, or
keep her in one place, just as we pleased; whereupon Shelvocke, who, like the old romancers, loved to make his
beauty coquet with the ogres, lowered his gaff-topsail,
hauled up the clew of the mainsail, and took in his flying-
jib, though even under this reduced canvas the *Tigress* had
to be luffed from time to time, and the wind shaken out of
her sails, to prevent her sinking the hull of the looming
hooker astern.

Yet I write in no disdain of this French ship, for she
was a noble-looking vessel, though dwarfed by distance
and surrounded by the deep, whose mightiness depresses

the grandest works of mortal hands into but a mean and little show. Through one of the powerful glasses, which were among the most useful of the *Tigress'* fittings, I beheld the French ship as clearly as though she lay within a quarter of a mile from us, and could have dwelt for hours upon the beautiful fabric peeling the green seas with her metalled cutwater into two bright, oil-smooth waves, which broke into glittering silver at her gangways; and upon the stateliness of her erect posture under the weight of her swelling canvas; and upon the snow-white line of hammock cloths topping the black bulwarks, pierced by the iron teeth of heavy guns; and upon the delicate black shadows thrown by the stays and braces on the brilliant sails, whose corners were softly shadowed.

By this time it must have been apparent to her people that they might as well endeavor to chase a seagull as the schooner; but they held on after us nevertheless, sailing full and bye, probably provoked into continuing a useless chase by the sight of our red flag. I believe they imagined we meant to fight them when they saw us shorten sail, for a puff of smoke broke out of her bows, and sailed away to leeward in a growing cloud, and after a while the boom of the report reached our ears. But as she was some miles distant, we did not trouble ourselves to look where the ball dropped.

I was amused by young Peacock coming up to me, and touching his cap, inquired if I knew whether Captain Shelvocke meant to engage the Frenchman.

"Why, you young fire-eater!" I exclaimed, "are you in a hurry to die that you ask such a question? One broadside from that chap would blow us into dust."

"I should like to try that scheme I spoke to you about, sir, and which Mr. Chestree ridiculed," said he, fixing his large, dark, melancholy eyes on mine with a look of earnestness in them that would have set many a girl's heart palpitating. "With the captain's leave I'd undertake to board her aloft, and douse her colors."

"I dare say you would if she gave you time. But we should have to get broadside on to her to enable you to gain her spars from ours; and how long, Mr. Peacock, do you suppose the guns of that ship would allow us to lie

alongside? Never fear but that you'll meet with something proper to practise your ideas upon, but if you want
to catch a shark you mustn't angle with a gudgeon-hook."

He walked forward, casting lingering glances at the
Frenchman over his shoulder.

Shelvocke looked at him as he left me, and crossing the
deck, asked me what he had been saying. I told him, and
he smiled.

"The lad has great spirit," said he, with the softened
voice and suggestion of fondness I had often noticed in him
when addressing the young fellow, or speaking of him.
"I doubt if he'd shirk the ugliest job you could put him
into. What think you of his face? He has a pretty look
at times, I fancy."

"I never met a handsomer nor a more interesting face in
a youth, sir. I question if he's purely English. There is
a southern tint in the skin, and a soft darkness in the
eyes——"

"Sail ho!" shouted a fellow on the forecastle.

There was no need to ask where away, for when I raised
my eyes they encountered the upper canvas of a vessel
about two points on the weather-bow. She was a full-
rigged ship, and making a due easterly course, and shortly
after she had hove in sight we raised another sail a little
to windward of her, that proved to be a brig.

We watched them anxiously, for if they turned out to be
Frenchmen we should, in all probability, find ourselves in
a pleasant little quandary, as by wearing and standing
down athwart our hawse, they could not only foil our
efforts to reach Guernsey, but force us to bring the wind
aft, in which case the line-of-battle ship astern would have
us at her mercy.

Suddenly the ship hoisted English colors, squared her
yards, threw out a couple of studding-sails, and, followed
by the brig, stood for the Frenchman, whom she had probably only just made out. We now saw that she was a
frigate, of what weight of metal it was not easy to guess,
as a vessel pierced as she was, for forty guns, might carry
more or less than that number; but though she was undoubtedly a crack ship of her class, she looked no match
for the huge liner whose soaring heights of canvas seemed

to sweep the very heavens, while the brig that accompanied
her had the air of an old collier with her badly stayed
masts, dark sails, and leaning bulwarks, which overhung
her decks like the flap of a Spanish sombrero.

As they came along, the brig about two-thirds of a mile
astern of her consort, the frigate threw out several signals:
each of them had her boarding-nettings triced up, and it
was clear that fighting was meant.   The gallant, dashing
manner in which they bore down upon their vast opponent,
shifting their helm and running for her with no more hesitation or swerving, as they bowled along under a press of
sail, than the slogster Mendoza exhibited when he stepped
into the ring, set most of our hearts beating quickly.

The magnificent intrepidity with which English seamen
—and I would speak particularly of the men of those times
—dashed into battle without stopping to reckon up the
enemy's strength and advantages, is a stirring thing even
to read about, but the seeing it even but once was enough
to give the heart the most inspiriting memory one must
hope to get out of this life.

I asked Shelvocke what he meant to do.

"Why, stand by to windward, to help our people if they
want assistance.   I would gladly give them a hand at once,
but those naval officers are as jealous as the very devil of
us privateersmen, and I remember the fable of the lion's
treatment of the jackass when the two went a foraging."

I had been watching the French ship, and doubting by
her keeping everything fast aloft whether she meant to
fight.   Once she starboarded her helm and went away to
leeward, a manœuvre that Shelvocke instantly took advantage of by putting the schooner about.   But the *Tigress* too
had not been five minutes settled down, and buzzing along
a course that would bring us close to the English brig, as
she followed in the wake of the frigate, when the Frenchman luffed, took in his royals and two topgallant-sails,
and hauled up his courses,—and at the same time let fly the
whole of his upper tier of starboard guns at us; they were
thirty-two pounders, and we had fallen within range of
them by backing; half the balls hurtled through the rigging
high over our heads, and the rest flew harmlessly astern:
nobody was hurt, but a good many ropes which had been

taut enough before were flying about in streamers, and the gaff-foresail came down with a run.

I saw by the expression in Shelvocke's face that he was about to order the salute to be returned; but he checked himself, and stood in silence watching the huge ship, while the crew sprang here and there, repairing damages and making sail.

Almost immediately after the Frenchman had closed us, the frigate shortened sail, took a reef in her fore and mizzen-topsails, and put her helm down, being about a mile to windward of the enemy. The brig was coming down slowly, though under a whole cloud of canvas, and as she neared us, Shelvocke wore the *Tigress*, shortening sail fore and aft in order to speak her. By this time the action between the frigate and the ninety-four had commenced, and the hulls of the two ships were enveloped in dense masses of smoke, streaked here and there with ugly bluish tints, and above which and jutting out like the spires of tall churches from a dense fog, might be seen the lofty mastheads of the vessels, with their pennants streaming against the pure limpid blue of the sky. The metal of the combatants was the heaviest at that time afloat, and the thunderous explosions of the guns resembled the raging of an electric storm; the very wind was stilled by the hellish uproar, and the waves appeared to have lost their buoyant play.

My attention, however, was diverted by the approach of the brig, and by Shelvocke springing on to the bulwarks and hailing her. They were at that moment shortening sail, and the rigging was dotted with men, while groups of half-naked seamen stood quietly at the guns; the suggestion of discipline was perfect; and the captain, a fine-looking young fellow, who answered Shelvocke's hail, spoke with the ease and composure of a man out on a holiday cruise.

"We are the English privateer schooner *Tigress*," sung out Shelvocke, "and I should be glad for instructions how to act in this engagement. I don't want to exceed what may be thought my duty."

"You had better heave to and watch us, sir," answered the captain of the brig. "I hope we may not require your

10

help; but should the need arise, I will summon you by hoisting a swallow-tailed blue-and-yellow flag."

Shelvocke waved his hand, and her helm was shifted; for by this time we had neared the frigate, over whom the balls of the Frenchman were flying as thick as peas, and flashing up the water to leeward of us.

By the time the schooner had been hove to clear of the cannonading, the brig had tailed on to the enemy, and added the thunder of her guns to the tremendous bellowing of the others. It was difficult to see the manœuvring, for the smoke clung like white sheets to the spars and hulls of the ships, and filled the whole theatre of the action with a fog that shut out the very heavens for the space of a mile on either hand of the combatants. The cannonading was furious—a man had hardly time to draw breath between the explosions; the glancing of the flames from the guns upon the pall of smoke was so incessant that one might have thought a great fire was burning upon the water between the vessels, and the deck of the schooner trembled like a house when a heavy wagon passes the door. From time to time one could just catch a glimpse of the English vessels twisting around the French ship as one may have seen a couple of dogs snuffling and running round a tree up which a cat has fled, while whole hurricanes of fire belched forth in double and even in treble lines at a time from the sides of the great liner, who reminded me—as she manœuvred, so as to avoid being raked, while the spray leaped about her bows and hung in trails from the stem—of a huge boar brought to bay and turning upon its pursuers.

Presently I noticed the frigate put her helm up and head for the Frenchman's quarter, with the evident intention of boarding; at the same moment the brig was preparing to take up a raking position right athwart the enemy's hawse. But the big ship was admirably handled; I had never imagined that anything approaching such seamanship was to be found in the French navy. She drove ahead, dropping the frigate astern as she did so, and giving her the whole strength of her broadside as she passed. The fore and main topmasts of the frigate fell under the discharge, as though men had been sent aloft to saw them off. A few moments after, the Frenchman's jibboom forged over the brig's forecastle under the topmast-stay; the brig had backed her yards for a stern-board, to escape the collision that threatened to cut her down, and the enemy's jibboom, like a giant's hand upon the stay, bore down the little vessel's fore-topmast with a crash and uproar of splintered wood. The brig dropped to leeward, carrying the Frenchman's jibboom with her, and with her bow dead on end to the liner's broadside that was let fly at her, with what effect I could not imagine, though I judged it as deadly a raking as any vessel ever received from another. With an alertness that would have done credit to the best commander in our navy, the Frenchman was got before the wind, flinging the fire of his port-batteries at the frigate as he passed her, and leaving her a mere confused heap of wreckage aloft. Cloth after cloth was thrown out, and with every spar standing save the mizzen topgallant-mast, the enemy stood to the southeast, running up her studding-sails in her eagerness to escape, and with crowds of men aloft splicing, knotting, fishing, and in every practicable way balsaming the rigging that it might carry them home.

The two English vessels, like men who had been knocked breathless and blind, hung uselessly upon the gleaming surges, and it was a sight to see the smoke of the finished battle floating in a huge wool-white cloud away ahead of the Frenchman, whose canvas shone like marble against it.

I noticed Shelvocke pacing in short turns at the extreme end of the quarterdeck. He beckoned me to him with a toss of the head, and said hurriedly:

"I should like to follow that ship. Her capture would beautifully turn the tables on the epaulets," his nickname for naval officers, "who cheated me out of the honor of beating the corvette. But," glancing at the huge square tower that was fast drawing toward the horizon, "she is too strong for us alone, and those vessels are as useless as cocked-hats now. Starboard your helm," he exclaimed to the fellow who was steering, "and let her drop under the frigate's stern."

As we approached the two vessels which lay within pistol-shot of each other, we got a better notion of the mischief the Frenchman had done them. There were some hands over the side of the brig examining the shot-holes, her

pumps were working furiously, and streams of water, colored crimson by the carnage of the decks, gushed from
every scupper-hole.  There were several dead bodies floating under her bows, their arms and legs and their heads on
the limber necks tossing with horrible and extravagantly
grotesque gestures on the wobbling waters.  Her port amidship bulwarks had been shattered to fragments, leaving exposed the deck that exhibited a ghastly spectacle of dead
and dying and wounded men, mixed up with splinters of
spars, heaps of rigging, sails, timber of boats, and a hundred other things whose wrecked condition left them unrecognizable and nameless.  A small group of men, naked
to the waist, and bespattered with blood and black with
the grime of the guns, were working the chain-pumps;
others were making some half-hearted efforts to clear away
the raffle, but I could not count above twenty living persons in all, though her decks, God knows, had been full
enough when we hailed her on the way to the engagement.

On the other hand, while the frigate looked almost as
complete a wreck aloft, her hull was comparatively uninjured, nor did she appear to have many men hurt.  Her
crew still made a great swarm, and they were all hard at
work repairing damages and rigging up a pair of shears,
and making ready to sway a jury-topmast aloft, while her
officers ran to and fro singing out orders, and the boatswain
and his mates piped like canaries in different parts of the
vessel.

The captain, a tall, gaunt, yellow man, with a ring of
hair round his face that gave him very much the appearance of a Madagascar ape, sat on a skylight rubbing the
top of his left knee, that had probably been grazed by a
shot.  As we glided slowly past, Shelvocke hailed him to
know if we should be of any use, and was answered by a
surly "No!" the fellow scarcely deigning to glance at us as
he replied.  The blood flushed Shelvocke's face, and with
a quick gesture of the hand he motioned the helm of the
schooner to be put down.

"Get all plain sail made, Mr. Madison!" he sung out.
"The play is over, and there is nothing more to keep us;"
and presently the *Tigress*, with her head to the northwest, was stealing along the waters which were quieting

down with the falling breeze, and growing a deep pure blue, over which in the south hung a sky of exquisitely delicate amber, that reddened into purple where the sun was sinking without a cloud to obstruct his lonely and regal descent. The red and slanting rays of the glorious luminary seemed to be concentrated upon the two vessels, and a whole constellation of ruby-colored stars sparkled in the streaming sides of the brig, whose hull had sunk low in the water, and between whom and the frigate several boats were plying.

"How reluctantly a vessel goes to her deathbed," said Shelvocke, watching with me the sinking brig, and speaking in a low voice, as though subdued by the pathos of this ocean-picture of the mutilated frigate and her slowly vanishing consort, the leagues of lonely water around, the red glare of sunset that deepened the impressiveness of the scene by the lurid coloring it imparted to the vessels, throwing them into strong relief against the calm sweet amber of the heavens beyond; "one thinks of a ship as of a living thing at such a time, and the gurgling of the water in the hold is like the gasping sobs of a drowning man."

"There she goes, sir," I exclaimed, as the little vessel cocked her bows to the very forefoot of her out-of-water and buried her stern; in a few moments the hull vanished, and as her lower-masts stuck for a brief pause out of water, methought that the sinking brig might have been likened to some veteran sailor stretching his mutilated stumps to heaven in a last prayer as he went down to his rest among the sands and shells under the sea.

"The action was bravely fought," said Shelvocke, watching the frigate, who had set a fore-topsail and hoisted her boats, and appeared to be standing after us, "though it has lost England a vessel and the best part of a stout crew. The frigate was badly handled at the last. If ever I have the honor of meeting her monkey-faced captain I'll tell him so. Nearly the whole brunt of the battle was borne by the little brig, and had she been properly supported the Frenchman would now be under British colors. Did you notice the frigate's name?"

"Yes, sir; the *Andromache.*"

"I must find out who her captain is. Ill-manners always

make me feel malignant. Some day I may chance to be in his company, and I should be sorry to discover that I had missed the chance of calling him a bad seaman to his face for the want of knowing him."

"He sails his ship large, sir. He has bore away four points."

"Heading for Guernsey, and the best thing he can do," said Shelvocke, pulling out a cigar, a luxury that was rarely out of his mouth.

As the twilight faded we lost sight of the frigate, but when the night closed in the wind completely died away, and we lay motionless on a dark and breathless surface of sea, with an unclouded heaven over us full of stars whose light hung in unblemished yellow flakes in the still water.

It remained calm all that night, and when the sun rose next morning we saw the frigate almost in the same spot we had sighted her in before the darkness fell. The sea was as white as a cotton sheet under the thin, steam-colored haze that tarnished the blue sky, save in the east, where the reflection of the sun hung in the form of a gigantic silver cone. I feared from the aspect of the weather that we were doomed to spend another long inactive day, but shortly after breakfast the water in the south darkened under a rushing wind that crisped up the foam as a cook froths a syllabub, and it was pleasant to see the swifter currents of air shooting along the surface of the glassy water ahead of the dark line of the approaching wind, like eels snaking off in a hundred directions, and lengthening and contracting as they sped along.

The breeze came dead on end from the French coast, and this decided Shelvocke to quit that part of the Channel for an English port where he might hope to hear news of a French convoy. Accordingly the schooner's course was shaped for Dartmouth, and we bowled along smoothly before the warm strong wind that blew over our port quarter, until five o'clock in the afternoon, when we made out a large ship under easy canvas apparently standing up Channel. But the moment she sighted us she cracked on all the sail she could set, though without altering her course.

It was my watch below, but I was on deck, lounging in the waist, smoking a pipe and enjoying, as I stood in the shadow of the foresail—the foot of which made a noble curve from the foremast to the gangway—the cool blowing of the wind that recoiled and breezed down vertically from the hollow of the huge cloths. Chestree was examining the vessel ahead with a glass, and I sung out to him to tell me what she was like.

"Why, sir, if she's not an English East Indiaman, I'll eat my head," he answered. "I believe I have seen that ship over and over again, though for the life of me I can't think of her name. Will you look at her, sir?" and he handed me the glass.

"Hang me," I exclaimed, after a short squint, "if I don't think—God bless my heart!—of course! I see her now—she is the old *Bombay Castle!*"

"Ay," shouted Chestree, "that's her name, Mr. Madison."

"I see the red capstan of her forecastle—and the black hoops of her mizzen-mast, like the keys of a piano-forte—and the galleries over the stern big enough for the Lord High Admiral to take the air in!" I cried, much excited by this sudden stumbling upon an old friend. "Mr. Chestree, jump below and tell Captain Shelvocke that his old ship is in sight."

And while he was gone I overhauled the flag locker, where, among a whole pile of bunting—for besides our mercantile code we carried the colors of every nation that flew an ensign—I found what I sought—Hannay's house-flag, a large, square red flag with a yellow castle for a centre-piece, and a white star at each corner, and told Peacock to bend it on to the main halliards and hoist it.

In a few moments Shelvocke came tumbling up through the companion, and seizing the glass, worked away at the ship with it.

"Ay, poor old hooker!" he exclaimed in a soft voice, such as a man speaks with when he stands looking at the house he was born in, "that's the *Castle*, true enough; I'd know her among a thousand. Lord, Madison, what memories she recalls! I took my first voyage in her, and she's carried me thirteen times to the East Indies and back. What capers have I cut on her decks on moonlight nights to the tune of a fiddle and a guitar! How passionately have I adored certain ladies—both married and single, alas! alas!—whom we have carried as passengers in that tough old sea-chest! What gales have I weathered, what dinners have I eaten, what friends have I made in her! Old Peppercorn commands her now—he's commodore, and his broad pennant would be flying had she any consorts in sight. Why, see, Madison! she hoists her house-flag! has the old bucket got the scent of me? Round go her main yards! Surely nobody aboard of her has ever seen the *Tigress* before!"

He was greatly amazed until I pointed to the house-flag I had hoisted, and then the mystery of the Indiaman's manœuvring was explained.

Rakish and piratical as our schooner looked, the exhibition of Hannay's flag at the masthead abundantly satisfied the *Bombay Castle*, who, with her mainyards aback, her courses festooned in the buntlines, and her bulwarks radiant with the red coats of a small army of soldiers, lay waiting for us to come within hail.

She was one of those amazingly romantic, old-fashioned ships which survive only in the paintings of the last century, with a sort of castellated stern, and a round tower for a poop, and two tiers of guns (half of the lower tier "quakers"), a low-pitched forecastle terminating in bows absurdly complicated with huge beams of decorative timber, out of which forked at an angle of about thirty-five degrees an immense bowsprit and jibboom, rigged with a couple of spritsail yards, so that they resembled a *fourth* mast that had fetched away, and was suffered to lie in the position in which it had fallen. The sight of her took one back to the days of Anson; yet, as she lay in the mellow afternoon light, with her sails swelling into the blue heavens, and the line of redcoats topping the white hammock-cloths, and the sunlight flashing in her windows, while the green waters broke in foam against her tall sides without stirring the ponderous hull, and her scarlet flags soared at the peak and main like tongues of flame breaking from those delicate points, she made a picture that even the rudest and most ignorant of our crew stood staring at with admiration.

As we rounded to, Shelvocke, who was on the bulwarks holding on to a backstay, was recognized by a silver-haired,

gray-faced old sea-dog—a real ancient in a broad-skirted
George the Second style of coat, that forked out all around
him as though expanded by a hoop, and long boots over
jean tights, and a frill that stuck out of his bosom like the
back of a perch, who bawled out to him in a cracked old
pipe:

"Glad to see ye, Shelvocke; come aboard! come aboard!
plenty of traveled Madeery left, my boy!"

This was old Captain Peppercorn, whom I knew by sight,
having been aboard a ship he was in command of at Bombay.
A number of military officers and ladies—some sweetly
pretty faces among these last—stood around him, and the
forepart of the vessel swarmed with soldiers and sailors.
Coming upon such a scene as this suddenly, amid the solitude of the sea, so gay with color, and so charmingly human-
ized by the ladies in radiant apparel, was like turning out
of a dusty highroad, and stumbling accidentally upon a brilliant garden-party. Only darkness and music, and a few
strings of colored lamps, were wanted to have made a kind
of Ranelagh of that Indiaman.

Shelvocke ordered the gig to be piped away, and asked
me to board the old hooker with him.

"I only left her t'other day," said he, "but it seems
twenty years ago since I was in her. Come, Madison, we'll
hear the news and have a look at our old home."

I was nothing loth; and, after diving into our respective
berths to change our coats and polish our faces, we jumped
into the gig and pulled aboard the *Bombay Castle*.

Old Peppercorn stood at the gangway to receive us, and
to our amazement immediately congratulated Shelvocke on
his victory over the French corvette.

"Why, how in heaven's name got you that news, Peppercorn?" exclaimed Shelvocke. "Are you outward or homeward bound?" And he stared about him as I did.

Peppercorn had one of those dry, powdery faces which
look as if a gale of wind would blow the whole of the skin
off in a cloud-dust; his widest grin never yielded a wrinkle,
it was like a miller's smile; and bursting suddenly into an
uproarious laugh over Shelvocke's surprise that was certainly not particularly mirth-provoking, the sight of his face
with his mouth distended like the crumb of a loaf with a

slice cut out of it, and the tears hopping down his sandy, dry, unfurrowed skin, out of his small, bleared, pale eyes, was so irresistibly funny, that I burst into a shout which I was forced to humor and give free vent to, lest in my effort to suppress it I should make a complete fool of myself.

My laugh proved contagious, and Shelvocke joined in; the thing spread; a stout old major let fly with a voice like a crow; some of the ladies *hearing* him, and *seeing* me, broke into peals of laughter; and in a minute everybody on board the vessel was tossing about in uncontrollable fits of merriment.

"Lord, Shelvocke, man!" piped old Peppercorn, drying his eyes on a red cotton handkerchief as big as his main-royal, "how you have made me laugh, to be sure! I give you my honor I have never laughed so heartily since I saw Munden as Obadiah. But come along aft! come along aft! let me introduce the captain of the *Tigress* to the ladies."

And hauling at Shelvocke like a watchman carrying a thief to prison, he dragged him up to the passengers, where he scraped and flourished, and went through the business like a dancing-master.

I kept close alongside, for I wanted to hear how Peppercorn had got to know about our action with the corvette; but he would first send for wine, and ask a hundred questions about Hannay, and the *Tigress*, and home news, and though it was no unfamiliar sight to me, yet I found myself watching with great interest the faces of the passengers as Shelvocke told all he could remember about home affairs, and the health of the King, and what was doing in the House of Commons, and who was dead, and so on. I had often, myself, made one of a party of eager listeners, after a year or eighteen months' absence from home, and when the gruff voice of the pilot, usually the first bearer of news from England, was as sweet as music for the tidings conveyed, and I could sympathize with the attentive faces which thronged around Shelvocke. At last a pleasant-faced, well-bred woman, thinking (very wisely) that she could get more news out of me by asking a few direct questions than by listening to old Peppercorn's diffusive catechization of Shelvocke, artfully drew me aside, and before long I was surrounded by a dozen ladies, among them three of the

sweetest girls I had seen for many a day, whose eyes—I
speak of the whole of them—being all fixed on my face,
were tolerably disconcerting, as may be supposed, of a bash-
ful seaman. However, I did well enough to please them,
though I had never greater reason to deplore my social ignorance than when one of the three darlings—the sweetest
of the three, too, a creature whose violet eyes and auburn hair
filled my slumbers for several nights with more dreams than
there are knots in a log-line—asked me if I could tell her
whether Lady Olivia (Thingummy—I forget the other name)
had married again. Alas! I had never heard of her ladyship, but there was so much agreeable flattery in the impli-
cation that I *might* know, and the Beauty who asked the
question conveyed by her tone so complete a notion that
anybody with the least pretensions to breeding *ought* to
know, that I blushed to the roots of my hair when I looked
at her, and answered in a faint voice, "I had not heard."

Presently, seeing Shelvocke pull out his watch, I bowed
to the ladies and joined my captain, and after exchanging
a few final words with Peppercorn, we jumped into the gig
and shoved off for the schooner. On the way, Shelvocke,
who was in high spirits, and repeatedly waved his hat to
the people we were leaving, who returned his salutation
with hat and handkerchief, explained to me how Peppercorn had come to hear about our action with the corvette.

He said that a few hours before the *Bombay Castle* had
made Scilly, she sighted a shallop that was tossing upon
the water without sails or oars. On coming up to her they
discovered five men, who by motions and gestures expressed
great suffering and entreated to be taken aboard. They
proved to be the survivors of the crew of a French brig that
had been fired into by an English cruiser but had managed
to escape; but, shortly after losing sight of the enemy, the
brig sprung a leak and filled so fast that before the boats
could be launched, she went down. Five of the crew managed to reach the shallop that had gone adrift when the vessel foundered, righted her, and baled her out, and they had
been in her fifty-five hours without food or water, or any
means of approaching the land, when the *Bombay Castle*
hove in sight. From them Peppercorn had learned the story
of the *Tigress'* action with the corvette, and out of grati-

tude to their preservers the poor fellows had volunteered
more news than Peppercorn had any interest in; one of
the items being that a convoy of sixty-eight sail, bound for
one of the French West India settlements, was to start
shortly from Brest, under the protection of a line-of-battle-
ship, two frigates, and four heavily-armed privateers.

It was this piece of intelligence that had put Shelvocke
in good spirits.

"The old *Bombay Castle* was always a lucky ship to
me!" he exclaimed, "and this is a bit of news I am superstitious enough to own I would rather have got from her
than from any other source. We have two clear days to
run down to Brest in. I shall give up Dartmouth. Only
let that convoy get to sea, and I'll warrant the British
cruisers shall not bag our share of the booty."

"And what is going to balk that charmer when once you
give her the scent, captain?" said I, pointing with a glow
of pride to the *Tigress*, whose superb hull, topped by the
towering masts, and the folds of canvas tingled by the pink
light of the setting sun, and the red flashing of her copper
as the green and foam crested surges rose and fell against
her sides, I had never beheld in greater perfection. "That
hawse-hole is like the dilated nostril of a swift and powerful beast, and the muzzles of those guns are eyes which
will look five hundred Frenchmen in the face without winking."

"That's almost bad enough for the House of Commons!"
said Shelvocke, laughing. "But bad as it is, I can make
it worse, by saying, that if those eyes did *not* wink when
they looked at Frenchmen, I'd pitch them overboard."

"So much for poetical imagery, captain. as the orator
said when he ducked his pate to a dead cat after a brilliant metaphor!"

In another minute we had gained the deck of the *Tigress*.

We hung in the wind in order to see the *Bombay Castle*
sail away. Her people knew we were watching her, and
went to work like boys under the shadow of a birch. She
swung her mainyards, and, having the breeze abeam, ran
up her studding-sails; and when I saw her reel over—with
the water dark with her shadow, and the tops of the waves
crimson with the evening glory, and all her passengers

grouped aft and looking at us over the taffrail, while her bulwarks flickered with the red line of uniforms, and the churned water to leeward flashed with a ruddy tinge along her depressed side that bristled with the short black muzzles of her guns—my heart went with her: a hundred glad memories of the life I had spent in the old frame rushed upon me. I recalled the silence of the sleeping ship upon tropical seas; the thunder of the hurricanes which filled her with groaning noises, and fogged her decks with flying spume; the toasts of the mess-table; the lonely night-watches; the faces I had met aboard of her, and had forgotten until now; the friendships and the enmities begotten in her—and I thought of the fears and the hopes which had vanished, the dreams which had been dispelled and for the extinction of which my maturer life was thankful, and of the unsuspected things which had come to pass.

Even that receding ship pointed a moral, and I felt myself the better for letting my thoughts run loose upon her.

We waited until she had got well away, and then fired a gun and dipped the ensign three times to her—a piece of maritime courtesy that she immediately acknowledged with two guns and her ensign. A few moments after the schooner's head was pointing down Channel, and the news was whispered fore and aft that we were bound for the neighborhood of Brest, and for the wake of a rich convoy that was to cross the Atlantic.

# CHAPTER VII.

## THE DROIT MARITIME.

To fetch the latitude we wanted to make we had about a hundred and thirty miles to run; we had therefore much more time on our hands than we needed. At least that would have been the notion, with the breeze that was blowing when we parted with the *Bombay Castle;* but about half an hour before sunset the wind dropped, veered to the west, and expired after a few faint puffs.

I was below in the cabin, talking with Shelvocke over the old ship we had just left, and he was laughing over Peppercorn and mimicking the way in which that tough-and-dry old chap had bragged about his pluck in giving the slip to H.M.S. *Gipsy,* that was convoying him and five other Indiamen home.

"As if there was anything particularly heroic in a man risking a run without protection from the latitude of St. Helena, with two hundred and eighty troops aboard, sixty seamen, and fourteen long nine-pounders, not to speak of six *quakers!*" said Shelvocke.

"He matches his ship well," said I. "His parched face and old brown scratch and flapping skirts are in perfect keeping with the hooker's mountainous stern and house-windows. Captain Peppercorn doesn't look like a man who will die the usual death; he'll fossilize, sir: and should the old *Bombay Castle* outlive him his executors would do well to hand him over to Hannay & Co. as a figurehead for the ship."

"You don't fancy the old fellow thinks of dying, do you?" exclaimed Shelvocke, laughing heartily; "why, he's going to be *married* as soon as he gets ashore. The lady was aboard, he told me, but he wouldn't point her out. I begged hard for a sight of her, but he only dug his elbow into my ribs, and grinned until I thought his eyes were quenched forever. Imagine the rogue having the impudence to get married! I asked him what his age was: he reflected and answered that he believed he was the wrong side of fifty; 'but,' said he, 'when I was born the registration of children's ages was a very imperfect job, so perhaps I'm not so old as I suppose.' Now, I *know* he won't see his seventy-second year again. 'Really, Peppercorn,' said I, 'you look wonderfully young for your age.' 'D'ye think so, Shelvocke?' said he, in his old cracked fiddle. 'Ay, wonderfully young; and let me assure you, Peppercorn,' said I, 'it comforts me to feel you are not old enough to firmly believe that your sweetheart admires you *only* for your beauty. That solace is reserved until you shall be turned seventy!' 'Ah! there is no telling what I may believe should I live to attain so great an age,' quavered the old hypocrite; but for all that he wouldn't point me out his affianced one. From which I suspect she's a chicken."

"Not one of the three beauties, I hope!" I exclaimed; and I was about to sing the praises of violet eyes and auburn hair, when Chestree thrust his ugly mug into the cabin, and said that the boatswain wished to speak to the captain.

"Well, Mr. Tiptree, what is it you want?" inquired Shelvocke of the fine, well-made fellow who stood at the door, cap in hand, his face shining like the top of a mahogany dining-table, while drops of perspiration, induced as much by nervousness as the heat, trickled down his cheeks into his enormous whiskers, which extended from under his ears to the corners of his mouth, and looked like a couple of door-mats slung by laniards athwart his jowls. His silver pipe hung just below the point where his open shirt disclosed his mossy breast and a throat whose massive and muscular proportions might have been copied for a painting of a Roman gladiator. Over his shirt he wore a short jacket, braided at the sleeves, and breasted with double rows of cloth buttons, while he occasionally plucked at the band of a pair of white drill bags flowing down to his small well-polished shoes in expanding folds like a ship's wake, that broadens the farther it goes astern. He was, I think, as perfect a type as any seaman that ever I met, of the better class of the mariners of that age, alert as a cat, tough as a spar of upland spruce, fearless less from native resolution and force of character than from what I have sometimes thought an *instinctive* indifference to death, extremely fond of rum, capable of doing the work of five men at a pinch, and hating the French like poison.

"If you please, sir," said he, going through various preliminary manœuvres in the shape of shifting his quid out of one cheek into another, tricing up his trousers, looking into the bottom of his cap, and wiping his heated forehead on the sleeve of his jacket, "the men have begged me for to come, Captain Shelvocke, to ask if your honor 'ud object to their having a bit o' toe and heelin' forrard—a kind o' all-round tom-foolin'. They can muster two wiolins, sir."

"Why not put your real question straight, and ask for a can of grog to shove some spring into the fellows' toes? You know that is what the crew mean," said Shelvocke good-naturedly, Tiptree being a great favorite of his. "How's the weather?"

"Quiet as the bottom of a well, sir," answered Tiptree, grinning broadly, and not without an expression of admiration at the skipper's sharpness.

"Well, you may tell the steward to serve out a glass of grog to each man, and as it will be getting dark soon, you can get the lanterns ready for slinging. See that the humor don't get too boisterous, Tiptree."

"Ay, ay, sir;" and evidently much gratified by the quick success of his errand, the boatswain withdrew.

"It's just this sort of sympathy with the crew that makes Tiptree the valuable fellow he is," said Shelvocke; "there's not a man aboard that wouldn't risk his neck to serve him. You had better get on deck, Mr. Madison, that your presence may stop any excessive horseplay; and let the mates keep a bright lookout around, for it won't do for an enemy's ship to bowl down upon us with a breeze, and find us dancing."

The sun was half immersed when I reached the deck, and I stood a few moments watching the glorious sight, and thinking that if ever a glimpse of the Paradise of Christians —"and the building of the wall it was of jasper, and the city was pure gold, like unto clear glass"—is obtained by us dwellers on earth, it is when the semi-sunken sun flashes upon the western sky a thousand heavenly hues—ruby and

amethyst, and opal and pearl, and violet, with the soft melting of the warm orange into the pale amber—when the hovering clouds make a vista of golden-edged porches which provoke the eye into searching through them the infinite depths
beyond, whose light is "like unto a stone most precious,
even like a jasper stone, clear as crystal"—when the blinding glory upon the sea appears rather the reflection of the
opening Paradise in that mirror of Eternity, the Deep, than
the flashing of a luminary upon water. Such a sunset I
was now witnessing, and I stood fascinated by its magnifi-
cence, watching the upper limb of the sun growing smaller
and smaller until but a tiny fragment of it glowed upon the
polished water-line, like a red-hot cinder, while the radiant
reflection shortened as though a band of bright gold were
being drawn away from us along the water, until the last
spark vanished, and the colors began to fade.

"Beautiful!" I exclaimed, unconsciously speaking aloud.

"Beautiful indeed, sir!" echoed a melodious voice at my
side; "who can look at such a sight as that and believe that
the bright home beyond the skies that has been promised to
men is a superstitious fancy?"

"Why, Mr. Peacock," said I, struck by the peculiar
melancholy in his large dark eyes, "it is strange that you
should put my very identical musings into words. But I
suppose the thoughts bred in you and me by that sunset are
not peculiar to us two. What makes you even suggest that
heaven may be a superstitious fancy? The most generous
and the best faiths a man has belong to his boyhood, and
though you are no longer a boy in years, let me advise you
to remain a boy in religion. You may take the word of
wiser men than I that you will want more brains than yours
or any mortal skull is likely to hold to improve upon your
mother's creed."

"My mother was a Catholic, sir," he replied, as though
he fancied that would rather confound my reckoning.

"And what of that? I hope you are not ashamed of your
mother's faith?"

A dark blush came into his face, and a dangerous devil
into his eyes. I once saw such a look in a very handsome
young Spanish captive who was being twitted by an ill-bred
English officer for wearing a silver crucifix under his shirt.

11

"I *am* ashamed of it, if I *must* speak the truth," he exclaimed. "I am ashamed of having been born a Catholic, though I am a stanch Protestant now, sir. Perhaps *you* may be a Catholic, Mr. Madison, but I shall not apologize for what I have said; I *hate*——" He seemed about to deliver some mighty violent sentence, but checked himself, touched his cap and walked over to the gangway, where he stood watching the movements of the men, apparently with great interest.

I thought all this very curious, and it was more so to my mind that I can well make clear by the significance imparted to every word and look of the youth by his beauty, his melodious voice, and the refinement and breeding that were exhibited in his person and manners.

The steward was on the main deck serving out a gill of rum to each of the crew from a huge can filled with the dark liquor, and it would, at any other time, have amused me to watch the men coming up with grave faces, some of them tipping down the grog raw from the steward's pewter measure, but most of them carrying the dose forward in tin pannikins, while those who had been already served were busy in clearing up the decks, slinging the lanterns for lighting, and making ready for the dancing. But my mind was full of young Peacock, and knowing that Chestree had been shipmate with him in one voyage, if not two, and observing that worthy standing near the launch gaping around the sea, with his cap at the back of his head, and his immense mouth open, like a newly landed fish, to catch every draught of air from the occasional gentle flap of the mainsail, I went up to him, and broke ground by telling him not to attend to the dancing, but to help me to watch for any wind that might come, and for any sail it might bring along with it.

"I doubt if there'll be any wind this side of midnight, sir," he answered; "but let it come when it will, I'll report it fast enough if I'm on deck."

"I've just been having a little talk with Peacock," said I;—"now *don't* stare at him, Chestree—and I have been rather surprised by a smart exhibition of prejudice. How comes a young fellow like him, who has been half his life at sea, to be troubled with 'longshore antipathies of any kind? Who is he? or rather, what *was* he—do you know?"

Here I thought, but it might have been my fancy, that Chestree grew grave; but it was difficult to interpret the thoughts of a man from a face that, in consequence of the heat, was nearly all mouth.

"Why, sir, all that I know of Peacock is," he answered, "that he's a love child. Who his mother was I can't say; but she wasn't English. I remember a big apprentice aboard the *Fattysalam* smoking the poor little chap—he was a little chap then, sir—and asking him what port his mother hailed from, and if his father knew he was out, until all on a sudden the boy seized a knife and sprang upon the bully; just as in Bombay once I saw a little slip of a Hindoo Shylock fly at an Englishman, and catch his throat in his teeth, and hold in that way until he was dragged off with a pound of bleeding flesh between his lips. The apprentice roared murder, and fell sprawling on his back, and that saved his life, for young Peacock was seized with the knife poised ready for the heart of the brute who had goaded him. I think little Peacock was raving mad for some minutes, but his treatment of the apprentice shut up all jokes after that. How we got to know he was a natural child, and that his mother wasn't English, I am sure I can't say. It's astonishing what lots of things, which one can't ever remember particularly hearing, *are* known to one!"

At this point a fellow, seated like a tailor on the drum of the forecastle-capstan, began to scrape a fiddle, and I crossed the deck to see if the steward had finished serving out the grog to the men.

It was not yet quite dark, but the twilight obscured the schooner, and the horizon of the sea was a dark, dream-like shadow; but the night was very calm and lovely, with a new moon in the west that cast a faint trickle of silver upon the sea, and a heaven overhead and in the east crowded with stars, and meteors which glided like illuminated bombshells through the air, and vanished in little puffs of bright smoke.

However, the mystery and beauty of this "visible darkness" were speedily put to flight by the men lighting the lanterns, and presently the deck was all aglow with the radiance of threescore candles, and it was a pretty sight to see the light flickering upon the small-arms in the racks,

and in the brass garnishings of the pumps, and giving a
yellow color to the shrouds for about the height of a man
above the bulwarks. This dance by lantern-light was a
very unusual departure from the customary order of sailors'
festivities, which are nearly always celebrated in the dog-
watches; but the novelty of it gave it nearly all its relish.
The two fiddlers proved very tolerable scrapers, and made
the air resonant with their miaulings; one sat, as I have
said, on the forecastle-capstan, and the other atop of the
galley; they played the same airs, kept good time, soon
worked themselves into a fever of excitement, and their
elbows quivered like the reflection of a stationary fish under
a running stream, while the crew hopped and sprang about
in all directions in couples, making the deck boom under
their shuffling and toeing and scraping, laughing uproariously the while.

One really good dance was a hornpipe performed by four
men, who had rigged themselves out in regular theatrical-
Jack fashion—flowing breeches, open breasts, jackets round-
ing over their quarters like the foot of a tautly set topsail,
hats on nine hairs, as they say, and shoes with heels which
they rattled like castanets. Their messmates knew their
*jigging* qualities and stopped their own dancing to gather
in a crowd, leaving an opening so that we quarter-deck
people might see. The capstan fiddler scrambled alongside
his brother-scraper on the galley that the music might be
concentrated; but finding the four men waiting and all
hands looking aft, I suspected the reason of the delay, and
went below to tell Shelvocke that the crew wanted him to
witness the hornpipe. He came on deck at once, and drew
close to the crowd, who raised a cheer when they saw him
that immediately started the fiddlers, and in a moment the
four sailors were quivering about in a fashion that set me
shouting out of hand, and I never stopped laughing until
the rascals ended their fooling. It was the best bit of
dancing that ever I saw, and the gravity of the fellows contrasting with the crowd of grinning faces around and the
shouts of mirth which broke forth, would have made a saint
split his sides.

I have seen many landsmen, actors and others, attempt
the hornpipe, and some have danced it very well indeed;

but the landsman never yet was born that could give the
real sailor's shuffle in that dance—the swing and bend of
the legs, as if the flowing breeches covered a pair of springs
—the whirring and twinkling of the toes—the flashing of
the feet as though, like those of the god Mercury, wings
grew at the heels. The landsman dances the hornpipe with
his head, body, and arms, as well as his legs; but when Jack
dances, only the lower part of him is concerned—from the
band of his breeches up he might as well be a torso mounted
upon a pair of human shanks.

The four *Tigresses* trod the deck to perfection: with their
arms hanging like dead limbs down their hips, the fingers
of their horny hands partially curled as though they still
grasped a rope, their heads so steady that not so much as a
streak of hair was tossed over their foreheads, their faces as
immovable as carved wood, they formed into a line, separated, danced at each other, then back to back, then face
to face, then in a circle, then sideways, their heels keeping
time to the fiddles like a band of drummers, while shout
after shout of applause broke from their admiring shipmates, and Shelvocke clapped his hands like a boy at a
pantomime.

The four harmonious figures; the swarm of excited faces,
all of one color in the lantern-light; the foreground full of
the grim details of heavy guns, and the huge mainmast
soaring into the darkness; the two fiddlers in shadow saw-
ing at the catgut and rocking in their seats and threatening
every moment in their excitement to plump over the side of
the galley into the crowd; the silver horn of moon in the
west; the sparkling sky overhead, and the lonely leagues of
water lying as breathless as a lake as far as the eye could
pierce—formed a beautiful and impressive picture.

This harmless revelry lasted until half-past nine; and
then tired and hot, but all in as high good-humor as if they
had been spending a merry time at Greenwich fair with
their Sukeys and Polls, the sailors one by one drew away
to their hammocks for a quiet smoke, the fiddlers came
down from the top of the galley, the lanterns were extinguished, and by ten o'clock the schooner lay wrapped in
silence and darkness, with nothing moving aboard of her
but the figures of the lookout men or the shadow of the

great mainboom, as the occasional roll of the vessel swayed the ponderous spar athwart the luminous haze around the skylight.

It was my watch on deck, and, missing Shelvocke, I supposed he had turned in; and so I paced to and fro with Tapping, who, despite the pugnacious pose in which nature had cast his figure and face, was an exceedingly good-tempered and agreeable fellow, and, so far as I had opportunities of judging, an intelligent seaman and full of sterling pluck. Young as he was, he had seen some strange things in his time—but what sailor had not in that age of adventure and fighting?—and was interesting me with an account of a mutiny, which, by the way, he was relating with real dramatic power, when he suddenly broke off, and went to the gangway, and, on looking around, I perceived the glowing tip of a cigar near the figure of the man at the tiller.

"The cabin is like a bakehouse!" exclaimed Shelvocke, whom I had approached on seeing. "How the deuce Chestree can sleep, I don't know; but that he is sleeping you can hear."

And certainly a most horrible sound of snoring came up through the skylight. The fellow who was steering smothered a laugh.

"It's like a church organ with something wrong in its inside," I said, almost awed by a snore that could pierce through a stout bulkhead and be audible so far aft as where we stood.

"This won't do, Madison," said Shelvocke, looking around him at the darkly pure space of water that was only determinable from the sky by the long, tremulous white flakes of light which the stars shed upon it. "If this calm lasts we shall have to give up our Brest scheme."

"I hope not, captain. It's about time to do something again. There was a heap of luck in the first few hours of our cruise, and if, as the French say, it's only the first step that costs, the rest of our work ought not to make us grumblers."

He quitted the spot where we had been standing, probably not wishing the man at the helm to hear us, and we leisurely patrolled the deck. Hearing Chestree snore as we passed the skylight somehow brought young Peacock into my head, probably because the lad was in the second officer's watch.

"What a very strange youth our fourth mate is, sir," said I.

"Young Philip Peacock, do you mean?" he answered quickly. "In what way strange? What has he been doing?"

"Why, nothing, sir; I judge him by his talk—though, to be sure, he gave me little enough of that to go by. I happened to say that a man can never do better than stick to the religion his mother believed in, and he whipped out against the Roman Catholic faith so passionately, with so much fire in his eyes, that I was honestly surprised."

Shelvocke remained silent.

"It seems queer that a young fellow like him, who has spent all his life at sea, should have shore-going prejudices of that kind. I suppose you know his history, sir?"

He still kept silence.

"I asked Chestree, who was shipmate with him in an Indiaman," continued I, "who he was, and he told me that all he knew was that Peacock was a love-child."

"Chestree knows that, does he?" said Shelvocke coldly, after two or three hard pulls at his cigar. "Has he spoken to Peacock about it?"

"No, sir, nor is it likely he would."

"He nad better not. Be good enough, Madison, to tell him from me he *had better not.*"

"Chestree has too good a heart to stand in need of such an injunction, sir; but of course I will tell him, since it is your order."

"How comes a circumstance that concerns no living creature but Mr. Peacock to be known to a man like Chestree?" exclaimed Shelvocke in a tone of deep annoyance that he strove ineffectually to disguise. "Nevertheless," added he, softening his voice, "it is true enough, Mr. Madison, though the boy is a fool to allow his sensitiveness to challenge curiosity, as he appears to have done in your case. Of course I do not suppose there is the least unworthiness in the interest Peacock appears to have excited in you."

"I should be sorry if you thought there was, sir. I have all along been attracted by the lad's beauty and refined manners, but I never should have dreamt of inquiring about him had not his sudden burst of temper on a subject that on would have supposed a young sailor like him would not trouble his brains about induced me to speak to Chestree. However, I shall be glad of your permission to change the subject."

"Nay," answered he, with some of his old good-nature in his voice, "as he excites your interest there can be no harm in my telling you what I know of his story. His mother was an Italian, and a remarkable beautiful woman. An Englishman, who was staying at Cantanzaro, where she lived with her mother, fell in love with her, and they secretly betrothed themselves. The priests got hold of the mother, and they went to work to separate the girl from a heathen who did not attend mass; but their efforts, of course, only served to deepen the girl's affection for the man, and so they had him poniarded—but, malheureusement pour mademoiselle, not killed. He was in bed a month, and his nurse was his sweetheart, who left her mother's home to be with him. Our true Briton requited the girl's admiration by ruining her. He promised her marriage, but suspecting, I suppose, that he could get on very well without marriage, he never kept his promise. There is a romantic story of the girl wasting away and breaking her heart over our faithless hero, and dying amid the fogs of London, whither the Englishman had carried her. More likely she died of bronchitis or lung-inflammation: but those are not diseases to adorn a tale with. At all events, she died—but not having your curiosity, or, to put it more humanely, not finding the lad so fascinating as he appears to be to you, though I took great interest in him when he was brought to me to be apprenticed to a maritime friend of mine, I asked very few questions."

It was my turn now to be silent.

"So there!" he exclaimed, with a rather unpleasant laugh, "you have as much of Peacock's story as I can give you. But what on earth there can be about a youth like that to excite the curiosity of an old stager like you, you must really forgive me for not being able to see. However, you can guess now why the boy bounced out about the Roman. Catholic religion."

"Because the priests had a hand in the stabbing of his father, I suppose."

"*No!*" he answered, with impetuous emphasis; "because he hates his mother's memory and everything belonging to her—like all natural children."

"Like all unnatural children, I should say, captain."

"It is no business of mine nor of any other person's," he replied, throwing the end of his cigar overboard; "and so you will oblige me by requesting Mr. Chestree not to talk about Mr. Peacock. The boy is under my care, and I'll not have him pained."

Tired of the subject and regretting my folly for having started it, I went to the side to look into the north, where a haze was gathering, and felt a little draught of air upon my hot face. It filled the lighter canvas, and a shower of dew fell from the cloths. It died away, but a few minutes after a stronger breeze frosted the sea with broken starlight, the sails grew steady, and the ear was refreshed by the bubbling of rippling water along the sides of the schooner. I called to the watch to trim sail, and by the time this was done the schooner's masts were sloping to a pleasant wind, and a line of froth was whitening the black surface of the sea astern. Before eight bells were struck it had breezed up into a fresh wind with clouds sailing across the stars; and when I left the deck, the *Tigress* was smoking along the quick, short surges with a single reef in her mainsail and foresail, and the decks forward black with the flying spray.

At daybreak, however, as the deuce would have it, the wind dropped again into mere light currents of air, and a hot and dazzling morning threatened to dry up the small breeze that remained, and leave us roasting on a surface of glass.

This was extremely disappointing, for putting aside our chance of fetching Brest in time to catch the skirts of the outward-bound convoy, this stagnant weather was holding everything that swam upon the surface of the sea idle. While the water-line was as polished as the edge of a worn shilling, there was nothing to watch for nor to hope for.

The calm, coupled with the heat, made us all surly. Forward the men were grumbling in their gizzards and whistling through their teeth as they hung over the bows, and

we of the after-part of the vessel could scarcely have been
more dogged had we passed the night in arguing on religion.
Shelvocke was particularly meditative, and sat smoking
cigars the whole morning, with a broad-brimmed straw hat
over his nose, and his feet on the skylight. He had a book
on his knee, though he seldom glanced at it; but from a
sheltered spot in the waist where I had hidden myself to
smoke a pipe, I noticed that he constantly followed Peacock about with his eyes.

However, by dinner-time our tempers had been improved
by a pleasant little wind that hit the schooner's best sailing
point, and sent her cheeping through the water with rounded
sails and breezy decks. Added to this was the cordializing
influence of the wine. Shelvocke shed his scales, and
"stood confest" the blunt and genial sailor nature had made
him. Corney was of our party, and favored us, for the first
time, with an astonishingly clever imitation of two Frenchmen quarreling. We quitted the table more amiable if not
wiser men, and the sight of the waters playing to windward
in quick glancings of froth, as though shoals of mackerel
leaped from the cool green into the sunshine, sustained our
good temper by making us hopeful.

Shortly after we had come on deck, Shelvocke walked up
to me, and said in a low but pleasant voice:

"I forgot to ask you, Madison, if you spoke to Chestree
about Peacock, as I requested."

"I did, sir, last night."

"All right," he answered, and went away, much to my
relief, as I was afraid he would pursue the subject.

Half-past three had just been struck on the silver-clear
bell we carried on the main-deck. I was standing on a
gun-carriage looking over the side at the passing water.
The soft creaming of the foam, as it raced past with its
outer edge sparkling blue and green and yellow in the sunshine, like diamonds strewn upon snow, and beautifully defined by the luminous emerald hue of the water beyond,
mingled with the tinkling of large bubbles as they exploded,
and the cool splashing of the polished arch of water curling from the stem, fell with a delicious refreshment upon
the senses; and the rich warm wind pouring out of the
mainsail swept past the ear with a mixture of vibratory

sounds which seemed like the notes of a far-off band of music.

Whenever the schooner had way on her, it was always our custom to have a hand stationed aloft on one of the fore-yards. This lookout startled me from a deep reverie ·I had fallen into by hailing the deck.

"Hallo!" I exclaimed.

"A sail on the port bow, sir!" he sang out.

"Can you make out which way she is standing?"

He shaded his eyes and had a long look, and answered that he believed she was heading our way.

"You had better take the glass aloft, Mr. Madison," said Shelvocke.

I did as I was ordered, and presently found myself along-side the lookout on the topgallant-yard. The sail was per-fectly visible from this great elevation, and on examining her through the glass I made her out to be a large three-masted lugger, but her hull was still below the horizon. I called out to Shelvocke to let him know what her rig was, and added that I would stay aloft until I could command a better view of her.

"She should be a lumping boat, to judge by the size of her mainsail," said I to the man at my side—a fellow of the name of Wilkinson, one of the smartest men in my watch, so tanned by long exposure to the sun that his face looked as if it had been painted with iodine, and who sat on the yard (the sail of which was furled) with his legs dangling down before it, and his hands buried in his breeches-pockets, and taking his ease on this eminence of a hundred and thirty feet above the sea-level as coolly as a landsman in an armchair. "But she has only her main-sail set. I can't make out what she would be at. She looks to be hove right up in the wind's eye."

"She'll crack on sail when she sees us, sir—leastways if she is a Frenchman," said the man, politely covering the weather side of his mouth with his hand while he discharged some tobacco-juice into the air.

I jammed the glass into the bunt of the topgallant sail, and threw my leg over the yard to make me a comfortable posture with my back against the mast.

I have often wondered, in reading that magnificent description of a giddy height of cliff in "King Lear," how the great master would have described a view from the masthead of a lofty vessel. Say what you will of a survey from a mountain-top or from the edge of towering cliffs; in my humble judgment the most thrilling impression that great elevation can produce is (leaving of course the balloon-car out of the question) to be obtained from the slender yard of a tall ship in the middle of the sea.

For here you get an element of *isolation* that, in spite of the lonesomeness of craggy land, is qualified, if not extinguished, when surveying a scene from any sort of height ashore, not only by the sight of land all around you, but by land being under your feet. But at the masthead of a ship you stand upon a slender rope or bestride a spar that looks no stouter than a knitting-needle from the deck, and you gaze around upon a mighty surface of water; for the narrow and familiar horizon beheld from the deck is magnified into an immense ocean, and a whole hemisphere of heaven leans away into the prodigious distance, while below is the narrow shape of the hull on whose surface the seamen crawl in size no bigger than flies, and you are amazed that so slender and tapering a fabric should support the sky-searching height of mast and canvas from the summit of which you look down. *Here*, I say, a man gets that sense of isolation which no land eminence can yield, and it is complete enough even when the seas bask brightly and calmly around, when the sails are gently drawing, when the sweet winds blow softly, and the blue sky looks blandly upon the deep in whose bosom it pictures its azure beauty. But it is *supreme* when the tempest is around you, when the heavens are full of sooty clouds, whirling in convolutions like the smoke of a newly fed furnace crowding in black, fat volumes from a factory chimney; when the torn sea spreads like a vast surface of wool for leagues and leagues, and the huge surges plash in sheets of blinding spray over the streak of hull that races, far beneath you, like a shadow through the white haze of storm-driven spume, and reels under the shocks with a quivering that sets the mast on which you are poised trembling like an old man's hand; when the gale is roaring in thunder out of the strip of sail stretched upon the yards a long distance below you, and the din of clashing seas and the yelling of the tempest in the sky perfect through the ear the scene of grandeur and terror beheld by the eye.

"Topgallant-yard there! Mr. Madison, are we rising the sail ahead?"

"Yes, sir, fast; she's a very large lugger: apparently not far short of our tonnage," I answered, bringing the glass to bear upon the hull that was now hove up clear upon the smooth water-line. "She looks to me to be deserted," I said to Wilkinson. "Watch her a bit, and you will see how she comes to and falls off;" and handing him the glass, I hailed the deck and told Shelvocke to luff the schooner a point, as the lugger was forging ahead, and would be to windward of us.

"She certainly don't look to me as if there was anybody at her helm," exclaimed Wilkinson. "But there ain't much doubt as to her character sir; she's a large French privateer chokeful of men, I dessay, though it's surprising they don't appear to see us coming, and wake up."

I descended the rigging, and on making my report to Shelvocke the order was given to see all clear. The great mainsail and spars of the lugger were by this time visible from the deck, and after working with the glass for some moments Shelvocke turned to me with a puzzled expression.

"Really, by the look of her, Mr. Madison, I am disposed to agree with you that she is abandoned," said he. "She is neither hove to nor ratching. One might suppose she would have made us out long before this—yet I cannot imagine there is any trick meant."

"I should say not, sir. She was in the same posture when we first sighted her."

Meanwhile the *Tigress* was slipping through the water quietly but very nimbly, and as the lugger lay athwart our hawse, apparently shooting a few fathoms to windward as her mainsail filled and then curving round into the wind again and lying motionless, it was like running down to a stationary object, and in less than twenty minutes her hull was distinctly visible from the deck.

"Seven guns of a side, by Jupiter!" exclaimed Shelvocke. "But I see no men."

"Unless they are all at quarters on their hams under the

bulwarks, sir. You remember how the picaroon was caught by the troop-ship who kept her soldiers hidden until the privateer ranged alongside, and then discharged a broadside of three hundred muskets and six rounds of grape into the thick of the buccaneering crew?"

"Ay, we must mind what were are about,", he replied, glancing along our decks at the men grouped at the guns, and at the crows, handspikes, rammers, sponges, powder horns, and train-tackles which garnished the sides of the grim black pieces. We watched the lugger with keen intentness, expecting every moment to see some movement aboard of her. There could be no doubt she was a Frenchman. I thought it possible that her people might have mistaken us for a consort for whom they were waiting; but though we were near enough to her now to have her very clearly in the glass, nothing living could be perceived. I watched her bulwarks with the closest attention to see if anything moved, but she looked as dead as a water-logged hulk. She was a very large and handsome vessel, coppered to the bends, painted black, and heavily sparred. She seemed to chafe like a tethered racehorse as she filled and shook her cotton-white canvas, and, like a creature of instinct, appeared to know her danger, and to make short and ineffectual efforts to escape.

"Do you notice that she has her tompions in, sir?" I exclaimed; "that does not look as if she meant to receive us ungraciously."

"She is evidently deserted," answered Shelvocke. "Get the launch and the two cutters piped away, Mr. Madison. But mind how you board. I have known a tempting gangway rope explode a pistol in the magazine, and blow a ship and the boats alongside her into staves."

We held on with the boats towing, until we were within half a mile of the lugger; a number of men heavily armed then tumbled into the launch, of which I took command, and we shoved off, followed by the other boats, each of which contained ten men.

As we advanced I watched the lugger keenly. This was not an ordinary boating expedition. When you are prepared for resistance your nerves are braced up, you can pretty well guess what is going to happen; with a crew of Eng-

lishmen at your back you foresee the spring of the men on
to the sides, the slashing and the nettings, the ugly thrusts
of the boarding-pikes, the clash of cutlasses, the fierce growl-
ing and wild shrieks of the deadly scuffle, the deafening explosion of small arms at your ears, the murderous crash of
tomahawks. But here was a powerful vessel wrapped in
the silence of death. Her bulwarks hid the decks, and it
was impossible to tell what lurked under the tall shelter.
A shower of grape would have been a welcome relief to the
highly wrought feeling of expectation inspired by the grim
and silent lugger. Our men, who would have looked five
times their own numbers unflinchingly in the face, seemed
almost scared by the unusual sight of a long and heavily
armed craft, seemingly abandoned, and suspecting some hellish design to underlie this spectacle of the helplessness and
desertion, were continually glancing over their shoulders at
the vessel as they rowed.

We had approached within a musket-shot of her, when
I saw a human head rise above the bulwarks and remain
for a few seconds gazing at us, during which it swayed to
and fro like the ball of a pendulum. It disappeared, and
immediately after a man with his hair over his eyes, and
with his clothes in wild disorder, scrambled on to the rail,
fired a pistol at us, and, with a laugh like a madman's, flung
the weapon toward my boat and vanished, falling backward
in such a manner that the last we saw of him was his quivering legs. At this extraordinary sight Tapping, who was in
charge of the cutter immediately astern of me, burst into a
hoarse guffaw, like the bray of an ass.

"A strong pull, men!" I shouted. "There *are* people
to receive us. Board her astern, cutters!" I cried, turning
to address the hinder boats; "her bows are my chance."

We dashed alongside simultaneously, scrambled over her
bulwarks like a cloud of bluebottles swarming on a piece
of carrion, and in a trice had possession of her decks.

As strange and monstrous a scene as ever human eye encountered presented itself. So far as I could judge by hurriedly running my glance over them, there lay upon the
decks about ten or eleven men in the last stage of beastly
intoxication. Some reclined like logs upon their backs,
with the full light of the sun pouring upon their crimson

faces, their mouths open, snorting stertorously like persons
in an apoplexy, and the glazed whites of their eyes looking
like slips of blank paper between their half-closed lids.
Others nearly as helpless, and quite as embrutalized as
these, but still preserving some dim glimmering of human
reason as one might suppose, faintly struggled to rear their
bodies on their elbows, but fell back with horrid smiles and
a sputtering of inarticulate words. There was only one man
—he who had fired at us—who appeared equal to the task
of gaining his feet. He rose from the side of the carronade
slide where he had fallen, and seizing a boarding-pike gave
a drunken shout, and reeled toward us with the weapon
couched in the posture of charging; one of our men sprang
forward, but before he could grapple him the brute tripped
over a coil of rope, and fell with such a mighty whack of
his forehead upon the deck that I was quite sure, even if
he had not killed himself outright, he would give us no
further trouble.

Against the coamings of the main hatch, that was covered
with a tarpaulin over it, was a tub half-full of undiluted
rum. The mere sniffing up of the ardent spirit with the
fierce rays of the afternoon sun beating upon my head and
back made my brain dizzy. A couple of tin vessels were
sunk in the tub, and half-a-dozen utensils of a similar kind
lay scattered among the prostrate men.

Of all beastly pictures—I hope to be forgiven the violent
word—these intoxicated sailors made one of the worst—I
had almost written *the* worst—that ever shocked and pained
and disgusted human eyes. Some of them had evidently
been concerned in a scuffle, for their clothes were in rags,
and they lay half-naked. One dreadful-looking creature,
with red hair in a tangled mass over his forehead, and the
whites of his eyes giving an extraordinary character of horror to his purple face, his gibbering, bluish-colored lips
churning out a stream of froth that flowed down his chin,
one hand under his back, and the other across his breast
with the fingers working convulsively, like the antennæ of
a dying "long-legs," and his legs doubled under him as
though the bones of them had been taken out, and his bare
breast and a portion of his shirt stained with a quantity of
rum that appeared to have been flung over him, was a sight

"And seizing a boarding-pike, gave a drunken shout and reeled towards us with the weapon couched in the posture of charging."

—*Page 176.*

that even the horror-loving eye of Hogarth would have shunned, and alongside of which Caliban would have looked a fair and pleasant creation.

"I believe there are more of them below, sir," rattled out Tapping, slewing his head about over a small closed skylight in his efforts to see through the panes which the flashing of the sun converted into a looking-glass.

"Mr. Chestree, capsize that tub of rum," I exclaimed. "Man the pumps, some of you, and drench these beasts—there are buckets forward there; mind you don't drown them."

While this was doing I threw open the skylight, first taking care to group a number of men with loaded pistols around it ready to fire down should any show of resistance be made by the inmates of the cabin. The skylight was pitched right amidships of the cabin ceiling, and on putting my head down, I saw five figures in various postures upon the floor, all motionless, and as dead drunk as the men on deck; one of them lying capsized backward in his chair, his head on the floor and his heels on the table. A perfect stench of rum came up in a cloud; it was like holding one's nose over a distiller's vat.

I was in the act of descending the companion-steps, when I was loudly hailed by Chestree, who stood forward.

"Mr. Madison, will you step this way, sir? I believe there's a whole cargo of men under the fore-hatch here."

I immediately ran toward the forecastle.

"Listen, sir!" exclaimed Chestree; and standing close to the small covered hatch, that was situated a few paces abaft the foremast, I heard a noise of knocking accompanied by sounds which resembled the distant moaning of a number of wounded animals.

"Belay that pumping!" I called out to the men, who were dashing water over the senseless bodies with a glee that betokened high enjoyment of the work. "Six of you keep watch round the companion, and the rest come forward. Look to your small-arms, men: there seems a whole shipload of human beings under these decks."

They immediately flung down their buckets, and formed into a compact square round the forehatch, the cover of which I now ordered them to lift.

12

Scarcely had this been done, when there a rose a wild and frightful din of agonized voices. May God spare me from ever hearing the like again! A rush of hot, fetid, suffocating air followed the opening of the hatch, and made every man who had bent forward to look down recoil.

"My God!" shouted Chestree, "they are French prisoners, Mr. Madison! Look! there are a dozen suffocated bodies under the feet of the living!"

He raised his voice into a shriek, and a deep groan broke from the seamen who stood around.

The cabin or forecastle was about six feet deep; the ladder had been drawn up, and when I looked down into this black and suffocating pit I beheld a whole surface of upward-gazing faces, glimmering yellow amid the twilight, with dark prostrate forms beneath them, while yell upon yell burst from the lips of the miserable sufferers. "*De l'eau! de l'eau! de l'eau!*" this was the one burden of the dreadful raving.

"Silence!" I shouted in my bad French, that was made worse still, just as my voice was rendered hoarse as a raven's by the agitation and horror I was under. "We are here to succor you. Tell me your numbers."

"We were forty. There rests but twenty-five living," came the answer.

"Quick, men!" I shouted to my own brave fellows; "hand up these poor creatures. Lean over as many of you as can find room, and let them catch your hands. They'll scramble up well enough with that help."

Half a dozen of the strongest men flung down their weapons and dropped on their knees, and as one by one the prisoners were drawn up, they fled to the scuttle-butt and fought for the dipper like famished dogs over a bone.

They had all the same semi-asphyxiated look, distended eyeballs, whitish lips, and the veins standing out like whipcord upon their throats and temples; while the perspiration had drenched the very coats on their backs, and so slimy were their hands that our men had to catch them by the wrists to get a fair hoisting purchase.

Hardly had the first-comers on deck assuaged their thirst, when they turned upon the bodies of the drunken seamen, whose nationality I had not yet been able to determine, though I was very much afraid that they were Englishmen. They brandished their fists over them, howled and cursed them, and spat upon them, and were only restrained from tearing the inanimate brutes to pieces by a determined movement aft on the part of the men.   One of the prisoners pulled a long knife from his breeches-pocket and made a sneaking stride toward the red-haired monster whose appearance I have described, grasping the haft of the knife so that the blade forked out of his shaking hand astern; and by the look of his face he would, I believe, have stabbed the intoxicated sailor to the heart before I could have had time to rush upon him, had not one of his companions gripped his arm and muttered fiercely in his ear, and dragged him violently back.

On the other hand, there were some among these wretched captives who, after they had drunk and recovered their minds, appeared overcome with the horrors from which they had been released.   I saw three of them weeping like children, others hiding their faces in their hands, and two on their knees crossing themselves and praying.   I glanced my eye over them as they stood near the scuttle-butts in a group of twenty-five—the number they had named, though how they had been able to take stock in the black and stifling forecastle was and still remains a great mystery to me—and noticed that they were all seamen, dressed in the picturesque costumes of the French buccaneers of that period, most of them with colored caps, the points of which fell over their ears, and red shirts, and duck or fine canvas breeches, and short sea-boots with overhanging flaps.   They were in general small men (though there were three or four strapping fellows among them), with keen, dark, savage, bearded faces, and many of them wore large earrings, and silver rings on their fingers.   They were unarmed, it is true: but there were pikes, cutlasses, and pistols in abundance, both upon the decks and in the racks, and these men, naturally ferocious, had been converted into wild beasts by the shocking treatment they had received.

To deprive the demons in them of any chance of an outbreak, I divided them into four gangs, each one of which was guarded by a number of my own men, and ordered

Chestree to hail the schooner and request Captain Shelvocke to send the pinnace to me along with Mr. Corney.

The *Tigress* had ratched some way to windward of us under her foresail only, but on perceiving the signals made by Chestree, Shelvocke at once put his helm up, and ran down. While the schooner was approaching, I called to a couple of seamen and entered the lugger's cabin. I found myself in a tolerably roomy box-shaped place, pierced by the foot of the mizzen-mast, with a couple of berths aft, the doors of which were open. There was a row of shelves affixed to the foremast bulkhead, full of china plates, glasses, and things of that kind, and the ceiling was garnished with a number of muskets, cutlasses, and a weapon I had never before seen—a truncheon of the length of a man's arm, terminating in a knob of *spiked iron* of about the dimensions and weight of a four-pound roundshot. There were three or four overturned chairs upon the floor, a quantity of broken glass that crunched under every step I and my men took, and the planks were slippery with rum, the smell of which was quite intolerable in the close and muggy atmosphere; and the sides of the table, which were rimmed to the height of an inch to prevent the crockery from sliding in rough weather, were afloat with grog, like the scuppers of a ship in a gale of wind, that drained off first at one end and then at the other, as the vessel swayed.

I now observed that there were six men in this cabin, the man that had escaped the glance I had taken through the skylight being jammed up in a corner, where he sat upon his haunches, with his arms hanging all abroad and his head fallen over his knees. Some of them snored through their pipes like men attacked by bronchitis; but the fellow who lay capsized in his chair made no noise and was motionless. A broad glare of the lateral sunshine that streamed through to the skylight fell upon this recumbent figure, and I would not like to say that the repulsive red-haired monster on deck made a more monstrous object than this man, whose face was black with suffocation, whose eyes protruded from their sockets, and over the rim of whose tight jacket-collar the flesh had swelled into a hard puffed-out circle, the color and appearance of a gutta-percha ring.

I ordered my men to raise him, but on seizing his arms,

they found him stone-dead; so we let him lie on his back, and I went on deck again, sick with the sight and dizzy with the spirituous stench of the place.

By this time the schooner had floated to within speaking-distance, I jumped on to the lugger's taffrail, and sung out the particulars of the capture to Shelvocke, and recommended that the prisoners should be divided between the two vessels.

"Very well," be called out. "You may send as many as you think proper abroad the *Tigress.* Corney will be with you in a few minutes."

I waved my hand, and ordered Tapping to tell off five men to hand up the bodies out of the forecastle. This was a most ghastly and painful business, but humanity demanded that it should immediately be executed, as it was just possible that life was not extinct in some of them. I suggested that the easiest and the quickest way to hoist out the dead was for one man to descend and attach lines to the bodies, which the others could then haul up. This was done, and before Corney arrived we had removed the whole fifteen bodies and ranged them in a row under the bulwarks, and I shall never forget the groans and cries which broke from the survivors of the miserable French crew as one by one the corpses of their shipmates were raised. The sight lashed them into a fury that nothing short of the cocked and levelled pistols of our men could have restrained.

Next to the expression on the face of a man who has been killed by a pike thrust, the most terrible that I know of is that of death by asphyxia—at all events when that kind of death is produced by the slow operation that killed these most miserable creatures. All the horror and anguish of the slow approach of extinction, the agony of the difficult breathing, the dreadful despair following the mad and unavailing fight for life in darkness and in the midst of a steamy and putrescent atmosphere, were expressed in these men's half-closed eyes and parted blue lips, from which a reddish froth was oozing, and the greenish yellow of the puffy skin, and in their blackened finger-nails buried in the palms of their hands.

On Corney's arrival, he immediately fell to an examination of these bodies, one by one. The Frenchmen watched

him intently and in profound silence at first; but as he
passed from one corpse to the other, shaking his head, half-
smothered execrations broke from the prisoners; and when
Corney had inspected the last body, and glanced around at
me with a look on his face that was unmistakable, a wild
chorus of yells and curses broke from the Frenchmen; they
all cried out together, and the sound of their voices was as
much like the snarling of wild beasts as the imagination
could conceive; there was a short rush from one group
toward some of the intoxicated men, and a few hard blows
were exchanged between them and the *Tigresses;* one of the
prisoners was knocked down, and a pistol exploded in the
scuffle.   However, the poor devils stood but a small chance
with eight-and-thirty determined Englishmen armed to the
teeth.   I ordered ten of them into the pinnace, and the
remainder I mustered aft, where they were suffered to remain with a strong guard over them, while I dealt with the
drunken scoundrels who littered the decks and the cabin.

Though I have dwelt at some length on the particulars
of this strange and ghastly adventure, yet not more than a
quarter of an hour had been expended from the moment of
our boarding to the time when I sent away half of the
prisoners.   Some of the drunken men were now beginning
to show signs of life; one or two of them struggled until
they gained their feet, but immediately fell down again,
and lay looking at us out of their bloodshot eyes and with
sickly imbecile smiles.   Some made an effort to crawl on
their bodies to the carronade slides or the foot of the masts
out of the sun, where they sat up with their backs propped
by the spar, in which posture they watched us with lolling
heads, and their hands lying lifeless upon the decks, and
their legs twisted into a manner of drunken shapes under
or around them.

I told Chestree to take some of our seamen below and
bring the men who were in the cabin on deck.

"Bundle the brutes up as they come," said I; "and, Mr.
Tapping, get the pumps manned and give some of those
breathing logs there another drenching."   And while these
orders were being obeyed, I called to Corney and requested
his help to question the Frenchmen, whose story I was
anxious to hear.

Although, as I have said, I pronounced the French language very ill, I was well enough acquainted with that tongue to understand it fully when spoken by others. I had, therefore, no difficulty in following the short and simple story related to Corney by one of the prisoners, whom I suspected to be a mate by the way in which he acted as spokesman for the others and the respect that was suggested by their manner toward him, though there was nothing to distinguish him in his dress from the rest of his shipmates.

He said that the lugger was named the *Droit Maritime*, and that her crew, when she left Granville that day a fortnight previously, had consisted of a hundred and sixty men. Of these, sixty were away in prizes when the lugger fell in with, and engaged, a large English polacre brig, who, after killing and wounding forty of the Frenchman's crew, hauled down her colors. Of the Englishman's crew only fourteen or fifteen remained unhurt, and these were put aboard the lugger, who sent ten of her own men into the brig to carry her to the Tregnier Roads. But a few hours after this engagement a small vessel hove in sight, which the French captain determined to pursue; he chased her to the northward for thirteen hours, but losing sight of her in the darkness, bore up again to follow in the wake of the captured brig.

This brought the time down to two o'clock on the morning of the day in which the adventure I am relating befell us; at which hour, a number of the Frenchmen being in the forecastle of the lugger, the English prisoners managed to break out through the main-hatch, under which they had been confined in the airiest and roomiest part of the vessel. The attack was so sudden that the people on deck, being utterly unprepared, were immediately overpowered, and flung overboard, "alive as they stood!" said the man who told the story, and his face grew dark with passion as he added that the hatch was put over the men who were sleeping in the forecastle, and that in that hole, without light, without air, without water, forty human beings had been confined for *fourteen* hours, while the ruffians who had become, not their jailers, but their murderers, had broken open the spirit-room, and drank until they had reduced themselves to the condition in which we found them.

"And they are our countrymen!" I exclaimed in French, looking with horror and shame at the brutes, whose contortions were reptile-like as they endeavored to roll away from the buckets of water which the *Tigresses* were sluicing over them, and snapped their teeth and gibbered in their drunken passion.

"Yes, they are English," answered the Frenchman, "but not such English as I have been used to meet," he added, with more tact than I should have expected to find in such a scowling, black, and savage-looking creature; and then with a world of moving passion in his voice, and with wild and pleading gesticulations, which amazingly increased the pity his dreadful tale provoked, he poured forth in rich dramatic accents an account of the terrible sufferings they had endured; how some of them had sucked the blood from their own arms to quench their raging thirst; how one by one fifteen of them had sunk down, dropping without a moan, until the living had no space for their feet, and were forced to stand upon the soft and soaking bodies of the dead. He described them tearing the very nails off their fingers in their efforts to force the hatch, so as to obtain, not liberty, but one little draught of pure air; the horrible sound of the grinding of teeth, the choked and husky hum of voices, the deadly struggle to keep or obtain a place under the hatch, where a tiny crevice showed a faint gleam of daylight.

I remembered the heat of the weather—the heat that had rendered the well-ventilated cabin of the *Tigress* almost unbearable—while he was speaking!

They could hear, he said, the Englishmen singing on deck and afterward fighting, until the silence assured them that the wretches had drunk themselves senseless, on which they abandoned all hope, for they knew that every miserable inmate of the black and choking forecastle would be dead before the Englishmen recovered their minds.

"I do honestly believe, sir," exclaimed Corney, drawing a long quivering breath as the man ended, and turning to me with a face as white as a ghost, "that this is the most horrible thing that has happened in my time, and I am forty-one this month."

At this moment I was hailed by Shelvocke, who had ranged the schooner within a musket-shot of the lugger.

"What are you doing now, Mr. Madison?"

"There's a whole mob of drunken Englishmen aboard of us here, sir," I answered; "and we are fishing the last of the tribe out of the cabin. These scoundrels will want watching as well as the Frenchmen, and I think you had better allow forty of our men to remain in the lugger."

"Very well," he replied. "Dispose of the men as you think best. How many of our seamen have you aboard now?"

"Thirty-eight, sir."

"I will send a couple more in the pinnace, and she can bring the other boats back with her. Let Mr. Tapping and Mr. Chestree return with them, and you can remain as prize-master. Get sail made as soon as possible, for I want to be off."

"Ay, ay, sir."

The disgust that had been excited in our men by the drunkenness as well as the brutality of the English seamen, was amusingly exhibited in their handling of the fellows whom they hauled out of the cabin. They dragged them up the companion-steps heels foremost, some of them, and rolled them along the decks like casks with their feet, and it was almost impossible to keep one's gravity over the postures the drunken fellows threw themselves into, and the imbecile expression of their faces as they were bundled unceremoniously over the hatch and dropped, one on top of the other, into the gloomy hole from which we had liberated their captives; but more merciful than they, we left the hatch open, and this made all the difference between a black and noisome grave and an ordinary forecastle.

The Frenchmen were now got under hatches and stowed amidships of the lugger, where there was plenty of room and light, and sentries posted at each hatchway; and as nothing remained to be done but to bury the dead, I dispatched a number of men to get as many hammocks on a deck as there were corpses, while the rest made sail on the lugger.

By this time the sun was low upon the seas, but there was the promise of a beautiful evening and a fine night in the soft blue of the sky, and in the high shreds of white vapor which mottled the heavens in the east, and there was a cool wind blowing. The sixteen dead bodies—fifteen Frenchmen and one Englishman—made a most repulsive and ghastly spectacle of the deck, and I ordered them to be thrown overboard as fast as the men could lace them up in the hammocks, taking care, however, that some show of reverence attended these precipitate burials. I felt easier in my mind when the last body was gone, and when I could look along the wide deck that sloped upward like a smack's toward the bows, and witness only the familiar sight of the rows of guns, and the seamen at work, and the sentries standing with drawn cutlasses and loaded pistols in their belts by the open hatches. Sailors are superstitious about the dead, and are always uneasy while they are shipmates with a corpse. Besides, fifteen of the unhappy creatures had died so horrible a death, that the mere thought of their last sufferings turned the heart sick; and the depression of spirits the sight of them bred in us was as reasonable an excuse as we needed to give them an informal and hurried toss.

Next to a schooner, I think a lugger the usefullest if not the handiest rig afloat. I had never sailed one before, and now I was in charge of a lugger of above two hundred tons, built and owned at St. Malo, and as fast and powerful a boat as any that ever hailed from that nest of privateers. Whatever injury she had received from the guns of the polacre had been made good, and when we had mastheaded her enormous gaffs a whole ocean of canvas looked to be spread overhead.

Shelvocke sung out that he wanted to try the schooner against her, but fast as the lugger unquestionably was, giving one a sensation of skimming rather than sailing, she was no match for the schooner, who walked away from her as though she had her tow-rope aboard, and had no difficulty in keeping her position abreast of us under her mainsail and jib only. And how glorious *she* looked! glancing her copper along the dark green water with the red sunset levelling its warm, rich light at her over our mastheads and rosily tinting her graceful sails and streaking her bright masts with lines of fire, and giving a reddish tinge to the froth that rolled along her black side like a line of wool unwinding from her bows; while her bristling guns and

high and gleaming bulwarks, and the massive though beautiful sheer of her from the gangway to the cathead, gave
one such an idea of the formidable figure she must make in
the eyes of an enemy as I had never before realized.

When we were fairly sailing along with the decks washed
down, and the ropes coiled away, and the guns carefully
looked to, in the event of a sudden call to arms, and while
the crisp slice of moon was doing battle with the reddish
twilight in which the figures of the men, as they hung with
pipes in their mouths over the bows of the lugger, loomed
large; and the sentries round the hatches were like statues
seen within a dimly lighted museum; and the form of the
schooner about a quarter of a mile away on the weather
bow, might, at the first glance, have passed for an optical
illusion, and set one winking to look again, so vague and
airy was the shape of her on the running water, and so
spectral the pallid canvas that seemed in the act of melting
away on the indigo of the eastern sky; methought—for
what should all this fine writing preface but a rank bit of
commonplace?—that I would sup. And so down I went
into the cabin, which, having been cleansed and swabbed,
had lost much of its rum-breathing atmosphere, and set a
youthful *Tigress* (who counted as one of the forty men) to
hunt about for something to eat: and presently he had
furnished out a very comfortable supper-table, on which I
beheld an excellent ham, a piece of cold brisket of beef that
looked to have been fattened on English grass, some capital
sea-biscuits, a cheese, and a bottle of wine—the fruits of a
well-stocked larder or pantry which I believe only a boy
would have stumbled on, for the door of it was a sliding
panel in the foremost bulkhead, and was as mysterious a
closet as anything of the kind I ever read of in the Anna
Maria and Rose Matilda romances.

I so little relished sitting down to this supper alone, that
in casting about me for a companion—Corney unhappily
had returned to the schooner with Chestree and Tapping—
I thought of the fellow who had acted as spokesman when
we questioned the Frenchman, and whom I took to be
mate: "Come," thought I; "the poor devil has suffered
enough at the hands of Englishmen; I will ask him to sup
with me."

So I went on deck to speak to the Frenchman down the main-hatch, as I knew there was no man aboard who could have delivered any message they would understand.

I called out, "Messieurs, I wish to speak to you;" whereat a whole crowd of them came and stood under the hatchway. There was just twilight enough to enable me to distinguish the faces of the poor creatures, for whom all my pity revived as they stood gazing up at me, and among them I noticed the man I wanted. So, addressing myself to him, I made shift to let him know that I should be glad if he would join me at supper.

He put his hand on his breast, and made me a bow full of grace, though his dignity was somewhat fluttered by the seamen who guarded the hatch having to hoist him on deck by the arms. Before I went aft I said to him in in a voice I wished his companions below to hear, that I was anxious the prisoners should want for nothing it was in my power to give them: and any desire they expressed to the sentries should be attended to, if reasonable. It was my duty, I said, to atone for the inhumanity of the monsters who were imprisoned in the forecastle, and who would be delivered up to justice on our arrival in England. He understood me, for I helped out my meaning by the gestures which make up the better half of the French language, and thanked me very gratefully, and looking down the hatch, exclaimed:

"You hear what this *bon monsieur* says?"

"Yes, yes; he is a comrade to be proud of—he has a French heart—he is an honest man," the poor fellows answered.

"Here, Parell," I called to the boatswain's mate, who headed my detachment of the *Tigresses,* "see that these Frenchmen are well treated. I have told them to make their wants known to the sentries, but of course if you have any doubts you will come to me for instructions. As to the brutes in the forecastle, if you hear any murmuring among them, tip them a few buckets of salt water."

The man grinned and touched his hat, and, followed by the French seaman, who did actually prove to be the mate of the lugger, I led the way to the cabin. I pointed to a seat, but he looked at his hands and down his shirt with a half-apologetic smile.

I nodded, as much as to say "I see what you want," and motioned toward one of the after-cabins, in which I had already taken care to assure myself the things he required were to be found. I admired his tact in leaving the door wide open while he bathed his face and passed a comb through his long black hair. Although dressed only in a shirt and trousers and a red sash round his waist, his brief and meagre toilet appeared to have given him as much confidence and ease as a new suit of clothes would have done; there was even a well-bred air in his manner as he stepped out of the berth smiling and lightly humming a tune, with his hands clasped in front of him, and his white teeth gleaming under his jetty mustache, and his black eyes shining.

He insisted on my sitting first, and bowed to me when he took his chair, and with the gayest air in the world told me that yonder berth, which I had been good enough to let him enter, had been *his own*.

"But, monsieur," said he, toying with his glass that I had filled with wine, "the corsair's toast should be always —*La guerre!* His enemies are his friends, and he is an imbecile who would grumble at the fortune who hates him to-day and caresses him to-morrow."

He chinked his glass against mine, and emptied it with a fine theatrical flourish. But though I was amused and even pleased with, I was not to be deceived by, this holiday politeness. The wisdom of having a loaded pistol in the side-pocket of the coat I wore had much weight given to it, not alone by the array of deadly weapons which glittered over the head of my friend within easy reach of his hand, but by the inherent fierceness and rascality in the fellow's face, which his smiles only lighted up, and the peculiar prowling roll of his gleaming eyes whenever he was silent for a few moments.

Indeed he was a complete realization of the popular idea of the picaroon, privateersman, corsair, pirate, or buccaneer—the world has never stinted the trade in titles—dark as a half-caste, long, black, curling hair, thick eyebrows, which formed an angle, the point of which was in the indent betwixt the brow and the nose, long mustaches, the ends of which overhung the short bristling beard, a thick neck and square throat, which suggested the heaviness of the concealed jaws, with the cheap exterior trappings of earrings, finger-rings, and an ebony crucifix, the head of the silver figure on which glittered just above the open shirt on his olive-colored skin. His manners were mild enough with me, but it was the amiability of a dog whose ears are uncocked because you carry a thick stick, and who wags his tail while he languishingly eyes your throat.

He ate very heartily, and enjoyed himself after the philosophy of his countrymen. No outsider would have guessed his situation from his manner, nor have supposed him other than one of our men, or at least a passenger. The talking was mostly on his side, for the very good reason that I had not enough of the language to sustain a dialogue, and he did not know a word of English except " Yash," which he meant for " Yes," and which he repeatedly uttered.

Having supped, I pulled out a pipe and a paper of tobacco, which I offered to him. He thanked me with a laugh, and said that if I would prefer a cigar he would be happy to fetch a box.

" Where are they to be found?" I asked.

He pointed under the table, and on peering at the deck, I observed, close at my feet, a trap-door about four feet square with an iron ring affixed to it.

" There are not only cigars there," said he, " but you will find some boxes, the contents of which would keep the whole of the men in this lugger, and in your schooner, too, supplied with cigars, ay, and *grogue* also, monsieur, for a hundred years, were they to live as long."

I looked at him earnestly.

" Monsieur does not know what his schooner has captured?" said he, with a bitter smile.

" I should be glad to hear," I answered.

" What does it matter *now?*" he cried, with a fierce shrug, and apparently thinking aloud. " But at least *your* crew will have the booty—the monsters who would have destroyed us will not share."

I was not very sure of this, so I made him no reply, merely keeping an interrogative stare fixed upon him.

" About these cigars?" said he. " Shall I fetch **a** box?"

"I will not give you that trouble," I answered. "Ransom!" I shouted.

The boy who was sitting on the top of the companion steps ran down.

"Tell Parell to send a couple of men aft, here, with a lighted lantern."

Although I believed there was no treacherous intent in the Frenchman's offer to procure the cigars, it was assuredly not my business to trust him. The powder-magazine was, in all probability, situated somewhere under our feet; the ruffianly Englishmen, who had killed fifteen and tortured the rest of this prisoner's shipmates, were still aboard the lugger, and the temptation to blow *them* as well as *us* into fragments might prove stronger than the consideration that he would also be destroying himself and his fellow-captives. Be this as it may, I would not trust him; but my evasion of his offer did not at all offend him. He merely said, and not satirically either, "Monsieur is very polite," meaning that I was polite not to allow him to take the trouble to fetch the cigars.

"Pray," said I, while we waited for the men, "will you have the goodness to tell me what those cases which you have spoken of contain?"

"One hundred thousand Mexican dollars," he answered promptly.

I looked at him amazed; in truth I believed the man was joking, and the expression of my face must have said as much, for he immediately added:

"We found the money in one of the prizes we took this day a week, monsieur. My captain transferred the chests to the *Droit Maritime*, as he believed the silver would be safer in our charge than if left in the custody of the small prize crew whom we sent to France in the captured vessel. One would have thought," he exclaimed, with his face darkening under a sudden gust of passion that at least convinced me he was speaking the truth, "that the captain of a vessel with such a booty on board would have made haste to land it. Instead, my captain, not content with risking this sum of money in the encounter with the polacre brig, must needs chase a small vessel who carries him within a few leagues of British waters. And for what? The chase escapes us! our prisoners rise, murder my captain and a number of men, and this rich lugger becomes your prey without costing you a struggle! I remonstrated—I cried out against my captain for his madness in chasing that small vessel. 'We are rich enough for this voyage,' I exclaimed; 'let us at least make for Granville, and start afresh with a swept hold.' He threatened me! he called me *boute-feu! mutin!* And now behold us!"

He dashed his clenched fist upon the table with all the extravagance of an infuriated Frenchman: but hearing the footsteps of the men on the companion-ladder, he recovered himself with an astonishing effort, and exclaimed in his former light-hearted voice, taking the neck of the bottle in his hand:

"Monsieur, your glass is empty. I know this wine—it will not hurt you."

Before I could answer him the men sent by Parell entered the cabin. One of them carried a lighted lantern, which I bade him set down while he helped his mate to run the table up the stanchions on which it slided, and to raise the trap-door. When this was lifted I peered down and noticed a row of steps nailed to a narrow bulkhead, and the rays of the lantern piercing the blackness faintly disclosed the outlines of a number of chests, bales, casks, etc., carefully stowed and apparently ranging forward past the narrow bulkhead on either hand to a considerable distance.

The Frenchman approached and looked down the trap-hatch for a few seconds, and then retired to the end of the cabin, and seated himself with his arms locked upon his breast.

"This man," said I, addressing the seamen, "tells me that there are chests down there full of silver. Try the weight of one of them, and also look about you for some boxes of cigars."

One of them dropped through the trap, and the other, after lowering the lantern, followed. With their bodies curved so that they looked on all-fours, and the lantern jerking the shadows of their faces here and there as they crawled about, the men rummaged as only sailors can, squeezing themselves into narrow corners, and accommodating their bodies to all manner of excruciating angles, puffing and blowing as they groped, and squirting tobacco-juice right and left, while through the stillness of the hold one could hear the gurgling of the passing water, and the sharp jar of the rudder on its pintles.

"Here be the seegars, sir, I think!" presently shouted out one of them; "aye, dozens on 'em!" and prizing open the batten of what looked like a crate, he forked up a box of cheroots.

"I can guarantee them fresh from the Manillas, sir," said the Frenchman from his corner.

"Will you please help yourself?" said I, giving him the box.

He opened the lid with the prong of a fork, and lighted a cigar, saying, as he resumed his seat, that tobacco was the best remedy for despair.

"It's blasted hot down here, sir!" bawled one of the men. "There's no moving of these cases, sir. Might as well try to lift a first-rate's bower."

However, I was determined to test the truth of the Frenchman's statement, and told Ransom to send Parell aft with a hammer and prizing-bar.

"What do you make in those canvas bundles, men?" said I. "Snip a bit of the lacing, but mind how you do it."

This was done.

"Why, what the deuce is it? yellow bunting?" I called.

They thumbed it, and peered at it and smelt it, and then rattled out:

"It's yaller silk, your honor—like what you see in Chaney, sir!"

And so it was, thousands of yards of it, packed (as only the Chinese *can* pack) in fine canvas covers. I turned to the Frenchman, who sat with his legs crossed, and his head thrown back, stroking his mustache, and puffing out tobacco-smoke.

"You have evidently the cargo of an East Indiaman in this hold?"

"The richest part of it, monsieur; silver, silk, some chests of ivory, and about sixteen tons of tea. The rest we left in the prize."

13

"A nice little haul for the *Tigress!*" thought I; and I was nearly shouting "Hurrah!"

Presently appeared Parell with the implements I had directed him to bring. The lamplight glistened in his perspiring face, and I noticed the honest fellow bestow a distrustful scowl on the French mate after letting his eyes rest on the grim decorations of the cabin-ceiling.

I gave him the Frenchman's report of the contents of the hold, and bade him jump below and open one of the heavy chests that we might prove the value of the capture by our own eyesight. His face cleared when I talked of ivory and silver and silk, and swinging himself down the trap, he fell to work upon one of the heavy chests, and after some mighty hard hammering—for the corners were strongly clapped with iron—wedged open a split board. The lantern was raised, and the light sparkled upon a surface of white coined silver.

"That will do," said I. "Replace that board, Parell."

The three of them came out of the hold, the trap was closed, and the table lowered.

"Here, Ransom, give Parell and these two men a glass of grog apiece. How does the schooner bear, Parell?"

"Steady on the starboard bow, sir."

"We *Tigresses* are in luck, men. If you add this capture to the corvette, our pockets won't hold our shares."

"Ay, sir," answered Parell, "and I reckon the gells have the news already, for they've got the tow-ropes in their hands, and the two wessels are giving 'em all they can do to haul in the slack."

Here they drank my health.

I sent the men forward to give the news of the value of the prize to their shipmates.

"And mind, Parell," said I, "to keep a strong guard at both hatches, and on no account allow our men to converse with the English prisoners—that is, when the brutes are sober enough to talk."

"I hope monsieur is satisfied that I spoke the truth," said the French mate when the men had left the cabin.

"Perfectly satisfied," I responded, lighting my pipe in preference to a cheroot, for, of all abominations, the flavor of Manilla tobacco is to me the greatest.

" Were you ever in France, sir?"

"Never."

" Nor I in England. I would to God that my first visit to your country were under other circumstances! I have heard that your prisons are detestable, though your jailers are more humane than ours."

" You must look forward to a speedy exchange," said I.

"Not as corsair!" he exclaimed vehemently, with a sweeping passionate gesture of the hand. "Monsieur, who has a kind heart, will doubly pity me when he hears that I have been married but one little year. My poor wife called to me when I was leaving the house the last time, crying, 'Jean, our baby is awake; come and kiss its eyes before thou goest.' My house is near the cathedral; and when I was nearly swooning in that abominable forecastle before your men admitted the air, there were two sounds ringing in my ears—the cathedral bells, which were chiming as I turned back and leaned over my baby's cradle, and the cry of the little one as it was fretted or frightened by this iron beard," taking his chin in his hand and looking at me with the tears in his eyes.

" Are these crocodile tears?" thought I, for truly, to behold such sentimental drops on his dark fierce visage was as confusing to all theories of "fitness" as the association of the homely sweetness of wife and baby—of the spiritual gentleness of marital and paternal love, with the scowling, be-sashed and be-ringed figure of the maritime bravo.

" Will monsieur listen to me?" he suddenly exclaimed, dropping his cigar on the deck, and clasping and extending his hands with a gesture of moving energy. "I have at my house, at St. Mâlo, a sum of fifteen hundred pounds (*livres*), the whole of which I would give for my liberty."

I smoked my pipe in silence.

"Monsieur," he continued, after a short pause, and speaking with such *intensity*—to use the only word that expresses the concentration of purpose in his voice—that, like a physical effort, which indeed you may be willing to reckon it, it bedewed his forehead with large sweat-drops, and kindled an extraordinary brightness in his black eyes —" is it impossible for you to enrol me amongst your crew —to exclude me from the prisoners you will send ashore?"

"Impossible," I interrupted with a sternness I did not care to conceal, seeing what his entreaties were leading to, and rising as I spoke.

He sprang to his feet, and flashed a look at the weapons over his head. The menace was more than I could brook. I whipped the pistol from my pocket, and pointing it toward the companion-steps, I told him to be good enough to go on deck. He made a stiff inclination of the head, and with a light defiant swing of the body ascended the ladder, I at his heels; and it was with a feeling of real relief that I saw him walk to the main-hatch and jerk himself down among his fellow-captives. Such was the abrupt ending of my well-meant kindness; but in truth I was getting tired of the man, and my stock of French was all but expended.

Calling Parell to me, I bade him increase the guard at the main-hold by two men, and to train one of the smaller carronades against the aftercoaming, so that our friends might understand that though we did not intend to stifle them, we had no intention of giving them their own way either.

"Is there any movement among the men in the forecastle, Parell?"

"There's a lot of snoring going on, sir, and one of 'em shouted out just now, but I don't reckon he meant it, or knew that he did it. Yet I fancy they's be rallying soon, for they seems to be growing oneasy. They'll be sure to wake up parched thirsty, sir. If they ax for water, are they to have it, sir?"

"Certainly; and you had better get a small cask filled ready for lowering down to them, along with some pannikins."

I filled my pipe again and walked aft. The new moon was hanging over the sea in the west, and the breeze had freshened with the darkness. The black form of the schooner hung steadily on the weather-bow; they had fixed a lantern on her taffrail, the import of which I thoroughly understood, and she was leading me on a course from which I judged it was Shelvocke's intention to fetch Plymouth.

It was a novel sensation to me to gaze around on the unfamiliar deck of the lugger, and at the immense lugs which swelled out overhead. She was sweeping through

the water in grand style, churning up twice as much foam
as the schooner threw up at her fastest, and to have looked
over the sides and the stern at the tremendous spread of
rushing froth, that widened away into the darkness like
the tail of a comet, one would have supposed our pace
something unheard-of. But what were my feelings when,
my sight having got used to the gloom, I perceived that
the *Tigress* was keeping her distance and holding her station under her mainsail, jib, and staysail only! I never
felt prouder of the beautiful craft than at that moment.
All the renown that the French luggers had obtained was
almost entirely centred in their speed, for their cowardice
was a by-word among English seamen; they bolted from
the sight of the smallest cruiser, and limited their depre-
dations to the badly armed merchantmen. But here was
as powerful a lugger as St. Malo had ever equipped and
dispatched, with all sail clouded and with the wind right
abeam, so that every cloth was drawing, unable to keep
pace with the *Tigress*, who showed only a third of the canvas she could unfold.

Our prisoners filled the sleeping-quarters of the lugger,
and my men had therefore to take their rest upon deck;
but this was no hardship on a fine warm night. Some of
the seamen had already disposed themselves near the guns
and under the bulwarks, with coils of ropes for their pil-
lows, their cutlasses upon their hips and pistols in their
belts; while at least twenty others kept watch at the
hatches, or stumped the sloping deck of the forecastle on
the lookout.

I kept watch until midnight, during all which time the
breeze remained steady, and the schooner held her station
with remarkable precision ahead. I then roused Parell,
who slept with enviable soundness in a sitting posture,
with his back against the skylight, and told him to take
the lookout while I lay down. But first I visited both
hatches and listened: all was still in the Frenchmen's quarters, though once I fancied I heard the sound of a hoarse
whisper; but it might have been the chafing of the sheet
of the great main-lug, whose foot arched transversely across
the wide deck. From the forecastle, however, there arose
various sounds of gurgling and sleepy grumbling, with an

occasional hoarse and barking yawn, and two of the bestial
inmates called to one another, but in such drunken accents
that I gave no heed to what was said.

"Keep a smart eye upon these fellows, men," I said to
the sentries. "When they come to they will want closer
watching than the Frenchmen."

And so saying, I went aft, and pitching on a spot near
the tiller, I spread a big French ensign for a mattress, and
lay down upon it, being much too anxious to bury myself
in the cabin.

It was this anxiety, I suppose, that put it into my head
to compare the interior of the lugger to a volcano, and
assuredly the comparison was sufficiently apt, seeing the
mass of human combustibles that filled it. But the fancy
set me dreaming of a volcano, to whose summit I had
climbed with very great labor, for no other object than to
be able to say I had sat upon it. I was enjoying the prospect of smiling country that stretched around, and speculating upon the nature and causes of volcanoes quite as
cleverly, I dare say, as many wide-awake philosophers,
when I felt the mountain throb under me very much as
though some imprisoned giant was hammering inside, and
I began to topple about in my seat. The smiling country
grew rather tipsy, and cut a variety of ornamental capers.
I held on in a high state of alarm, while I was jerked
about like a man astride of the hump of a terrified camel.
"Good Lord!" thought I. A volume of smoke rushed up
all around me, accompanied by a tremendous explosion, that
was no doubt intended to drive me several miles high in the
air, had I not cheated my ingenious imagination by opening
my eyes and springing to my feet.

"What was that?"

The whole of my men were standing in groups near the
hatches, but the crowd was densest at the forecastle, through
whose open hatch there issued the muffled but hellish din of
a fierce struggle. I rushed forward.

"What is it, men?" I shouted.

"The Frenchmen have broken into the forecastle, and
a·e killing the Englishmen!" was the answer.

The uproar that had reached me with a subdued note in
the after part of the vessel was fearfully distinct here.

But the full horror of it did not strike me until my men had opened a passage and enabled me to get close to the hatch, down which I looked. Parell held a lantern, but the gleams penetrated the gloom but a short distance, and merely revealed now and again the glimmering figures of men tearing at one another like wild beasts, while the whole interior of the lugger rang with shrieks and drunken yells, and the crunching of bodies flung against the massive bulkheads and sides of the vessel.

"Madmen!" I shouted, "back to your quarters, or, by heaven, I will sweep the hold with grape! Men! train a carronade forward—depress the muzzle into the forecastle!"

The slide roared along the deck as it was dragged up to the hatch with a force that nearly ripped up the coaming. I had hoped the sound would still the monstrous combat; but, like oil upon fire, it only appeared to make it rage more furiously.

"Parell! lower that lantern! small-arms men, take aim and shoot every Frenchman you can distinguish."

The boatswain's mate bent a rope's end on to the lantern, and lowered it; scarcely had it sunk three feet below the deck when a blow shivered it into fragments, and the light was extinguished. What was to be done? It would have been sheer and brutal murder to fire among the seething mass who fought and yelled amid the blackness; but the consideration that the men whom the Frenchmen had fallen upon were half of them stupefied with drink, and that they were but sixteen opposed to twenty-five, so infuriated our seamen that Parell and myself had to threaten them with loaded pistols to stop them from leaping into the forecastle to aid the English.

"Bring another lantern," I shouted. "Parell, take fifteen men and get down the main-hatch, and carry a couple of lanterns with you. You will take the prisoners in the flank, and shoot every man who refuses to come out of the forecastle."

This order was immediately executed. Meanwhile a second lantern had been lowered down the forehatch by a seaman, who covered the light with a pistol. The horrible struggle still raged, and I thought it the more deadly because it had become less noisy. The combatants had no other weapons than their hands, but by the dim lantern-light I could perceive that they fought with their teeth and feet as well as their fists; and what with the drunken ferocity of the Englishmen on one side, and the mad revengeful spirit of the Frenchmen on the other, the scene of grappling and twisting figures, of motionless bodies stamped upon as a laborer beats down the earth with his hob-nailed boots, or wrestling forms whirling into the sphere of the rays and vanishing into the darkness beyond, aided by the snapping of teeth, the groans of the wounded, the fierce breathing, the sudden thrilling cries of pain, was one of such abounding horror as no man could imagine the like of who had not witnessed it.

"Let ten men follow me!" I sung out. "Use your cutlasses only. Hold that lantern steady, my man, and jump down with it as we drive the prisoners aft! The rest remain to guard the hatches."

Snatching a cutlass from the hand of one of the seamen, I sprang into the forecastle with a string of *Tigresses* after me. It is impossible to describe the scene that followed. It was one of those wild, impetuous, confused struggles which give a man no chance of noticing what happens. My object was to drive the prisoners out of the narrow forecastle into the roomier 'tween-decks, where we should at least find space to swing our arms in. The instant I gained my feet I fell sprawling over a body; but quickly recovering myself, and making a sweeping blow with the flat of my cutlass at the arms of a ferocious Englishman who was probably still too drunk to distinguish between friends and foes, and who was levelling his huge claws at my throat, I formed the men into a line, and by dint of thrusting with our hands and feet and pricking with our cutlasses, we bodily drove the combatants past the fittings of the bulkhead, which the Frenchmen—who knew their vessel better than we—had removed, where, as they arrived, they were seized by Parell's men and pinioned with lines flung down the hatchway for the purpose. The Frenchmen offered no resistance, but the English fought like cats, and when their arms were bound behind them and their legs secured they snapped at my men with their teeth, and spat at them in the impotence of their passion.

In truth, they were rendered perfect devils by the drink; they took us to be a portion of the Frenchmen who had broken in on their drunken sleep, and their brute courage operating as an instinct, and being all of them very powerful men, we had so much difficulty in pinioning them that I was in momentary fear of the temper of the *Tigresses*, and had several times to warn them not to use their cutlasses.

The lanterns illuminated an extraordinary picture. On one side of the deck were the Frenchmen, some of them bound back to back, some singly pinioned, standing or sitting, their quick savage breathing filling the hollow 'tween-decks with a sharp rushing noise, many of them covered with blood, their clothes half torn from their backs, and whole clouds of steam issuing from their bodies, as you may have seen the smoke rising from the hide of a driven horse on a winter's day. On the opposite or starboard side were the Englishmen, a small and brutal-looking band, writhing on their bellies, or straining at their bindings as they lay prostrate on their backs, but every man bound by turn upon turn of rope round his limbs, so as to resemble a mummy, or, better still, a fly after the spider has revolved him two or three times.

I do believe that a low inebriated Briton—this word gives a place to Pat as well as John Bull—offers the ugliest picture of intoxication that can be found the whole world over. Frenchmen, Spaniards, Italians, Russians—I am speaking of the lowest orders—may be more malignant and dangerous in their cups; but for vileness, vulgarity, brutality of language and conduct, and for a remarkable capacity of making every hair on his head and every rag on his back, and the very toes which peer out of his broken boots look as drunk as his eyes, face, limbs, and motions, the low-bred Briton, who never will be a slave—except to the bottle—is without a rival. There lay these reeking savages, shouting and cursing, and rolling their horrid eyes about them, and working themselves into a white-hot fury as they struggled in vain to free their arms and legs. Expostulations, entreaties, commands, were of no earthly use; like savage beasts they would have continued yelling at us with the muzzles of our muskets at their foreheads.

Some of them had received terrible injuries; like the

Frenchmen they were covered with blood, and their clothes were in ribbons. I counted them and found the number eleven, while three of the Frenchmen were missing. .Followed by Parell I entered the forecastle, observing as I did so that the bulkhead consisted of stout movable panels, the removal of which left a clear space from the mainmast to the head of the vessel; and here lay a number of bodies. I never would have believed it possible that unarmed human beings could mutilate their fellow-creatures to the extent these prostrate figures indicated. To look upon the torn flesh and broken limbs one would have imagined that half a dozen jaguars had been at work. The curses and cries and barking sounds uttered by the Englishmen beyond the bulkhead added a new element of horror to the ghastly scene, and the men who had followed us stood looking on with pale faces and aghast expressions, as Parell, holding a lantern, moved about this floating charnel-house, examining the countenances of the bodies.

However, it was necessary for a second time to clear this dismal and tragical forecastle, and the bodies were accordingly handed up and placed in a row on the deck. A strong muster of our seamen then seized the English prisoners, and dragged them, howling and shouting, and bound as they were, into the forecastle; the bulkhead was replaced, and a guard stationed to keep the two gangs of captives separated.

I went on deck with a reeling step and a giddy head. My nerves had stood the carnage of the forecastle, the struggle, the sight of the wounded men, the monstrous spectacle of the bleeding and torn Englishmen; but the scene of dead illumined by the wavering rays of the lantern had nearly proved too much for me, and I leaned against the mizzenmast trembling like a half-drowned poodle. But the cool night air braced me up, and a glass of grog, which I ordered the boy to smuggle through the skylight, gave me back my old strength.

"Well, Parell," said I, as the honest fellow, catching sight of me, came over to where I stood, "what of those miserable creatures? Are they *all* dead?"

"Two of them are alive, sir," he answered; "but the rest look to be clean done for."

"Who could have supposed that a movable bulkhead divided the men! Why, this is ten times worse than an engagement. How goes the time?" I looked at my watch. "Ten minutes to two. I had a mind to signal the schooner and hail her to send the surgeon; but we shall be having daylight soon, and meanwhile we will wait to see if more of those bodies there show any signs of life."

And when daylight at last broke, never was the dawning gray of the east more gladly welcomed by me. I watched the horizon darkening into a deep black line against the pallid heaven, and the gradual unfolding of the waters away on the port beam, and the slow shifting of the sky from the cold indigo of night into a tender azure that was growing pink in the east, until at last the whole surface of the restless and creaming deep was exposed, with the sloping form of the schooner ahead trailing a long line of snow astern of her, and the foam falling away from her weather side, and her cloud-like canvas swelling from the tapering spars whose topmost points presently caught the silver fire of the rising sun, and as the glorious luminary sailed above the sea, there flashed star-like points of exceeding brilliance upon the schooner's bright masts and in her streaming sides, and the sallow hue of her canvas changed into a glossy whiteness, like the breast of the albatross. "Ah, Master Shelvocke," thought I, with something like a pang of envy, "little wot you of the hideous nightmare your prize crew and their officer have been forced to dream this blessed night, now most mercifully gone!"

I called to one of the men:

"Hoist this French flag at the main. So—let it blow out a few feet below the truck."

The signal was immediately answered on the *Tigress* by the ensign at the peak; the clew of her mainsail was hauled up, her jibsheet flowed, and presently the two vessels were side by side.

"Schooner ahoy!"

"Hallo!" shouted Chestree, who stood on the lee bulwarks with his arm around a backstay.

"There has been an affray between the French and English prisoners. Eight men killed and wounded. Send Corney aboard. I will heave to when you are ready."

He tossed his hands with a gesture of amazement. Presently the boatswain's pipe sounded, and at the same moment Shelvocke's fine figure upreared itself on the rail.

"You can heave to, Mr. Madison!" he shouted, his powerful voice coming down upon the wind like a bugle-call. A boat was lowered, and in a few minutes Corney stepped on board the lugger.

I had no fancy to attend the surgeon while he examined the bodies, and therefore stood leaning over the lugger's side watching the *Tigress* as she lay with her sails quivering in the wind, gently pitching upon the emerald-green seas.

After some time Corney came aft and told me that only two of the men were alive.

"I never saw death in a more terrible form," said he, evidently much shocked. "They must have fought like fiends. Had a bluelight burned in the forecastle when these men were fighting, looking down the hatchway would have been like peering into the infernal regions.

"It was like hell itself, Corney. It wanted no bluelight."

"I would recommend the bodies to be thrown overboard at once, Mr. Madison."

I gave the necessary instructions, and then proceeded to acquaint Corney, for the information of Shelvocke, with the value of the lugger; whereat the consternation that the sight of the dead had raised in him melted out of his face, and was replaced by an extravagant grin of satisfaction.

"One hundred thousand dollars!" cried he. "And ivory and tea, and silk, too! God bless my heart! If this goes on, I shall be able to fling my surgical instruments overboard."

He waited until the dead had been dropped over the side, and then returned to the schooner, singing out to the boat's crew, as he flopped into the sternsheets, that the lugger was full of minted silver and silk and ivory, and begging them to give way, so that the news might be immediately given to the captain. As soon as he had shoved off, the sails of the lugger were trimmed, and we were once more pushing through the sparkling waters.

It was an amazingly inspiriting morning, and my men,

in spite of their hard night's watching, were in high spirits as they bustled to and fro, clearing up the decks, and cracking marine witticisms on the guns and rigging of the lugger, and peering into the hatchways, some of them stripped to their waists forward, dashing buckets of water over one another, while others lighted the fire in the little caboose for breakfast.

I watched the *Tigress* hoist in her boat, and fall off before the wind and come tearing after us, with the bright surges bursting away in smoke from her keen stem; and as she tore past us, her men sprang upon the bulwarks and gave three hearty cheers, which their shipmates in the lugger instantly responded to.

"Keep her smoking, Madison!" roared Shelvocke; "both anchors must be down in Cawsand Bay before sunset."

And this actually happened; for at four o'clock that afternoon the *Tigress*, who headed us by about a mile, hoisted her ensign and fired two guns, the meaning of which was presently rendered apparent by our heaving up a blue film on the starboard bow that proved to be Bolt Head. The sun was setting as, under a press of sail and with a strong northeasterly wind blowing, we swept along astern of the schooner, passed Mewstone Ledge, with Penlee Point on the port bow and the shores of Cawsand Bay looming dark against the red evening sky, and throwing into noble relief a fleet of eight large merchantmen who were riding in groups upon the dark-blue tumble.

Plymouth Sound lay open to us with lights springing up ashore and flashing fitfully across the running waters, as the air darkened and the stars sparkled and faded among the driving clouds like the revolving lantern of a beacon. Swirling past the merchantmen who occupied the Bay betwixt Cawsand and the Broady Coves, and whose forecastles were crowded with men who watched the lugger much as a crowd of flies might be supposed to stare at a captured spider, we rounded to under the stern of a dashing frigate and let go our anchors, and never before had the splash of iron flukes and the tearing of the hemp through the hawse-holes fallen more gratefully upon my ears.

Shelvocke boarded the frigate, and presently returned, followed by her launch, pinnace, and first cutter full of seamen and marines, who, to my inexpressible comfort, cleared the two vessels of their prisoners, and carried them away to the port-admiral's ship up Hamoaze; and within an hour and a half of our bringing up, I was in the cabin of the *Tigress* enjoying a good supper, some excellent cold grog, and a lively chat with my worthy captain.

# CHAPTER VIII.

THE hope of reaching Brest in time to fetch the outward-bound convoy could no longer be indulged, though, considering the value of the lugger, none of us had any fault to find with the cause that had stopped our project. Yet rich as the prize proved—her cargo being actually assessed at thirty-five thousand pounds—no capture ever gave more trouble than that of the *Droit Maritime*. The owners of the polacre brig that had been taken by the Frenchmen and sent into Granville, claimed the lugger and cargo on the ground that she was in possession of a part of the crew of the brig when we boarded her. This was true; but our contention was that the said crew, at the time we boarded the lugger, were drunk and incapable, and that their condition was tantamount to the virtual abandonment of the vessel. I cannot remember more of the arguments of the lawyers than this: but I know we were detained three weeks at Plymouth, during which time I must have kissed the Bible over not less than a dozen affidavits; and I got so sick at last of the visits of the attorney, that whenever I saw him coming I used to hide myself. I may as well say that the case was decided by Lord Stowell, some months afterward, in Hannay's favor; but what become of the English seamen, who in my opinion richly deserved to be hanged for the death of the wretched Frenchmen, I did not inquire at the time, and so cannot now say.

While we lay at Plymouth, the *Tigress* was visited by a great number of persons; for the value of the prize and the lawsuit about it had made some noise, and the name we had earned by our action with the corvette was not yet forgotten.

Among half a dozen invitations received by Shelvocke

and myself to as many different houses, was one to a ball given by an old rich knight, in celebration of a remarkable victory obtained by his son, who commanded an English sloop-of-war, over two large French frigates. This ball dates the beginning of as romantic an experience as was probably ever encountered by a sailor.

Invitations to it had been sent out for the night preceding the day on which we sailed; and as I was immensely fond of dancing, I had eagerly looked forward to this chance of having a regular sailor's frisk with a lively partner.

"Rather unusual for privateersmen to be asked into select companies," Shelvocke had said to me dryly. "Hope we shan't frighten the dandies."

I hoped so too; and to provide against any likelihood of a scare, we took some trouble over our togs; and whatever figure I may have cut, I will say that Shelvocke, with his masculine rugged breadth of forehead, sunburnt face, tawny beard, and noble stature, that was improved with the inimitable grace of the sailor's movements, impressed me, as he stepped forth in full fig, as one of the handsomest and most manly creatures it had ever been my fortune to behold.

It is so many years since I was at Plymouth, that I cannot clearly recall the geographical position of our host's residence. It was about a quarter of a mile out of the town, and was a small but very nobly wooded estate, and the house like a castle. The owner, Sir William Tempest, had caused the beautiful avenue that led to the house to be hung with colored paper lanterns, a great number of which glimmered among the trees which extended on either hand; and the effect of these lights twinkling in blues and greens and yellows among the deep shadows, and the dense volumes of the lofty trees towering against the bright stars, and the newly risen moon silvering the upper stories of the castellated building and lying in delicate jasper-like lines upon the lower walls which received the pure beam through an opening here and there in the trees, and the contrast of the mellow illumination of candles upon the tall windows with the vista of colored lamps along which the eye roved to the house—formed a night-scene of soft and peaceful beauty that was immensely heightened to the senses by the rich smell of leaves and dew-moistened sward, and great beds of lilies and roses and other sweet flowers.

We were among the late arrivals; so that, when we entered the long and lofty drawing-rooms, we found nearly all the company assembled, and many persons dancing to a capital band of music. Of course, two-thirds at least of the males were naval officers; and their sparkling epaulets and bright buttons and laced collars, mingling with various military costumes and black civilian coats, and the gleaming satins and silks and the white shoulders and arms and the flashing diamonds and the flowers of the ladies, made a brave and brilliant show under the blazing candelabra and the rows of sconces.

There were upward of two hundred people present, but the large rooms would have held another hundred without the least crushing. The walls were hung with banners, and an immense red English ensign drooped at each end of the room; and in a large recess opposite the beautifully carved old-fashioned chimneypiece there was an emblematic contrivance that was probably considered appropriate to the occasion, though I did not much admire the taste that suggested it. It consisted of a small boat carronade, with a cleverly constructed lay figure of an English seaman in the act of discharging the gun, and a large number of projecting poles, on which were suspended the flags of all nations, the whole topped by a tall staff, upon which was midway hoisted a mutilated French flag, and above it the English colors. This piece of nonsense was meant to typify Britain's supremacy over all the countries of the world, and more particularly over Monsieur Crapeau. Some of the naval officers appeared to admire it, but for my part, as I have said, I thought it a twopenny affair, fit only to amuse little boys; and as it stood upon a fragile draped scaffold, I was vicious enough to hope that some of the dancers would capsize it before the night was out.

We were received with great kindness by Lady Tempest, whose white hair, fresh complexion, motherly smile, soft eyes, and winning confidentiality of manner, as though she had so much to say and would so immensely enjoy a quiet chat with you, made her one of the pleasantest-looking and nicest old ladies a man could wish to meet. She kept us

14

talking just long enough to mention her son's name, and I could have hugged Shelvocke for the pleasure he gave her by his hearty, honest, generous applause of Captain Tempest's gallant conduct.   Then her husband, a timid, gentle, little old man, in black silk stockings and metal buttons on his long-tailed coat, came up and welcomed us, and took Shelvocke over to a knot of naval officers, while her ladyship, catching me with a pretty gesture by the hand, led me up to a haughty young person who was studying her fan under Jonathan's stripes and stars.

She was the handsomest-dressed woman in the room, and I have no doubt the worst-tempered—quite insolent in her questions; so that presently I grew resentful, and learning from her that her father was a rear-admiral and a lord, I recollected the learned Doctor Samuel Johnson's behavior on a like occasion, and said that although I was a sailor, I never pretended to be anything better than a pirate, that I got my bread by plundering merchant ships and dispatching honest men : that polite people termed me a privateer, but that I liked to call things by their right names.

After this we danced like automatons, and she then asked me to be good enough to take her to her papa, a puffed-out, red-faced old man in an embroidered naval uniform, the breast of which was covered with decorations.   I made her a low bow, which she returned with a sublime courtesy, the overwhelming *sweepingness* of which was no doubt meant to cover me with confusion and awe, and I believe that no couple ever got rid of each other more rejoicingly than she and I.

Seeing Shelvocke standing alone, I joined him.

"I rather suspected," said he, "that when the epaulets found me out they would serve me with the cold shoulder. 'Give privateersmen the stem!' is the cry, you know, among those fellows.   But heaven has blessed me with uncommon fortitude, and success teaches patience."

"Why don't you dance, captain?   There are surely enough pretty women in the room to console you for the neglect of your own sex."

"The reason why I don't dance is extremely simple—I can't dance.   By the way, who, think you, makes one of yonder group?" indicating with a movement of his head the officers to whom Sir William had introduced him.

I looked, and answered I could not imagine.

" You remember the surly captain of the frigate who left the little brig to do all the hard work, and missed the French liner after all?"

" Perfectly well."

" Well, there he stands.  His name is Monk—that ring-faced man to the right of the tall gray-haired chap."

" I see him, and now I remember his face."

" Singularly enough," he continued, "they were talking of this very engagement when Sir William introduced me. I heard one man say, 'Monk, your *Andromache* was not up to the mark: her Astyanax was *not* saved from the flames; 'tis a bad reading of your "Iliad," but—' I lost the rest, but the word *Andromache* made me look at my man, and I then recollected him."

I watched Captain Monk while Shelvocke spoke, and noticed the ludicrously pompous airs he gave himself as he stood, apparently engrossing all the conversation, in the midst of half a dozen naval men.

" You remember how extremely rude the fellow was when I proffered such assistance as was in my power?" continued Shelvocke.  " I thought of his impudent boorish manner as I listened to him talking about his action with the French-man, and determined to take him off his own peg and hang him upon one considerably lower down.  So addressing myself to him, I said I had witnessed the action from the deck of a privateer *I had the honor to command*—always put on a cocked-hat, Madison, when you talk of your own calling; if I swept a crossing my broom should never lack importance from my lips;—and that I was much impressed with the gallantry with which the vessels swept down upon their huge opponent; and having oiled him with this feather I applied the clyster.  I praised the brig up to the skies; I said it was deplorable that so much bravery should have been left unsupported by the frigate; I should have been only too glad," I continued, "to have brought the schooner into the conflict had not the captain of the brig requested me to remain a looker-on, and I explained my sensitiveness in the matter of interference by relating the story of our

engagement with the French corvette; there was no lack of
courage on the part of the frigate, said I, but she was so
unskilfully handled as to make me hope in the interests of
the naval service that Captain Monk had not omitted to
represent the incompetency of the sailing-master in his dispatch to my lords.    That was corrosive enough, wasn't it,
Madison?"

I laughed and thought to myself, no wonder they have
given him the cold shoulder.

"You would have split your sides to see the man's face,"
said Shelvocke.    "One or two of the officers walked away,
either afraid of their gravity or of a 'scene.'    But there
was no fear of the latter.    I was much too courteous for a
riot, and passed my criticism so interrogatively that I believe the man scarcely knew whether I talked to insult him
or from an honest thirst for information."

At this moment Sir William brought up a middle-aged
gentlemanly man, with whom Shelvocke immediately and
cordially shook hands, and who proved to be an East India
merchant who had twice sailed with Shelvocke to and from
Bombay.    I was glad to see the captain in tow of an old
friend, and one I had already noticed as shaking hands
and appearing on very friendly terms with some of the
highest naval and military officers in the room: but as I
had come to this ball to dance I hauled off from the quarter-deck yarn these two men began to spout, and presently
had the luck to obtain an introduction to a young lady
whose frank and beautiful eyes had previously attracted my
attention and won my admiration as she executed a very
dull and solemn dance hand-in-hand with a glittering, jingling, youthful third lieutenant.

An English *lady* is the first woman in the world for
manners, and one hour of her spiritual elegance and bland
and soothing graces is worth whole years of the quilted
dignities and cultivated airs of foreign grand dames.    I
don't like to be poetical—the popular idea of Jack is so intimately blended with rum, tobacco, and vulgar bluntness,
that a sailor is almost afraid of appearing in any other
character than the one which novelists and actors have invented for him, lest he should not only wound a deep-
rooted prejudice, but even be snubbed as an imposition;

therefore I don't like to be poetical: but I scarcely know how to convey the impression Miss Madeline Palmer—for that was her name—produced upon me, if I may not say that talking to her and looking into her face was like breathing the fragrance of a beautiful flower. So there you have it.

She was young—not more than nineteen—with a rich contralto laugh that had more melody in it than many a fine singer's voice: yet fresh and womanly as was her face, with the large, wistful, honest gray eyes, and soft, faintly flushed complexion—like the hue of clear flesh in a pink light—and arched upper lip, and the nose slightly, but how slightly! *turned up*—have we no romantic definition in our vocabulary of this delicious stroke in the face of beauty?— like the fascinating organ of Lady Cleveland, as I have beheld it in the portrait of that amorous romp, and the square, snow-white forehead, topped with a glorious thickness of golden-brown hair, divided on the right side, glittering with the gold dust that in those days ladies sprinkled over their heads with great effect, and hanging with a breezy look, and sparkling in golden threads over her brows, the starboard one of which was decorated with a sweet little mole designed by nature to contrast the exceeding whiteness of her skin; while her plump yet maidenly figure was dressed, as it should be, in white satin with short sleeves, and a light green drapery of crape fastened on the left shoulder with an amber brooch, folded so as to conceal the left side of her figure in front; and long, white kid gloves, between the top of which and the green chenille trimming of the sleeves the white, firm, round flesh of her arms looked like a carving in finest ivory; and exquisitely fitting shoes of green silk; and around her throat a string of pearls and a small cross of diamonds, concealing, but suggesting too, the little hollow, of which the swelling satin that rounded away from this point, and curved back again into a tapering waist was the reserved but sufficient expression; I say—but, bless me, what *was* I saying? Ah! I have it; that sweet and womanly as were the face and form of this girl, yet these outward and visible signs, as constituents of her fresh and fascinating being, were as naught compared with the indescribable graces of her cordial, ten-

der, modest, and most winning manners. No airs, no sim-
pering, no stupid observations: we danced, and then saun-
tered into a brilliant anteroom full of flowers, and tables
covered with refreshments—how true is Horace:

" Difficile est proprie communia dicere !"

how is a man fresh from the study of a woman's beauty to
describe *eatables!*—where we sipped wine and coquetted
with the jellies, while we fell into a talk that missed me
two dances.

She proved to be the daughter of a Colonel Palmer, whose
regiment had been for some time in Jamaica, but the last
letter she had received from him warned her that his health
was bad, and that it was probable he would be forced to
return home by the end of the year. Since the receipt of
those letters she had met a friend of the colonel, who had
alarmed her by saying that her father was looking seriously
ill, and that he ought undoubtedly to act upon the advice
of his doctor and return home.

"But papa is a very obstinate man, Mr. Madison," said
she, "and is quite likely to linger on in that dreadful climate with the idea that he is serving his country by ruining his health, until it will be too late for him to receive
any benefit from a change of air. So I am going out to
bring him home. I am his only child, and his objection to
my remaining in the bad climate of Jamaica will be sure to
induce him to come home with me if I refuse—which I
mean to do—to return alone."

I asked when she sailed, and she said in a day or two;
the vessel in which she had taken her passage had that
morning arrived in Cawsand Bay. For the last fortnight
she had been Lady Tempest's guest, but her home was near
Canterbury, in Kent.

On my telling her that I had been mate of an Indiaman
for some years, she asked me many questions about the life
on board ship, and listened to me with such graceful, kindly
interest, that I was induced to prolong my conversation beyond the warrant of good manners. I know not how it
came about, nor what there was in me to merit so high an
honor, but she talked to me with as little reserve as she
could have shown had I been an old friend, and seemed

almost reluctant to leave the comparative quiet of the refreshment room when I offered my arm to conduct her out
of it. ·

I found other partners, and whisked through several
dances; but the moment I saw Miss Palmer alone again, I
went to her, and the rest of the night I spent almost entirely at her side.    I never passed a pleasanter, happier
time.    The rooms were full of pretty women, the dancers
among the men had no difficulty in finding partners, love-
making grew general as the night advanced, and these little conditions of this delightful ball enabled me to keep
Miss Palmer very much to myself.    I talked to her about
my privateering experiences, asked her if she was not
frightened to dance with a corsair, told her (when she asked
the question) that yonder tall, powerful, handsome man
was Captain Shelvocke, the commander of the vessel I was
first officer of, described to her our fight with the corvette,
and my experiences aboard the *Droit Maritime ;* and she
chatted to me about her Aunt Matilda, and her pretty home
near Canterbury, and her dear papa, whose name she pronounced with exquisite fondness, and her mother, who had
been dead seven years.

Indeed no two people could have found more to talk
about than she and I.    As the hours wore away, and the
spirit of the revelry grew strong, the scene of the ballroom
was amazingly brilliant with the glitter of uniforms among
the gleaming dresses of the ladies, the flash and play of
white arms and white necks, and gaudy turbans and stately
feathers, and medals and dress-swords, and sweet, fair faces
looking one way, and sunburnt, handsome faces looking another way;    while the banners swayed under the breezing
of the sweeping skirts, and here and there a picturesque
background was formed of grave dowagers nodding to the
music and watching the dancers, and stiff old sea officers
in costumes of a Rodney pattern, figged-out old sea-mon-
sters, one with an empty sleeve, another with one eye; and
a sprinkling of military coats and gold lace and bullion
fringe and warlike whiskers.

The supper was really a magnificent affair, in a wing of
the house that was all one room, and as big as a church,
and not unlike the inside of a church either;    hundreds of

candles, more flags, flowers everywhere; long tables crowded
with silver and crystal wherein the candles shone like the
sun in a calm sea, and dishes of things the mere sight of
which would have kept an alderman smiling in his sleep
for years; champagne fizzing in all directions like the froth
through the scupper-holes of a wave-swept ship; fellows
in liveries tumbling against each other; old gentlemen and
old ladies eating, young gentlemen whispering, young ladies
giggling; and, to crown all—bear me witness, some Plymouth centenarian!—speeches!

The King's health was drunk. General A—— quavered
out thanks for the army: "It always *had* done its duty: it
always *would* do its duty." Admiral B——, who rose
with a napkin pinned over his decorations, grumbled out
his thanks in a deep-sea note for the navy: "Hearts of oak
—Frenchmen afraid of us—St. Vincent—the Nile—hurrah!" But the toast of the evening was Captain Tempest
(at whose name we all cheered until the vaulted room rattled to the cordial broadside), whose absence was explained
by his having been ordered to join the North Sea squadron
with urgent despatches. His health was proposed by the
port-admiral—a fine, jovial-faced old man, with a head like
Collingwood's—in a bluff speech that set dear old Lady
Tempest crying with pride, and made her modest little husband blush like a purple dahlia, and when the port-admiral
wound up by exclaiming, with kindling eyes, and holding
a full wineglass over the turban of a stout lady on his right
as if he intended to pour the libation among her feathers
before he sat down, that the fine young officer had given
one more proof by the gallant fight he had made that Nelson's immortal signal before the battle of Trafalgar (*Hip,
hip, hurrah!*) still flew wherever a British man-of-war was
to be found, we cheered again and again, springing to our
feet and shouting at the top of our voices; in the middle
of which, and producing an effect that raised our enthusiasm (backed as it was by champagne) to fever-pitch, five
twelve-pound guns (the concussion of which, by the way,
broke several windows) were discharged on the lawn in
front of the house, the ladies shrieked, dress-swords were
jingled, and a military band outside struck up "Rule
Britannia."

After all this we were invited on to the lawn to view the fireworks; there was a rush for shawls, and I had the happiness to robe the beautiful shoulders of Miss Palmer, and to follow the clanking, rustling, sparkling, and nodding line of guests with this delightful girl on my arm.

> "And 'twas pretty to see how, like birds of a feather,
> The people of quality flock'd all together."

The night was calm and cloudless. The moon, who, like other middle-aged ladies, had risen late, floated with half her silver disc obscured; but her sweet beam was too mild to vex the gayety of the clusters of colored lanterns which hung in festoons all round the wide lawn where the cannon had been fired, and where a military band (by kind permission of the Roman-nosed colonel who had sat opposite to me at the supper-table, and drank champagne enough to launch a bomb-ship in) was rattling out martial music. Away beyond the lawn was a magnificent denseness of towering trees, amid the intricacies of which the lanterns glimmered like fire-flies.

Of all fine effects I never witnessed anything more striking than the aspect of our numerous and vari-colored assembly, when all on a sudden, a number of red, blue, and green fires were burned, as a hint that the pyrotechnical drama was about to begin. The sudden stopping of promenading groups; the quivering of the prismatic hues in jewels, buttons, bullion-fringe, sword-hilts, and bright eyes; the ghostly coloring of faces; the star-like sparkles of the dew-drops upon the grass; the long double shadows cast by the mingled light of the moon and the colored fires upon the sward on which we stood; the boughs of the nearer trees which seemed to writhe and twist like snakes forking out from the huge trunks, as the fires waned and brightened; the sickly uniform pallor of the flowers, as though some deadly breath had passed over their petals, and extinguished their bright hues—it was the best part of the fireworks.

"Enough to make one think of the last day," said I to Miss Palmer, "when some of our decorated braves will be wanting to dodge the light that shows their stars and medals to be fashioned out of human blood, when the biggest diamond among us will not be reckoned half so beautiful as a pauper's tear, and when all the feathers our turbans can muster shall not furnish the lightest-weight lieutenant with a pair of wings."

"Rather profane but true, Mr. Madison," she answered; "and it only shows how wicked even the nicest people must be when a little red and blue fire makes them look like— imps."

The fireworks were excellent, but a little of that sort of buzzing and fizzing and banging goes a long way with me; and Miss Palmer being of my mind, we presently found ourselves wandering after a few detached couples among the flower-gardens to the right of the house, where the strains of the band reached us with a softened note, and where we had an excuse to pause often over the dewy fragrance of the beds of dahlias, lilies, starworts, pinks, roses, pentstemons, and all the rest of them—I never can remember the names of flowers, nor the months in which they flourish—which lay in pale spaces on either hand of us.

When the final rocket exploded, the band played "God Save the King," which was immediately followed by the drawing-room fiddlers striking up a piece of dance music, for we had not strayed so far but that these notes reached us as they floated through the open windows; so we returned to the house, and for the rest of the night I danced with nobody but Madeline Palmer, who seemed perfectly happy and satisfied with her partner; and when the ball broke up amid the twittering of birds, and in the pink haze of the budding morning, before I parted from my sweet companion I begged a flower from her as a memorial of the delighted hours I had passed in her society, saying romantically, and, as I apprehend, collectedly, having regard to the hour, and how redolent the air was of champagne, that it would sweeten with its fragrance the rough life I should be renewing in a few hours, and that nothing would better emblemize the happiness she had given me.

"Because it will fade very soon, do you mean?" she said, with her rich laugh, but taking the flower from her bosom and giving it to me cordially, and without the least embarrassment.

I bowed, she courtesied, and, as much in love as any fool could well be at first sight, I went to look for Shelvocke.

I found him waiting for me outside the avenue, and the moment we got under weigh he lighted a cigar.

"Well, Madison," said he, "do you come away with a broken heart?"

"Pooh, pooh! my dear sir, when a man gets to my time of life he doesn't allow a little harmless flirtation to affect his happiness. I have danced, I have drunk, I have been alarmed by the explosion of guns, I am immensely indebted to the most hospitable of ladies for one of the most delightful of nights, and to-morrow—nay, by George! this very blessed day, captain, we go in quest of more booty." Here I heaved a deep sigh.

He took my arm, but as I imagined that he did so to steady me, and as I did not consider I required any support, I wriggled away from him, whereat he laughed, and offered me a cigar. I halted to light it at the cigar in his mouth.

"Would you kindly keep your cigar steady, captain?" I exclaimed, as I found the glowing tip dodging first this side and then that, and eluding all my efforts to fix it; "or can it be the effect of the dancing lingering in my feet? Any man might suppose that we are still shaking a leg,"— here I caught his cigar, and at the same moment his eye, the expression in which made me break into a shout of laughter. The laugh did me good, and methought I took the ground with a steadier stride.

He continued to rally me somewhat, saying that my partner was the prettiest girl in the room, that he had watched me flinging my nautical heels about with envy and admiration, and wondered where the deuce I had got that trick of making love, so to speak, with the part of my face that was turned to the young lady, while the other part that was exhibited to the public gaze expressed the utmost modesty and the most genteel consideration for other people's feelings.

To calk his banter, I asked him if anything more had passed between him and Captain Monk.

"Why, yes," he answered quietly. "A good deal more. He came up to me on the lawn during the fireworks—I was alone—and asked me in the most impertinent manner in the world what my object had been in cross-examining

him on the subject of his action with the line-of-battle ship.
He was rather *fou* as the Scotch say, for it was after supper, you know.   I answered that I asked for information.
'If that was your motive,' said he, 'you might have saved
yourself a great deal of trouble by confessing your intention
at once, and I should have been glad to refer you to a three-
and-sixpenny treatise on the mariner's calling, which would
have acquainted you with all the professional duties of
which you appear to be ignorant.'   'I am surprised,' said
I, 'that you should know of any such treatise, after the
specimen of seamanship I was a witness of.'   After insult-
ing each other in this fashion for some minutes he walked
away.   While I was waiting for you, a naval officer saun-
tered up to me, said, with a bow, he believed he had the
honor of addressing Captain Shelvocke of the privateer
schooner *Tigress*, informed me that Captain Monk claimed
satisfaction for the affront I had put upon him, and desired
me to refer him to a gentleman who would act as my second.   I begged permission to waive all ceremony—the fact
is, Madison, I had not the heart to lug you from your
charming companion into a business of this kind—and assured the officer that if he would appoint a place and time
I would very punctually attend upon Captain Monk and
bring a friend with me.   'We sail at noon,' said I, 'and I
have therefore to request that the affair be dispatched
quickly.'   So it was arranged that I should meet Captain
Monk at seven o'clock, at a secluded spot neat Catwater.
I am to land at the flagstaff, and the officer will conduct
me to the shooting-place.   I have to ask you to be my second, Madison."

"Certainly, captain."

"I am not a vindictive animal, but there is something in
this Monk that is detestable, and if I can put a bullet into
him I will," he said.   "I have ascertained that he has the
character of a tyrant, and to judge by his seamanship the
service can well afford to lose him; though, mind, I will
always say he brought his frigate into action gallantly."

"Rather sharp work, sir," said I, pulling out my watch;
"it is already past four.   One moment toppling about with a
lovely partner through halls of dazzling light and amid scenes
of more than Eastern splendor, and the next—Oh, Lord!"

"What's the matter with you?"

"Why I have put the lighted end of my cigar into my mouth, sir. By the way, captain, what about pistols?"

"I have the weapon I require on board."

"Really, sir," I exclaimed, beginning to feel maudlin, "that is an unfortunate business. I hope the man's a bad shot. If you should be winged, captain, or made a sheer hulk of like poor Tom Bowline, whose face was of the manliest beauty, what's to become of us *Tigresses?*"

"Steady, my friend, steady!" he sung out, as I lurched up against him. "Here, take my arm, man; nothing like a leeboard for a craft that sails three sheets to the wind."

I held on to him fondly, and felt so excessively sentimental that I could have shed tears.

"If you have any commands, captain, if you have any last injunctions, any dear ones you would like me to wait upon, any sealed packets, pieces of hair——"

"Thank you: if I fall my lawyer will know what to do," he answered, with his face as grave as a judge's, and in a most serious tone of voice. "Being alone in the world is thought a poor lookout by many people, and mothers with marriageable daughters will paint the horrors of celibacy in lively colors. But loneliness confers some fine privileges, and at this moment I would not be a married man if my wife were Venus, and Plutus had made his will in her favor."

"And yet it must be a pleasant thing to have a wife, sir; to feel that there is always a plump little goddess with gray eyes and soft lips sitting at home and thinking of you; to be the owner of a girl like Madeline Palmer for instance, or such a beauty as that romantic young Italian girl you once told me about—little Peacock's mother, captain, you know—eh? Pray describe her to me, sir. I am in the mood to talk about pretty women."

"Come along, come along!" he exclaimed rather sternly and very impatiently, nipping my wrist as though he held it in a vice under his arm, and making my legs feel like corkscrews as he hauled me over the ground. "It will be eight o'clock before we get aboard at this rate. I am sorry I did not accept my friend's offer of a lift in his carriage—but he had left before I was *called out.*"

The length and impetuosity of his stride effectually silenced me, and we walked as if for a wager. The sun had risen, and such a morning had broken as would have made a man in love with a saunter along the country road we had taken in order to fetch the place opposite which the *Tigress* was anchored, by the shortest cut. After the heated rooms, the revolving dances, the champagne and the flirting, the smell of the hay, the sweet scents of the wild flowers, the breath of the full-leaved hedges, were refreshing beyond all expression. However, the hard walking cleared my head, and by the time we had reached Bottlenose Point (I think it was) I was collected enough to regret the nonsense I had talked to Shelvocke.

Right opposite to us lay the schooner, calmly resting upon the blue water that reflected her beautiful form and gave back the lustrous sheen of her copper. Shelvocke hailed her, and was immediately answered by Tapping, and in a few moments a boat was lowered.

The Sound was a beautiful picture with its verdant shores, and a group of motionless ships at anchor in Jenny-cliff Bay, and a few small, creeping, white-winged vessels taking advantage of the land-breeze that was making the water tremble toward the sea, though where we stood scarcely a blur tarnished the blue mirror; while, on our right, we could see the mastheads of the ships and the grouped town of Plymouth and the hills to the north of it, and Catwater sparkling like quicksilver as it rounded to the eastward past Catdown; while the whole glittering scene of still, blue water, and green and brown land, and ships with their tall masts trembling in the faint haze that the sun was drawing from the shores, was made singularly impressive by the night-silence which the young morning had not yet broken, and by the lifelessness of the silver-bright and beautiful picture which the crawling sails on the water away toward the sea, or the cry of some hidden workman hailing a fellow-laborer, or the striking of a ship's bell, seemed rather to heighten than disturb.

The water buzzed under the stem of the gig as she swept toward us, and in a few minutes we were aboard the schooner. Shelvocke was somewhat grave, otherwise his usual manner was unchanged. He ordered the gig to re-

main alongside; and after giving a few instructions to
Tapping respecting the preparations for sailing shortly
after noon, he went below and remained in his cabin until
it was time to be off.

A plunge over the side and a twenty minutes' swim completed the cure that my sharp walk with the captain had
commenced in me. I drank a cup of tea, and, pipe in
mouth, waited for Shelvocke's summons to start. I was
depressed; for I thought it a monstrous pity that the life
of a man like Shelvocke should be risked in a pitiful and
inglorious encounter with a person whose surly reply to our
hail from the deck of his frigate might very well have been
passed by with contemptuous indifference. However, re-
grets were of no use; and, at twenty minutes to seven,
Shelvocke came on deck with his pistol-case concealed
under a light cloak, we jumped into the gig, and started
for a place of meeting.

The men looked inquisitively from Shelvocke to his cloak
that lay beside him, as though they suspected his errand,
and I was heartily glad to see no signs of a man-of-war's
boat in waiting upon Captain Monk; for, owing to the
press-gangs which (now that the war with America had
added to our numerous engagements of a similar nature)
were bearing with heavy severity on merchant-seamen, an
epaulet in the eyes of mercantile Jack was as bad as a
crime in its wearer, and collisions between the crews of
merchant ships and naval vessels were repeatedly occur-
ring, and often with lamentable consequences. However,
as I have said, nothing resembling a boat was to be seen in
the neighborhood of the spot toward which we were heading. The distance altogether was two miles, and given
any other errand, the row would have been a delightful one.

My recollection of Plymouth has been greatly dulled by
time, yet I did then, and do still, think the view of the
Sound—the town, the forts and heights down as far as the
eye could reach, to Staddon Point, ay, and even to Reny
Point, and the hilly shores of Penlee opening, as we rowed,
far away behind Drake's Island—the most romantic and
beautiful bit of coast scenery mortal eye could wish to look
upon, even low on the water as I was, when I turned my
head and looked over the stern toward the slip of Cornwall

promontory, upon whose green and yellow fields the soaring sun was pouring his lustrous silver.

"There's a flagstaff," said Shelvocke.

"And there's a man," said I, pointing to a figure that was walking by the margin of the water under cover of a tall bank.

"Monk's second, I suppose," said Shelvocke, looking at his watch. "He is punctual enough; it wants ten minutes to the hour."

The oars creaked and the boat flew along; every stroke enlarged and sharpened the figure of the man. Presently we could distinguish his face, and see the buttons glittering on his coat. He stood watching us, and as we approached, raised his hat and pointed to a ledge of soil or sand that jutted into the water, as much as to say, "You had better land here." The stem of the boat grounded, she swung to the ledge, and we stepped out.

I put the pistol-case under my arm, and wondered how far a distance we should be taken by the naval officer, who had the look of a free and hearty, yet well-bred man, when, again raising his hat, he requested me to step aside with him. I did so at once, leaving Shelvocke standing with his back toward us, and rolling a cigar between his thumb and forefinger, as if considering whether he should light it.

"I am much concerned, sir," said the officer, "that it was out of my power to save Captain Shelvocke and yourself from undertaking a fruitless journey. The fact is, on my arrival at the house where Captain Monk is staying, I found that he had been struck down by an apoplexy. There were two doctors in attendance on him. Of course, his presence here is impossible."

I made him a bow, and walked over to Shelvocke, and gave him this message. The expression on his face did not alter in the least. He approached the officer with a cold inclination of the head.

"Unhappily," said he, "I sail to-day, and cannot possibly fix or suggest a time for another meeting should your friend recover. But if you will favor me with Captain Monk's address, I will take care that he be kept furnished with such accounts of my movements as the owner of the *Tigress* will receive from me; and you may tell him that I shall be willing to fight him at the earliest possible opportunity that may offer, in any part of the world, with any weapon he likes to name, and at any hour in the whole circle of the twenty-four he may take it into his head to fancy."

The officer—I forget his name—replied with a haughty bow; the half-suppressed contempt and chilling deliberateness of Shelvocke's manner and voice were a behavior in a privateersman which our naval friend did not at all relish. But there was nothing in Shelvocke's language that he could resent. He named a place at which Captain Monk could be addressed, and added:

"I will deliver your message, sir, and you may rely upon it that nothing short of an apoplexy will cause Captain Monk to disappoint you when the opportunity for another meeting *does* occur."

I had some difficulty to keep my face when he said "nothing short of an apoplexy,"—as if there were no other illness calculated to stop a man from fighting a duel. We again saluted one another, and there being nothing more to say, he walked in the direction of the town and we returned to the gig.

"Shove off, my lads; give way now," said Shelvocke; and turning to me as he lighted a cigar, he exclaimed with a quiet smile, "I shall be able to smoke this out, after all."

15

# CHAPTER IX.

THE chimes of the church-clocks striking the hour of noon came down upon the pleasant northeast wind; and as the ship's bells clanked out the time, it was like the tinkling you hear among flocks of sheep. The piercing pipe of the boatswain summoned all hands to get the schooner under way; a strong gang manned the capstan; some were aloft loosing the square canvas, others out on the bowsprit and jibbooms, and groups at the running rigging.

With ninety men and a small ship there was no excuse for the least want of smartness; besides, we lay full in sight of Plymouth, and the shores all along were alive with critical naval eyes, the mere notion of which nerved our seamen into uncommon dexterous activity. The main throat-halliards were taken through a snatch-block hitched to an eye-bolt abreast of the tiller, so as to give the fellows who manned them the whole run of the deck; there were hands by the topsail, staysail, and jib halliards; twenty men had the handling of the square rigging, and so soon as ever the cable was up and down, the boatswain chirped his pipe, the beautiful schooner flashed as if by magic into a broad tall surface of white canvas, another turn of the capstan raised the anchor, and the *Tigress* was under way.

I strode about apparently full of business, singing out here, shouting there, but all the time I was thinking of a green and beautiful estate away beyond the red tiles and church tops, and of the sweet and graceful girl who had stood with me in those same grounds last night and watched the fireworks. I cannot express the gloom that dropped upon me as I looked again and again at the diminishing town and the country that opened behind it as we drew

away, and thought that it was a thousand to one if ever I
met Miss Palmer again, and wondered how long a time
would elapse before I should gaze once more upon this
noble space of blue and golden scenery, the recollection of
which in my heart would be eternally associated with the
cordial, melodious, sweet-eyed Madeline.

Which of those three vessels in Cawsand Bay was *her*
ship? I wondered. They were all West Indiamen. In
truth, sentiment was making a perfect fool of me. I felt
that I should have been quite content to become Madeline's
ship's figurehead for the whole voyage to Jamaica merely
for the happiness of being in the vessel she was aboard of.
The duel, or rather the programme of it, had given my
mind so much occupation that my sentiment had fallen
into a mere smouldering condition; but it was forking up
into a blaze now that there was nothing particular to dis-
tract my thoughts from the contemplation of the girl I
might never see again.

Long before we were abreast of Cawsand the ropes had
been coiled down and the decks cleared, and a number of
seamen (like myself) were leaning over the bulwarks
watching the passing shores, or gazing moodily with their
faces turned toward Plymouth, where they too, in all probability, had been enjoying some ardent flirtations, though I
dare say their memory was busier with the grog-shops than
with the Sukeys and Salls who had sat on their knees.

"What are those vessels—West Indiamen?" said Shelvocke, coming to my side and pointing to the three ships
in the bay.

"I think they are, sir. Miss Palmer told me that the
ship she was to sail in for the West Indies had arrived off
Cawsand, and I suppose the three yonder are to make part
of a convoy."

He pulled out his watch with a very grave face, and
holding it in his hand, asked me if I knew the hour when
Lady Tempest's ball broke up.

"About four o'clock, sir," I answered, wondering at his
discursiveness.

"Say five-and-twenty minutes past four, Madison," said
he; "and that will make it exactly eight hours since you
bade good-by to your pretty partner. Is it possible," he

added, pocketing his watch, "that you remember her after all these hours?"

"My dear sir——" I expostulated.

"Madison," said he, "you're a wonder! What—a sailor remember a girl eight hours after he has left her! Why, man, do you know what you are doing? You are revolutionizing our choicest professional traditions. You will be leaving the Dibdinites nothing to rhyme about, and driving poor Ben Incledon, a man who has never injured you, off the stage! Lord help us, Madison! turn your quid and get rid of this longshore swash, or you'll be writing verses before you know where you are."

"I'll tell you what it is, captain," said I manfully: "you didn't dance with her, sir—you didn't see the sparkling of the fireworks in her eyes—you didn't take a moonlight stroll with her among the flowers. Must a night's rout end in battle, murder, and sudden death? Is duelling to take the place of dancing? When a man is asked to a ball, must he limit his enjoyments to the tweaking of surly naval captains' noses? Give me a beautiful companion, I say. Give me, in preference to arguments on naval manœuvring, impassioned murmurs up in a corner, white shoulders before epaulets, and a moonlit trance among lilies and roses before the cutting civilities of a conversation with a bloodthirsty second!"

"That will do, Madison. Rest your fame as a speaker of the highest order upon that, and say no more. But, doubt my good-nature as much as you please, I do now freely admit that I *did* snatch a horrid enjoyment from the browbeating I gave the surly Monk." That we shall fight yet, I do not doubt, unless another fit of apoplexy comes between us. It is high time that we merchantmen vindicated our titles as gentlemen and seamen from the contemptuous usage every little snobling in blue cloth and bright buttons thinks himself privileged to give us. When there is a storm, cannot we meet it? When we are in danger, cannot we brave it? When we are confronted by an enemy, do we wince? Is not the mercantile officer as good a seaman as his cocked-hat despiser? Is not he sometimes a handsome man and a fine fellow? Play to him, will he not dance? Pipe to him, will he not pull and haul? Is not he beloved of sweet women? Rogues! if you say we are not like you in the rest, we will resemble you in that."

" Worthy of Kemble!"

We were soon clear of Rame Head, with the blue waters of the English Channel stretching before us, and after our three weeks' spell of the ground-tackle, it was almost strange to feel the heave of the sea under our feet. It was a pleasant day, the wind cooled the sunbeams, and over-head was the finest sky I ever beheld; the high clouds lay in fine white veins—portions resembled lace—from east to west stretched this lovely exhibition of vapor; indeed, it was like looking up at a dome of marble. The blue lay with a lovely softness of color amid this vaporous spray; and when I called Shelvocke's attention to the beautiful appearance, he was so much struck that he stood gazing like a man before a picture.

By dinner-time we had run the coast into a mere shadow. The men had been mustered and divided into watches, and our sea-life was fairly commenced.

"After all, gentlemen!" exclaimed Shelvocke, address-ing Chestree, and myself, and young Peacock (who had been asked to dinner), as we took our places at the table— which the steward had equipped with flowers, and which was as radiant as a looking-glass with the flashing of the sun's rays through the skylight upon the plate and glass, and purple and yellow wines in decanters—" there is more real happiness to be got at sea by the poorest sailor, than can be purchased ashore by the wealthiest lord. Madison, a little of this soup? First of all, there are no women to tease him. His sleep is never broken by the cries of a baby. There is no post. There are no tradesmen to vex him with their trifling accounts. Steward, some bread for Mr. Peacock. Money is of no use at sea. There are no shops—there is nothing to buy. Then again, there are no troublesome next-door neighbors. And best of all, there is no news."

"And a man needn't shave unless he pleases," said Ches-tree.

"And besides, sir, where are you going to get this beau-tiful buoyant, up-and-down feeling ashore?" exclaimed

Peacock, half closing one of his handsome eyes, and looking with the other through a glass of sherry at Shelvocke. "I never seem to walk comfortably on dry land. There is no spring in the earth."

"Try dancing," said I.

"Even then it's like having your boots soled with lead, sir."

"Give me dry land," observed I. "The sea is very well; but put me where I can humor my artless fancies, gentlemen. I will at this moment pawn all the privileges the captain's prodigal and beneficent sea yields the humble sailor for a cottage and an acre of land—just out of Plymouth; a cow; enough hens to give me as many eggs as will garnish two rashers of bacon of mine own curing, and make me every day a pudding; a ten-ton yacht to scour the Sound, and——" the rest was lost in an irrepressible gape, for which I immediately apologized. "We have neither of us been in bed, you know, captain, since the night before last."

Here Tapping's head darkened the skylight.

"There's a sail right ahead, sir, coming down upon us."

"All right, Mr. Tapping. Get your colors ready for hoisting," said Shelvocke. "Madison, your yawn interrupted your sylvan discourse; your cottage and your cows and your hens are very well, but who's going to cook your bacon and make your puddings?"

"A proper little maid, sir; wages ten pounds a year, and cold meat on Sundays to enable her to go to chapel," I replied, perfectly understanding the twinkle in his eye.

"Mr. Chestree, try a glass of that port," said Shelvocke, who was in high spirits. "Pray, my friend—forgive my inquisitiveness—were you ever in love?"

The second mate's face looked like the rising moon on a hot summer night, as he answered in a sort of cracked voice that made Peacock burst into a laugh, "Once, sir."

"Only once!—surely you forget?"

"No, sir; on my honor, only once," repeated Chestree, with great gravity.

"Did you marry her, Mr. Chestree?" I asked.

"No, Mr. Madison," answered Chestree, who was an extremely literal person, and the most accurate man in his

statements that ever I met; "I didn't fall in love with her
with the intention of getting married, but for the sake of
having somebody to keep company with when I was ashore."

"That was a very unsettled view of life on your part, Mr.
Chestree," said Shelvocke. "Had she a mother?"

"No, sir; she hadn't a mother, but she had a father. I
lodged in his house, and that was how I got acquainted
with the girl. He was a wooden-legged man, and very
often in liquor. He lived in Limehouse, sir, and kept a
toy-shop. When he was drunk, his behavior was extraordinary. Imagine, sir—it was his habit, when he got intoxicated of a night, to go into his shop and wind up all
the spring toys and set them running about the floor. He
dealt largely in that kind of goods. He would fling the
Indian-rubber balls and dolls against the walls, set the tops
spinning, wag the babies' rattles; in fact, he'd start everything that made a noise, sir—cursing and swearing himself
all the time at the top of his voice, and rolling among the
hoops, boxes of soldiers, and the tambourines. The louder
I'd knock overhead, the more things he'd set going. I
put up with him as long as I could for the girl's sake, but
I was driven away at last, and you'll hardly believe me,
Mr. Madison, when I say that the moment I shifted my
lodgings the trollop passed me in the street as though I had
been a mile-post."

"A rent in the affections," said I.

"A week's rent," exclaimed Shelvocke. "A fine com-
mentary on tearing a passion into tatters."

"She came to tatters at last, sir, I believe," said Chestree; "for her father destroyed so many of his toys that at
last he had nothing to sell. They locked him up for debt,
and Susan went to—" He checked himself, drained his
wineglass, and stared at Peacock.

"Pray, Captain Shelvocke," said I, smothering another
yawn, "might I be so bold as to ask where the *Tigress* is
bound to?"

"Certainly. I intend skirting the French coast as far as
d'Oléron, and then head for the West Indies. But how is
it possible for privateersmen to have a programme? To-
morrow may see us burnt, or sunk, or captured or—a live-
lier fancy—convoying a noble prize back to that very

Plymouth you, Madison, are fretting over. By the way, did not I understand you to say that Miss Palmer is going to Jamaica?"

"Yes," said I, blushing a little in anticipation of some banter.

"And did you not endeavor to dissuade her by a picture, such as your active and amorous genius should very well know how to paint, of that hobgoblin the Yellow Jack, the Jamaica Charon, the fugleman of the noisome battalion of snakes, mosquitoes, bats, blood-suckers of many kinds, sharks, guanos, negroes, and Yankee skippers? But no matter. Fill your glass—and you and I, as eye-witnesses of her beauty, will privately and in elegant silence toast her. That she and you may meet again I ought not to hope: the feelings of a friend should prompt the heart to kinder aspiration; but still, here's to your wish, Madison— as the good old song says:

> "Here's to your wish! let it run as it will, boy!
> Bad it *can't* be, as it makes us both fill, boy!"

Honest Chestree stared at all this, for neither he nor I had ever seen Shelvocke in such good spirits. No doubt the excitement of the night, the release from an engagement which the braver a man is the gladder he will be to get easily and honorably quit of, and the glee which the prospects of a new cruise raised in him, caused his present overflow. Be this as it may, I never liked him in any mood better than in this. His freedom gave no offence. The kindness that underlay his joking was always apparent, and the worst-tempered wretch that an enlarged spleen and a congested liver ever exacerbated would have been soothed into blandness by Shelvocke's hearty ringing laugh.

Tapping's pugnacious face again darkened the skylight.

"Please, sir, the fellow ahead is a line-of-battle ship. She's either lost or struck her topgallant masts."

"How far distant is she?"

"About three miles."

"All right, Mr. Tapping; I'll come and look at her presently. What a very odd language sailors talk, Mr. Chestree. Did you hear Tapping speak of the *fellow* ahead, and call him *she?*"

"Well, sir, now that you call attention to the contradiction, I see it, captain. But what is a man to say? They corrupted the sex of ships when they called Government vessels men-of-war. You might as well christen a baby-girl Bill."

"Very true, Mr. Chestree. Gentlemen, if you have finished your wine, we will go on deck."

I was excessively sleepy, and the *Tigress'* sherry had not lightened my eyelids. However, I thought I would take a squint at the liner before lying down, and followed the others on deck. The breeze had slackened somewhat, and the schooner was slipping through the water with the quick, sinister, piratical, and sneaking motion that was one of her distinctest qualities. The sail was right ahead, and looked like a wreck under her double-reefed topsails and thick topmast heads.

She was a very large line-of-battle ship, with three tiers of ports, the lower ones of which were closed; and our impression was that she had been partially dismantled by a gale of wind, until she was near enough to show a whole constellation of shot-holes in her bulwarks, her yards and masts fished in numerous places, her lower rigging knotted, and many other signs of a recent severe engagement. The most noticeable thing about her was the streams of bright water spouting from her sides, and trailing their lines of foam upon the sea as she went slowly, and wearily, and heavily forward.

I once witnessed a prize-fight, and watched two muscular savages pound each other for an hour and a quarter. It was a disgusting sight; but no part of the ferocious and unnatural exhibition impressed me more than the appearance of the victor after his blue, and blind, and bleeding opponent had been carried away. The skin of the conqueror's face was in rags, one eye was hermetically sealed, one arm broken: nevertheless, he made shift to flourish a large white and red pocket-handkerchief; and with a hoarse, spluttering cheer in his throat, the wretched creature staggered round the platform to let his backers see how gamely he endured his punishment.

The recollection of this maimed and heroic—brutally heroic, no doubt, but still heroic—figure was in my mind as I watched the battered, splintered, leaking, patched-up line-of-battle ship go past us, with English colors at the peak, and the water rushing from her scupper-holes under the action of the pumps like the gutters of a house after a thunder-shower. She appealed to us as a human being might: it was the courage of the broken and mutilated prize-fighter waving his handkerchief, and limping to his home; but how ennobled the picture by the character of the tremendous struggle that had driven this sinking and injured ship to the refuge of her own ports! We lowered our ensign, and in obedience to a signal from Shelvocke, every seaman on deck sprang into the rigging, and gave the ship three hurricane cheers. An officer with his arm in a sling responded by raising his hat, but no other notice was taken of us.

"Is she one of the Channel squadron, I wonder?" said Shelvocke, watching her with great interest. "If so, there has probably been a general engagement, perhaps off Finisterre, where our fleet were last heard of. Mark how she lifts to the swell! Saw you ever such sickly rolling before? She must be half full of water, and it is strange there is no tender in company. I would not undertake to navigate a vessel in that condition twenty leagues."

Her rolling was made all the more impressive by the swell being very light; she swayed to and fro like a round-bottom vessel, that, being depressed on one side, continues its oscillations for a long time in the smoothest water. I stood watching her until she was a long way astern, and then went to my cabin and slept for four hours like a top.

And now for the space of a fortnight not a single adventure of any kind befell us. It seemed as if all the luck that was to attend the *Tigress* had been squeezed into the first few days of her cruise, and that nothing more was to happen. We sailed along the coast of France as close in as we dared venture, and on one occasion were so well inshore —this was off the Pointe de Penmarch—that we could see a number of soldiers and villagers looking at us from the top of the cliffs, and a French man-of-war at anchor in the bay that opens the river upon or near which the town of Quimper is situated.

Indeed, our audacity grew with our disappointments, and I have often thought over the hundred chances we gave the enemy of capturing us. The truth was, the numerous reverses that France had suffered at sea had almost emptied the ocean of her merchantmen. I believe half the privateers would have given up this year had we been concerned in no other than the French war. Two-thirds and perhaps more of the merchandise of France were being carried in neutral bottoms, and, as Shelvocke had all along said, referring of course exclusively to France, the only chances which the English Channel offered to privateers were recaptures like the *Hanover*, or the inglorious sport of hunting down small craft like the lugger we chased and sank between Dunkirk and the Goodwins.

At last came a morning when Shelvocke's patience gave way. The Vendee coast was a clear green, and brown, and white-streaked outline on our port-beam; a fresh breeze was blowing over our port quarter, and the schooner was chopping slowly through the surges which ran way ahead of us in burnished surfaces a short distance before they broke into sheets of sparkling foam, under her mainsail and jib only.

"Look around you, Madison," exclaimed Shelvocke; "was there ever such a wilderness! There is not a sixpenny bit to be found in these seas. Will any man believe that this schooner has been coasting the best-armed of the French seaboards without encountering a single vessel of any kind or description?"

"Ay, and without provoking a single Government ship to come out and have a closer look at her."

"Where are the English blockaders, I wonder? where is the Channel squadron? A month ago I know that the offing for leagues swarmed with our cruisers. Has peace been signed? Why, this is worse than Churchill's Scotchmen feeding

"'Like half-starved spiders upon half-starved flies.'

There is not even cold porridge for us here."

He shaded his eyes with his hands, and bent a steady, scrutinizing look upon the French coast and away around upon the sea-line.

"Not even a fishing-smack," he said. "And the men are spoiling. All their old merchant-service instincts are budding upon them like funguses upon trees. They'll lose their taste for fighting if this lasts, and will forget how to load a gun. See their idle, sprawling postures, like the boatmen of a fashionable watering-place."

He made a few quick turns along the deck.

"I have had enough of it," he exclaimed. "It's time to give the Yankees a turn. So get all sail made, Mr. Madison. Helm, there! let her go round, and keep her at southwest!"

"Make sail, the watch!" I shouted. "Crack on all, men! Jump aloft and loose the square canvas—every stitch of it!"

In a moment all was bustle. The great mainsail jibed as the schooner swept round on the port-tack; the froth spat and buzzed alongside: as cloth after cloth was extended to the strong breeze, the slope of the deck grew a sharper angle. Presently the schooner was a lofty, broad, and beautifully symmetrical surface of canvas, the little snow-white skysail topping the great column of canvas forward, the jibs curving from the jibbooms, the mainboom over the quarter. The rush of the vessel was felt in the thrilling of the deck, and with a mile of silver-bright wake astern of her, and the smoke and flashing of spray across the forecastle, the *Tigress* fled across the heaving waters of the Bay of Biscay for the great Atlantic deep beyond.

"Where away now in such a hurry, sir?" asked Tapping.

"For the West Indies—the latitudes of rich freights, man!" I answered; and in a few minutes the news that we were bound for a long stretch of salt water was all over the schooner.

# CHAPTER X.

THE morning of the first of September broke with a
lowering and gloomy sky. We had left the coast of France
a long distance astern of us, but from a privateersman's
wish to make a beam-wind of the northeast trades when
we should have run into them, and with the hope of netting
one of the numerous contraband Guineamen crossing the
Atlantic for the Spanish Main, or some of the French Indiamen homeward bound, Shelvocke had made a much more
southerly course than was necessary for the run to the West
Indies.

All through the night it had been so sultry as to drive
the men out of their hammocks under the decks, and force
them to take their rest alongside the guns and under the
boats, where they were kept rather uncomfortably cool by
the showers of dew which fell from the sails, and by the
humidity of the air that whitened the rigging and the fife-
rails and every other part of the vessel where the damp
lodged in lines, with millions of crystal globules which
streamed away in water on being touched.

I was on deck when the sun rose, and could scarcely
credit that the bleared, rayless, reddish disc that was hove
out of the broken and swelling deep was the familiar day
luminary. The sea was a dark, sallow-green heaving plain,
of this one gloomy and ugly color on all sides, not a break
of froth to relieve the menacing monotony of its stormy and
chafing aspect. The sky was a mere space of leaden gray,
like the sea, unbroken by a single point of light or relieved
by the shadow of darker clouds; in a corner of which hung
the newly risen sun, like a reddish ground-glass globe over
a dull argand, shedding a trickling reflection, as pale as the
light of a crescent November moon, on the sickly green

swell beneath it. There was a small draught of wind blowing from the east, but every roll of the schooner shook the
current of air out of the sails, and the tumblification was
sometimes so furious that we had to hold on with our hands
to save ourselves from being dashed from one side of the
deck to the other. The water burst through the scupper-
holes in smoke, and poured through the hawse-holes as the
vessel pitched, and washed high as the keel of the gig over
the stern. One moment you could have touched the water
over the taffrail, the next it was like looking down from
the top of a mountain. Men who had been to sea all their
lives, and to whom a jumping deck offered a securer footing than the steadiness of the land, went sprawling in all
directions, the moment they let go with their hands.

I had noticed Tapping uncommonly pale, but could not
conceive the cause until the *Tigress* giving a courtesy that
dished a green sea over the forecastle, and sent a number of
fellows racing aft, rolling and blowing, and laughing, and
shaking themselves, as they rushed floundering into the
waist, I was amazed to see my friend dart to the lee bulwarks, giving me, as he ran, a most woebegone glance with
his bilious, bloodshot eyes, over which he hung as sick as
a Frenchman, and like a Frenchman, groaning and convulsing his body, and taking a squint along the deck, first on
one side, and then on the other, every time he sacrificed, to
see if anybody was watching him.

The strain aloft, however, was getting rather more than
I thought good; so I ordered the main topmast to be struck,
and not having great confidence in our own new hemp, I
had the lower rigging swiftered; the mainsail was then
lowered, as it was of no use, and bade fair to chafe to
pieces, and the schooner was left to tumble about under her
jib and gaff-foresail.

And, indeed, it was the most uncomfortable experience of
the kind she had yet given us. Tapping was not the only
man she had nauseated. The cook was too sick to attend
to his duty, and the only thing hot we were promised for
the cabin breakfast was coffee; but even this small luxury
was denied us by the cook falling head over heels down the
companion-ladder with the coffee-pot in his hand. So we
had to make out a meal with cold grog and a piece of salted

brisket, and a mighty unpleasant meal it was. The ledge of the table saved the plates from sliding on to the deck, but there was nothing to prevent the contents of one's plate from rolling into one's lap; and after forking up for a fifth time a piece of beef from between my knees, I begged Shelvocke to excuse me from using a knife and fork any longer, and finished the meal with a bit of beef in one hand, and a biscuit in the other.

"Now," said I, as Chestree crawled from under the table with the mustard-pot, that had fetched away down his legs on to the cabin floor, decorating his unmentionables in its passage with a very tidy streak, as you may believe, "will any gentleman sneer at the preference I ventured to express at this same table some time ago, for a garden and a cottage ashore, to a heaving, sickening, muddling, tumbling, however beautifully constructed, machine like this schooner, that sends Tapping to hang his face over the side, and starts Chestree to crawl upon his knees after the breakfast things?"

"I have always looked for a dance of this kind whenever old Neptune took a fancy for a frisk with the beauty whose home is his bosom—there's a passage in your line, Madison!" said Shelvocke. "But how can any vessel of this tonnage help rolling with such a top-hamper of iron as grins along our decks? Go and build a tower atop of your little cottage, and I'll warrant you the first gale of wind will hoist you out of your bed, and make you hungry for the safety of the sea."

"Do but listen to the groaning of the timbers, captain!" cried Chestree. "If one will but think of it, sir, man must be a courageous animal to build a hollow ark and sit in the midst of the sea, and eat and drink and joke. You would not catch a beast of the field adventuring such an exploit, sir."

"Excuse me, Mr. Chestree, there is a large blob of mustard on the front of your shirt. Well, Mr. Madison, how is this going to end? In a gale, do you think?"

"I do, captain. As you judge of a man's temper by the expression in his eye, so I look at the sun to observe what sort of a mood nature's in. That bleared bloodshot orb shows that nature's in a rage. Feel the panting of her mighty breast under us, sir. Chestree, kindly catch my glass before it capsizes over you."

"Where can this abominable swell be coming from?" exclaimed Shelvocke. "Either there must be a tempest close to us or a storm has very recently passed. It's as bad as one of the lulls off Cape Horn."

The motion was made more impressive—I had almost written startling—by the uproar it occasioned throughout the vessel, and which we in the cabin could hear to perfection. The swell, as it struck the schooner under the counter, boomed through the hollow fabric as though a thirty-two pounder had been fired under our feet, and one of these swells hove us up to such a height that every movable article on the table went clattering and jingling away to the foremost end of it, and while the three of us swung with our arms round the stanchions like drunken lords to lamp-posts, Shelvocke bawled out:

"Madison, you can now understand what Gulliver felt when the eagle flew away with the poor little chap's cage!"

The bulkheads strained as though they must burst asunder; every timber, every plank, every bolt had something to say on the subject of this crazy, walloping usage, and the small arms rattled like a regiment of charging dragoons in the rack against the foremost partition. Indeed, it was like being rolled down a hill in a barrel into which a bucket of oyster-shells had been flung.

I was not sorry when Shelvocke left the table. However, instead of following him on deck, I entered my berth, as it was my watch below, and I was too old a seabird not to turn in while there was a chance of getting some rest, more especially in the face of a storm that threatened us with a long spell of wakefulness. And, indeed, I do believe that only a sailor or a baby could have slept amid such an uproar of groaning beams and thumping and booming water as filled the cabin. I left my door open ready for the first call, and lay down in my boots; and in a short time was, I dare say, contributing to the general hullabaloo.

A loud cry sounding through the skylight aroused me. I heard the whistling of the boatswain's pipe and the running about of men. I looked at my watch and found I had been asleep an hour and a quarter; but it was so dark I had to bring the watch close to my nose before I could read the dial. The motion of the schooner was much less violent than it had been when I lay down, also it was evident to me that there was no wind, though the activity of the watch on deck betokened a change of some sort at hand.

Considering that it was ten o'clock in the morning, the evening gloom that prevailed was not a little ominous and alarming. It was like an eclipse of the sun, and though the watch below had received no summons, I tumbled out of my bunk and went on deck.

Never before in all my life had I witnessed such a sight as it was now my fortune to behold. Stretched across the whole surface of the sky lay a dense, dark cloud, the malignant bluish hue of which as much resembled a quantity of ink smeared across a sheet of paper with a brush as anything I can imagine to liken it to. But this was only the canvas or ground upon which nature had worked a most terrific piece of cloud tapestry. Right round the horizon was stretched what sailors would call a "grummet" of sooty vapor—dense, motionless—like some gigantic chimney's outpouring that had settled low upon the sea, and choked out of the heavens the very air that should have scattered it. But in the east there hung, as though poised upon the upper line of this horrible inky circle, layer upon layer of huge clouds, each layer overhanging the other like the scales of old armor, the lower tiers being of a blackness that projected, by the sheer relief of the contrast of hue, the portion of the sooty vapor upon which they leaned their ponderous and dreadful burdens. Under this sky, the awful character of which no pen could express—for what language could convey that *reactive* quality which informed it with its peculiar horror, the awe, the amazement it excited in the mind, the shock that the first sight of it gave to the nerves?—under this sky, I say, the sea lay as dark as you shall have beheld it in the twilight, the horizon swallowed up in the gloom and the haze, so that the schooner appeared to be heaving on a small surface of water in the interior of a globe of cloud.

Such indeed was the darkness that the eye could not follow the run of the swell above half a mile distant from the vessel. Every stitch of canvas had been furled with the

16

exception of the close-reefed gaff-foresail, and the men were employed in snugging the decks, hauling taut the running rigging, looking to the gun-lashings, and making every preparation for the coming tempest. I particularly noticed the manner in which they glanced up at the sky and in the direction of the ponderous cloud-layers. Probably no man among them had ever witnessed such a sight; and now that no more running about was necessary, their subdued manner, their alarmed faces, their voices toned into awed whispers, exhibited with singular impressiveness the influence of the portentous heavens upon them.

"Did any one ever see such a sight before?" said Shelvocke, who had noticed me the moment I came on deck, and now joined me. "I hope it may not cost us our guns. I thought at first it would end in rain; but the gathering of that ring, and above all the upheaval of those giant clouds yonder, undeceived me. That black, horizontal circle is a real phenomenon. It has taken a whole hour to gather; but for the last ten minutes, and even longer, it has not risen, I was going to say, an inch. We are in the centre of a regular belt. I believed it an atmospheric illusion while watching it at the beginning. There must have been a swirl of wind to have caused it; yet for the last hour it has been a dead calm here."

"It has given us time, sir, and we are ready for it. That's one good job. But it's enough to quail a man. Do you notice the cowering attitudes of the crew, sir? The worst of this sort of thing is, you never can tell what's coming."

"Imagine a battle like Trafalgar amid this gloom!" exclaimed Shelvocke. "See!" he added, as a flash of lightning sparked out from the lower strata of the piled-up clouds and glanced a dull blue glare across the sky, "there's the first gun of a bigger engagement than human enemies are ever likely to be concerned in."

Presently the boom of thunder came down slow and faint. It grew gradually darker and darker; it was impossible to trace the masts to their topmost points; the binnacle lamp was lighted, and the candle flame threw a haze upon the air just as it did at night. The watch below had turned out alarmed by this Egyptian darkness, and blackened the decks with their figures as they stood whispering or shuffled uneasily from place to place.

It is bad enough on land to find one's self under a dense thunder-cloud and waiting for the first flash. At sea the suspense is increased out of all comparison by the feeling that one's vessel is, perhaps, the only point upon the ocean for leagues and leagues for the lightning to aim at. When I first went to sea, the ship I was in was becalmed one afternoon in the Bay of Bengal, in company with a small trading vessel. A storm gathered, there was a fierce flash of lightning, almost simultaneously followed by an explosion—the whole air seemed to be filled with live embers—and then came a crash of thunder as though heaven were echoing back the deafening explosion of the country-wallah. Such fatalities are, happily, rare; but I had witnessed one of them at a time of life when the impressions a man gets are usually deep and lasting, and I viewed with uncomfortable misgivings these sooty, stooping, overburdened masses of vapor, and the early night their shadows had flung upon sea and sky.

"Is that you, Mr. Madison?" exclaimed Shelvocke, who had walked aft and stood near the binnacle.

"Yes, sir."

"Call all hands."

"All hands are on deck, sir."

"Then get the hatches on, and stand by to let the lee-foremast and aftermost broadside guns go overboard should the order be necessary."

These were significant instructions. The hatches were battened, and hands told off to stand by the guns. And now we had not long to wait.

First came the rain; it plumped down as though a travelling waterfall had taken us on its way. The suddenness and weight of the downpour were astounding, and the noise of the gushing and cascading and sluicing of water was as bad as half a dozen great cataracts. A blinding flash of lightning streamed across this water veil and made hail of it, which pounded and hammered and beat down upon us as though buckets of grape and canister were being emptied on our devoted heads. The roaring of this fall was scarcely silenced by the peal of thunder that crashed immediately over us, and the lashed sea looked like snow under the fierce and shattering discharge.

This ceased with the same alarming suddenness with which it had begun, and the moment I could squeeze the water out of my eyes and look about me, I saw the wind coming. There was no need to sing out, for every eye was upon it. The sea was like molten lead everywhere but in the east, where the horizon appeared to be lifted into a bluish-white ridge, immediately over which the black clouds were twisting and flying like the rushing and eddying of a ship's wake, or a fierce current full of whirlpools; while to right and left of these tumultuous vaporous masses there was an opening, not indeed of blue sky, but of the sky as it appears when discolored by a thin body of smoke, through each of which, but for a brief while only, and travelling toward us like the spoke of a revolving wheel, there slanted a sickly, yellow, unearthly looking sunbeam, the light of which seemed to blast the very water over which it fled. It was a glimpse, and merely a glimpse, of one of those spectacles of terrific, I had almost said supernatural, grandeur which a man must go to sea to behold. In an instant the tempest had changed the scene into a heaven of flying black vapor and streaming lightning, and an ocean as white as wool, the very swell of which was hurled flat by the fury of the blast, amid which lay the *Tigress*, with the mere shred of gaff-foresail she had exhibited in rags, her lee bulwarks under the foam, her lee fore-topmast rigging standing in circles like iron half-hoops, motionless upon the level froth; as you might paint a vessel stranded on her bilge on an Arctic plain of snow.

I had posted myself near Shelvocke, in order to receive his instructions, and we stood clinging to the backstays watching the behavior of the schooner. What angle her mast made I could not guess; but I know that for some time the foaming sea to leeward was up to the main-hatch, and the whole of the starboard guns and the bulwarks were out of sight under the water, and the men up to their necks.

And this, be it remembered, with no other canvas exhibited but the rags of the close-reefed gaff-foresail.

The helm was jammed hard over, and after an interval

the noble little vessel began to pay off, as though, like some creature of instinct, she had been willing to test the strength of her grappling enemy before running. I looked at Shelvocke as the schooner, in wearing, righted, and he shouted, "Magnificent!" And so it was, for had she been one jot less worthy, the hurricane would have had her on her beam-ends and her masts along the water with the first blast.

As her jibbooms swept around her decks became level, and with the water up to one's knees gushing overboard from every part of her, and her guns like polished jet with the wet, and huge flakes of spray flying over her stern and ripping through the rigging like a storm of snow, and the men clinging to whatever came to their hands with the conformation of their bodies ribbed and lined upon their soaking garments, the *Tigress* raced like an arrow along the seething surface of the deep, piling the foam as high as her catheads, while the hurricane yelled through her rigging and roared under the pitch-black sky that the lightning was tearing asunder from horizon to horizon.

"Get a new foresail bent," cried Shelvocke, with his mouth close to my ear, and shouting at the top of his voice, "and let us heave the schooner to before the sea rises."

I went forward to execute his orders, but at every step I took I had to seize hold of a belaying-pin, or a coil of rope, or a gun-tackle, to prevent myself from being dashed down upon the deck by the violence of the wind, and so prodigious was the propulsion of the hurricane, that it required my utmost strength to maintain a grasp of the object I seized. It was as though half a dozen men were endeavoring to thrust me forward, and by the time I reached the waist I was soaking with perspiration.

With incredible labor a new sail was reefed and bent, and a shred of it hoisted, and the schooner was brought to the wind, and lay with her lee-bulwarks buried, straining upon a sea that was every moment growing heavier, and almost hidden by the showers of spume which flashed like feathers over her. Meanwhile, the sky had grown a shade or two lighter, there was no more lightning, and the huge layers of clouds which had risen in the east had all gone away to leeward, and lay in a pitch-black pile upon the horizon.

But never had mortal eye beheld a wilder, stormier,

gloomier picture of warring winds and waters watched by a more scowling sky, than the scene that we surveyed from the deck of the *Tigress*. The seas had grown into livid coils as high and menacing as the combers which the westerly gales of the Pacific heave in thunder upon the shores of that mighty deep. Far as the eye could reach the ocean resembled a boiling caldron, and one could follow the huge lifting of the creaming surges against the leaden sky of the horizon. The schooner rode with wonderful buoyancy, with the most expert helmsmen aboard of her at the tiller; but ease her as they would, from time to time the head of a towering sea would strike her midway between the gangway and the bows, before she could lift to it, and whole tons of glittering green water would swoop through the rigging and fill the decks with a foamy current which the next heavy *send* to leeward would swirl like a cataract over the bulwark into the raging waves beyond.

I was standing holding on to a rope's end near the aftermost gun, listening to the hooting and roaring of the gale, and watching the frenzied ocean with awe and amazement, and contrasting man's physical littleness with the astounding genius that enabled him to live through, if not to defy, such a furious combination of powers as were now hurling their full and treacherous forces against us, when I was startled by a loud and fearful shout from a group of men who had secured themselves to the mainmast; and looking in the direction toward which they pointed, I was horrified to observe a large ship with her fore-topsail in rags, heading directly for us at a distance of not more than half a league.

Scarcely had my eye rested on her when another loud cry was raised, and the schooner soaring at that moment on the summit of a huge sea, I saw to the right and left of the approaching ship no less than eight large vessels, some of them close together, all of them tearing furiously before the gale.

"A convoy!" roared Shelvocke, who stood close behind me. "See! there's a line-of-battle ship—and look there! and there!" he pointed first toward the weather-bow, and then toward the weather-quarter, and sure enough at each point the water was studded with rushing ships, some barely visible in the distance, some stretching like clouds of smoke athwart of our hawse and away along the horizon astern. There were sixty or seventy of them; they looked as though the London Docks had fetched away, and the ships in them blown out to sea.

But no one thought of counting them then; no one thought of the wildly picturesque show they made. The great black ship that had been first sighted was swooping down toward us with the velocity of the very hurricane itself. She did not appear to see us, and as we watched her, utterly powerless to help ourselves, there was not a man who did not reckon that his life was to be counted by the few minutes which would pass before the ship struck us. The horror and danger of the hurricane were forgotten; we only thought of the ship that threatened to dash into and sink us.

I looked at Shelvocke. His eyes were on the vessel, and by the expression on his face I knew he not only expected the worst, but was ready for it. He had planted himself in one of those set, determined attitudes which resolute men will involuntarily fall into when a great danger is upon them; his teeth were locked—I could see that by the swell of the temple over the brow—his arms were tightly folded, and his right leg thrown forward.

In truth, there was nothing to be done; there was no time for the schooner to pay off even had we been willing to meet the certainty of our decks being swept and run the imminent hazard of the vessel foundering under our feet. The approaching ship upon which every eye was bent, and whose coming I watched with suspended breath, dashing the spray from my eyes as the raging wind hurled it against my face, was fully eight hundred tons in burden, with a high keen stem that divided the water into two hills of foam, each as high as her forecastle-rail; and every time her stern sank and her bows were hove up, I could see the copper, streaming with white lacings of spray, down to her forefoot; and then the whole broad, black, and massive hull would disappear behind a great sea, and nothing be visible but her masts and her long black yards, which swung from side to side as the gale struck the slackly braced spars on one yardarm and then on the other, while I could hear the flogging of her torn topsail sounding like an endless succession of musket-firing; and in a few moments up she would be hove again, thrown toward the scowling heaven like a little toy upon the summit of a sea, until the whole fabric seemed to be flung out of water, and we looked up at her with white faces as pinioned men would gaze at some nodding rock about to fall upon them from a mountain-top.

Some of the seamen who crowded the waist shrieked; some of them pulled off their boots and coats; some watched and waited with stony faces; some, as I imagined, as if calculating their chances should they leap for her bow.

I turned again to look at Shelvocke; he tossed his hands with a wild dramatic gesture. The motion instantly sent my eyes toward the ship, and I saw that she had shifted her helm, and that, although she was almost aboard of us, she would clear us.

I sprang on to the bulwarks, defying the hurricane, holding on with both arms round a backstay, and watched her go by. There is no describing in words the impression her passage produced. She was half as lofty again as we, and she swept past our stern like a huge floating tower in a haze of spray and froth, lifting when she was broadside on to our counter, so that we looked up her sides as people on a beach look up a cliff, passing so close to us that she hove half her bow wave over our taffrail, that swept the men at the tiller off their feet, grazing our main-boom with her fore-channel, and carrying away our peak signal halliards with her cross-jack yardarm. Her decks might have been crowded with people for all we knew, but her bulwarks hid every-thing, and not a human being was visible. Her gun-ports were closed, her boats slewed inboard, her running rigging as slack as a watchguard; the hooting of the hurricane among the ropes was deafening; but it was just a furious rush, and the thing was over; it was like seeing a cartload of snow flash from the housetop past the window through which you are looking.

Scarcely had she travelled six times the distance of her own length, when she put her helm down with the intention of heaving to. I got off the bulwarks, and, crouching under their shelter, watched her. She was obviously acting in obedience to a signal from the line-of-battle ship, who had rounded to, and whose example many of the vessels were following, though others, whether from helplessness or fear of broaching to, swept wildly on, and were one after another swallowed up in the spray and gloom of the near horizon. As her broadside came up to the wind, she lay over to such a degree that I shouted to Shelvocke she was foundering. The enormous seas which were now running swept over her as though she had been a rock. Every time the surges swung up giddily into the air I could see the hull of her exposed to within a few streaks of her keel. I believe that her cargo had shifted, for her lee lower yardarms were in the water, and she appeared to have no more buoyancy than a water-logged vessel.

Meanwhile, astern and to windward there was to be seen such a sight as few men have had the fortune to behold. The whole ocean, all that way, was covered by vessels of various rigs and sizes—ships, brigs, snows, tartans, schooners, pinks—hove to, some under storm staysails, some under bare poles, some with shreds of canvas streaming from the jackstays. The line-of-battle ship was astern of us; near her were two large Indiamen; abreast of us was a small frigate, and beyond, a whole squadron of vessels, wildly plunging upon the foaming seas, some being buried while others were hurled toward the sky, every vessel shrouded from time to time in vast veils of spray, a few of them going to pieces aloft, and two with the English ensign jack down in the rigging. It was enough to scare a man to see all these ships appearing on a sudden amid a raging surface upon which our schooner was the only visible object a few minutes ago.

"I never remember a worse hurricane than this," cried Shelvocke, squatting alongside of me under the bulwarks, in which position we were not only sheltered from the weather, but could command a windward view through the gun-port near which we crouched, as well as survey the whole scene to leeward. "These surely must be the May convoy from China and the East, or what should they be doing here? I fear that some of them are doomed ships."

"I thought we should have been the first to go just now, sir."

"Ay, there never was a narrower shave."

Sheltered as we were, yet such was the hellish hooting through the rigging and the roaring of the tempest through the sky—a sound as distinct from the other as a clap of thunder is from the moaning of wind through a window-casement—that we had to yell out our words to make each other hear; small wonder, therefore, that we did not talk much. Indeed our thoughts were engrossed in watching the behavior of the schooner and the movements of the numerous ships which, as if by a stroke of magic, had suddenly crowded the waters around us.

As for the *Tigress*, she rose and fell like a cork, scaling the watery acclivities as a sleeping albatross would, and freeing herself with an alertness that resembled the instinct of that bird from the falls of frothing water which, helped by the wind, ran faster than she could rise, and tumbled like a scattering of thunderbolts over the forward deck.

But the poor ship—she that had nearly run us down! She lay sheer on her beam-ends with the seas flying over her, as though she were stranded. Whether she was under-manned, or her people were lubbers, or consisted chiefly of Lascars, who at a time like this would, I knew from experience, be skulking and praying in corners, I could not guess; but apparently no efforts were made to right the vessel; the braces were slack, the hurricane had whipped the yards round, and as not only her royal-yards were crossed, but all her sails were very ill-stowed, the pressure aloft must have been enormous.

Presently a man swung himself into the mizzen-rigging, holding a small red ensign. Hardly had he reached the second ratline, when a sea struck the ship just under her mizzen-channel, and ran up to a height of twenty feet in a dark green, sparkling column before the wind dashed it into smoke. The man, clinging to the rigging, and looking more like a soaked rag than a human being, climbed another foot or two, and then attempted to seize the flag with the jack down to one of the shrouds; but he had no sooner secured one corner of the flag than the seizing gave way, the bunting flashed from his hand and was swept toward the clouds, resembling as it went a flash of fire.

"Why don't they cut away her masts?" roared Shelvocke.

"Why don't they cut away her masts?" roared Shelvocke.
"My God! she can't last another five minutes in that posture."
—*Page 250.*

"My God! she can't last another five minutes in that posture!"

As though the exclamation had been uttered on board the ship herself, he had hardly spoken when several men climbed, evidently with great difficulty, over the slanting, almost horizontal bulwarks, and got into the channels, where they fell to hacking and hewing the laniards of the shrouds and backstays. A blinding sea smothered the unhappy vessel; at the same moment her fore and mizzen topmasts broke short off under the topsail-yards, and hung with all their complicated hamper down the lower rigging. I looked for the men who had severed the rigging, but only two were struggling over the forward bulwarks, and the *main chains were empty.*

The ship righted a trifle, but not to the extent she should have done, and I was now sure that not only had her cargo shifted, but that she was taking in water fast. It was a sight to sicken the heart to see that she was doomed, to know that she must founder, and to feel that no help could be given her. It is bad enough to behold a vessel sinking under your guns, even mitigated as the sin of destroying human life is to your conscience at such a time by the intoxication of your triumph. But to witness in cold blood a noble ship struggling with a raging sea, gradually losing her buoyancy until she tosses with the inelastic action of a dead body, settling lower and lower until she suddenly vanishes, amid the ear-splitting yells of the mass of human beings congregated on her decks, is a spectacle calculated to give more anguish to the beholder than any other picture of human suffering.

Except the men who had scrambled into the chains, no living creature had been visible aboard of her, in consequence of her high bulwarks and her tremendous list, that probably huddled her people into the scuppers; but now that she was indubitably sinking, a sudden rush of figures blackened her rail to windward; they clustered like flies along her side, and, in spite of the gloom and the fog of flying spray, the figures of numerous women were clearly distinguishable. The shrieks of the poor creatures rang through the thunder of the hurricane; we could see their frantic gestures, the passionately lifted arms of the women,

the mad beckoning of the men for the help that could not
be given. Some scrambled aloft, some in tossing their
hands lost their balance, and fell headlong into the sea.
The wrecked mast, the yards swaying wildly with every roll
and harpooning the lee-side and shrouds of the ship; the
crowds of miserable creatures raving and motioning upon
the bulwarks of the hull whose staggering movements were
like the reeling of a drunken man; the ceaseless pouring of
the surges over her in whole acres of green water which
broke as they struck her decks, and were swept upward by
the hurricane in clouds of spray, like the stream of water
thrown upon a burning house, and the black heavens overhead, under which masses of sand-colored scud-like clouds
were driving with incredible velocity, and the mountainous,
seething, roaring waters like ink in contrast with the foam
of their breaking summits, formed such a picture of wild
devastation and enormous fury, as not the oldest seaman
among us could ever remember hearing or seeing the like of.

She had sunk by this time as deep as the thin white line
that ran under the gun-ports, and I was watching with a
wildly beating heart and difficult breath the blood-freezing,
the dismal, the most dismal spectacle of the crowds of men
and women motioning to us, and shrieking in their horror
as they stood, so to speak, on the very brink of the tremendous and appalling grave of boiling and roaring waters
that was opening under their feet, when a loud shout from
Shelvocke caused me to look to windward, where I beheld
a monster sea—the Mont Blanc of the liquid Alps around
us—a whole league long, as I should imagine, stooping its
emerald-green unbroken crest as though fearful of brushing
the sky, and rushing at us at the sped of a race-horse in
full career. The men had barely time to fling themselves
down upon their breasts under the weather bulwarks when
the schooner was on her beam-ends and running up the
watery steep. The sensation was that of being shot by an
irresistible power into the air—I mean, that one felt to be
disconnected altogether from the schooner, and to be soaring
alone through the gale. I never experienced anything like
it before nor since. The faculty of thinking was suspended;
one could only hold on with a kind of dull amaze, and listen
to the roaring and feel the mighty upheaval and the more

terrible sensation of sinking. At one moment, namely, when the schooner had been swept to the summit of this prodigious sea, she seemed to be revolving so as to bring her keel up; a plummet dropped from the port rail would have grounded on the starboard-rail; the deck was up and down like the side of a house; another instant and she was rushing down into the black and howling valley that was scooped out by this astonishing height of water, with her deck making a perpendicular line with the zenith in the other direction. It was incredible that any fabric made of human hands could have encountered such a wave and lived through it; yet such was our fortune, or such the buoyancy of the beautiful vessel, that she did not ship so much as a single drop of water, though assuredly had the gigantic sea *broken* before it reached us, we should have been overwhelmed, and in all probability gone to the bottom like a lump of lead.

I watched it as it rushed toward the ship; I saw the sodden helpless hull partially rise, as though making one struggle to let it pass under her. In an instant she was rolled completely over, and her copper bottom gleamed amid the ocean of foam that broke round and about her; the spray filled the air; there was just a glimpse of her dark spars lying aslant upon the water; the monstrous sea, uniting its mountainous green ridge again where it had been divided by the hull of the ship, rolled roaring along the sea, and its gigantic form might have been traced for miles. The great track of snow-white foam left behind was broken up by the hurling surges, which leaped into it like a band of wolves into a sheepfold. I thought I saw the hull of the ship glancing amid the hollows, but it was only the outline of a dark wave. The ocean all that way was a blank, and every vestige of the ship and her freight of human lives had vanished.

And now, as though this dreadful sacrifice had partially propitiated the storm-fiend, the heavens in the direction whence the hurricane blew lightened into a squalid sulphur color, and the horizon opened, but there was no lull in the wind; on the contrary it seemed to come with a new edge, a fresh spite. From time to time one of the windward vessels would put her helm up, and under a shred of canvas,

rush like an affrighted thing from the tremendous scene of
warring sea and dark sky, and vanish upon the waste of
hurling waters to leeward in a fog of foam. Most of the
large ships had suffered terribly; one was totally dismasted,
and in the most dire peril; another had only her foremast
standing; the line-of-battle ship had lost her foretopmast
and jibbooms. She lay about a quarter of a mile astern of
us, and there was something *sublime* in the spectacle of her
large hull soaring and vanishing, glancing through a storm
of spray as she was hove up, until she stood nakedly exposed
against the leaden sky, poised on the summit of a sea like
a ball balanced on a finger, and then sinking until nothing
could be seen but her topmasts sloping out of the pea-green
ridges heaped about her.

Strangely enough, the little vessels had proved the most
weatherly; only one of the eight or nine that I counted
appeared to have suffered aloft, and she could scarcely have
exceeded eighty tons. It was like watching a wherry. I
never should have believed it possible that any vessel could
be so flung about and live. Every time she vanished I could
have sworn she was gone for good, yet up she would come
again as regularly as a buoy.

A little after four bells in the afternoon this hurricane
began to slacken its fury; the sooty pall of cloud that was
stretched like a carpet across the whole surface of the visible heavens broke up into large masses of vapor with prim-
rose-colored patches between them, and anon narrow spaces
of watery-blue opened and let down hazy beams of sunshine
here and there, which touched the dark surface of the mountainous waters with a troubled yellow brightness. By four
o'clock the wind had decreased to a moderate gale, and a
quantities of smoke-like scud were sweeping under a blue
sky marbled with small prismatic oyster-shaped clouds,
which were moving slowly and bodily away to the northward, athwart the course of the gale, and through which
the windy sun was forcing his ardent beams and giving a
beautiful green sparkle to the tumbling seas, and a flashing
whiteness to their seething crests.

We hoisted a small English ensign to let the war-vessels
know our nationality, and watched the line-of-battle ship
repairing damages, and signalling to the convoy like a hen

calling around her the survivors of her brood after a hawk has been among them. As for the *Tigress*, she was in the same taut and uninjured condition as the hurricane had found her in; not a spar was sprained, not a rope had carried away; there was not an inch of water in the well; under a close-reefed foresail the noble little craft rose and fell upon the gradually subsiding seas, as sound in masts and hull as if she had just come out of dock, with the decks whitening in all directions as they were dried by the sun, and the crew busy clearing up, seeing to the guns, swabbing down the scuppers, opening the hatches, and so forth.

I stood with Shelvocke watching the vessels to windward.

"Madison," said he, "this will, I fear, prove a memorable gale. I should not like to be prevented from sleeping until I had counted in guineas the value in ships and goods that has gone to the bottom this blessed day."

"I would to God, captain," said I, "I had not seen that ship founder. The yell of her people will ring in my head to my dying day. It is a horrible trial to be obliged to helplessly watch one's fellow-creatures miserably perish."

"It is so; but is it not monstrous that men who will shudder over such a sight as we have witnessed would, without a single compunctious visiting of remorse, make a holocaust of whole shiploads of human beings merely because the ambition of one potentate thwarts or obstructs the ambition of another potentate? We are aghast at an act of God; we are horrified by the visitation of that Being in whose mercy we declare our faith upon our knees; but our own hellish wickedness, our own unnatural, fiendish cruelties we exult over—we crown—we behymn—we monumentalize!"

"My dear sir," I exclaimed, much astonished, "how, with these sentiments, can you have the heart to command a privateer—a vessel licensed by the authority of one of those potentates you name, whose ambition covers mankind with sin, to destroy, capture, burn, and the rest of it?"

"Because, young man, being born of woman, I am inconsistent, weak, vain, and insincere," he answered. "Besides, I am a sailor, and what the dickens have *I* to do with longshore moralities? The turn of a spoke just saved our lives when that foundered ship was rushing upon us.

What is the use of sentiment to men whose existence depends upon the angle described by a piece of timber? When that great sea took us, what premium do you suppose an insurance office would have charged you for a policy on your life? Could a diagram of the vessel as she hung on the crest of that Andean wave be submitted to some of your scientific bodies, not a member but would swear that she ought to have been upset, and that, instead of taking the liberty to discuss the subject, you and I should be making love to the Atlantic mermaids, some thousands of fathoms deep. Men who go about with a halter round their necks, which at any moment may be hauled taut, can't be bothered with philosophy. I am one of those who go where the devil drives. Sometimes I may try to sneak on a drag. Sometimes I may whip out a bit of morality and expose it as a man might a flag to show that he sails under honorable colors. But the devil keeps hold of the reins all the same; and it is in this fashion that a large number of us are going virtually to hell."

A flash, followed by a loud report.

"A gun from the liner, sir!" I exclaimed. "With whom is she parleying with those flags?"

Presently the frigate that lay abreast of us, but a long way off, replied to the signal. Then came another gun from the big ship, and more signals, which were evidently addressed to the merchantmen, for every vessel that had masts hoisted the answering pennant. The import of these signals was speedily shown by the various ships making sail: and a brave and handsome show they made, as in twos and threes they sheeted home the reefed canvas and came rolling and foaming toward us upon the swelling surges: the large Indiamen looking like men-of-war with their square yards and tiers of ports, and their lengths of white hammocks, and their tall poops and forecastles crowded with men, and the little craft toppling about like toy brigs and schooners, rolling their gunwales under water as they buzzed along, while the rays of the sun which streamed down in a mass of lateral lines, for all the world like a heavy shower of molten gold, and seemed to veer from one point of the compass to the other under the swarming of the flying scud, illuminated the various vessels in turns, kindling red fires in their glossy sides, and veining their masts with purple lines, and flashing up their decks like diamonds on a motioning hand, as the brass-work and skylights caught the rays, and making a perfect magic-lantern show of the windy, tumbling, and foaming scene, by the swift alternation of violent shadows and yellow brilliance.

The line-of-battle ship set her main-topsail and foresail, and advanced toward us with slow, ponderous, and lordly movements, as much as to say, "I have had my eye upon you, my friend, and take the first opportunity to have a better look at you." Nor was her curiosity unreasonable; in spite of the small ensign at her peak the *Tigress'* low, long, powerful, and heavily armed hull, and piratical sweep of spars, were hardly of a kind to reassure a commodore in charge of a rich and numerous convoy.

She approached us within pistol-shot, and was indeed so close that the recoil of a sea from her huge side sent a shower of spray over our quarterdeck. Groups of officers stood with glasses levelled at us, and gazing at them was like standing in the pit of a theatre and looking up at the gallery. I remember noticing her gigantic cutwater as she ploughed the green seas, curling an immense wave away from her with every plunge of her heavy, enormously thick bows, and the vast spread of her lower shrouds, terminating in tops as big as the floor of a room, and the little figures of the men who looked down at us from these platforms.

I thought they would hail us; but I suppose they reckoned us honest enough, and shifting her helm the huge fabric rolled away from us, in the direction pursued by the merchantmen, leaving the frigate to look after the injured ships.

"'Tis an ill wind that blows nobody any good," said Shelvocke, after sweeping the weather horizon with the glass. "Yet this hurricane would have been more obliging had it blown up any other convoy than an English one. However, get a reef shaken out of the foresail, Mr. Madison, and set the standing and inner jibs. The course is west sou'west."

In half an hour's time we were foaming along on the strong swell left by the hurricane, every vestige of the convoy vanished, a bright sun shining over our starboard bow,

17

and a heaven out of which the smoke-like scud had vanished, leaving instead a sky of brilliant, small white cloud flecked with orange in the west, and blue overhead, and violet in the east, as it arched toward the sea whose tossing surface seemed to have been purified into the most lovely and transparent green by the hurricane that had ravaged it.

# CHAPTER XI

"WHAT is all that smoke forward there, Mr. Tapping?" I sung out as I came on deck, after changing my wet clothes.

"It's the cook bothering with some damp wood over the galley fire, sir. I suppose you know the men haven't had any dinner?"

"Then that accounts for the odd sensation just here," said I, laying my hand on my waistcoat; "that has been bewildering me for the last two hours. Why, none of us have dined."

"No, sir, and the men are like wolves. It's a sight to see them sharpening their knives on the soles of their boots. I shouldn't like to be the cook if the water don't boil soon, sir."

I went up to Shelvocke, who was puffing a cigar with a thoughtful face, on the grating abaft the tiller, and asked him if he was aware that neither he nor any of the rest of us had tasted food since breakfast—nine dismal hours of abstinence?

"Upon my word!" he exclaimed, throwing his cigar overboard and jumping up, "the hurricane must have been strong indeed to blow the very appetite out of a man. Call the steward, Madison."

The man came on deck.

"What is there to eat, steward?"

"There's cold beef, sir, and cold 'am, and a piece of pickled pork——"

"No more words," interrupted Shelvocke. "Make the best show you can with the cold provender—we can't wait for the cook; and take my compliments to Mr. Corney and the third and forth mates, and say I shall be glad to see them to dinner."

The steward bustled off, and presently we were all pegging away at the substantial and plentiful sea fare that
loaded the table, while a boatswain's mate stumped the
quarterdeck in charge of the schooner.

But there was a gloom upon some of us that the wine,
freely bandied about as it was, could not lighten.  I wondered at the depression of my own spirits almost remorse-
fully, when I recalled the perils we had escaped and glanced
up and beheld the mild blue heaven beaming over the skylight, and the golden evening sunshine streaming in rays
upon the small-arms rack, and flashing in the musket-
barrels and cutlasses.

"You look as glum as a sick monkey, Madison," exclaimed Shelvocke.  "Are you still haunted by the spectacle
of that foundering ship?  One would suppose you had a
sweetheart aboard of her.  And you, Peacock, have you
seen a ghost that you sip your wine as solemnly as if you
were drinking to the memory of the dead?"

"There's nothing the matter with me, sir," answered
the handsome young fellow, rousing himself apparently
with an effort; but the unusually thoughtful and dejected
expression came into his face again a moment after, and he
fixed his large dark eyes dreamily upon the table.

"Captain, what state of mind ought a man to be in after
a narrow escape?" said Corney.  "Ought he to feel awed,
and wonder that such a rascal as he was thought worthy of
another chance of mending his life, or take his luck dispas-
sionately and conclude that his escape merely meant that
his time hadn't yet come?"

"Why, Mr. Corney, that will depend upon whether he's
a Christian or a Mussulman."

"But how ought a Christian to feel, captain?"

"My good sir, do you suppose that Great Britain sup-
ports four archbishops—Armagh counts for one, don't he,
Madison?—four archbishops I say, and a whole squadron
of dignitaries from London to Sodor and Man, that such a
question as yours shall be answered by the skipper of a
privateer?  Give me ten thousand a year and a palace, and
I'll engage to reply to your inquiries."

"What is meant by a narrow escape, I wonder?" observed
Chestree.

"When the toyman's daughter jilted you, that was a narrow escape for you or Susan," said I, feeling that I ought to say something. "You might have married her."

"Why, that's very true, Mr. Madison," responded Chestree gravely. "But was that a narrow escape because I *knew* it to be an escape, or would it have been a narrow escape whether I knew of it or *not?*"

"Good Lord!" cried Tapping, "what *do* you mean, sir?"

"Pray explain yourself, Chestree," exclaimed Shelvocke.

"As your proposition stands," said Corney, "it is the most unintelligible thing that has come to my ears since my first schoolmaster asked me if a bee was a fly, would a blue-bottle make honey."

"Why, really, gentlemen," said Chestree, blushing like a girl after staring at one and the other with his great mouth open like a newly landed cod, "what I said is extremely sensible. What *is* a narrow escape, I asked? For instance, here we are sitting in this cabin. At this very moment one of the boys may have wriggled himself into the powder magazine that is almost under our feet, and be skylarking among the cartridges with a lighted candle. A spark from the candle would blow us into smithereens, but the candle is accidentally extinguished, the boy sneaks away, and no harm is done. Is this a narrow escape, captain?"

"Of course it is."

"Whether we know it or not?"

"Certainly. What the deuce has your *knowledge* of the danger got to do with the risk you run?"

"But, good heavens, sir," pleaded Chestree, "at this rate every moment of our existence, more or less, involves a narrow escape. I am sent aloft; in my hurry I skip a ratline; had I footed that ratline, I should have tumbled overboard. But I got up and I come down safe, and I knew nothing of the risk I have run. Do you mean to call that a narrow escape?"

"If by taking that ratline you would have been thrown overboard, your skipping it would assuredly be a narrow escape."

"Whether I knew it or not?"

"Certainly," said Tapping.

Chestree drew a deep breath.

"It's no use, gentlemen; I see you don't understand me."

"You don't understand yourself," said Corney, wondering at the blockhead.

"You'll excuse me, Mr. Corney," replied Chestree, with a wandering eye, "but I hope you don't think, because I am not able to amputate a man's leg, that I'm an ass, sir?

"And I hope you don't imagine, because I *can* amputate a man's leg, that I'm unable to tell when a man talks nonsense, sir?" said Corney.

Shelvocke gave me a faint wink, and glanced at Peacock. I imagined that he was willing to encourage a quarrel between Corney and Chestree merely that it might awaken Peacock out of his melancholy. At least I knew the real, if furtive, interest he took in the lad, and his glance at him exactly conveyed the impression I have written.

"'Nonsense' is rather a strong term to apply to man's opinion, Mr. Corney," said I.

"What other word," replied Corney warmly, "will describe the reasoning of a person who says, in effect, When I pulled off my coat before going to bed, I found that somebody had chalked 'Fool' upon it; but so far as I was concerned, no such word was on my back until I pulled off my coat and read the word, because I didn't know it was there?"

"I think he has you there, Chestree," said Shelvocke. "That's a strong argument against Chestree, don't you think, Madison?"

"Strong for its impertinence, sir; but as a piece of reasoning not worth *that!*" shouted Chestree, with a loud snap of his fingers.

"Oh, pray don't talk of impertinence, Mr. Chestree!" exclaimed Corney, rather hysterically, and cocking his nose in the air, with the nostrils working like a pair of bellows. "The man who sneers at a gentleman's profession isn't the right kind of individual to speak of impertinence. Impertinence!" he continued, warming up, with Chestree's reference to the amputation of legs evidently rankling; "why don't Mr. Chestree refute me, captain? My idea of the word 'fool'——"

"*Your* idea of the word 'fool'! *My* idea of the word

'fool,' you mean, sir!" shouted Chestree. "Ask me for a definition of that word, my young friend, and no living artist shall give you a neater portrait of yourself than I will."

"Gentlemen, gentlemen!" interposed Shelvocke; "not so personal, please."

"Captain Shelvocke!" exclaimed Corney, "I desire, sir, to take this opportunity, in the presence of the commander and officers of this schooner, of stating that in my opinion Mr. Chestree is a man of no origin."

"Here's a pretty surgeon! here's a fine cutter and carver, gentlemen!" burst out the literal Chestree, with a deafening *neigh* that was meant for a laugh, "not to know that every human being born into this world *must* have an origin! No origin! Ha! ha! And yet I dare say the fellow thinks himself qualified to argue on anatomy!"

There was no standing this acceptation of Corney's affront; the high convulsed features, the dancing eyes, the broad open mouth of the second mate, and the purple countenance and quivering nose of the surgeon, were too much for our gravity. Shelvocke, Tapping, and I burst into a roar of laughter, which Chestree joined in to his heart's content, evidently imagining the joke to be on his side.

"Gentlemen," said Shelvocke, "we have had enough of this discussion. Now that you are evidently both of one opinion, you will oblige me by drinking each other's health. Mr. Tapping, fill Chestree's glass. Corney, the decanter is at your elbow."

The apparent good-humor of this request did not make the tone in which it was delivered less imperative; but the look that the two men gave each other as they grasped their glasses, as if they intended to fling them at one another's heads, started me off again.

Presently Chestree left the table to attend to his duty on deck, and was followed by Peacock. The young fellow had not spoken half a dozen words during the whole time we were at dinner.

"What's the matter with the boy, Madison?—do you know?" asked Shelvocke. "Is he ill?"

"I don't think so, sir. A little capsized, perhaps, by the sight of the sinking ship, as I am—or *was*, I ought perhaps to say."

"That is it, no doubt," remarked Corney; "and an awful thing it was to see. I suppose if Chestree had been asleep when she foundered, he would swear it couldn't have happened because he knew nothing of it."

"Oh, pray don't get upon that subject again, Mr. Corney," said Shelvocke. "Do you know, Madison, I think I have made a mistake in coming so far south."

"Why, sir, I always thought the contraband Guineamen would give us more trouble than they're worth, should we succeed in capturing one or two of them," I answered. "But we are heading now for the Yankee tracks, I take it, and I think the helm has been wisely shifted."

"The sea has dropped miraculously, considering the frightful severity of the hurricane. Mr. Chestree!" he shouted, sending his voice through the open skylight, "how looks the weather?"

"Very fine indeed, sir, and clear as glass in the north. The breeze has shifted three points since I have been on deck, and I reckon it will be failing us altogether at sundown."

"Likely enough," said Shelvocke, emptying his glass, and glancing at the tell-tale compass that swung over his head.

We had more wine and sat chatting a while, and then Shelvocke got up and went on deck, and I repaired to my cabin, where I lay thinking over the hurricane, and the sinking ship, and Corney's and Chestree's quarrel, and Miss Palmer and Lady Tempest's ball, and many other such matters, until I fell asleep; but was awakened by the excessive heat, that bathed me in perspiration and made the berth like a forcing glass-house in the dog-days.

It was more than I could stand, so I filled my pipe and went on deck.

The sun had set, and though there was a rich red flush in the west, the night—as it does in these latitudes—had gathered a few minutes after the luminary had vanished, and the effect of this blood-red space upon the darkly pure heavens in which the large yellow stars were shining like little moons, was extremely beautiful and strange. There was a faint breeze blowing from the south, scarcely enough to steady the sails, and a swell that would have kept the schooner rolling uncomfortably enough but for the unusually long intervals between the watery heavings.

The first person I noticed on arriving on deck was young Peacock, who stood upon one of the guns, leaning over the bulwarks, and looking into the black water alongside. He was so utterly lost in thought that though I remained at his side for some moments he had no knowledge of my presence, and when I addressed him he started so violently that the light straw hat he wore fell from his head into the sea.

Trivial as this incident was, I cannot express the effect it produced on me.

"It's gone for good," said I, watching the pale circumference glide astern, "and you'll never wear that hat again this side of the promised land. What caused you to jump so wildly?"

"Your voice startled me, sir."

"Go fetch another covering," said I; "the dew falls like rain."

He went below, and presently returned, and stationed himself alongside the gun on which he had been standing.

"Aren't you well, Peacock?"

"Quite well, sir," he replied, a little irritably; "what makes you think I am not well, Mr. Madison?"

"Because you are so extremely glum, my boy. Nothing has annoyed you, I hope," said I, thinking of Shelvocke's story about him, and wondering whether Chestree or Tapping had said anything to pain him.

"No, sir. A fellow cannot always control his feelings. I have felt dull—I shall wake up presently."

"What should make a lad like you *dull?*" I exclaimed, rather disposed to think him sentimental—a weakness that is bad enough in men, but odious and disgusting in boys. "You're nineteen years old, I think you said; and any man who can be *dull* at that age must be cracked—nothing but a list in his brains ought to excuse him. What were you looking for in the water alongside just now?"

He made no answer. I could not very clearly distinguish his features in the starlight; but I *did* see, and was astonished to behold, his large dark eyes glittering with tears, as he raised them toward the sky, and stood in that posture for some time quite motionless, breathing quickly.

"What ails ye, Peacock?—tell me, my boy," said I, softening my voice and addressing him very earnestly.

He suddenly threw his arm along the fife-rail, and buried his face in it and sobbed like a girl, yet very quietly; indeed so gently, that had I stepped back a pace I had not heard him.

"A touch of hysteria—highly delicate organization—deplorable sensibility! Poor boy! quite unfit, as I have always felt, for a rough sea-life," thought I, watching him and waiting until his emotion was spent before I addressed him again.

Presently he looked up, and said, "You see how it is, sir; I cannot control these moods of mine."

"Go and ask the steward for a rummer of cold grog," said I. "Nothing like a glass of grog to haul taut one's nerve-strings."

"No, thank you, sir. Give me a little time and I shall be all right."

However, what with the curiosity my knowledge of his story had aroused in me, and· the interest he had all along excited, I was not in the temper to let him go without a little further probing.

"Look here, Peacock," said I, "why the deuce won't you answer a plain question? No man sheds tears without a reason. If it's on the nerves, let him get the head-pump rigged and stand under it until he's better; if it's in the mind, let him unburden himself. What's the matter with you?"

He folded his arms and tapped on the deck with his little foot.

"What would be the good," said he, in a low voice, of my telling you, Mr. Madison? You will only laugh at me."

"Not I, man."

"I know you ridicule everything superstitious, sir."

"How do you know that, my friend?"

"Mr. Madison, I will tell you the truth if you promise me to keep it secret."

"Of course it has no relation to what you would very well know to be my duty as chief officer?"

"Oh dear no, sir."

"Then, on my honor, I will keep your secret."

He pulled off the cloth cap he had substituted for the headgear that had gone astern, and wiped his forehead; but instead of replacing it, he held it in his hand—and there can be no doubt that he did this expressly, as though his story were too solemn for him to relate with his head covered. The starlight was in his eyes as he fixed them upon me, and he spoke in a voice scarcely raised above a whisper, sometimes catching his breath hurriedly like a person in pain.

"It was in the morning-watch, sir; half an hour after I had come on deck this morning. It was very thick all around, and black as pitch. The men had stowed themselves away under the boats, and forward the decks looked deserted. Mr. Chestree, who was right aft, told me to bring him a draught of water from the scuttle-butt. It was so dark all about the foremast that I had to walk slowly and pick my way for fear of treading upon the men; and when I reached the scuttle-butt—the one just before the galley, sir—I stood groping about for the dipper. I was feeling with my foot for it, as I fancied that it might have capsized off the scuttle-butt, when a pale, faint, yellowish light was thrown suddenly upon the deck; and close up against the foremast I saw a wavering yellow outline that grew quickly into the likeness of a woman, with hair all over her shoulders, of the color of the light, and large black eyes: and her hands were clasped like those of a person's beseeching you, but all below her waist flowed away in a sort of trembling yellow mist that faded into the darkness when it was within a foot of the deck. As soon as ever the phantom became distinct, it unlocked its hands and made the sign of the cross with the first finger of its right hand, and then pointed upward; and though no sound came from it, yet I could see by the movement of its lips that it pronounced the word Philip. It faded away, with its finger pointing toward the sky; and I stooped and picked up the dipper that I had noticed when the light first broke, and filled it and carried it aft to Mr. Chestree."

At this point he was seized with a violent trembling, and I could judge the extent of the fit by the shaking of his hand as he raised his cap and placed it on his head.

I was never a superstitious man, although one of a class

who, as a body, are reckoned so; but though I did not in the least believe that any such spectre as Peacock painted had appeard to him, yet what with gleaming eyes and the darkness, and the moan and wash of the water alongside, and the solemn shining of the stars, added to the story itself, and the horror that possessed the youth in relating it, and his difficult breathing and the quivering of his body, I do admit that I was stirred and affected to a degree I could scarcely have believed possible in a mind so healthily fixed and (in spite of Shelvocke's good-natured ridicule) so purely prosaical at bottom as mine.

"Did you tell Chestree what you had seen?" I asked.

"Oh no, sir. I have mentioned it to no one but yourself."

"Was it a dream, do you think? dreams are sometimes so life-like, and so muddle one's waking experiences, that I have often asked myself whether such and such a thing really happened, or whether I had dreamed it."

"No, no, it was not a dream, Mr. Madison," he answered, shaking his head slowly, but with deliberate decision. "I saw the dipper by the light the figure threw, so that I knew exactly where to put my hand upon it when the light faded."

"Was the woman's face known to you?"

"No, sir; I had never seen the face before."

"And pray, Peacock," said I, knocking the ashes out of my pipe with a sharp rap, and feeling a little irritated by the involuntary sympathetic interest I had taken in this bit of ghostly nonsense, "why should this spectre give you any disturbance? what do you want to pretend that a thing of this kind signifies?"

He made no answer.

"See here, Peacock; suppose, after worrying yourself over this matter until you felt inclined to hang yourself, you should find out that, at the very moment you spied your vision, a seaman had lighted a candle for one of the lanterns at some point of the deck from which the flame would fling such a light as you saw; and suppose you could satisfy yourself that—the cause of the light given—all the rest of the phenomena of yellow hair and flame-colored cheeks, and black eyes and moving hands, was caused by your startled and morbid imagination working upon a coil of rope, a couple of belaying pins, a background of bright mist, and a few twisting shadows; wouldn't you laugh at yourself for a donkey in allowing an illusion scarcely alarming enough to frighten a female cook, to depress and agitate you?"

He said he would be glad enough to find out that the thing he had seen had been caused in the way I suggested; and perhaps it might be as I supposed, too; any way he had told me the truth so far as he was concerned, and begged me to remember my promise not to repeat his story.

"Certainly, you may trust me," I replied. "And now, my lad, don't go hanging over this matter as though it were a thing of consequence. Treat it as a mere waking dream; one of those visions which come before a man with his eyes open. We're all of us dreaming, day and night; and for my part, if I had my choice of dreams, I would ask to see handsome women with yellow hair and black eyes— a lovely combination, Peacock: that is if the skin be *fair*— not sallow like most of the foreign fair-haired women, as though a brunette should dye her hair golden—but whose native complexion is always stamped on the back of her neck, you know."

"Yes, sir, I know," he answered, laughing a little, though I don't suppose he *did* know; but I was glad to hear the laugh, and flattered myself my arguments had done him good.

At this moment eight bells were struck, and the watch below called. I went aft to take Chestree's place, and Peacock left the deck.

"Chestree," said I, as he was shambling rather sullenly toward the companion; his quarrel with Corney was not forgotten.

He stopped, and I drew near him.

"Will your memory carry you so far back as half-past four o'clock this morning?" said I.

He tipped his hat over his eyebrows to scratch the back of his head, and looked at me as if he thought I was going to quiz him.

"What now, sir? My memory's good for a few hours, I hope."

"Shortly after you relieved me at four o'clock, you sent young Peacock to get you a drink of water?"

"Ay, that's right," he replied, staring at me with surprise, and his arms hanging alongside of him like a recruit being drilled.

"Did you see anything in the shape of a light betwixt the galley and the foremast during the time the youngster was forward?"

"A light?" he exclaimed. "What, do you mean a lantern-light?"

"Yes."

"Such a light, for instance, as a candle would throw, sir?"

"Yes, Chestree."

"No, sir, I didn't."

"When Peacock brought you the water did he seem at all upset?"

"What do you mean by upset, Mr. Madison?"

"What's the matter with you to-night, man? I ask, was there anything peculiar with Peacock—anything odd—anything to strike you as unusual in the lad's manner when he came aft with the water?"

"No, sir."

"I'm a fool to ask these questions," thought I; "Chestree's an honest man, but a complete blockhead," and I was turning away, when, after screwing his head round to make sure that Shelvocke was out of hearing, Chestree said:

"Pray, Mr. Madison, have you any notion of what Corney meant by saying that I was a man of no origin?"

"It was only like hinting that your forefathers were not all of them probably members of the aristocracy."

"I have been pondering over that observation, sir, and although it is no doubt as stupid a thing as could be said of a human being, yet there's sometimes a great deal of malice even in stupidity, and I should like you to tell me, Mr. Madison, whether you think I ought to accept that remark from Mr. Corney as a reflection on my mother?"

"No, the man never thought of your mother. If any member of your circle was in his mind at all it would be your grandfather. A man without an origin—in England—is a person who can only hope, without being able to prove, that his father was born before him."

"Then you think, sir, there is nothing in Corney's remark that I should be justified in accepting as a reflection on my mother?" he inquired, with much anxiety expressed in his voice and posture.

"Nothing whatever."

"I am very glad to hear you say so," said he, and swung himself with some briskness through the companion.

Although I readily admit that old ruins, and churchyards, and desolate moors, and such places, are fine nurseries for human superstitions—shall I ever forget how the sight of a tall white goat browsing one evening on the green hillocks of an old churchyard made the sweat pour down my face, and started my heels as if the grapnel of a balloon had got foul of the hair of my head?—yet, if I wanted to enjoy what old midwives call the "creeps and crawls" to perfection, I would choose for the liberation of my fancies a quiet night at sea, with a reddish half-moon in the sky, and a slow, dark swell that is felt but not seen, as it rolls out of the mystical distances where heaven and ocean are mingled into one deep shadow, and when the illusion of the deep as a concavity in correspondence with the sky that arches overhead is rendered more impressive by the clear and unbroken sparkling of the stars in the water.

I was in the midst of just such a scene as I walked quietly to and fro the deck of the *Tigress*, thinking over young Peacock's story; and could I only have brought my mind to admit the possibility of such a spectre as the boy had declared he looked on, the gentle sighing of the light breeze aloft, the sobbing of the water under the counter, the soft flapping of canvas like the rustling and rushing of invisible wings overhead, the silent deck, and the flitting figures of the lookout men in the bows, whose shapes were only determinable by the stars which they blotted out, would have supplied my fancies with a more thrilling spirit than ever the ghostly windmill, the rustling brake, the moonbeams shining through the embrasure of a ruin, or the shadow of a wind-tossed yew upon a gravestone, furnished to the imagination of a belated ploughman.

"What a contrast with the scene of this morning, Madison!" exclaimed Shelvocke, coming up to me as I stood watching a white, gauze-like film creeping off the moon, and noticing how the stars in the immediate neighborhood of the pearly planet waned and died in the silvery blue as she brightened.

"Ay, sir, to look around upon this quiet night-scene makes the recollection of the foundered ship appear like a freak of the fancy. There is very little air abroad, to judge by the passage of that bit of haze across the moon."

"I am prepared for a calm. I am prepared for a long spell of inactivity. At least, I couldn't feel more despondent if I knew *for certain* that no luck was to befall us for the next six months. I exceedingly regret the southing we have made. We really had no business down here, at least on *this* side. How do the spirits of the men appear to you?"

"They seem lively enough, sir."

"I fancy this enforced idleness is telling upon the officers, though. If it had not been for Corney and Chestree at dinner, there would not have been a laugh heard aft to-day."

"I suppose the strongest-minded persons have their superstitious depressions at times, sir," said I, my previous thoughts taking my words that way.

"Superstitious depressions!" he exclaimed. "Who's superstitious? Not you, surely?"

"Oh, not in the least, sir. But don't you think despondency is always more or less superstitious?"

"I can't say I do. If I fret over the days passing without running us alongside a prize, I'm not superstitious, am I?" said he, chipping away with flint and steel for a light for his cigar.

"Do you believe in ghosts, captain?"

I expected a laugh for an answer, instead of which he lighted his cigar, stowed the box away in his pocket, and after a considerable pause said:

"You put the question so seriously, that 'Ill give you a serious answer—I do believe in ghosts. Not in hobgoblins; not in your saucer-eyed, long-tailed figments. But I do most firmly believe that the spirits of the dead revisit these cold glimpses of the moon, and that many persons have beheld such apparitions. Strange that you should have hit upon the subject, Madison. It's a strong faith in me, and has been with me as long as I can remember; though," said he, grasping his beard and slowly passing his hand down it, "no one would suspect a big barbed fellow like me, who has been to sea all his life, and knocked about in the rudest and most unsentimental calling known to mortals, guilty of such a weakness."

"Your confession certainly surprises me, sir. *I* do not believe in apparitions, but I really don't know why they *shouldn't* be believed in."

"There are two reasons for my belief," said he, seating himself with an air as though he relished the conversation. "First of all, from the very earliest times—so far as my reading goes—all through scriptural, pagan, modern history, down to the present hour, the idea that ghosts—incorporeal essences as the dictionaries describe them—have appeared to living beings, and that such existences are real has been deeply rooted; the one article of faith in which the votaries of all sorts of creeds are agreed. There is hardly a country you can visit but that you will find this belief a settled conviction. What stronger testimony would you have? I would to heaven there were the same concurrence of faith in deeper matters which puzzle me in the religion I belong to! But I have another and surely a very conclusive reason for my belief."

"And what may that be, sir?" said I, observing him pause.

By the moonlight, that was now exceedingly clear and bright, I saw him looking at me intently. He removed his cigar from his mouth, and said in a low, grave, and steady voice:

"Credit my words or not, as you please, Madison: I have beheld a spirit with my own eyes."

"*You*, sir!" I shouted, and I was rather thankful that I was too much astonished to laugh.

"Yes, I, my friend. I have seen a spirit when my mind was as calm and collected as yours is now, when my pulse was as temperate and steady as health could make it, when my brain had been tautened and set up by the luff-tackles of a long and refreshing sleep, so that neither wine, nor a late supper, nor any of the rest of the unpoetical causes to which the sceptics assign the creation of ghosts, could have been at the bottom of the tremendous visitation."

18

"Why, captain," said I, impressed by the subdued energy of his manner, "if you tell me that you are serious, I will most dutifully believe that you have seen a ghost, although any other man's most solemn assurance on such a subject would only set me laughing; for if I know you at all, you are certainly not a person to be duped by your own imagination into a conviction so opposed to common sense."

"I am speaking the sober truth, Madison. That I have seen a spirit I do most solemnly declare."

"You amaze me, captain. May I ask what shape the spirit appeared in?"

He swung his leg and looked down. I was not sure that he heard me. He had forgotten his cigar, and his posture was one of deep self-engrossment. I never regretted anything more in my life than the promise I had made Peacock not to repeat his story; as I should have amazingly liked to have Shelvocke's judgment on the lad's statement, the more especially as he himself was a believer in spirits, and took besides a strong interest in the boy.

"Who was it that described a ghost as something of a shadowy being, captain?" said I. "I suppose that is as exact a definition as could be ventured. But how can a shadow have a sex?—and yet you hear of male and female spectres."

"Oh, I can't follow you into the physiology of ghosts," he rejoined, pulling out his tinder-box again and hammering at it as though he kept time to a tune. "And now, let me ask how happens it that so poetical a mind as yours should not believe in the apparition of the dead? Know you not those magnificent lines:

> "'To-morrow, and to-morrow, and to-morrow,
> Creeps in this petty pace from day to day,
> To the last syllable of recorded time:
> And all our yesterdays have lighted fools
> The way to dusty death.'

What are our yesterdays but tombs?—yet will you tell me that out of those tombs the dead do not steal to stare you in the face, taking such form and substance, gazing at you with looks so full of pity or scorn or sorrow or reproach, that the fleshly eye beholds nothing completer in skin and

bone?   Suppose that the vessel in which Miss Palmer sailed
from Cawsand Bay had foundered, and all aboard of her
perished, a few hours after she had left the Sound—the girl
would be dead as a nail now, wouldn't she?   Yet think of
her, and observe how her face shall shape itself out of the
substance—be it sunbright or dark as this water—upon
which your eyes rest as you muse.   Is that so?"

"Yes, sir; but——"

"But me no buts; I can guess your objection.   You
want your spectres to turn out in the conventional costumes, do you!" he interrupted, in a lively mocking voice.
"You seek for your supernaturalism in scanty skirts, eh?
Your spirit must make its bow silvered over with a fine
moonlight light, like the theatrical angels I once saw hovering round a tragedy-woman's death-bed at the Portsmouth
Theatre.   If that be your theory of ghosts, Madison, you
need never lard your head to keep terror from stirring your
hair. . . . Ay, our beautiful luck!" he muttered, as the
mainsail flapped heavily; "let us be becalmed for a fortnight, and then get a breeze to blow us the news that treat-
ies of peace have been signed by all the Powers."

And so saying he got up with a yawn and a long stretch
of his arms, and, with a half-smothered laugh, lounged
lazily over to the binnacles, where he stood for some minutes courting the wind by whistling through his teeth, and
then went below, leaving me so much in doubt as to
whether his talk about spirits had not been mere banter,
in spite of his declarations of sincerity, that, to save myself
a heap of idle speculations, I let the subject fall from
my mind.

The light air that had kept the water tinkling against the
sides of the schooner now died completely out, and the long
swell rolled in lines like liquid jet along the glassy sea,
flashing back the silver of the moon as they passed under
her, and sweeping onward in black ridges into the distant
gloom.   The vessel lifted and sank upon these heavings as
noiselessly as a swing, unless now and again the canvas
gave a smart flap, or a block squealed like a rat among the
swaying spars; but the water for the space of a fathom
away all around was a beautiful sight, with the phosphorescent fires which, as the hull sank, shot out in tongues of

flame, or in fibrine forms like the wreathing of innumerable tendrils of plants, and which, as the vessel was hove up, faded into green clouds like puffs of steam illuminated by blue light. It was like looking into a kaleidoscope to see the graceful writhings of these lovely though weird fires, and never had I been in a better mood to watch the play of the mysterious radiance and to mark the wonderful luminous shapes which were formed—flitting, and fluctuating and nebulous visions, whose astonishing configurations admirably harmonized with the vast, unsearchable, and ebony-colored depths, on the polished surface of which they sported like brilliant summer flies on some stream that runs darkling under the shadow of trees.

However, some time before midnight sentiment had been tired out of me. The dew lay so heavy on the decks that the starlight sparkled in them as though a shower of rain had fallen. I went right aft and squatted myself on the grating, waiting with impatience for midnight to be struck.

Suddenly, the man who held the tiller with both hands astern of him, and lolled against the head of it as though weary of standing, shifted his posture, and I saw him rear himself on tiptoe, and peer eagerly into the darkness right abeam.

"What do you see, Andrews?" said I.

"Isn't that a sail away down yonder, sir?" he exclaimed, pointing with his long arm, so that with his projected head and eager attitude he looked as if he were calling down a curse upon some distant object.

I peered and peered. Presently I was sure, and went for the glass, and when the swell threw the schooner up, I could just make out a small dark shadow upon the gloomy water-line; but I lost it instantly, and before I could "fix" it again, as the Yankees say, eight bells were struck. There was a shuffling and snorting and yawning along the decks; a mass of human figures uncoiled themselves from behind the guns, from the scuppers, from the front of the galley; the deck was heavily thumped, and a hoarse voice summoned the port watch to turn out.

I went below and roused up Chestree, and told him that we had just sighted a sail away on the port beam, and desired him to arouse Shelvocke on the first appearance of a breeze. So saying, I entered my berth, undressed myself, and lay down, leaving the door open that I might get the benefit of the draught of air that circled through the open porthole each time the vessel rolled that way.

The wearing anxiety induced by the gale of the morning, coupled with the long and decidedly tedious watch I had just stood, had left me as sleepy as ever I had been in my life, and having consoled myself with the belief that there was small chance of a breeze springing up to close us with the vessel abeam, at any rate for the next hour or so, I dropped my head upon the pillow.

My senses were beginning to scatter, and I had lapsed into the imbecile stage of slumber when a man is sufficiently awake to hear a question asked, and sufficiently asleep not to know what he answers. Suddenly I found myself, with my eyes wide open, listening intently.

What was it?

A cry? a thump, as though a heavy block had fallen from aloft on to the deck?

Some peculiar noise had unquestionably startled me. I lay hearkening, but was too dead-tired to sustain that attention: my eyes closed again, and I fell sound asleep instantly, like a fortnight-old baby.

"Hallo! confound it—let go, will you?" I shouted, dreaming; and then sat bolt upright. "What's the matter now?"

The tall, gaunt figure of Chestree stood beside my bunk; he held a lantern in his hand, and the yellow light shining upon his face made it resemble the imperfect lineaments of some ancient portrait glimmering out of a black background.

"A dreadful accident has just happened, sir. Mr. Peacock has fallen from the foretopsail-yard, and I am afraid he is killed."

The news of a Frenchman or a Yankee being alongside would not have awakened me more effectually than this piece of intelligence. I jumped out of my bunk, and hastily clothed myself.

"Where is he?" I asked.

"I left him on deck, sir. Corney is with him. Shall I call the captain?"

"Wait until I hear what Corney says."

I sprang up the companion-steps, followed by the second mate, and ran toward a group of men who were assembled abreast of the galley. One of them held a lantern, the light of which shone upon the motionless figure of the poor lad lying on his back on the deck, with his head resting on the arm of a seaman, while Corney stood over him.

Of all the dreadful, heart-breaking sights that ever I beheld, none that I can remember equalled the spectacle of mutilation exhibited by this lad. His face, so greatly admired by me for the beauty of the large, spiritual, eloquent, dark eyes, the square white forehead shaded by the clustering auburn tresses, the straight nose and delicately carven nostrils, was a crushed, shapeless, unrecognizable bloody mass. The sickened and horrified eye sought in vain for any semblance of humanity lingering amid the ghastly wreck. And still he was breathing! Father of pity, that such an object should yet have life in it!

The seaman who held the lantern thrust it into the hand of one of his mates, and, covering his eyes, went reeling into the darkness, unable to stand the sight. Not a word was spoken. As I leaned forward, Corney looked up at me, and then fixed his eyes upon the boy, and in perfect silence we stood around, our ears tortured by the breathing of what veritably looked but a sod, while the dimly burning lantern kept the shadows dancing upon our ghastly and pallid faces, heightening by the capricious twitchings the expression of horror in the eyes which peered around.

The breathing of the poor, crushed lad was as vigorous as that of a healthy man; but all on a sudden it stopped—it stopped so abruptly that every looker-on gave a start; and a cry rose up from our feet, a short, thick, half-smothered cry, and then a sputtering, suffocating cough; a black stream that glistened like ink in the lantern-light crept from the head an inch or two along the deck; there was a sharp quivering of the limbs, and the boy lay dead.

Corney was the first to speak.

"It's all over, sir, and the Lord be praised that it's quickly over. The breathing of such a thing was shocking."

"How did this happen, Chestree?" I asked.

The poor fellow, who appeared quite broken down, looked at me as if he had the lockjaw.

"I sent him aloft," he answered, in a hollow voice, "to see what he could make of yonder sail. He went briskly enough forward, and I watched him jump into the fore-shrouds. A minute after I heard a crash, and a dark object rolled off the top of the galley on to the deck. I rushed forward, and saw"—his voice failed him, and he hid his face in his hands, trembling from head to foot.

"He struck the top o' the galley first, sir," exclaimed a seaman. "I was lying just here, and his body rolled over with the send o' the swell, and dropped close alongside o' me. He spotted my face all over with his blood," he added passing his hands over his bronzed cheeks with a quick gesture, half of disgust and half of fear, and then slewing round to examine his palms by the light.

A sheet was procured, the lad's hammock brought up from the cabin in which it swung, the body placed in it, and a couple of seamen were about to carry it below into one of the spare after-berths, when Shelvocke arrived on deck.

"What have you got there, men?" he called out. "What's the meaning of that lighted lantern? Where's the officer in charge?"

"Here, sir," responded Chestree, and sidling up to me, he exclaimed, "For God's sake, Mr. Madison, break the news to him! He was attached to that boy, sir. I'm an awkward fist at such work."

I immediately walked up to Shelvocke.

"Is that you, Madison?" he sung out, as I approached.

"Yes, sir."

"Why, what are you doing on deck in your watch below? What's going forward, eh?" he cried sharply.

"A dreadful accident has just happened, sir. Mr. Peacock has fallen from the foretopsail-yard, where he was sent to get a view of a strange sail, down yonder."

There was a pause—it seemed to me a long one, though at such moments as these impressions are always exaggerated.

"Fallen from the foretopsail-yard?" he exclaimed, turning his back upon the two men who had advanced as far as the main hatch with their burden, and stood there holding it between them and waiting for further orders. "Is he— is he *much* hurt?" he asked, in the voice of a man who forces himself to pronounce words he abhors.

"The fall. I deeply regret to say, has killed him, sir."

"*Killed* him!" he shouted fiercely, turning upon me with a swiftness that might have passed for an action full of menace. "Do you tell me that Peacock is *dead?*"

"Yes, sir."

Though the feeble starlight gave me no more of his face than the shape and whiteness of it, I could *guess* its expression as he stood for many moments like one transfixed; stock still, as though by some magic he had been converted into marble. A deep sigh broke from him, and his manner changed.

"Who sent him aloft?" he demanded.

"I did, sir," responded Chestree, who had drawn near.

"Then," said he, lifting his clenched fist as though he intended to strike the second mate, "you are his *murderer,* sir! his blood is on your head!" and rearing himself to his full height, he thundered out in a voice positively hoarse with passion; "How *dare* you order a delicate boy like him into that dark rigging?"

Chestree stood with his mouth wide open, utterly bewildered by this furious attack, and my own astonishment was supreme. That Shelvocke had a liking, nay, that he had even a fondness for the boy, furtively as it had been expressed, at least in my presence, I knew; and no reasonable expression of sorrow on his part would have surprised me. But to hear him attack poor Chestree as a *murderer,* and watch him wrestling with sobs which appeared to rend his frame, was indeed to be the spectator of an extraordinary exhibition, and I was pretty sure from that moment that there was something deeper in this matter than had met either my eye or my ear.

He seemed, however, to realize the insanity of his conduct, or at least of his abuse of Chestree, for his hand fell to his side, and he muttered apologetically:

"Gentlemen, this is a dreadful blow—it is the unexpectedness of it that deprives me of the power to meet it as I should."

"Captain," exclaimed Chestree, in a hoarse, tremulous voice, but very spunkily, "you were not fonder of that boy than I was, sir; and I would rather have lost my right arm than that this accident should have happened through my

" Then you are his murderer, sir !  his blood be on your head."
—Page 280.

agency. But if you call me *murderer* for doing that which
I have done a score of times, not in this schooner only, but
in the ship he and I sailed in when he was a little fellow,
you grievously wrong me, Captain Shelvocke—by heaven,
you do, sir! and I would rather lie in irons for the rest of
the cruise, and forfeit every penny of the prize-money I
have earned aboard the *Tigress*, than suffer such an attack,
such an unjust attack, upon my character at your hands
again, sir."

And the poor fellow sniffed and snuffled as though he
were shedding tears.

"Say no more, Chestree," answered Shelvocke in a
broken voice. "I was hasty—I ask your pardon; I know
you were fond of the boy"—the rest of the sentence stuck
in his throat. And turning to me he said, "Let the body
be taken below, Madison—placed in the spare berth next
to mine; and he walked right aft, and stood with his back
toward us, and never stirred from that posture until the
men returned from depositing their melancholy burden,
when he quitted the deck.

The calm was still as profound as when the watch below
had been called; the schooner probably had not drifted her
own length in that time. I took the glass to scrutinize the
strange sail in the northeast, but could make nothing of
the minute dusky patch. Some men were swabbing the
deck where the body had fallen, and as the lantern-light
by which they worked glanced upon the foot of the foremast, the recollection of the apparition that had appeared
to Peacock rushed upon me, and one of those swift shudders which seem to thicken the blood and make the senses
cold passed through me, though I promptly checked the
feeling and recovered myself.

Observing me to remain on deck, Chestree came out of
the waist, moving with such a slow, bruised, and dejected
air that the most expert mute in advance of a hearse could
not have carried himself more dolorously.

"Come, Chestree, take heart," said I. "You could no
more have helped this terrible accident from befalling the
poor boy than you could have stopped a cannon-ball from
killing him in an action."

"I know that, sir; but it is a fearful thing to be called

a murderer, Mr. Madison, and I do feel that Peacock would be alive now if I had not sent him aloft."

"For calling you a murderer, Captain Shelvocke has apologized, and his regret ought to satisfy you. You saw how deeply affected he was, and a man in that state of mind should not be held responsible for every word he utters. As to your assertion that Peacock would still be alive had not you ordered him aloft, all that I can say is you are the cleverest man in the world if your foresight can provide against other people's misfortunes. So forget Shelvocke's language, and clear your conscience of all sense of the responsibility of the lad's death."

"Well, sir, you are no doubt right; but it will take me some time to balance my mind afresh," said he, in a sort of groaning voice. "I've seen a number of accidents in my time, and some dreadful deaths by wounds; but nothing ever shocked me so much as this. I wouldn't mind if he had been killed by a ball or a pike at my side; a brave or fair death like that wouldn't make me feel that I would give ten guineas to be able to clear the tears out of my throat. But to fall like a sack from that fearful height," he exclaimed, looking up at the yards towering into the gloom: "to see his beautiful face mashed like a ripe pear chucked against the wall; to think of his plucky little soul being dismissed from this world by a mere *rigger's* accident —oh Lord! oh dear! it's enough to melt the heart of a shark!"

His grief was so lively that it twisted him about on his legs as though somebody were shaking him by the scruff of his neck; and he plucked at various parts of his garments with his long claws like a drunken man trying to undress himself.

"But who would have imagined," he continued, "that Captain Shelvocke would take it so much to heart? He didn't know him so well as I. *He* never boxed an apprentice's ears for saucing the poor little chap. *He's* never laid alongside of him hammock to hammock, and listened to him yarning about what he'd do when he came to be a man, as I have. But the Lord be praised! he leaves no mother to break her heart over his going. He's gone to a place where he'll hear no jokes about his parents, and never be made to blush for other people's sins, and where they'll not belay his singing, nor prevent him from looking as glorified as the other angels because he's a natural child."

And burying his nose in a large pocket-handkerchief he blew a loud and long blast, and, apparently relieved, looked around to see if there was any wind coming.

There was nothing now to detain me on deck; and though I did not feel particularly sleepy, I went below with the intention of lying down; but on reaching the cabin I saw Shelvocke issue from the berth in which the body had been placed, holding a small hand-lamp, and he called to me in a whisper.

I followed him into his own cabin. Apparently too overcome to speak, he pointed to a chair alongside a table strewn with papers, charts, and nautical instruments; and taking a flask of brandy from a shelf over his bunk, he poured out a full dram and swallowed it, though I was struck by the trembling of his hand as he raised the glass.

"I have just been to look at the body," said he, speaking in a low voice that his want of self-control might be the better concealed: "death must have been instantaneous."

"To all intents and purposes it was so, sir, no doubt."

"What a wreck! who could conceive that the missing of a rope, the slipping of a foot could crush God's most beautiful image into such—into *such* an object!" He passed his handkerchief over his forehead.

"Mr. Chestree is deeply affected," said I, "by this dreadful misfortune. I believe he was really fond of the lad, sir, though one would not suppose that much tenderness could lie in so uncouth a cover. He is also greatly pained by your grief, as indeed, I am, sir."

"My grief!" he exclaimed, looking at me with a singular expression. "I dare say you are both *surprised* as well as pained. It does seem strange, no doubt, that the captain of a vessel should be stricken down by the death of one of his junior officers. One does not look for such strong sensibility among plain seamen."

I made him no answer.

"But this boy had particular claims upon me," he continued. "I knew his mother, Madison. She died when he was a baby, and as he had no knowledge of his father, he was but an orphan, as you can see: and what is there under heaven more appealing than a little helpless orphan? His story interested me, and ever since his mother died I have watched over him, and I know now—I know *now* that I loved him. O my God! what is there more detestable than moral cowardice? What sort of a hero is he, who having the reputation of such bravery as gunpowder and cutlasses inspire in a man, fears to do an act of justice, shrinks from righting those whom he has wronged, and suffers his wicked selfishness to cripple, ay, and to blast, the happiness of innocent beings who love him? Ask me why the death of young Peacock has prostrated me even as you see:—*he was my son.*"

I looked at him steadily.

"What! you have guessed the secret all along."

"No, sir."

"He was the son of a woman whom I adored, neglected, and whose heart I broke. He never knew that I was his father, though had he survived me, my will would have proclaimed the truth. No! it was from no cowardly feeling that I held my secret from him. I kept my counsel to save him the shame of the discovery, hoping that I might be spared to such an age that, when at last the truth was told him, he would be a man in years, with a man's fortitude to meet and despise those sneers and shrugs which are so killingly cruel in boyhood, and with money enough to purchase that marketable thing, the world's esteem. He was a bright lad, as clever as he was handsome—he had his mother's eyes. God alone knows the pride I took in him, and how keen that pride was made by concealment."

"Yet it was certainly known to him that his mother was not a wedded woman, sir."

"I heard that from you first. The captain to whom I apprenticed him—the only man to whom I told the story—must have blabbed; otherwise how should the boy have known?"

"Unless," said I, making the observation merely to introduce the subject without violence, "he had learned it by the metaphysical means of which Macbeth speaks."

"What do you mean?" he inquired, staring at me fixedly.

"Why, sir, I believe he was a ghostseer, a quality in

him that your admissions last night and your confessions now make intelligible."

"How do you know?" he exclaimed impatiently.

"I asked him yesterday evening," said I, speaking almost in a whisper—for the mystery of that visitation, coupled with the proximity of the dead body, subdued me in spite of myself—"what was the cause of his depression. I think you noticed how dull he was at dinner. After some conversation I succeeded in getting him to confess that in yesterday morning's watch, before daybreak, he had gone forward on an errand, and while standing near the foremast he beheld a light that brightened into a human face, the lips of which pronounced his name, while she pointed up after making the sign of the cross."

"His *name!*" he exclaimed in a long-drawn thrilling whisper. "What name?"

"Philip."

"Merely Philip?"

"That was all, sir."

"Did he describe the vision?" he asked, while I saw the sweat gathering upon his forehead in large gouts.

"He did. He represented the face as pale, with black eyes and yellow hair."

"Ay," he muttered, "and she appeared to me too."

He clasped his hands tightly and leaned back, with his eyes lifted to the cabin ceiling. I rose, thinking I had stayed long enough. He looked at me with a lack-lustre eye and said: "Are you going, Madison?"

"Yes, sir."

"Well, I thank you for your sympathy. And now, from this moment, please let no further words pass between us on this subject."

I bowed. He extended his hand, and I shook it; but the moment I liberated it he locked his fingers afresh and lay back in his chair with his eyes raised; and this was his posture when I left him.

# CHAPTER XII.

I TURNED in again, wondering how long I should be permitted to rest this time, and mused over the events of the night and Shelvocke's confession, and ghosts, and the dreadful sight of the corpse, until my brain simmered over my fancies, like a saucepan on a hob.

The main source of my bewilderment was that Shelvocke as well as poor little Peacock should have been visited by the same apparition. Peacock seeing it I had attributed to an hysterical and morbid nervous system; but Shelvocke's evidence—the evidence of a matter-of-fact, healthy, sound-headed seaman like Shelvocke—proved that the spectral face that had risen upon Peacock was no cozenage of the lad's fancy; and the poor fellow being killed a few hours after the vision had by its motions prophesied his death, was such a confirmation of the ghostly story as might have scared a man more sceptical that I in such matters.

I was really not clever enough, however, to argue the subject out. My reason went one way, and my imagination the other. Certainly the hull of a privateer seemed an odd theatre for a ghost to act or threaten a tragedy on; though if tradition spoke the truth, the *Tigress'* was not the only deck upon which a spirit had walked, to the dismay of Forecastle Jack.

I lay for a whole hour thinking over supernatural things: the Flying Dutchman, composants whose blue radiance had blasted the life out of men, and left them hanging over the yards like bolsters, drowned cats who had reappeared at midnight and *mewed* up heavy contrary gales; until, cursing myself for an idiot, I shifted my position, screwed up my eyes, and forcing my mind upon pleasant thoughts, at last fell asleep.

I was aroused by the shrilling of the boatswain's pipe

calling all hands, and immediately jumped up and went on deck, noticing that it wanted five minutes to four by the cabin clock, so that my watch below was very near over. The first person I encountered was Shelvocke, who was giving directions in his usual voice to some men engaged in trimming the after canvas. There was a light breeze blowing, and every stitch had been set, and there was a very pretty little murmur of running waters.

Guessing the meaning of this bustle, I stooped to look for the sail I had descried some hours before. Shelvocke saw me, and said, "She is yonder," pointing on the lee bow. "See all clear, Mr. Madison," said he. "She looks to me to be a large brig, but I am not yet certain."

His tone was perfectly collected. In a few minutes the hands were all grouped at quarters, and I stationed myself aft with a glass to examine the stranger as we approached her. Shelvocke walked the weather side of the deck like a pendulum, sometimes coming over to my side and peering into the gloom ahead, and making some commonplace remarks about the weather, and speculating upon the character of the stranger. To judge from his present manner, no one would have credited that a short time ago he had appeared crushed and half-crazy with grief. Such an instance of self-control I should hardly have believed possible; and this surprising exhibition of nerve and will deepened the amazement with which I reflected upon his belief in spirits, and his assurance that one had appeared to him.

The southerly wind that had sprung up was very gentle, and being on the quarter, the schooner's progress was slow; and, when the dawn broke, making the horizon a line as black as ink against the ashen sky, the vessel was fully five miles distant.

As she stood hove up against the dawn, I never beheld a more clearly marked object. She looked like a vessel cut out of black paper, and pasted on a gray ground, and had all the brilliantly sharp minuteness you find on inverting a telescope and looking through the big end of it. She proved to be, as Shelvocke suspected, a large brig; but of all puzzling sights, the spectacle she submitted when viewed through the glass was one of the most singular, at least to a sailor's eyes.

The dawn brightened so rapidly, and her outlines were so beautifully clear, that her remarkable appearance was at once apparent. Every yard upon her two masts was braced to a different angle; she had both topsails set, each of them twisted contrary ways, as far as the bolt-ropes would let them go, through the canting of the yards; her foresail hung in rags which, in the brightening light, resembled long icicles depending from the yard; the outer jib (the halliards of which had been let go or carried away) was trailing overboard; her spanker was split in halves, and the huge rent opened to every swing of the boom, and looked, with the light sky coming and going behind it, like an immense eye blinking. Her hull was black and round-sided, somewhat low in the water, and her bows were graced with a long, projecting, finely curved stem; and these signs, added to her short lower-masts, and the raking stay of her lofty spars, strongly disposed me to consider her a Yankee, and a fighting vessel too.

But, in the name of conscience, what doing in that trim?

"Do you notice she is not sailing, sir?" I exclaimed to Shelvocke. "Did any man ever see yards braced about as hers are! It must have taken her people a long time to achieve such perfection of disorder."

"Can you make out any signs of life aboard of her?" said Shelvocke.

We both worked at her with our glasses. Presently I sung out:

"Aren't those men's heads moving about near the wheel, sir?"

"I believe they are," replied Shelvocke; "yes—I am certain now. Look all along her bulwarks, right away to the very eyes of her. Why, Mr. Madison, she's full of men!"

We dropped our telescopes and stared at each other. This was the first good view I had had of him by the daylight. His eyes had an extremely worn look, and his general appearance was that of a man who had been confined for some days to his bed by sickness. But there was nothing in his *manner* to indicate even a lurking grief or agitation. He was full of the strange brig now, and eyed me as if there was nothing else in the world to think of.

"She has the look of a slaver, sir," sung out Chestree to us from the other side of the deck.

"Thank you, Mr. Chestree; I believe your suspicion to be correct," answered Shelvocke, with a marked accent of kindness in his voice. "The crowds of heads along her side, Madison, can't belong to her *crew*, or surely they would not suffer her to remain in that condition."

I levelled the glass and looked again.

"She has six ports on this side, sir," said I; "but only three of them are filled. Why, see! is not that a naked black man standing on the rail abaft the main rigging, or does he merely *look* black against the sky?"

"Naked he certainly is," exclaimed Shelvocke, steadying his telescope against a backstay; "and for that same reason black no doubt. Why, surely she must be a filled slaver deserted by her crew."

By this time the sun had risen, and a league away to the right of the brig the water was flashing back his blinding beams and catching here and there a flecking of pink from the gloriously colored sunrise; the sparkling rays shone broad on the sails and hull of the brig; and the crowds of negroes, whose heads swarmed above the straight black bulwarks, were distinctly visible to the naked eye.

"Here's a dead body passing us, sir," suddenly shouted out one of the men stationed at the forecastle gun, craning his neck as he gazed over the side.

I put down the glass and looked over into the water; and sure enough, about a fathom's distance abreast of the port cathead there floated the corpse of a man on his breast, with the head immersed in the water and the feet drooping, so as to make a semicircle of the body. He was dressed in a blue shirt and white duck trousers, the ends of which were crowded into a pair of high yellow-leather boots, and a long sheath-knife rested on his hip, suspended by a broad belt that clasped his waist. His hands being stretched right down under him in the green water, and his face hidden, it was impossible to tell his color. He glided rapidly astern; but veering into our wake, the eddying of the water twisted the body in such a manner as to give one the impression that he was still struggling for life.

"That should be one of the brig's crew," said Shelvocke;

19

"and it looks uncommonly as though the slaves had risen upon her people. If so, the job has been a recent one."

This was evident enough from the proximity of the body to the vessel. But another five minutes placed the matter beyond all question. We had floated to within musket-range of the brig, and had rounded to, and there within speaking-distance lay this large and powerful slaver, her sides crowded with black faces and naked figures, and looking as woe-begone and helpless an object as the mind can well imagine, with her yards twisted in all directions, and her foresail in rags and her gear in the utmost confusion. She was, in one sense, hove to, if the slewing of her top-sails into corkscrews could be so considered; but in reality she was drifting, though softly enough, dead to leeward, as could be seen by the short, broad, oily wake that hung around her weather side from stem to stern.

So far as I could judge, there were at least two hundred and fifty negroes, negresses, and pickaninnies clustered along the bulwark of the brig, many of them exhibiting their full figures as they stood upon the rail holding on to the rigging. We were near enough to see the glittering of their eyes in the sunshine, and the flashing of their white teeth as they jabbered to one another and pointed at us, and, what was more ominous, the sparkling of the cutlasses with which a great number of them were armed. In spite of the wind being the contrary way, we could distinctly hear the hum of their voices, and now and again the shouting of one man—exceedingly like the vociferation of some outdoor holy hullabalooist one hears preaching in England on Sundays—as though they had a chief or leader aboard, who kept up their courage by clamoring at them.

"I suppose they don't understand the use of gunpowder," said I, turning to Shelvocke, "or surely they would have given us a dose from their small arms or guns by this time."

"I think that may be taken for granted," he replied. "Forecastle, there! keep your bow-gun covering the brig ready to fire."

"Ay, ay, sir."

"Put your helm up—ease off your main-sheet—steady; keep at that, now."

We ran down to within a biscuit's throw of her, and

rounded to again. The negroes imagined we meant to board them, for they brandished their cutlasses, and squealed, and yelled like pigs dragged along in sacks; the very children threatened us with their little black arms, and the thick line of black woolly patches bubbled and popped like boiling pitch, while dozens of full-length black muscular figures, standing upon the rail or the lower rat-lines, frantically motioned to us to keep off.

Their cries ceased when we put our helm down, but the same thick guttural voice that had before sounded rose once more, broken occasionally by a sort of deep acquiescent buzz, and there was a constant quiver of gleaming cutlasses.

"I see no signs of a white or even a yellow face among them!" exclaimed Shelvocke, looking considerably puzzled. He put his hand to the side of his mouth: "Brig ahoy!"

His voice produced the same effect that might have been expected from a cannon-shot; volleys of the most extraordinary shouts and shrieks broke from the negroes, and the former scene of brandished cutlasses, waving arms, and bobbing heads was repeated, this time with a little extra emphasis.

"Can anybody speak English among you?" sung out Shelvocke, when he could make his voice heard.

This second hail seemed to drive them mad outright; what they imagined we meant by calling to them I have no idea; but a broadside could not have thrown them into wilder antics. They hopped on and off the bulwarks with the agility of monkeys, slashing the air with their cutlasses, and menacing us with boarding-pikes, pulling one another off the rail in their eagerness to shake their fists or weapons at us, and making such an extravagant uproar that you might have supposed the noisiest denizens of one of the biggest forests were aboard of the brig.

"Main-deck, there! throw a shower of grape over her spars—but see that you don't hurt any of the blacks."

The muzzle of one of the carronades was elevated, and the piece discharged; the iron hail swept through the main-topsail, filled the air with chips of canvas, and brought down a whole bucketful of blocks and several ropes' ends. The effect of this explosion was comical; the negroes who were standing on the bulwarks sprang head over heels backward; there was a universal ducking of black wool; and above the rails not a sign of a human being could be seen, though through the open gun-port we could spy the black bodies of some of the affrighted creatures as flat as turtles on their stomachs.

"All this may be very funny," said Shelvocke, looking puzzled and bothered, "but I wish I had not stumbled upon this adventure. Common humanity won't suffer me to leave these miserable savages floating wherever the winds of heaven may waft them; but our boarding them will cost us more blood than I intend that my men shall lose or shed. See! nearly all the blacks are armed, and there can't be less than a hundred and fifty males. They have evidently risen and murdered the crew, and I know what sort of spirit is put into slaves who have once tasted white men's blood. They'll fight like demons."

He took another long squint at the brig.

"Why," he continued, "we should have to massacre half of them before we could get the rest under. See the crowds of women and children! It would be sheer brutal murder to fire into them. I cannot do it."

"It looks rather like a quandary," said I.

"A few wounds would make fiends of the unhappy wretches. You don't know what sort of foes kidnapped savages make after they have successfully risen upon their captors. Besides, the kidnappers themselves are destroyed, the vessel is no longer a slaver, and we have no excuse to attack her."

All this was quite true, but what was to be done?

"It seems to me, sir, that either we must sweep her decks with grape, or carry her, or proceed on our course and leave her to her fate. I really don't see what other choice we have."

"I have given you my reasons against firing into her," he answered; "and I am not at all disposed to decimate my men by an attempt to carry her. Leaving her to her fate is out of the question."

Then, thought I, what *is* to be done?

"How came she with that ragged foresail?" I exclaimed, "unless she were in yesterday's gale?—if so, she must have been tolerably well handled, for all her spars are sound. Aha! Massa Neger's courage is beginning to rise again," I added, observing a head like the top of a chimney-sweep's brush rise cautiously here and there along the line of the brig's bulwark. Presently the side of the slaver pulsated with swarms of black pates. "I don't know anything that is likely to bring them into our way of thinking but the want of water, captain."

"Ay, but who's going to wait until their casks are empty?" he answered, combing down his beard in real perplexity. "Madison, suppose you take a boat and see if you can make them understand you by signs."

No sooner said than done. The second cutter was piped away, and I jumped into her along with eight men.

Just as we shoved off, the wind puffed into a bright crisp breeze; the schooner bowed under it, and forged ahead by twice her own length before they could shake the wind out of her. It was always a difficult job to stop the *Tigress*, for I have known her to ratch with nothing on her but her standing jib, with the sheet over to windward. To check her slipping tendency every inch of canvas was taken in, and she lay floating under bare poles.

Meanwhile the brig was slowly drifting to leeward like a collier in ballast. The moment the negroes saw the boat approaching them their consternation and passion were startling to watch. Their ceaseless and convulsive movements as they jumped on and rolled off the bulwarks, the perpetual motion of their dusky arms and legs, and the intricate writhings of their naked bodies as they pressed to the sides of the brig, reminded me of an ant's nest stirred up by a stick.

But the noise! the whooping, the yelping, the outpouring of the thick and throaty African accents, through two hundred and fifty pairs (as I reckoned) of blubber lips all at once—the short, strange, infuriated screams, like sheaves of a block revolving on rusty pins, of the women—and the shrieking of the children, might have made a man suppose he had lighted on a vessel full of demons fresh from their Satanic port, and out on an excursion after fugitive mariners' souls.

That we might not be left in doubt as to the reception

they intended should we attempt to board them, about thirty negroes, strong, tall, and broad-chested men, some of them stark naked, and others with cloths wrapped round their loins, sprang on the bulwarks, every one of them armed with a boarding-pike which they held poised in their hands like spears, and from time to time essayed our distance by letting drive one of the pikes at us. Not only their agility but their strength was very unpleasantly illustrated by the space they made these heavy missiles cover. I doubt if there was a man aboard the *Tigress* who could have darted one of these boarding-pikes half the distance they were hurled by these limber, muscular, glistening negroes.

It was certainly a most disagreeably impressive scene: the row of stalwart, almost coal-black figures poising the long pikes, the whites of their eyes gleaming in their inky visages, and their ivory teeth shining as they yelled at us with their thick, purple lips rounded into immense holes; the surging, palpitating surface of black heads stretching astern of the front guard of warriors; the vessel heeling over, and drifting fast to leeward; the rags of her foresail flogging the wind; and the ropes' ends, which had been severed by our grape, blowing away beyond the masts like serpents.

We hung on our oars, and I stood up in the stern sheets of the boat.

"Mind that they haven't got a loaded musket among 'em, sir," sung out the fellow who pulled bow: "those niggers are more artful than monkeys."

I had thought of that when I stood up, and considered what a capital target I made *should* some among them know how to pull a trigger. However, I had to take my chance, and so I began to gesticulate.

I made all the signs my imagination could invent. I pointed to the schooner, and laid my hand on my heart to express our friendship. I pointed to their masts and then to the sky, and then at the sea, to signify that if a gale arose they would founder. I pointed to my throat, and pretended to drink and eat, and pointed to their vessel and shook my head, as much as to say when their water and food were expended they must perish. I took a cutlass

" The moment the negroes saw the boat approaching them their consternation and passion were startling to watch."

—*Page 293.*

from one of the men, and imitated the action of breaking it across my knee, and then held it up, shaking my head again, to denote that we did not want to fight.

But it was no good. The more I gesticulated the more they roared and screamed. Every motion of my arms increased their rage, which grew so lively by the time I had come to the pantomime of breaking the cutlass, that not only were several boarding-pikes launched at us, but the band of negroes in the bulwarks were dragged down to make way for their infuriated comrades behind, and the women sprang and sprawled about as though executing some religious dance, tearing their wool, dashing their fists toward us, and flinging their very babies into the air in the paroxysms of their fury.

"I wouldn't mind making any man a bet," said the fellow who had cautioned me against exposing myself, "that the poor devils think us the crew of the slaver come back to take charge of 'em again. I have sailed among kidnappers, sir," said he, addressing me, "and reckon I know something of the hignorance of niggers in a savage state. They can't tell one white man from another, and we'd have to cut 'em into bits afore they'd let us get possession of the brig."

I had shaken my head, and sawed with my arms, and convulsed my body until I was bathed in perspiration and every bone in me ached; and it at last struck me rather forcibly that I might gesticulate my limbs off and nod my head overboard without producing the least impression upon these savages. So I stood staring at them, and wondering what was the next card to play, while they swarmed along the sides, some on all fours, many of them running to and fro,—it was like a number of apes endeavoring to get at you through the bars of a cage.

"Hand me over that musket," said I, wishing to try the effect of another explosion. I pointed the piece at them and kept it in that position, but they did not show the least alarm, and I am persuaded that none of the poor creatures had any knowledge of the character of the weapon that was aimed at them. But the moment the musket was discharged (I fired over their heads), down the whole mass of them toppled as if they had all been shot dead. It would have taken months to drill a company of white men into such celerity and concurrence of action; the black crowd vanished like smoke before a sudden blast of wind, not a sound came from the vessel, and she appeared utterly deserted.

Hardly had the small white puff from the musket blown a dozen fathoms away, when, as though some distant mountain had echoed the report, the sharp crack of a small-arm came down to us upon the wind; and looking toward the schooner, that had managed to drift half a mile away from us, I noticed a signal flying for our recall.

Before the men could ship their oars, a gun was fired.

"That means urgency. Give way, men!" I sung out; the oars groaned in the thole-pins, and the foam flew scattering past us. What the matter was I could not guess, but as I watched the *Tigress* I could hear the piping of the boatswain's whistle, and sail was made with a rapidity that was strong evidence of danger being at hand.

We dashed alongside and sprang aboard; the boat was hooked on and run up. Shelvocke stood to windward, and answered the inquiring look I gave him by pointing to the horizon on the weather-quarter, where I immediately beheld the canvas of what was apparently a large, full-rigged ship. I levelled the glass at her, and at once saw by the spread and hoist of her sails that she was a war-vessel; but her hull was still below water, and it was impossible to form an opinion of her nationality.

"I can make nothing of those negroes, sir," said I to Shelvocke. "Either they don't or they won't understand signs."

"So I judged: but what made you fire at them?"

"I fired *over* them, sir. I wished to try the effect of another explosion; thinking that as noise appeared to terrify them more than anything else, we might manage to get at them by running the schooner close, letting fly a blank broadside, and pouring in upon them while they lay flat upon their bellies."

"That might have answered," said he: "but let us see what yonder vessel is going to prove before we trouble our heads any further with those niggers."

Every stitch of fore-and-aft canvas that the *Tigress* car-

ried had been piled upon her, but her way was checked by
her helm being kept down; by this means we drifted sufficiently to leeward to maintain to some extent our position
with regard to the slaver.

The negroes had regained their courage on finding that
our boat had left their neighborhood, and once more clustered along the sides of the brig. and I fancy by the character of their whooping, and the extraordinary postures
into which they flung themselves, that they were not only
defying us, but exulting over their imaginary victory. Of
all striking objects nothing that ever I saw exceeded that
brig as she lay, slightly heeling away from us, with the
dark green water lapping and creaming against her black
hull, the upper line of which was alive with the crawling.
leaping, motioning, and dancing figures of her sable freight.
whose black skins were startlingly relieved by the constant
glittering of the cutlasses in their hands.

However, I had not just now much leisure to admire effects of this description; my attention was quickly absorbed
by the vessel to windward, who, as she drew up out of the
water with a rapidity that betokened nimble heels. disclosed
the broad, long, and solid hull of a large frigate or sloop-
of-war, with short but tremendously broad courses, and
unusually tall topsails. She was swirling down upon us
under a heavy press of canvas, with topgallant, topmast,
and lower studding-sails out, and her sails shone like cotton.

Shelvocke and I kept our glasses fixed upon her, and I
was noticing the white line of hammocks along her side,
and the beautiful set of her canvas, and her short royal-
mastheads. and, indeed. beginning to view her with serious misgiving—finding something new and unusual in the
aspect of her—when Shelvocke dropped his glass; and exclaimed quickly. but in a collected voice:

"Jonathan! I suspected him from the first, I am sure
now. Mr. Tapping, get the American flag out, and hoist
it at the peak."

The stripes and stars were run up. We watched to see
if he would answer. A couple of minutes elapsed. and
then I saw a tiny black ball creep like a fly up to the main
royal-masthead, until it was hard against the truck. when
it broke into the bright and beautiful American flag.

"I am right, Madison, you see," exclaimed Shelvocke.

"Shall you fight her, sir?"

"Fight her!" he answered, laughing: "do you know that she may prove the *Constitution*, or the *Hornet*, or, worse still, the *President?* one of those vessels I'll swear she is; in which case she will be carrying over fifty guns and four hundred men. Fight her! what would you advise?"

"Who, sir, after our action with the *Diane*——"

"Ay, but that ship is not the *Diane*—cannot you see that?" he interrupted, watching the approaching vessel all the time he was talking: "and worse luck still, she is a Yankee."

A big ship she undoubtedly was, though, as she approached us stem on, I could only form my judgment of her size by the height of her masts, and the enormous spread of her canvas.

"Now, I'll make the slaver serve our turn," cried Shelvocke. "Helm there! keep her full—let her go!" he shouted.

The helm was starboarded, the canvas rounded, and with the muzzles of her lee guns trailing through the passing foam, the *Tigress* snored through the water. In spite of his flag at our peak, however, Joanathan instantly twigged us by this manœuvre. His studding-sails melted away from his weather yardarms like summer clouds upon the blue sky; in a few moments he was braced up on the starboard tack, bowlines hauled out, main-tack boarded, a whole flight of flat staysails between his masts; and as he swept round in pursuit of us, with the water smoking over his forecastle as he met the first of the sea, and his long, low, heavy black hull sliding like a water-snake along the bed of glittering froth churned up by his shapely bows, he let fly three guns at us.

"That shows you his calibre!" exclaimed Shelvocke, as the shot spurted up the water in three jets of foam within a few cables' length of our quarter. "Aim higher, old Doodle, next time, and look alive, or you'll lose our scent. Now, little *Tigress*, show them your metal, sweetheart! Mr. Tapping, haul down that flag, and exhibit English colors."

Then after a pause: "Are you ready?"

"All ready, sir."

"Then hoist away!" and as our own glorious bunting soared to the peak we slapped our two aftermost broadside long guns at the enemy.

"Now let us mind our eye!" shouted Shelvocke, flushed with the excitement of the pursuit; and sure enough, and as though our guns had aggravated the insult of our flag beyond Jonathan's endurance, he put his helm down, and as he brought his broadside to bear, the long black hull flashed into a blinding blaze, as though the whole ship had blown up; a dense volume of white smoke hid him; the sea was lashed into a fury of foam at precisely the same distance from the schooner where the first shots had fallen, and at the same moment a dull *thud* trembled through our vessel, as though she had grounded an instant on a shoal.

"Hulled, by Jupiter!" said Shelvocke; "confound him, what metal the villain carries!"

Heavy, indeed! and the worst of it was, he was out of range of our guns, so that it would have been merely wasting powder to answer him.

"I hope that confounded slaver hasn't brought us into a mess!" thought I; and as I watched the towering canvas and black hull of the heavy ship tearing through the water and curling out a high green wave that broke into foam abreast of the foremast, and swept aft to form the long wake that glittered like a silver ribbon upon the tremulous green seas astern of her, dismal fancies of American jails, Yankee hectoring, and an abrupt wind-up of our roving holiday crowded my mind, and I thought that Shelvocke had shown want of judgment in suffering the Yankee to draw so close to us before he gave his schooner the reins.

Assuredly if the big enemy only managed to wing us, our game would be up; against a big ship with twenty-four ports of a side—they could be counted now—her tops full of men, and her decks bristling with marines, the *Tigress* would be able to make but a very short stand indeed. Moreover, in Jonathan we had a smart sailor to cope with; not a Frenchman who could not put his helm down without missing stays, but a shrewd, bold, and determined seaman, who not only knew what a ship can do, but had skill enough to make her do it.

*This* particular Jonathan was sailing his ship magnificently: intent on holding the weather-gage, and yet never choking her; making every shred of canvas do its work; marking the distance of his luff to fire at us, with an expertness that scarcely lost him a fathom of way. Indeed, I never remember a ship better sailed; and when I saw how purely *British* was the science of her handling, and considered that her people were talking and speculating about us in our own language, that in all probability there were men bearing our own names aboard of her—Shelvockes, Madisons, Peacocks, and a host of Smiths, and Browns, and Johnsons, as any man might warrant—and that our own blood circulated in their veins, it seemed difficult to conceive that she was a bitter enemy, chasing us merely and solely to capture or destroy us; difficult, I say, until—pouff! the glare of a broadside, and the lashing into foam of a small circumference of sea, dispelled these peaceful fancies, and made me wish these *relations* of ours at the devil.

She had started after us when she was about a league to windward on our quarter; for some time she held her position, and there was a moment when my faith in the *Tigress* abandoned me. "She has more than her match yonder, both in weight and bottom," I thought, and my heart felt as heavy as a deep-sea lead in my breast. Ay, it was galling to me to a degree beyond the power of any landsman's sympathy to compass, to imagine that our beautiful schooner —she to whose lovely lines and surpassing heels my faith was as purely committed as a lover's to the honor of his sweetheart—was going to be outsailed by a big, square-rigged man-of-war.

I glanced at Shelvocke. He was lighting a cigar, leaning against the bulwark with his back turned upon the Yankee, in the easy attitude of a yachtsman enjoying a pleasant cruise.

"Is she not fore-reaching on us, sir?" I exclaimed.

"Fore-reaching!" he replied, with a contemptuous laugh. "Did you ever see an old woman make sail in a chase of a bad boy?"

"I hardly remember. But if the old woman had *her* agility," nodding toward the Yankee, "I should not like to lay many dollars on the bad boy's chance."

"Ay, but it is not *all* heels, my friend. Where's your staying power? The old woman may have the longer legs, but the boy has the lungs. But this is an illustration that will not serve my views so patly as the fellow's paternity. If he be the true Doodle I reckon him, his thoughts are with the brig astern and he draws a lengthening chain as he goes, the end of which will bring him up presently with a round turn. The imagination cannot figure the prodigious squint with which the commander of that ship surveys us—one eye on the *Tigress*, and t'other on the slaver."

But the truth is, Shelvocke's keen eyes had noticed what was not yet apparent to me, sharply as I watched: the schooner was drawing ahead of the American, slowly, indeed, for the enemy was not only an exceedingly fast ship, but she had a direct advantage over us in having a long weather-gage that enabled her captain to keep her chock full, and force us out of that close luff which would have thrown half her canvas aback had she attempted to imitate it.

About once a minute they let drive at us with one of their long thirty-two-pound guns, and it was the widening distances between the fall of these shots that at last unmistakably marked the superiority of our heels.

By this time the slaver was a mere dot upon the far horizon, and I had put down the glass after looking to see if the negroes had sense enough to take advantage of their being left alone, when Jonathan suddenly hauled up his mainsail, and let fly his head-sheets.

"There he goes!" shouted Shelvocke.

She rounded on her heel like a woman waltzing; and with a woman's spite, too, she gave us her parting blessing in the shape of her whole broadside as she swept into the wind; the storm of iron fell a long way short. In another minute she was on the port tack, showing us a back view of herself—the most elegant part of her hull she could have submitted to people in our state of mind—and foaming through the water under royals and boarded tacks toward the distant and just visible slave brig.

"Luff you may, now!" sung out Shelvocke, and the helmsman brought the schooner close to the wind. "A really lucky escape, Madison, and I give you my word I do not believe there is another vessel belonging to an English port that could have shaken off that fellow as we have."

"I wish him joy of the brig, sir. Those niggers will avenge us."

"Oh, he'll not treat them so fastidiously as we have. The nigger is only a man in the United States—not yet a brudder—and if Jonathan can secure a hundred of them by massacring a hundred and fifty, he'll reckon the bagging quite worth the cost of the powder. However, I am very happy that he should have taken so perplexing and unpleasant a job out of my hands."

He jumped into one of the boats which swung at the davits, and examined the schooner's side. Only one shot had struck the vessel, about a foot below the aftermost broadside gun-port; it had torn a thin strip of wood out, but the extent of the injury was limited to this very trifling defacement. The carpenter was sent for, and went to work to solder the wound; and performed his business so skilfully, that when, some time afterward, I looked over the side, I could not detect the spot where the ball had hit us.

We had run the slaver out of sight, the hull of the Yankee was low upon the water, and distance was giving an exquisite daintiness to the color and outline of her canvas; the broad and speckless ocean, with the morning sunshine streaming gloriously upon it, lay stretched before us; and last, and not least, it was half-past eight, and time for breakfast.

As I put my foot upon the companion-steps, I thought of poor young Peacock lying dead below. Alas! how easily is the saddest memory deposed! I had not given the poor dead boy a thought since I had been on deck.

Chestree and I took our seats at the table in silence, and in a few moments Shelvocke came out of his cabin. Depressed as I was by the sense of the proximity of the crushed and broken remains of a youth who, only a few short hours ago, was one of God's fairest creations, full of life and hope and the generous ambitions of manly boyhood, yet such was the hang-jaw and yellow lugubriousness of Chestree's face, as he gazed fixedly with lustreless eyes at Shelvocke, that, after the first glance at him, I did not dare look again for fear of forgetting myelf in a burst of laughter. I am sure the poor fellow felt Peacock's death acutely, as being, however innocently, concerned in the cause of it; but it was impossible that his distress could be half as acute as his dismal face depressed. The most hollow-cheeked mute that ever wept on the way to the grave, and got drunk on the way home again, never excelled Chestree's countenance of mourning on this occasion.

However, he made shift to stow away a large breakfast, though he looked as if he must burst into tears every time he drew his fork out of his mouth.

I was almost pained by the severity of the grip Shelvocke had taken of himself. He could not keep his grief wholly out of his face, but whether it was that he was ashamed to have manifested so much emotion before me in the night, or that he was resolved to conquer his new trouble, and to clear out of his heart every memory of a painful and unhallowed romance, he talked pleasantly, and at times even gayly, laughed over our experience of the slaver and Jonathan's discomfiture, and as greatly astonished Chestree by his apparent light-heartedness as he had before astounded the poor man when he called him Peacock's murderer.

Yet in spite of his manner—and he certainly carried it admirably—I was sure, by the look of him, that it would have done him good to talk of his dead boy, and hear us bemoan him. Why any man should take the trouble to suppress or conceal emotions of which only a swab could feel ashamed, I do not understand. What sort of pride or conceit is that, I wonder, which makes a man fancy that dignity is best asserted by a wooden face? I admired Shelvocke's self-control as a piece of acting, but I did not think him the better man for doing well what any provincial tragedy actor for half a guinea would have undertaken to do better.

Before going to my berth to get some rest during my watch below, I went on deck and had a look around me. The Yankee was out of sight astern, the wind had freshened into a glorious sailing breeze, and the brightest, gayest morning that had broken upon us since we quitted English waters was beaming over us. The heavens were full of steady-sailing clouds, blowing like puffs of steam, athwart us from the northeast; and the schooner was sweeping magnificently along the sparkling blue surges, with her hull careened by the warm strong wind to an angle that scarcely varied to the extent of a degree, so constant and uniform was the pressure.  I stood for some minutes admiring the sand-white decks and the groups of men at work on different jobs in various parts of the vessel, and the joyous scene of foaming waters, out of which from time to time there would leap a swarm of flying-fish sparkling out from the dark-green arch of a wave, and scattering as they flew like a handful of brand-new silver dollars flung broadcast into the water;  and then observing Chestree to be looking at me earnestly as though he meditated a conversation, I sidled to the companion, gained my berth, toppled into the bunk, and went to sleep.

I was awakened by Shelvocke, whose presence in my berth was so unusual that I stared to see him.

"It is close upon eight bells," said he, "so I have not defrauded you of any rest.  I wish you to oblige me.  Peacock will be buried at noon: I have given directions for all hands to attend;  for as one of my officers—and on that account mainly—all honor must be done his remains.  I have to ask you to read the service.  I am capable of some self-control, as no doubt you have remarked;  but this is a tax which, if I know my strength, I ought not to impose on myself."

His voice had slightly faltered when he mentioned the lad's name, but he immediately mastered it.

"I shall be happy to do what you wish, sir," I replied.

"I have not shown myself on deck since breakfast-time," he continued, "expressly that my absence from this ceremony may be explained by you to the men as owing to my indisposition.  I do not wish to set them wondering."

I bowed.  He seemed to have more to say, but a sudden rush of grief, that tossed his will aside as a current bursts through a barrier, darkened his face; he seized and pressed my hand, and went hastily to his own cabin.

The order had already gone forth, for when I reached the deck the boatswain's pipe mingled with the strokes of the "bell eight," and one by one the men, dressed as on

Sundays, came out of the hatchway and formed themselves in lines on either side of the gangway. After a few minutes the body, stitched in the hammock in which it had swung in life, with a twenty-four-pound shot lashed to the clews of it, was reverently handed through the companion, placed on a grating, and covered with the English ensign. Four of the boys of the ship's company then raised the grating, and stood with it at the gangway.

Although I do not claim more pathos for a funeral at sea than one ashore, yet one feature there is at sea that makes a burial there more solemn than I have found it elsewhere; and that is the crowd of silent seamen who are grouped around the body and behold the launching of their dead shipmate into the ocean, whose mightiness makes it a fit symbol of eternity. Otherwise I do not think a funeral at sea more affecting than that ceremony ashore. You have certain elements of horror ashore which do not enter into our service: the churchyard weeds, crazy and crumbling old stones, a swarm of persons (such as the undertaker's men), who attend as a matter of business or curiosity, the ugly hearse, and, above all, the dark new grave, with its mound of freshly turned soil alongside of it, amid which the attentive eye may often view the wriggling worm.

We are spared all this at sea: our grave is the eternal and boundless deep—our hearse is a grating or a board—our coffin the white hammock; no hired mourners in rusty black and spirituous tears surround our poor remains—no parish-clerk dodges us into the very Valley of the Shadow of Death for fees; we are plunged into the heart of that ocean whose breast has often rocked us, the whole deep is our grave in perpetuity, and our heirs have nothing to pay for our spacious rights.

Short as had been young Peacock's association with the men, they had got to like him as a kindly hearted boy who was always willing to do an obliging act, who was always blind to little harmless defects of duty; and besides, they were drawn to him by his remarkable beauty. The feeling was that a kind, brave, and handsome young officer had met with a cruelly sudden and dreadful death; that a familiar face was missing; that it was a pity—a great pity; and the quid stood out high in many a bronzed cheek, and

20

there was a heap of rough and homely moralizing at work in the eyes dwelling upon the outline marked by the full hammock on the graceful folds of bunting which covered the grating.

Yet how different the scene from the shore-going church-yard theatre of man's last performance in this world! There was nothing here to make death dreadful. The sun-shine was bright in the hollows and foaming crests of the speeding surges; the strong, glad wind swept through the rigging like a spirit-hand upon a harp, and the taut hemp rang out merry tunes; now and again a flake of foam would sweep like a handful of snow over the forecastle and glitter frostily for a few seconds; and life, deep, full, and abound-ing, was suggested to every sense by the rushing motion of the fabric on which we stood, by the sound of the hoarse pouring of froth forward, and by the steady streaming of the strong breeze out of the white and gleaming concavities of the spacious sails.

I stood close to the body, prayer-book in hand; and alongside of me was Chestree, with his dismal face hanging down, and close behind stood Tapping. On the other side of the grating were the boatswain, the gunner, and the carpenter; and the men, with their faces turned to the gangway, filled the decks down to the bulwarks, and from the companion to the main-hatch.

I am partial, of course: as we grow old we look back upon the past, and find that everything then was better than it is now—the men taller and handsomer, the women prettier and more honest, sailors and soldiers braver, relig-ion a deeper sentiment, our country more feared and ad-mired by the world, and so on. I do not myself share in such prejudices: he must be a stupid old man who judges of the excellence of things by his capacity of enjoying them, as if the most aged swab now living would not find as many fine things flourishing to-day as there were four-score years ago, if he only had the eyes, ears, and appetite of four-score years ago to bring to the banquet; but this I *will* say, that remembering the ninety men who stood along the deck of the *Tigress* when we buried Peacock, I do hon-estly doubt whether the present age could match me such another ship's company—such a set of seamen of the old,

salt, hearty, busby-whiskered, manly type—so active, so
sagacious, so determined. But let me remember the period.
It was a time that had produced the noblest set of seamen
our nation of sailors had ever given birth to. As, after a
long succession of gales, you will find the sea-shore strewn
with beautifully polished stones wrought to that perfection
by the turbulent seas, so the wars this country had been
engaged in had culminated, in the period I am writing of,
in the production of as perfect a race of tars as ever walked
the decks of English ships. That we shall never see such
men at sea again I do not say; but it must cost as many
years not only of hard but successful fighting to produce
the like of them.

The ceremony was soon over. I briefly explained to the
men the reason of the captain's absence, as he desired me;
and when I began to read the Office, the flag was hoisted
half-mast high at the peak, the end of the grating was
placed upon the bulwark, and one of the bearers stood by
to snatch off the ensign. The signal was given, the grating tilted, and the hammock sped from the side and clove
the green water; at the same moment a gun was fired, the
flag lowered, the white powder-smoke blew across the deck
and fled in a compact, gleaming cloud across the sea; the
boatswain tuned his pipe, the crowd of seamen broke up,
and in a few moments the decks resumed their usual aspect.

When I went below, Shelvocke called me to his cabin
and in simple words thanked me for discharging the duty
he had put upon me; and there the subject dropped, nor
did he ever again mention the name of Peacock, nor in the
most distant manner allude to him during the short time I
afterward remained in the *Tigress*. He took charge of the
boy's effects, which were brought to him by the steward
shortly after the funeral; and I cannot but suspect that he
came across something belonging to the poor fellow that
moved him particularly, for he remained in his cabin all
the afternoon, leaving Chestree and me to eat our dinner
alone; and when he came on deck a little before sunset, he
looked sorrowful and worn, much more so than he probably
supposed, or I questioned whether he would have shown himself by daylight.

And now, before I close this little incident of our cruise,

I should like to ask what is a man to think of such a story as both Shelvocke and Peacock related? Is it reasonable to believe that spirits do appear to men, or shall we explain the declarations which people have made, and solemnly and credibly made, of having beheld such apparitions, by assuming the possibility of an imagination powerful enough to dupe the reason by its fancies? Fortunately, it is a matter of no great consequence to human happiness, though I will not deny that such beliefs make life picturesque, and have even served directly useful ends, as, for instance, where an apparition has stopped a man from committing a robbery, and, better still, where a voice has caused a would-be murderer to take to his heels. Be this as it may, my log-book contains Peacock's story, and I have spun the yarn truthfully, and shall not attempt to make more of it.

# CHAPTER XIII.

A SMART ENGAGEMENT.

MONDAY (such and such a day), 1812; latitude 24° 2′ N.; longitude 54° 17′ W.

The day had broken beautifully bright and clear upon an ocean stretching like a swelling sheet of quicksilver to the sharply lined horizon. The wind that had carried us to this point had suddenly failed us; but we hoped it was coming again, when, shortly after the sun had risen, the sea away to the north darkened into a deep and lovely blue under a glorious breeze, the hoarse and rushing sound of which we could hear long before it struck us. It held for an hour, driving us smoking through the water; then, to our deep disgust, hauled round to the westward, and blew spitefully straight down the course we were heading. Worse still, it worked up a hazy atmosphere that narrowed the horizon with a driving mist that put me in mind of the North Sea in November, only the vapor was so exceedingly close and *muggy,* that by shutting your eyes you would have imagined you were passing through the steam of a hot tank.

"One almost seems to taste the presence of Yellow Jack, even at this distance from his home," said Shelvocke, sniffling and snuffling and wiping the humidity from his face.

He had once spoken of the Yellow Jack when talking of Madeline Palmer, and I suppose the mention of the subject recalled her to me. Strange, how widely different are the thoughts which chase each other through the mind! I was surprised to find how vivid was my recollection of her. How many weeks had rolled by since I had danced with her at Lady Tempest's ball? and yet my memory retained every point of her as accurately as though I held a minia-

ture of her to my eyes: the dress she wore, the flower she
had taken from her bosom (I had it in my cabin), her soft
gleaming hair, the black fan by her side, the soft laugh in
her eyes, her parted lips and sweet gravity when I spoke.
Such an impression was surprising, truly. I never would
have believed that any woman could, in a few hours, have
left so clear and lasting an image of herself on my memory.

"I say, Mr. Madison, mind you don't tumble overboard!
You had better lay hold of one of those backstays if you
mean to stop up there," sung out Shelvocke from the
weather-side of the deck: and wondering at the depth of
the reverie that had suffered me to clamber on to the rail
of the bulwark, and stand there holding on only with my
feet, without knowing how I got there, and why I was
there, I jumped down with a red face and walked aft.

Coming events cast their shadows before. Shakespeare
himself never wrote a truer line than that, thou prince of
lyrists, Thomas Campbell! The shadow of a coming event
was assuredly upon me then, or why should I have stood
pondering and musing over a girl whom I had only met
once, whom I was quite sure I should never meet again,
thinking over the dances we had danced together, of the
silver fires which had sparkled in her eyes as she stood
upon the moonlit lawn with me, and of the pensive little
equivoke that had slipped from her lips when she handed
me the flower I asked for?

"Why, I say? Why on *that* day particularly? Why
not yesterday, or a week or fortnight before? Jamaica
still lay a long distance ahead of us; my persistent thinking of her could not have been owing to the neighborhood
of that island, where by this time, I might take it, she was
installed, and viewing with accustomed eyes the black,
brown, and yellow population of that sweltering, verdant,
mountainous possession, and accepting the mosquito, the
snake, the guana, and the bald-headed noisome vulture, the
sudden deaths, the prompt funerals, as condiments specially
provided by a bountiful nature solely to increase the Euro-
pean's relish of tropical happiness.

"How does she go, Mr. Madison?" called out Shelvocke,
who was sheltering himself under the pinnace from the
moist blowing of the wind.

I started. *She*, thought I!

"West-nor-west, sir," I answered, after creeping up the greasy deck, and peering at the card.

"Turning wool-gatherer!" he exclaimed, as I approached him. "Are you sure it is west-nor-west?—or were you answering in Hamlet's vein?" *

"No, sir," I answered, laughing; "we are heading as I said."

Before Peacock's death he would have probed me to know what I was thinking of, and then have rallied me; but his spirits were low now compared to what they were, his joking mild and exceedingly short-lived.

"It is very strange," said he, after a short pause, "that we don't come across any vessels. Luck has been against us ever since we quitted the Channel, so that Hannay's advice to stick to those waters has, I am bound to say, down to the present proved sound. I have made my mind to run straight for Kingston and fish for news. It is certainly remarkable that nothing but that slaver should have hove in sight, considering the vast extent of water we have traversed."

"I believe we made a mistake in running south after leaving the French coast," I answered.

"I am sure of it. I ought to have stretched over into the American waters and worked off my parallels on that side. And here we are now bothered by a head wind. You had better get the outer jib stowed; it will make her drier forward."

"I gave the order, and the jib was hauled down, slatting violently and rattling the hanks like a shower of penny pieces flung upon a pavement. The wind was as strong as we needed, steady, and the sea moderate; the schooner was being sailed so close that the weather-leeches were rippling like flags, and the seas running almost straight at her made her chop up and down so viciously that her progress was marked by a surface of foam as broad and wild as a line-of-battle ship would have flung off.

The weather had certainly an odd look, a hazy blue sky overhead, thin sheets of mist which closed and opened, sometimes giving us a view of the natural horizon, some-

---

* "We must speak by the card, or equivocation will undo us."

times narrowing the visible circumference of the sea down to within a league; a fiery, confused sun, like the eye of a man angered by drink, flinging down a wild white light upon a space of leaping violet-colored seas lustrous with breaking surges. It was really tropical weather, however; I knew it well; the only two bad points of it were, it obscured the view and headed us out of our course.

The morning crawled away. At dinner-time the sea was still covered by the driving mist; constant showers of spray swept over the decks and made the planks smell like seaweed; but in spite of these cooling libations, the sun was so fiercely hot that the pitch betwixt the seams was as soft as putty.

"Positively," said I, as we seated ourselves at the dinner-table, "one might imagine that the sunlight to-day consisted of an endless succession of vicious insects. It is one long sting."

"Not an hour ago," exclaimed Chestree, "I clapped my hand on the back of my neck—the sun being behind me—under the full belief that somebody had stuck a mustard-poultice upon it. It was like having one's skin peeled off."

"Well, here is enough pricking—so let us hope that something wicked this way comes," said Shelvocke. "Pea-soup, I perceive, and boiling hot, of course," drawing hastily back as the steward whipped off the cover of the tureen and let a cloud of steam soar up. "A nice drink for this temperature!"

It was death to me to look at it, but Chestree passed his plate for a second helping.

"I am very fond of pea-soup," said he; and as he hung over the steaming fluid, I thought of Miss Hawkins's description of Samuel Johnson eating a veal-pie stuffed with "plumbs"—the perspiration, the veins standing in cords upon the forehead, the slop, slop of the spoon.

"Phew, captain! the windsail wouldn't be amiss," said I; "the atmosphere has been heated by twenty degrees since Chestree begun that second plate of soup:" and to my great comfort the order to hoist the windsail was given, and the big canvas funnel breezed sweetly into the hot interior.

"Happy is he," said Shelvocke, looking earnestly at Chestree, "whose stomach is not impatient of the equinoxes. The true Briton is a man who will eat anything anywhere; calipash in the West, curry in the East, pea-soup on the equator. The nearer he draws to the sun the hotter he likes his food."

"Pea-soup only makes you hot while you're eating it, sir," exclaimed Chestree, as if he thought an apology was wanted from him. "It cools you afterward."

"Still, though I sneer," said Shelvocke, "I am looking forward to my calipash. As you know, Madison, I am quite an alderman in my veneration for the turtle. Strange that so monstrous a conformation should enshrine such ecstatic fat. The man who first tasted him must have been a courageous creature. I should have required the experiences of at least three generations of digestions to have dared such a feat."

A step was heard on the companion-ladder, and Tapping, hat in hand, put his head down.

"There's a sail in sight, sir, about a point on the weather-bow. She is only to be seen now and again when the mist clears."

"Go and see what you can make of her, Madison," said Shelvocke.

I jumped up and went on deck.

"Where away is your stranger, Tapping?" said I, staring into the blank horizon ahead.

He pointed, and I peered, but nothing was in sight.

"The mist has rolled down over her again, sir," he exclaimed. "But you'll see her by keeping your eye on that part of the sea for a few moments."

I stood looking and looking.

"Very strange, Tapping; your ship is a long while heaving in sight. Surely you haven't mistaken some dark patch of mist—like that yonder—for a vessel," said I, pointing to a small circular shadow that I myself should have taken to be a sail but for the speed with which the long struggling wreath of vapor that held it was sweeping athwart our hawse.

"Why, I don't think I could have been deceived," said he, looking rather puzzled, however. "What I saw was uncommonly like a ship, and the mist opened her twice before I reported her, sir."

"Forward there!" I sung out: "did any one sight a sail on the starboard bow just now?"

"No, sir."

"Depend upon it, Tapping, you have been deceived by some flaw in the vapor yonder. However, keep a bright lookout;" and so saying, I dived below to finish my dinner.

"There is nothing in sight, sir," I exclaimed, resuming my knife and fork. "The fog must have misled Tapping. It's as thick as the lees of a bottle of loaded port. Chestree, kindly pass me the brandy."

"I thought the news of a sail being in sight was rather too good to be true," said Shelvocke ruefully.

At that moment I heard a voice on the forecastle hailing the quarter-deck. Tapping made some answer that I could not catch, and I saw Shelvocke prick up his ears. In a few seconds the windsail was shoved on one side by the third mate poking his head through the skylight.

"It *was* a ship, I saw, sir," he sung out. "The fog's hidden her again, but the lookout reported her this time, so there's no mistake."

"How did she seem to be heading, Mr. Tapping?" asked Shelvocke.

"She is on the starboard tack, sir, apparently going our way, but not lying so close; for she's right ahead now, rather to leeward, if anything."

We hastily finished dinner, and I followed Shelvocke on deck, where we stood, armed each of us with a glass, ready for the first glimpse of the stranger.

"Now if this wind would only shift a point we should have a clear horizon," said Shelvocke, impatiently biting the end off a cigar, and clasping his glass betwixt his knees while he irritably hammered at the flint of his tinder-box.

"There she is at last, sir!" I cried, as the mist thinned away on the horizon ahead, like the moisture of your breath upon a looking-glass, and displayed the hull and spars of a large vessel under easy canvas.

We both pointed our glasses. The ship was not more than five miles off, and we had her plain. The sun, being behind us, flung its misty radiance over our mastheads upon her, and the light sparkled in the windows and gilt carving of the high stern of what was seemingly a large West Indiaman. Her masts were focused into one from our point of view, but I could tell by her yards that she was a full-rigged ship. She had a single reef in her topsails, and a main-topgallant-sail set; but just before a whole cloud of mist blew over her and hid her, she set her mainsail and fore and mizzen topgallant-sails, and I could see some hands crawling aloft to shake out the reefs—as I surmised.

"Gone again, just as I was beginning to take her in!" cried Shelvocke, making his glass ring as he angrily drove the tubes into one another. "What do you suspect her to be, Mr. Madison?"

"A West Indiaman without doubt, sir; and an Englishman, I am afraid."

"Why English? deuce take her if she prove so! I'm in the mood for a change, man. I want to see a few foreigners."

We waited and watched. Presently there was the ship again heeling under all three royals, and foaming through the water about three points on our lee bow.

"Oh, ho! that's the time of day, is it?" shouted Shelvocke. "Tiller there! starboard your helm—starboard you may! so—keep her full now. Ease away that mainsheet. Lay aft some hands and set the gaff-topsail. She wants to get quit of us, does she? Ease off those fore-sheets! tail on to the outer jib-halliards—loose the flying-jib!"

He sprang over to the weather-side of the deck and cast an eager look at the trim of the canvas, and apparently satisfied, came back to where I stood, and exclaimed with a chuckle:

"We'll talk to her, be she what she will!"

Freed from the griping luff that had choked half the wind out of her sails, and with many additional cloths upon her, the *Tigress* rushed through the water like a comet; the whirring, crackling, sparkling foam fled past with a velocity that made the eye that watched it reel again; the wind boomed with a thunder-note out of the immense hollow of the mainsail, and every sail was as hard as stone under the pressure. The relieving tackles were manned, for the tiller kept the two powerful men who grasped it dancing like a couple of monkeys on the bough of a tree. The mist was blowing away fast, though from time to time lines of it would sweep across the ship ahead, and obscure her, but not so as to embarrass our pursuit. Her press of canvas was dragging her channels under. It was a sight to witness the foam fly out at right angles with her hull in long glistening streams, like jets from a force-pipe, as the chains ripped up the water, while to windward her black side and the copper under it glanced against the white tops of the deep green of the waves—the ebony chased with gold and ivory.

"We are overhauling her fast!" exclaimed Shelvocke, in a voice ringing with excitement. "Pipe the hands to quarters" (there was no beating of drums aboard the *Tigress*); "get the nettings triced up, and close the hatches. Were she English she would face us."

As the crew were bustling to stations, I caught sight of a spot of color on the taffrail of the ship: it fluttered, struggled, soared, and stood out like a board at the peak.

"The stripes and stars, as I am a man!" cried Shelvocke. "But we'll have no juggling this time; so hoist away our ensign, Mr. Tapping, and let them know the worst."

"In spite of that Yankee flag, sir," I exclaimed, after narrowly inspecting the ship with the glass, "I will *swear* that she's English. Indeed I am greatly mistaken if I have not seen the vessel before. If she prove to be what I suspect she is, then we may suppose that she has hoisted the American flag under the impression that we are one of Jonathan's privateers."

"She has the truth now, anyway," answered Shelvocke, with a glance at our ensign: but she's not English, I tell you, or she'd shorten sail and receive us—she wouldn't run; or if she's an English vessel, she has a foreign crew aboard, of that I'm *certain*."

"Time will prove," said I, ogling the ship's stern shrewdly, in the hope of finding her name; but if any letters were there, they were so involved in ornamentation as to be indistinguishable.

We gained on her foot by foot, and when within range let fly a gun at her as a hint to heave to; but she paid no attention to this challenge. Nobody was visible aboard of her but a fellow dressed in a white jacket and jean pantaloons and a red cap, whose tall figure, as he stood upon the rail over the weather quarter-gallery, with his arm round the vang, watching us, made a conspicuous object.

The dress of this man, however, went a long way to confirm Shelvocke's suspicion that, if the ship was an Englishman, she had fallen among thieves.

All at once they let go the royal and topgallant halliards and hauled up their courses, put their helm down, and, throwing their vessel almost athwart our hawse, fired a broadside of seven guns at us. The manœuvre—full of reckless audacity, as it not only imperilled their spars, but very nearly put the ship in irons—was executed with an abruptness that would have taken away the breath of any man less alert than Shelvocke: but almost simultaneously with the shifting of their helm, he motioned to the men at the schooner's tiller. The *Tigress* fell off, and the ship's broadside discharge flew wide of the mark to windward of us. There was a pause of a minute or two, while we flew down upon the enemy, who was slowly paying off. The instant she presented her stern at us, we raked her with five guns. Heavy as was the thunder of the explosion, we could hear the grape and round shot tearing along her decks, the smashing of glass, the splintering of wood, mingled with loud shrieks; and at the same moment that we fired, the sail-trimmers whipped half the canvas off the schooner, and there were we to windward, under jib and foresail only, and within hailing distance of the ship.

So close, indeed, that we could clearly distinguish the faces of the half-naked men surging about the gun-ports as they worked the cannons. The man in the red cap, who had been watching us, was evidently in command; flourishing an immense pistol, he darted here and there, and his cap seemed to twinkle in half-a-dozen places at once; he was a giant in stature, and brandished his arms like a windmill. Through the gun-ports we could see a number of mulattoes and negroes among the crew, and some white men and negroes were clustered in the maintop, and discharged muskets at our decks as fast as they could load them, and a constant succession of tiny white puffs of smoke blew away from among them through the topmast rigging.

It was as clear as the sun now that the ship was an English West Indiaman, in charge of a prize crew—whether Yankee, French, or pirate could not yet be known. But there was no time for observation or conjecture. The moment we took up our position to windward, guns of each vessel began their infernal din. How can any man describe such a scene! It was all crash and fury, the sparkling out of tongues of red flame, a smother of choking, sulphur-flavored smoke, a dull trembling throughout the length and breadth of the schooner, the whistling of hurtling iron missiles, the cracking of wood, and a roaring of human voices. The very wind seemed awed by the fiendish hullabaloo, and the smoke from our guns drove sluggishly down upon the enemy, and, mingling with the white clouds which rose from her decks, sailed in a large fog along the green waters to leeward.

"Aim at that red-capped fellow, some of you small-arms men!" shouted Shelvocke, pointing to the giant, who, regardless of the danger of the exposed position, had jumped on to the bulwarks before the mizzen-rigging, and stood there yelling to his fellows, and pointing with his pistol to us.

Half-a-dozen muskets were levelled; they flashed at the moment our two after-guns were fired; the man leaped in the air and vanished behind the bulwarks. Now, thought I, the rascals are without a leader: when lo! there was the cap twinkling over the rail again, and presently the whole giant forked up, and stood vociferating and motioning to his men upon the identical spot from which I imagined we had shot him down.

Crash! down topples her main-topgallant mast.

"How come your shot to be flying so high? Hull her, men—hull her!" roars Shelvocke.

What is that object swaying to and fro as it slowly soars to the maintop? A boat's gun, by Heaven! And see those black rascals up there fling down their muskets to steady the tackle, and make ready to sway the piece into the top! I noticed the men stationed at our foremost carronade elevate their gun: the live fuse touches the priming, and the gaping muzzle belches forth an ocean of fire and smoke; a ringing cheer peals forth, and when I look the boat-gun has vanished, the tackle idly beats the mast in whips, and a wounded black, shrieking in his agony, and lolling head down, and hands hanging over the edge of the top, suddenly shoots heels over head and whizzes through the air. A murderous discharge is at this moment fired at us from three of the enemy's forward guns: the shower of white splinters fly from our forecastle-rail, and the parted foretopgallant-stay swings quickly in to the mast; the gaff of the foresail floats down with the white folds of the sail, and smothers a group of small-arms men in the waist.

"No matter, my lads! The sail's a rag, and well doused. Aft here, and rattle up this mainsail!"

By this time the two vessels had drawn close together. There was not half a ship's length between them. Our shot had already knocked two of the enemy's gun-ports into one, her sides were studded with shot, and her bulwarks were like a sieve. What the slaughter was we could not see. On the other hand our hull was badly hurt; moment after moment our men were being taken away; and it was easily seen that, if this battering was not soon terminated, the ship would fight herself clear of us.

Indeed, such fierceness and obstinacy on the part of the enemy was quite unexpected by us. They were fighting their ship like demons. We could see the men flinging the dead and wounded, as fast as they dropped down, out of way, as if they were sacks of biscuit. Though the vessels were so close together that the flames of the enemy's guns scorched our people away from their quarters at every broadside, the men of the Indiamen never swerved from their stations, though just before we boarded I saw a whole fathom of fire dart out of one of our amidship guns into the thick of a cluster of the Indiaman's crew, and blast and wither and shrivel up half a dozen of the unhappy wretches into olive-colored rags, yet the survivors held their ground, and rattled their gun out again, and exploded it with a derisive yell. Our metal was heavier, but they had the advantage of elevation; and resolving to end the bloody and fiery business by a *coup de main*, Shelvocke motioned for the helm to be put over, and the next moment the two vessels were grinding their sides against each other.

A dozen blacks and white men, headed by the giant in

the red cap, succeeded in tumbling into the waist, where a furious hand-to-hand struggle commenced. Aft, Shelvocke was the first to spring aboard the enemy, I was next him, and behind were thirty or forty of the *Tigresses*.

Of what followed I cannot pretend to give a close account. I remember hacking and hewing with my cutlass at the netting, clambering over and through it, and tumbling down on my nose over the bulwarks of the ship; gaining my feet and seeing Shelvocke and a number of men making the air brilliant with the gleaming sweep of their cutlasses; joining them, and finding myself stabbing, thrusting, parrying, half-blinded by blood, whether my own or other people's I did not know, opposed by a furious mob of human beings, half of them negroes, most of them naked to the waist: and yet in this moment of wild excitement, stunned by the hideous yelling of the blacks, and the fierce execrations of the whites who cursed and raved at us in our own tongue, stumbling over corpses, ropes, boarding-pikes, sliding about on grape-shot rolling over the deck, stunned one moment by the weight of a heavy body flinging against me in a headlong fall—even in this moment, I say, certain minute occurrences and things were vividly flashed upon my perception, just as a man takes note of objects during a glare of lightning. I remember, for instance, the demoniacal expression on the face of a herculean negro as he let drive a boarding-pike at my breast, my momentary sense of despair as I dropped my cutlass to catch and wrestle with the weapon, and the joy that gave me back tenfold my strength when he tossed up his hands, leaving the pike in my grasp, and coughed and sputtered up a fountain of dark blood, and fell backward, shot through the lungs. I remember looking at Shelvocke, though the glance must have been instantaneous, and observing the prodigious strength expressed by his towering form, as, with his coat wrenched off his back, his massive, knotted arm bared above the elbow, his face dark with blood and the grime of powder, he *mowed* with his cutlass among the writhing, struggling, hooting mob, whom foot by foot we were driving forward.

"Aloft, some hands!" he shouted, "and clear those vermin out of the maintop!"

I turned to lead the way, but Tapping was before me; he was followed by half a dozen of our men, and I forgot them a moment after, as I rounded again to the demons who opposed us.   A fierce-faced, bearded, white man, rendered ghastly beyond description by a wound across his forehead, that had let fall a flap of skin over his left eye, levelled a pistol at me; I ducked, and the shot flew over my head.   I sprang at him, and then—— "Oh God!" I remember crying, and consciousness fled from me in a flash of fire.

**21**

# CHAPTER XIV.

## THE NAMUR.

I OPENED my eyes, and the first object they rested upon was the highly whiskered, brown, and honest face of Parell, the boatswain's mate, who headed my watch.

"Mercy on me, Parell, where am I?" I exclaimed, as he whipped his body erect with astonishment on finding me alive. "Here, give me your hand, my good fellow;" and seizing his fist, I hauled myself on to my legs, staggered, reeled, was caught by the man, and lodged safely on the step of a carronade slide.

The fight was over; the West Indiaman was ours: but great heaven, what a sight were on her decks! Blacks and white men—and alas! alas! among the latter I beheld many of our own people—lay so thick, that a man on stilts could not have picked his way along the starboard side of the maindeck without treading upon the corpses.

Directly facing me, and seated on a carronade slide that corresponded with the one to which Parell had led me, was Shelvocke, with his hands and face smeared with blood, supporting his head on his arm, without a hat, his shirt in rags upon his back, his naked arms black with powder, breathing violently, and apparently terribly exhausted. Around the forehatch were grouped a half-dozen of our men, armed to the teeth; a dead body hung across a ratline in the lower fore-rigging; ropes lay strewn across the deck and upon the sides of the ship in bights; portions of the bulwarks were crimsoned with blood; here and there a prostrate body quivered or moved, and low thrilling murmurs from the wounded in their agony, from the dying in their last struggle, broke upon the ear.

"I have a drop here, sir, that may pull you up a bit," said Parell, producing a flask of brandy, how obtained I

did not inquire. I put my lips to it and swallowed a dram;
but it was like pouring liquid fire down my throat.

"Water!" I gasped, half choked. He made his way to
a scuttle-butt near the mainmast, and brought me a tin pint-
measure full. Oh, the sweetness, the delicious coolness of
that blessed draught! Topping the spirit, it made another
man of me. I got upon my feet and found I could stand.

A dull aching pain on the top of my head caused me to
raise my hand. I found I was without a hat, and my fingers touched some hard stuff that felt like pieces of mortar.

"Why, what in heaven's name have I here?" cried I,
bringing my fingers away and looking at them. "Blood!
. . . to be sure! I was felled just now by some scoundrel, wasn't I?"

"It's only a little blood that's thickened your hair, sir,"
said Parell. "A touch o' warm water 'll set that to rights."

Ay, that is it: but the sun, though declining fast, had a
fierce bite, so I tied a pocket-handkerchief round my unfortunate pate, and walked over to Shelvocke. He looked
up.

"Good Lord, what a face, Madison!" he gasped out.
"But welcome back to life. I thought I saw you dead."

"And you, sir?"

"Untouched, though almost dispatched by my own exertions. But see—but see what a number of our brave fellows these murderous Yankee pirates have cost us!" and
he ran his grieved eyes over the prone bodies.

"And how long can I have been dead—do you know,
sir?"

"Why, not above five minutes, I should think. We
have only just driven the last of the batch below. How
they fought! Those blacks are fiends! in their very death-
agonies some of them buried their teeth in the flesh of our
wounded. What enemies to oppose to white men!" he exclaimed, still fetching his breath with labor. "Has the
schooner suffered much? My eyes so smart with the powder-smoke that I can hardly see out of them," he added,
nodding toward the *Tigress*, who had drawn ahead of the
ship by about a cable's-length, and lay hove to with her
canvas shaking.

"So far as I can make out, her rigging is a good deal cut

up, and her mainsail is a perfect Milky-way of shot-holes,"
I answered; "but her spars look all right, sir."

"The Lord be praised for that!" said he, rising. "The
last two broadsides were ferocious enough to drive us out of
water. But heaven and earth, what a massacre!" he cried,
clasping his hands with a vehement gesture as he ran his
eyes over the deck. "Look, I can count seven of our men
dead between this and the main-hatch!"

"Surely there cannot be many prisoners below sir," said
I. "There is slaughter enough here to account for the
whole of the ship's crew."

"We drove about a dozen or twenty of them under," he
answered. "There should have been two-score at least
when we boarded, but they melted away as we slowly settled them forward like a handful of sand through the fingers. You had better take some men below, Madison, and
explore the cabin, while I signal the schooner. Have you
seen anything of Tapping?"

"There he is yonder, sir, near the fore-hatch."

He hailed the third mate, who limped heavily as he made
his way aft.

In the mean time I called to Parell, and another seaman
named Bowman, to follow me; and picking up a cutlass I
descended the companion-steps and entered the cabin. I
advanced cautiously, for there was no guessing who was
below, and what reception awaited the first explorer of those
regions. We found ourselves in a large deserted cabin, or
saloon, most luxuriously and handsomely fitted. Accustomed as I was to the sumptuous cabin-trappings of Indiamen, I was astonished by the beauty and taste exhibited in
this place. The bulkheads were furnished with tall mirrors;
rich curtains hung in front of the doors of the berths which
were partitioned off from the cabin; trays of flowers and
globes of fish swung from the ceiling; the mizzen-mast, that
pierced the two decks, was painted and decorated so as to
resemble a column of elaborately-carved marble; and what
with velvet chairs and sofas, sparkling brass lamps, skylights enriched with ferns, dark and lustrous oak-panelling,
and a tall, picturesquely ornamented pianoforte at the back
of the mizzen-mast, the cabin seemed like a drawing-room
in a royal residence.

There were some decanters of wine, glasses, plates, a dish of biscuits, and a cold ham on the table; where they looked to have been hastily placed and hastily left; there was a fork with a piece of ham stuck on it upon a plate, and a biscuit alongside of it with the mark of a bite, and a wineglass lay on its side amid a little pool of sherry.

All these things were noted by me as I advanced, but on facing a mirror I came to a dead stop, aghast at the monstrous figure reflected in it.

"Good heavens, Parell!" I muttered, observing the two fellows grinning behind me. "Can that fearful thing be ME?"

My face was covered with grime and blood that had hardened into a black mask over my eyebrows and on my left cheek; but shocking as this discoloration and the *character* of it made my countenance, the whole expression was rendered inexpressibly hideous by the stained white pocket-handkerchief I had tied around my head and knotted under my chin, so as to cause my beard to project like a frill, or the dorsal fin of a shark. In addition to this my shirt, like Shelvocke's, hung in several rags from my shoulders, and the left leg of my trousers had been split up as high as my knee. My horror of my own aspect so heightened the ghastly appearance of my face, that the proverbial extremes met. I looked, turned away, and burst out laughing.

"Lord, what a ghost I should make!" I shouted. "What a Banquo—what a Hamlet's father—what a Witch of Endor!

"'Approach thou like the rugged Russian bear,
The arm'd rhinoceros or the Hyrcan tiger,
Take *any* shape but that——'"

I stopped short, petrified by the apparition of a long yellow face projected beyond one of the curtains that quivered like a blowing flag in the shaking hand of the individual who had drawn it aside. The face was yellow as butter, and had the moist shine of butter, too; it had a long aquiline nose, perfectly round, black, bloodshot eyes, and was crowned with a mat of intensely black hair. It looked at me, and I looked at it; it dodged once or twice, like the head of a person who makes a feint of hiding; it then forked out, slowly drawing after it a long, thin figure, dressed in black, supported upon a pair of knock-kneed legs, cased in stockings like a bishop's, and terminating in a pair of square, flat shoes, freighted with enormous silver buckles.

"Gracious goodness!" he ejaculated, looking at me from top to toe. "Are you a man or a walking corpse? God have mercy upon us! Such horrors, one after another, might turn the brain of the unthinking beast of the field!"

I immediately perceived that he was a passenger, and as there was no time for parleying, I explained who I was, and the character of the vessel that had captured the ship. I never saw any human face more agitated than his when I told him that we were Englishmen, and that the ship was our prize. He rushed at me with extended arms, clasped his hands round my neck, and sobbed out the wildest exclamations of joy like any woman in hysterics.

"And you tell me that the American pirates have been vanquished? and that this ship is in possession of honorable Englishmen?" he shouted, breaking away from me and shooting about on his long, thin legs; and then darting aft, he drew back the curtains hanging in front of the berths, one after the other, with a vehemence that made the rings rattle again on the brass rods, and flung open the doors, shouting as he turned the handles:

"Colonel Bray, we are saved, sir! Mrs. Montague and family, we are in the hands of Englishmen and friends! Miss Palmer, Mr. Johnson, Mr. and Mrs. Solomons, come forth, come forth! We are saved, I tell you! The pirates are defeated! We are under British colors once more! Hooray!"

He uttered three distinct and vigorous cheers; and such was the contrast between his extravagant joy and his solemn costume, the carnal raptures expressed by his legs and their spiritual structure, that nothing but the reflection of my person in one of the looking-glasses, and my annoyance that ladies would be among the spectators of my deplorable figure, could have restrained my laughter. Indeed, I had never contemplated the possibility of ladies being below when I undertook to explore the cabin, nor, until a mirror confronted me, had I any idea of the frightfulness of my appearance.

However, I was too late to escape, though when the yellow-faced men fell a-bawling to the others to come forth, I cowered behind Parell and his mate, who, grimy as they were, looked civilized and Christian men alongside of me.

A number of ladies and gentlemen came running out of the berths until the cabin seemed full of people. I bobbed behind the seamen, looking at the passengers as they emerged, all talking at once; but my eye lighting on a face —pale, gray-eyed, full of sweetness, sorrow, and fear—my heart seemed to stop beating, the blood tingled through me until my fingers felt as if buried in an ant's nest.

"Merciful powers!" thought I, "it is Madeline Palmer!" I could scarcely believe my eyes—but there she stood, to the right of the mast, the outermost figure of the little crowd, gazing at me and my men, with eyebrows arched with horror. My stupefaction passed quickly. "Pish!" I said to myself, "she'll never know me in this figure:" and parting the two fellows who had stood right in front of me, I stepped forth.

The ladies screamed, and there was a general recoil, more especially on the part of Mrs. Solomons—an immensely fat West-Indian Jewess, who backed so violently into the waistcoat of a slightly built gentleman, who turned out to be Colonel Bray, that she pinned, crushed, and nearly suffocated him against the bulkhead.

"I am sorry," said I, "to be obliged to appear before ladies in this trim; but the engagement has been a severe one, and I have really had no time to change my clothes. However, ladies and gentlemen, pray do not be alarmed. We are Englishmen, and have regained this vessel, which we supposed was captured by an American privateer. Your persons and property are safe, and you will be under way for Kingston, Jamaica, as soon as the decks are cleared and the vessels refitted."

I looked hard at Miss Palmer as I spoke, to see if she "twigged" me, but, though there was plenty of speculation in her beautiful eyes, there was no recognition. All horror had left her, however, and she was one of the first to press forward to grasp my hand.

And then began one of those ordeals I abominate. In all, there were eleven passengers, including a baby; and I

was nearly suffocated by them as they pressed around me.
Such sobbing! such short peals of hysteric laughter!—
everybody shaking hands; women kissing; the baby taking
fright and squalling; Mrs. Solomons swooning away and
recovering, at the expense of her gown, that had to be cut
off her back; Mr. Johnson, a bald-headed, fat little man,
bouncing up to me again and again to grasp my hands and
thank me for his life and liberty; Colonel Bray forcing
wine upon me and my men; the yellow-faced man cutting
capers around me, and calling me his guardian angel—it
was more than I could stand.

"Gentlemen, we have our work on deck; meanwhile I
will ask you to remain below with the ladies, and on no
account to suffer them to leave the cabin until the ship is
cleared:" and so saying I made a bow, and mounted the
companion-steps, thankful to heaven to have escaped Miss
Palmer's recognition, and horribly distressed that any woman's eye should have beheld my blood-stained face and
torn garments.

I found Shelvocke watching Corney at work among the
bodies, separating the dead from the wounded; and as fast
as he pronounced a body dead, some men attached a shot to
its feet and dropped it overboard.   There was no time for
ceremony: the sun was within an hour of his setting, the
heat increased as the wind failed, much work was needed
aloft; but it was necessary to clear the decks first, and
cleanse the ship of the ghastly relics of the struggle.

"There are eleven passengers below, sir," said I to Shelvocke.

"Ladies?"

"Five ladies, a nurse and a baby, and four gentlemen."

"And what did they take you to be?" said he, glancing
at me with a smile, that the grime on his face made exceedingly odd.   "You look like a portrait of old Mother Ship-
ton with that handkerchief around your head.   I hope you
stopped them from coming on deck?" running his eyes over
his own clothes.

"Yes, sir, and I have posted a man half-way up the the
companion-steps, in case their curiosity should master them.
Whom think you makes one of the ladies?"

"I have no idea."

"I am sorry," said I, "but the engagement has been a severe one, and I have really had no time to change my clothes."

—*Page 327.*

"Miss Palmer—the young lady I danced with at Lady Tempest's."

He looked hard at me to see if I was in earnest.

"Strange indeed!" he exclaimed: "and yet not so very strange either, considering that she was to sail for the West Indies much about the time we quitted Plymouth. Did she know you?"

"I hope not."

"Anyway she couldn't have seen your blushes. Curious things do happen in this world, which is much smaller than people think, even at sea. Look at them tossing the dead overboard! So many of our men, too! I dread the hour for the muster-roll to be called. I am sorry to say that Chestree is badly hurt—stabbed by the red-capped ruffian who boarded the *Tigress.*"

"It has been a bloody business, captain."

"It has indeed. How does your head feel?"

"As though a little warm water would freshen me up, sir."

"Then see here, Madison; jump into that boat, and get aboard the *Tigress* and dress your head. You can afterward return and relieve me. Be as quick as you can, as I want you to take charge here."

"Ay, ay, sir," said I, mightily thankful for the chance of boarding the schooner. I dropped into the gig that lay alongside with three men in her, we shoved off, and in a few minutes I was in my cabin.

The steward brought me a can of warm water and bathed my head; the wound was on the scalp, very sore indeed to the touch, and I had evidently lost a great deal of blood: however, I felt pretty hearty when I was washed and my clothes changed. I told the steward to make up a small bundle of linen and throw it into the boat; and while he did this, I peeped into Chestree's cabin. The poor fellow was asleep, but looked so ghastly, I thought he was dead, until I put my ear to his mouth. I closed the door gently, bidding the steward give an eye to him; and as I went to the gangway to get into the boat, I saw a pile of dead lying against the galley, and some of the crew of the schooner swabbing the deck while others were at work aloft. I called to the boatswain and asked after the wounded.

"There are eight dead, and nineteen down, sir; and of them I fear near half a score'll never see the sun rise again. It's been a murderous action!" he exclaimed sadly.

"I am glad to find you unhurt," said I. "The wounded have been seen to, I hope?"

"Yes, sir, after a fashion. Mr. Corney has coopered 'em as well as time allowed. I suppose there'll be a boat-load aboard the prize?"

"Ay, the slaughter there has been dreadful. What are those dead yonder?" I asked, pointing to the bodies near the galley.

"Most of 'em the chaps who boarded us, sir. Not a man escaped. But that red-capped cove must ha' been Satan himself. I don't know as ever I see or heerd of any man fighting like him, nor giving so much trouble to kill. I shot him twice, another stabbed him in the back, another cut him over the shoulder, and I see the cutlass jammed there so as not to be drawed out, and the man went on fighting some minutes after that, and stabbed Mr. Chestree afore he dropped. As to the niggers, they was like sharks. Had you cut 'em into twenty bits, it's my belief that every piece would ha' gone on fighting in its own account. Talk o' the Mericans not having spunk! they're bulldogs in breeches, sir; and jine 'em with British sailors, and the whole world made into one fleet couldn't resist them."

"No doubt, no doubt. Keep close to the ship, bo'sun; the captain will be aboard of you shortly;" said I, and jumped into the boat and was rowed back to the prize.

I found Shelvocke at the gangway waiting for me, and the moment I stepped over the side he laid hold of the side ropes in his impatience to be gone, and stood talking to me with one foot on the ladder.

"All the dead are overboard," said he, "and you will now send the wounded in charge of Corney to the schooner as fast as you can. I find there are thirty of the *Tigress'* men aboard here, of whom you will keep fifteen; but let the whole thirty turn to at once and solder your spars and rigging. There are twelve prisoners whom you had better send to me. You may also tell the passengers that they are at liberty to remain with you or shift themselves into the schooner."

I touched my hat, and he dropped into the boat.

The evening that had insensibly stolen around us was as lovely and clear as the morning had been thick and unsettled. The wind had slackened into a gentle breeze that was just brisk enough to cool one's face and keep the water twinkling. The setting sun was filling sea and sky with heavenly colors, purple in the west and amber in the east, and a haze of pink that left the water-line sharp as the rim of a glass lens all round the horizon, and overhead a deep, unspeakable tropical blue, and under us a sea of melting green.

My first and pressing duty was to dispatch the wounded in the schooner's cutter, but the job of getting the poor creatures into her was one of the most painful I had ever undertaken. However, it was imperatively necessary that they should be transferred to the *Tigress*, as there would be no one to doctor them aboard the ship when Corney was gone. It was touching to see how tenderly their shipmates handled them, whispering soothing or encouraging words as they lowered them one by one over the side. Nor were they one jot less humane in their handling of the wounded whites of the ship's crew; but though they were merciful enough with the blacks and mulattoes, their abhorrence of them was strongly expressed in their faces and their sharp disgustful recoils when addressed or touched by them.

"You wouldn't believe how they fought, sir," said Parell to me. "One of them was found dead with his teeth locked in the hand of Jim Baines, and afore they could get the poor fellow's hand out of the brute's mouth, Mr. Corney had to lash a couple o' marlinespikes together like a pair o' shears, and even then it took two of us to prize the nigger's jaws open."

A dismal boatload they made: to this day my memory is haunted by the white men's low moans, the peculiar short, thick grunts of the negroes, the hollow suffering faces, the bloodstained clothes, the rolling eyes of the blacks, and their shining fangs gleaming betwixt their bulbous drawn lips and giving a most unearthly character to the ashen-black of their faces. Thankful enough I was when, the last man having been lowered, I gave the order to the boat's crew to shove off. I then turned up the rest of the men to refit, and went below to offer a choice of vessels to the passengers.

My heart thumped as I descended the companion-steps. I had not had much time to think of the strangeness of this meeting of mine with Miss Palmer; and though, as you know, she had often been in my thoughts, the idea that in all human probability we should never meet again had stopped me from realizing the tenacity of the hold taken by the grapnel she had flung into my heart from the very first moment of our getting alongside of one another at the Plymouth ball. I appreciated the strength of that grip now, and understood its significance by the uncomfortably nervous flutter that bothered my brain, like an angry popple under a light craft.

But shove ahead, men—shove ahead! So down I went, wondering whether it was my nerves or the temperature that made my face burn, and plumped headlong among the passengers, every one of whom—baby and all—was assembled near the table, sitting or standing.

Hat in hand, I made them a polite bow, and immediately perceived that not one of them recognized in me the ghastly figure that had confronted them three-quarters of an hour before. Miss Palmer was standing near Colonel Bray, and the moment I hove in sight she fixed her eyes upon me— that much I saw—and I also noticed that she eyed me intently, and that a little color stole into her cheeks.

"I am deputed by the commander of the schooner, ladies and gentlemen," said I, "to inform you that both vessels will be under sail shortly, and that if any of you would prefer to occupy the schooner for the remainder of the journey, you will be very welcome to such accommodation as she has to offer."

The gentlemen looked at one another, and then at the ladies.

"We are extremely obliged for the offer," said Colonel Bray. "I have the pleasure, I presume, of addressing one of the officers of the vessel to whose gallant crew we are indebted for our rescue?"

"I am her chief mate, sir," I replied with a bow.

"I have been examining your schooner through my cabin window," continued the colonel, "and observe that she is a very beautiful, powerful, and well-armed boat. After our disastrous experience in this Indiaman, whose crew, I regret to say, struck to the American privateer without firing a shot—without firing a shot," he repeated warmly and indignantly—"I, for one, am strongly disposed to accept your captain's polite offer to use his vessel."

"But will the gentleman be pleased to tell us whether we run any danger by remaining in this vessel?" exclaimed a dusty-looking, big-nosed, black-eyed old man, whose yellow fingers were brilliant with rings, and under whose highly flowered waistcoat there hung, by the bight of a chain, enough seals and gewgaws to furnish out a jeweller's shop.

"Mr. Jonas Solomons, sir," said Colonel Bray, introducing the old fellow to me with a wave of the hand.

"Why, Mr. Solomons," I replied, "the schooner is not only the better-armed, but she will be the better-manned vessel. But as she will convoy us, and as the run to Kingston cannot prove a very long one, I do not see, as regards the security offered, that there will be much to choose between the two vessels."

"You hear what the gentleman says, Jonas," said Mrs. Solomons, fanning her fat, treble-chinned face, and resembling an inflated balloon in the green silk dress she had substituted for the gown that had been ripped off her back. "Mind, I leave it to you!"

"Who will command this ship, thir?" asked Mr. Solomons.

"I," I replied.

"What do you say, Mr. Culpepper?" observed Colonel Bray, addressing the yellow-faced man in gaiters.

"Why, I am certainly for placing myself under the guardianship of our brave rescuers," replied Mr. Culpepper. "In simpler language," he added, pulling out a snuff-box, "I'm for the schooner."

"And so am I," said Mrs. Montague, a red-faced, rather untidy-looking woman, slackly rigged about the bosom and with her cap awry, as if most of her time was spent in nursing the baby and fighting with it. "When I think of the risk my blessed tootle-torums has run, I vow I would rather finish the voyage on a bare raft in company with our brave rescuers than in this dreadful ship;" and here she snatched her baby from the nurse, threw her spare arm round the neck of a girl of about fourteen years old, was clasped round the waist by another daughter who looked like a full-grown woman, and a most pathetic tableau was formed, the effect of which was considerably heightened by both daughters sobbing and the baby screaming.

"You will please understand that some of the men belonging to the schooner will act as prize-crew under me in this ship," said I, when the baby had done crying, and looking as I spoke at Miss Palmer; there was a little smile in her eyes, and I saw that she knew me. "I merely say this in order that those among you who decide to remain in this vessel may know that they will be under the guardian-sihp of a portion of the people whom Mr. Culpepper is good enough to call your brave rescuers."

"I should prefer the schooner," said Colonel Bray.

"And that is my choice," exclaimed Mr. Culpepper.

"Ladies and gentlemen," said I, "I have to ask that those among you who wish to be transferred to the schooner will be good enough to immediately collect such articles as they may wish to take with them. Darkness will be upon us shortly, and time presses."

Colonel Bray, Mr. Johnson, Mr. Culpepper, Mrs. Montague and family rushed into their cabins. Mr. Solomons flung himself down upon a chair, and was immediately attacked by his wife.

"Now, what do you mean to do, Jonas?"

"I am very comfortable here, and I shall stop, my dear."

"Mind what you say! The pirates that's been turned out of this ship aren't the only ones on the sea."

"I don't care about other pirates. All my goods are in this ship, and here I stop."

"Was there ever such a man! He thinks of his goods as if he hadn't got a life to lose. Do you hear what I tell you, Jonas?"

Here Tapping, limping heavily from a wound in his foot, came stumping down the companion-steps like a wooden-legged man.

"The boat has returned, sir, from taking the wounded to the schooner."

"Very well, Mr. Tapping. Arm the men, and get the prisoners on deck. They are to be transferred to the *Tigress* at once."

"Right, sir!" and he went up the steps again. As I looked around, Miss Palmer came up to me with her hand extended.

"Do not you remember me, Mr. Madison?" she exclaimed.

"Indeed I do, Miss Palmer," I answered, holding her hand. "I saw and knew you when you saw but did not know me."

"No, do not say that. I recognized you the moment you entered the cabin, though I was too much surprised to speak."

"Surely you did not recognize me when I had a handkerchief over my grimy face?" I exclaimed, laughing.

"Was *that* you!" she answered, much astonished. "Why, it looked like a dying man! *You* are not wounded?"

"Very slightly—nothing worth mentioning. Miss Palmer, you cannot imagine how proud and glad I am that the little *Tigress* should have been the instrument of saving you from a voyage to America, and God knows how long a detention there. But tell me now—for time presses—which vessel would you prefer to remain in?"

"I would like to be guided by you, Mr. Madison," she replied.

"As I am to take command here," said I, feeling that I blushed a little, but talking on pretty bravely, "you may guess what my wish would be. But I should not like to influence. I may say, however, that as the *Tigress* will hold us in sight, and as the journey to Kingston will not occupy much time, you may believe that you will be as safe with me as with Captain Shelvocke."

She turned to the couple who were arguing at the table.

"Mrs. Solomons, do you intend to stop in the *Namur?*" she asked.

"Yes, yes, miss, we shall stop," responded Mr. Solomons.

"Listen to the man! he thinks only of his goods!" rattled out Mrs. Solomons. "Does he *know* what he means? Be pleased to tell him, mister, what he risks by stopping!"

"He really risks nothing that I know of," I answered, seeing the importance of prevailing upon these people to stay where they were, as it would be out of the question that Miss Palmer could stop unless some other lady remained also.

"You hear him, my dear; now don't bother me any more," remonstrated Solomons, shrugging his shoulders, and extending his hands, and looking very worried.

"Mind, then!" exclaimed Mrs. Solomons, "this is your doing. I have left it to you. It's you as decides. If harm comes, it'll be your fault, Jonas: so mind!"

And she bustled into Mrs. Montague's cabin, where I heard her abuse her husband to that lady as a weak-minded old man.

"As they have decided to remain, I too will take my chance with you," said Miss Palmer, addressing me with a smile. "I am sure I shall be as safe here as in the *Tigress*, and certainly more comfortable, as I do not suppose your schooner will have a cabin like this."

"No, indeed," I replied, overjoyed by the prospect of her company.

She must have remarked my delight, for she looked away with a little tremor of the eyelids—not a smile, and yet with more significance in it than a smile could have held, which so confused me that to remedy my embarrassment I went the round of the berths, bidding their inmates make haste and join me on deck, and then quitted the cabin.

I was in great spirits; my heels never felt lighter; I would have foregone all my prize-money sooner than this meeting with Miss Palmer. And yet, what was she to me? Worse still, what was I to her? Could I be ass enough to suppose that she had ever given the young fellow she had danced with at Plymouth a single thought from the moment I had said good-by to her down to this particular hour? What on earth, then, was there in her arranging to stop on board the ship that was like to set me whistling for happiness as any school-boy would?

Here I knocked my hat against the top of the companion, and crushed it over my nose, and when I raised it I was on deck confronting the American·privateersmen, who had been brought up from below, and stood in a group near the gangway, and their lovely countenances speedily clapped a stopper on my romancing.

There were twelve of them, two coal-black Africans, a few mulattoes, and the rest white men; and of all the rascally creatures I ever beheld, I think these were the worst. Tapping had taken the precaution to pinion their wrists behind them as they emerged one by one from the forehatch, and it was impossible to see their scowling, gleaming eyes wandering upon the weapons in our men's hands without applauding his discretion. The blacks and mulattoes were nearly naked; the white men wore shirts; they were all of them exceedingly powerful men especially the negroes, upon whose naked flesh the muscles stood out as you may see them on the shoulders and haunches of straining cart-horses. They were handed over the side like carcasses, and deposited in the boat, half of them aft and half forward, a number of armed seamen stood over them, and presently they were alongside the schooner.

By this time the passengers had arrived on deck, and I sent some men below to bring up the parcels and cases which they desired to take with them to the *Tigress*. They appeared to realize their rescue here more completely than in the cabin. I saw Mr. Culpepper look around him with strong emotion expressed in his face; Mr. Johnson grasped my hand and held it, without speaking; indeed, by a hundred nice tokens which cannot be expressed in words, they all of them appeared deeply affected by the sudden and happy change that had been wrought in their condition.

Miss Palmer went to the rail and leaned upon it, watching the schooner. The sun was still above the sea, but he would vanish in another ten minutes; the great and peaceful glory in the west, the calm, soft blue of the sky overhead, the graceful shape of the schooner rolling gently on the swelling green of the water that was gradually transmuted into a sheet of flashing gold as it neared the sun, formed a scene that must have given a particular richness to the sense and relish of the liberty that had come to these people who, a short time ago, were prisoners on their way to a bitter exile in an enemy's country.

"Is that the vessel, mister, that fought this ship?" asked Mrs. Solomons of me, pointing to the schooner.

22

"Yes, that is she, madam," I replied, accepting the inquiry as a preface to something laudatory.

"Well, when I looks at her," says she, "I don't know but what Jonas is right after all. She's but a little ship, mister, and I dare say rolls fearful."

"Ay, she rolls fearfully, Mrs. Solomons: you'd never be able to keep your footing in her. However, I'll say nothing about the smallness of her cabins, and the heat of them, and the cockroaches, ma'am, for they cannot concern you now that you have been clever enough to decide on remaining in this large, roomy, cool, and beautifully furnished ship," said I, determined to disgust out of her any lingering wish she might have to accompany the others—for, as I have said, if *she* went, Miss Palmer would have to go too.

She nodded cunningly, and I rather think she winked.

"Ah," she whispered, "Mr. Solomons is no fool. He knows what's good. Are you the captain of this vessel, sir?"

"I shall have charge of her, as I think I informed you."

"Well, I'm pleased to hear it. You looks a good sailor. Lor', to think of our being rescued from them savages, and me calling upon death this very day sooner than be carried off to Ameriky along with two thousand o' pounds worth of goods belonging to Mr. Solomons, and which he was only saying to me just before your ship took to. firing at us— 'Rachel,' he says——"

The interesting creature's confidences were interrupted by a fellow in the maintop bawling out "From under!" and I had just time to trundle her out of the road, before the port mizzen-topsail brace, the end of which had been accidentally let go, unrove itself and fell heavily in a heap where she had been standing. Uttering various exclamations of alarm, and fanning herself violently, my porpoise-shaped beauty waddled or rolled to the companion, and disappeared in search of her Jonas.

Presently the cutter returned from the schooner, and the passengers entered her, shaking hands with me as they went over the side. The sun sank as they put off, and the darkness came rolling down upon us like a curtain out of the east. But by this time most of the refitting aloft was completed; the running-gear had been rove afresh, new fore and mizzen topsails bent, tackles got on to the injured standing rigging, and the decks so effectually cleared that, beyond sundry dark stains here and there and splashes upon the paint of the bulwarks, no relic of the dreadful carnage that had made a very shambles of the Indiaman was visible.

Once more the cutter returned with orders from Shelvocke to me, to keep fifteen men and Parell, making sixteen, as a prize-crew, and to send the rest of the *Tigresses* back to the schooner. At the same time some written instructions from Shelvocke respecting day and night signals, etc., were placed in my hand. The men were mustered, a prize-crew singled out, and the remainder repaired on board the *Tigress*, who fired a gun as a signal for us to brace round the mainyards; and in a few minutes the ship was gliding slowly through the water, with the dark shadow of the schooner blotting out the stars to windward, and a thin, greenish, fiery wake trailing slowly away under our taffrail into the dark waters of the east.

# CHAPTER XV

## MY PASSENGERS.

THE night came down very dark but clear, and the sky was so crowded with stars that scores of them were blotted out by the meteors as they broke and vanished in clouds of silver dust. The men had come from aloft, and were in the forecastle, swinging their hammocks and taking a spell of rest after the heavy exertions of the day; the ship was under three topsails, courses, and fore-and-aft canvas, in deep shadow, save where a bright light burning in the galley threw a glare across the deck—a yellow beam that floated upon the darkness like an elongated *ignis fatuus*—and threw up a short length of the rusty links of the chain-cable, and glanced upon the half of a large water-cask, and a coil of rope slung over a belaying-pin, and a space of the perpendicular bulwarks heavily fractured by a cannon-shot.

"Is that you, Parell?" I called out.

"Yes, sir;" and as he emerged from the darkness and passed through the glare from the galley, he looked like a figure cut in ebony.

"What sort of a job have the men made of it aloft?" I asked.

"As good a job as can be expected, sir. I rather think there's a square topgallant-mast among the booms, and if it's fine weather to-morrow we might make shift to rig him up and cross the yards."

"Yes, that and other jobs can be done to-morrow. Who's that in the galley, there?"

"Peter Larkins, sir, he's getting the men's supper for them."

"He's a bit of a cook, I've heard, and you had better appoint him to the galley. Also let young Ransom wait upon us aft. Have you heard what has become of the officers and crew of this ship?"

"Why, sir, I believe Mr. Corney fished out some news from one of the wounded, and it was this. The wessel that attacked this ship was a large Yankee privateer brig, and the *Namur's* skipper struck to her without firing a shot. The 'Merican captain came aboard and ordered the whole of the crew as well as the officers to be shifted into his brig, no doubt in the hope of getting 'em to sarve under the stripes and stars, which was likely enough they'd do without much persuading, seeing what curs they proved theirselves when they were called on to surrender. He likewise took out three passengers—males—one of 'em a chap with a title. In the room of the *Namur's* crew he put in fifty of his own beauties, twenty-five of 'em negroes and colored men, and gave command to the chief mate—him with the red cap—and ordered him to make the best of his way to Chesapeake Bay, which they calculated they was doin' when the *Tigress* stepped in and altered their course."

This information was no doubt accurate, and it explained away one source of puzzlement that had pretty considerably bothered me since I had found time to look around; I mean the total disappearance of everybody barring the passengers, who were in the ship before she was taken by the privateer.

"Very well, Parell; keep a lookout while I go below and get something to eat. Send Ransom aft, and be careful to keep the schooner's light well in view;" and after taking a peep at the compass I made my way into the cabin.

The lamps had been lighted some time before, and the cabin looked amazingly brilliant with its tall sparkling mirrors, and the gleaming, marble-colored mizzen-mast, and the shimmer of the lights in the rich, dark panelling. The table was still littered with the ham, plates, decanters, and biscuits; but the disorder of these homely articles did not impair the drawing-room elegance and charming air of refinement that characterized this richly cushioned, carpeted, and delicately colored interior. Miss Palmer, who had left the deck shortly after dusk, was seated in a low arm-chair, with her hands folded upon her lap, and apparently lost in thought. Opposite her, in another chair, with his feet cocked up, lay Mr. Solomons, fast asleep, and snoring with a noise like a straining timber. Mrs. Solomons was in her berth, and I could hear her talking to herself as she shambled about.

Miss Palmer looked heartily pleased to see me. Her face brightened up, and she warmed quickly and gracefully into life out of her reverie like a flower under the rising sun. (Rather poetical, this, for a nautical man; but I never can think of her without drifting into garden fancies.)

"I am afraid you will find the rest of the voyage dull, now that no society is left you but——" and I motioned with my head to old Jonas.

"Dull, Mr. Madison? Do you imagine I am dull because you find me sitting here with my hands before me? Were you to ask me how I feel, I should not be able to tell you. I can hardly believe that I am not dreaming. Last night I nearly cried my eyes out in thinking of my father. I remember telling you he was ill, and that I was going to Jamaica in the hope of inducing him to return with me. When I thought of my being forced away into another part of the world, at a time when our voyage was near its close, and that months must pass before he and I could meet—if ever we met in this world again—and that he might die without knowing what had become of me—was it not enough to break my heart, Mr. Madison? And now that I am with friends again, and a dreadful time—oh, how dreadful a time!—past, and once more on my way to my dear father—can you suppose me dull? Surely that is like charging me with cruel ingratitude: though how grateful I am, to God first for His merciful providence in bringing you to our ship, and to you next, and your brave men, for your noble and heroic struggle, only my own heart knows— no words could express my thankfulness."

She rose from her chair with her eyes swimming, and grasped my hand with both hers and held it, unconsciously caressing it in the plentitude of her gratitude and emotion. The touch of her hands set my heart beating so furiously, that for the life of me I could not immediately have spoken to her. Fortunately she was as much moved as I, though in a different way, and did not (as I believe) observe how consumedly upset I was.

"You told me you had been slightly wounded," said she

presently, resuming her seat. "I hope only slightly, and that you are quite well again?"

"A little tap on the pate—just here, Miss Palmer," I answered, touching the top of my head. "Not enough to let out my foolishness, nor to admit some of the intellect I stand in need of. Have you had anything to eat to-day?" said I, struck by an idea.

"Nothing since breakfast—though I really should not have known we had not dined but for your question," she answered, smiling. "We were all too miserable to eat."

I looked at the ham on the table.

"Oh!" she exclaimed, following my glance, "the odious man in a red cap who took command here when our captain was carried away, called for those things, and was beginning his meal, when somebody came down to say that a sail was in sight—your schooner, as it afterward proved. He jumped up, and left those things as you see them. Oh, Mr. Madison, what a horrid—horrid—*horrid* creature he was!" she added with a strong shudder, and putting an almost vicious energy into the last "horrid;" "so rude, so hideous, so gross!"

Here Mr. Solomons, as if sympathizing with her language, gasped loudly in his sleep, wheezed, and gargled through his nose, "Not them goods, thir! they're mine: two thousand pounds worth. Rachel was with me when——" *snore.*

"Happy old man that!" said I. "The one beautiful thing about old age is its quality of indifference. Here, Ransom!" I sung out, in so loud a voice that old Solomons woke up in a fright, and stared at me with his eyes rounded like an owl's; and at the same moment Mrs. Solomons came bundling out of her cabin; "get the cloth laid here, my lad. I'll show you how to place the knives and forks. Yonder's the pantry—overhaul it and make the best show you can, and bear a hand."

The youngster whom I had noticed flitting at the head of the companion-ladder came trotting below, and went to work with more adroitness than I had expected. It is true he set the glasses upside down, and the plates in the middle of the table, and the cold meats which he found in the pantry he lumped together like a dozen colliers which had parted their cables and gone adrift in a body; but Miss Palmer and I soon effected such a distribution of the crockery as made the table very hospitable and glittering, and I presently had the happiness of seeing my three passengers making a good supper.

"Now, Rachel," exclaimed Solomons, pegging away at a cold fowl, and talking with his mouth full, "isn't this comfort? What more would you have? Did you want to box me up in the little wooden cabin of a butter-rigged schooner?"

"Not butter-rigged, Mr. Solomons," said I.

"Well, well," he said with a shrug, "then she *shan't* be butter-rigged; but you won't pretend that she has such a cabin as this, sir?"

"I don't say I wasn't a little hasty, Jonas," answered his wife, whose enormous person, as she sat at the table, completely overhung her plate, and obliged her to look at her fork every time she lifted it to know what she was eating. "Mister, might I trouble you for a bit of that tongue?"

"Miss Palmer," said I, holding up a bottle of champagne which Ransom had discovered in the pantry along with various other bottles of wines and spirits, including two of Jamaica rum, all of which he had very faithfully and honorably put upon the table, where they stood in a lump like a wine-merchant's "order" ready for delivery, "when I last had the happiness of drinking champagne with you, I little thought that our next meeting would be on the high seas, and amid the thunder of a sterner kind of cannon than those which Sir William Tempest fired in honor of his son. Will you let me fill your glass? Such a triumph as ours over the Yankees deserves to be drunk in an elegant wine."

She smiled with a pretty color in her face that made her eyes sparkle; but the poetry of drinking wine in champagne with this sweet girl was balked by Solomons calling for the bottle. I verily believe the old fool thought I had proposed a toast. The result was we all drank to one another, and I was nearly convulsed by the bow and smirk Mrs. Solomons bestowed on me. A bow did I call it? It was rather the compression of a balloon, or like standing a feather-bed on end, and squeezing down the top of it. There was no inclination forward: it was merely a lowering of the head, and a surprising increase of the rotundity of the body; and her very gown shone under the tightening effect of her laborious amiability.

"I see that you have met Miss Palmer before, mister," said Solomons. Both he and his wife evidently thought the "mister" as polite a form of accost as the strictest good-breeding required.

"Yes, Mr. Solomons, I have had that pleasure," I replied, glancing at Miss Palmer, and receiving a smile from her.

"I met Mr. Madison at Plymouth a few days before the *Namur* sailed, Mr. Solomons," said Miss Palmer. Her voice was so full of music, that it was a greater treat to hear her speak than to listen to a good singer. "It was but a short acquaintance, Mr. Madison."

"Acquaintances are always short when they're first made, my dear," said Mrs. Solomons, with an encouraging nod. "But I dare say, mister, you was very surprised when you saw her here, wasn't you?"

"Sailors soon lose the faculty of surprise," I replied coldly, not relishing the direction the conversation was taking in her hands. "I have not yet looked into the berths, Miss Palmer; can you tell me if our shot have done much damage?"

"Damage!" cried Solomons; "Lord bless your heart, I should say there's not less than twelve pounds' worth of windies broken."

"Several windows are broken, Mr. Madison," said Miss Palmer, keeping her face with admirable breeding. "The window in my cabin was broken by one of the first shots the *Tigress* fired, and a whole shower of glass fell over me."

"I was sitting," said Mrs. Solomons, in a well-soaped, confidential voice, and nodding her head at every other word until her chins quivered over her collar like jellies to the tread of dancers, "talkin' to Mr. Solomons, and he was calculating how much it would cost him to get us out of prison after he was in Ameriky, when a cannon-ball hit the back of the ship just against the wall where my cheer was. The blow was that violent it throwed me on to the floor, and when I begged and prayed of Mr. Solomons to help me up, where do you think he was, mister?"

"I cannot guess."

"Why, in bed, sir; with the counterpane pulled over his head, and the toes of his boots sticking up at the other end?"

"A very good place to be in," said I, looking at Solomons, who was picking the leg of a fowl with a dogged face. "I understand from one of my men, Miss Palmer, that the privateersman carried off three of the passengers. Why was that?"

"I cannot imagine, Mr. Madison. The American captain came into this cabin with a number of men, and ordered Captain Salmon" (the skipper of the *Namur*) "to produce his passengers. We were desired to stand up in a row, as though we were felons," she said, with her face flushing with the memory of the indignity, "and were then asked our names."

"True; every word of it, mister," interrupted Mrs. Solomons; "and Mr. Solomons was for calling himself Levi."

"And wasn't I right to try to cheat 'em?" shouted Solomons. "Rachel, don't quote me any more, for God's sake. I'm sick of hearing you."

"After we had given our names," continued Miss Palmer, "the American captain ordered Captain Salmon and three of the passengers—one of them Sir Sampson Jardine, a judge, and the other two rich plantation-owners—to go on deck. They did not return and we saw no more of them. We were afterward told they had been sent to the privateer."

"Did not the *Namur* make one of a convoy when she left England?" I asked.

"Yes; but we met with a heavy gale of wind that dispersed the other vessels; and we had been alone four days when the privateer attacked us."

These answers put the story before me intelligibly; and I further learned from Mr. Solomons that the freight of the *Namur* consisted of a general cargo; but he could not tell me the nature of it, unless I except two thousand pounds' worth of house-furniture belonging to Solomons. The ship's papers had either been carried off or destroyed; for I afterward searched high and low for them, but without success.

Supper being dispatched, I looked into the cabin that

had been occupied by Captain Salmon; and finding a cot swinging in it and several other conveniences, I ordered Ransom to prepare it for me. I also got Miss Palmer to shift her quarters into a cabin which the *Tigress'* shot had left untouched, and then went on deck to settle the watches.

The starlight had brightened somewhat, and the night was clearer than it had been when I went below. The wind was exceedingly soft and refreshing, and the sea quiet, black, and gleaming; the dew kept the decks cool like constant showers of rain; and the slow passage of the ship through the sea was appreciable to the ear alone of all the senses by the soft purring and creaming of the water around her stem. Ahead of us, broad on the starboard-bow, loomed the shadow of the schooner, the bright light on whose stern baffled every effort of the eye to determine her outline. That her people were watching us like cats, I knew by the regularity of the distance from us they maintained. And indeed, when I considered the value of the *Namur*, and the slenderness of her crew, I was anxious enough, as you may believe, that the *Tigress* should keep us well under her eye.

I told Parell to pipe the men aft; thirteen grouped themselves on the quarter-deck, leaving one at the wheel and Ransom in the cabin. I counted and divided them, making seven in Parell's and eight in my watch. I then sent the starboard watch below; and lighting a pipe—the first bit of tobacco I had tasted that day—I planted myself on a gun-carriage to enjoy a quiet smoke.

It was a true remark of mine to Mrs. Solomons that a man who goes to sea as a sailor soon loses the power of being surprised. Indeed, the whole life of a sailor is a chance, and the unexpected is the only thing he can safely reckon on. Consequently, my transfer from the *Tigress* to the temporary command of this large West Indiaman did not in the least astonish me. Her spacious decks, her lofty masts, the numerous points of equipment which distinguish a full-rigged ship from a topsail schooner, had grown familiar to me, I may say, almost as soon as I had found myself amid them; and had I sailed in the *Namur* from England I could not have surveyed her with an eye more totally unimpressed by the novelty of my surroundings.

But my professional incapacity of surprise ceased with the ship. My astonishment began when I thought of Miss Palmer. It was certainly amazing to find myself aboard the ship she had taken her passage in, commanding that ship, intimately associated with her who had occupied much of my thoughts, in the happy position of having been one of the instruments of the rescue of a girl who had grappled my admiration—to say no more—with hooks of steel, from the horror of a prolonged exile from her father and her home.

The silence, broken only by the creaming of froth forward; the imponderable lower darkness, over whose topmost heights the starry heavens were sparkling in widespread glory of silver fires; the hush upon the faintly breathing bosom of the deep, in whose darkling surface a faint throbbing of phosphorescent radiance mingled with the white crystalline reflection of the greater stars; the shadowy decks, with here and there the figure of a man standing still as a figure of bronze, and the faint haze of a lantern slung on the forestay, throwing up a coal-black pillar of the gigantic foremast—these were influences to subdue me into a pensive mood; and my thoughts strayed from Madeline Palmer to the events of the hours which were passing away, and my heart melted in gratitude to my heavenly Father for the merciful protection He had vouchsafed me throughout the fierce and murderous struggle of the afternoon.

A footstep caused me to look around.

"Is not that Miss Palmer?"

"Yes, Mr. Madison; surely it is not so dark but that I am to be distinguished from Mrs. Solomons?"

"Is she on deck?" I asked, rising and gazing about me.

"No; but her husband will be here in a minute. Pray do not put down your pipe."

"Shall I fetch you a chair, or will you walk?"

"I would rather walk."

In spite of the haze thrown upon the air from the lamps under the cabin skylights, the outlines of our figures only were visible. The occasional slight roll of the ship gave me an excuse to offer her my arm, and she took it.

"This has been a rare day of surprises, Miss Palmer,"

said I. "It is strange that of all the convoy dispersed by the gale, the *Namur* should have been the only one reserved for the *Tigress* to overhaul, and not a little astonishing that you and I should meet again under conditions so extremely different from what any prophet with the least regard for his reputation would have dared to predict. But the most amazing part of it all to me is, that this very morning you were so incessantly in my thoughts that positively Captain Shelvocke noticed my abstraction, and twitted me on it. Considering that your ship must have been within a few leagues of us at that time, one ought to be superstitious enough to suppose that there is more in this than mere common-sense can perceive."

This very simple and candid speech ought perhaps to have embarrassed her; had she shown any embarrassment I should probably have seen how very simple and candid it was; instead, she laughed pleasantly, and answered:

"You have a wonderful memory, Mr. Madison, considering you are a sailor."

"At all events I don't forget Lady Tempest's ball," I answered; "and if we were aboard the *Tigress* I could prove the sincerity of my memory by showing you the flower you gave me."

"Yes, I remember," said she. "The fireworks were very pretty, and the night was even finer than this, for there was a moon, was there not? How peaceful and beautiful those heavens seem!" she exclaimed, raising her face that looked shadowy and vague as some lovely spirit's, with the starlight gleaming in her soft large eyes: "what a tranquil close to such a day as we have gone through! I should like to have seen Captain Shelvocke—do you remember pointing him out to me at the ball you have spoken of? He ought to know how grateful I am—how grateful we all are to him and his brave men. But I shall doubtless meet him at Kingston, where my father will be able to add his thanks to mine."

And then she talked of her father, and her anxiety about his health, and the eagerness with which she looked forward to their meeting. Indeed, the love she bore her father was delightful to hear her talking about, and I listened to her voice as a man listens to a nightingale. She conversed with the same cordial, well-bred candor that had fascinated me when we first met, and it was the pleasanter to me to hearken to because it implied the best compliment a girl can pay a man. Yes, I own I am never better pleased than when a well-bred woman bestows her home feelings upon me. Let her favor Jones or Jenkins with her festive hopes and memories, and chatter to them of dresses, lovers, balls, and Italian singers; she charms me most when she talks of baby's first tooth, her boy's cleverness—when in short she takes me into the nursery, ay, and into the kitchen, my boy, of her life; passing over the drawing-room, where those fine fellows, Jones and Jenkins, sit in polished boots and burnished waistcoats.

My sweet companion gave me a description of the red-capped Yankee privateersman; how he would come into the cabin, fling himself into a chair with his cap on, and leaning his long arms over the back of it, while his legs stuck out like a pair of compasses, the points of which were riveted in a couple of immense rusty boots, heap—through his nose, and with his mouth full of tobacco—every possible abuse that could be coined by an American ruffian upon the British people: how, by way of giving emphasis to his contempt for the British people, he would pull out a pistol and point it at those male passengers whom he particularly addressed: how on one occasion he invited a number of blacks to breakfast, and made the ladies take their arms to the table, in order to show, as he said, what an American citizen's notions of liberty were. Her voice quivered as she told me these things; and that grosser affronts had been offered her than she knew how to tell me I was sure by her suddenly withdrawing her trembling hand from my arm and burying her face, leaving me swelling with helpless indignation, and passionately deploring that it had not been my hand that struck Master Red-cap down.

However, she rallied presently, as I did when I reflected that the scoundrel *was* dead, and that of his fiendish crew only a handful were preserved for the gallows; and after I had soothed her a bit she put her arm again into mine, and held as though she clung to me—an unconscious action on her part, though it moved me strangely; and in a few minutes we were once more talking quietly on cheerful matters, pausing now and then to watch some bright meteor flash over our mastheads, or the quivering of the yellow light thrown by the lantern on the schooner's stern into the visionary darkness of the water under her, or the passage of the stars gracefully sailing through the faint tracery of the rigging as the shadowed and silent ship leaned gently with the swell.

There is no place in the world where a charming girl's society is more enjoyable than on the deck of a vessel on a quiet starlight night, when there is just wind enough to keep the sails asleep, and when the *shaling* of the water, broken by the pushing stem, runs like a tune through your whispers and the silences between, and when every sound seems muffled by the darkness—the jar of the rudder, the murmur of men talking forward, the creak of a block high up in the gloom.

Poets may sing of love-making in sylvan scenes, of Delia listening to Strephon amid the twinkling shadows of leaves, of Chloe hearkening to Damon blowing his pipe while lambkins skip in the distance and Zephyr wantons o'er the enamelled mead; by all means let Strephon enjoy himself *sub tegmine fagi*, and let the lambkins shake a foot to Damon's oaten pipe; but if Delia and Chloe want to taste a bliss in flirtation beyond all that the poets have told, let them choose for a theatre a roomy ship's deck, a star-spangled night, a soft, tropical air sweetened to every sense by refreshful showers of dew falling with every melodious flap of the alabaster-like sails, and a surrounding space of mighty waters reaching down to the further heavens, and yielding out of their vast and gloomy distances a high and magical coloring to the thoughts.

Do not I speak from experience? for a whole blissful hour Madeline Palmer and I patrolled the spacious quarterdeck of the *Namur*, and with but one brief interruption from Mr. Solomons, who, with an immense cheroot in his mouth, asked me if I could tell him how fast we were going. I looked over the side and gave a guess at the speed, whereupon he got upon the aftermost skylight, and pillowing his head upon his arm, lay on his back and troubled us no more.

At last Miss Palmer said she must wish me good-night

now; it was nearly ten o'clock; she had much enjoyed her walk and conversation.

"Indeed I am afraid, Mr. Madison, I have tired you with my incessant chatter."

"Indeed you haven't, and I hope you don't believe you have. Your society gives me so much happiness that I should only make a fool of myself if I attempted to express my gratitude. You cannot imagine what a delightful break your company is to a poor sailor whose horizon has for weeks been a sea and sky."

"I believe you, Mr. Madison, as you must believe me," she exclaimed, pausing in the soft radiance that streamed through the open skylight, whereby I beheld her eyes fixed earnestly on me, and her sweet face very pensive and thoughtful. "Unmeaning compliments would be a cruel pastime after our experiences this day. When I think of what your presence in this ship means, my escape from sufferings I dare not dwell upon, I can only wonder that my full heart suffers me to speak at all."

"Ay, but you mustn't let the past trouble you. If I chose I could make myself as sad as the ghost of a murdered man, by reflecting on the number of brave, hearty, kindly shipmates whom the rascally buccaneers have sent to their account this day; of my plucky messmate, the second mate of the *Tigress*, tossing, with a dangerous wound in him, in the close atmosphere of the schooner's little cabin; of the narrow escape I have had from sounding these dark and melancholy depths, on whose surface you and I are exchanging our fancies. But surely I am wiser in preferring to dwell upon the happiness that has grown out of to-day's thunder—the happiness, I mean, of having helped to rescue you from the Yankees, and of passing a few days, at least, in your society."

"One cannot forget the past at will," said she, shaking her head; "and I have not your power of fixing my attention on things I ought to think of."

However she smiled as she said this: and then, holding out her hand, bade me good-night.

"God bless her!" thought I, watching her go down the companion-steps; and when her bronze-colored hair caught the light as she descended, it sparkled as though she shook a shower of gold-dust out of it. "A charming girl, indeed! a frank, womanly, affectionate lady!"

Here I went on tiptoe to the foremost skylight, and peered into it to see her as she passed along the cabin. She stopped at the table to fill a glass from a jug of water on one of the swinging trays. The shawl she had over her shoulders dropped off as she stretched forth her hand to take the jug, and her wide sleeve slipped down below her elbow and exposed her beautifully moulded arm that was as white as ivory, and gleamed like bridal silk in the beams of the lamp that hung to the right of her. Not being a linen-draper, I could not tell you what material her dress was made of. It was white, and *bolted* with black velvet, and fitted her like a glove; and a narrow, black, silver-mounted belt, to which her sandalwood fan was hitched, marked the circumference of her waist with lovely precision against the swell of her bosom as she leaned across the table as flexibly as a sportive panther crouching for a bound.

Suddenly she looked up, and saw me before I could dodge my head. It was very annoying to be caught watching her.

"I was just going to advise you to put a dash of sherry into that water, in case it shouldn't have been filtered," said I, keeping the shadow of the skylight on my face that she might not witness my confusion.

"The water is very clear," she answered, looking into the jug, and for my satisfaction, poured out a glassful, and held the glass up to the light for me to see; and as she stood with her face upturned, and her hair gleaming on her fore-head, and her lifted hand poising the sparkling glass to the lamp, and giving her figure the sweetest posture it could have taken, methought a fairer picture was never offered to mortal eyes than that which this skylight framed.

She bowed and moved away, and to comfort myself for her loss I pulled out my pipe and lighted it.

"I don't know if you are aware, Mr. Solomons," said I, going to the after-skylight, where the little man lay as quiet as a suit of clothes, "that every time you suck your cigar the reflection of the glowing point sparkles in your face as though it overhung a pool of water: strong proof that the dew falls heavily;" and I scooped along the top of the sky-light with my hand, and flung a cupful off it on to the deck.

23

"I'm obliged to you for the hint, thir," he answered, getting up. "I've been wondering what made my small clothes feel so heavy on my legs."

"Let me advise you to change them—pray stand in this light for one minute; ha! I thought as much: the dew has turned your waistcoat into brown paper."

"Whoever would have thought it so damp!" he exclaimed, smearing himself down with both hands. "Is my wife on deck, mister?"

"No; she has been below all the evening."

He went to the companion and stood staring around at the dark sea.

"There is no danger of any kind about, is there, thir? nothing, I mean, to prevent me from going to bed properly?" said he.

"Nothing more than you see," I answered.

"I haven't worn a nightcap for two nights," said he, "and sleeping in my clothes always makes me feel as if I was a man in possession."

"That must be rather a queer thing to feel like," I observed.

"Well, it isn't so much the clothes being on you, as their obliging you to lie awake and listen, and to think every sound that strikes your ear to be some one moving goods. However, I shall sleep comfortable to-night, thank God, and so I wish you *bong swore*, mister."

He faded down the ladder, creeping with great caution and clinging fast to the handrail, and I was left in lonely possession of the deck.

I was no sooner alone than an unaccountable depression fell upon my spirits. Whether it was due to the blow I had received on the top of my head, or to the events of the day which took advantage of my solitude to crowd upon my memory, and to flash upon my mind's eye the dreadful picture of carnage these decks had exhibited after the fight, I know not, but I do remember that a most heavy sense of foreboding weighed in me, a nervous apprehension of coming evil, that my utmost resolution was unequal to combat.

I went aft to the man at the wheel and spoke to him; but I had better remained alone, for after exchanging a few

words, the poor fellow began to speak of our action with
the Yankee privateersman, and then told me that his
brother—whom he had sailed with voyage after voyage, for
fifteen years, during which time they had always managed
to be in the same watch, and even to swing their hammocks
alongside of each other—had been run through by one of
the men who had boarded the *Tigress,* in the waist, and
instantly killed. His head drooped over the spokes of the
wheel which he clutched, as in rough and broken tones he
told me of the affection that subsisted between them, how
neither of them had married, that their wages might be
wholly appropriated to the support of their mother, and I
saw the tears glance from his eyes past the binnacle-lamp
as he muttered that he did not know how he should be able
to break the news to the poor old woman, and that it was a
pity the Lord had not taken him instead of Joe, who was
ten times the better man, "the finest sailor, your honor, in
the whole world, every finger a fish-hook, his courage like a
lion's, and his heart as soft as a girl's."

I had no consolation to offer him; indeed, I was only fit
to make him more miserable; so I left him and went to the
side and hung over it gloomily, watching the schooner and
heartily wishing it were an hour earlier that I might persuade Madeline Palmer to come on deck again and cheer
me up with her company.

All this time there was a light breeze gently blowing on
the quarter, and our progress was marked by the slow
passage of little eddies whose presence in the deep black
water was denoted by the phosphorus that circled in them.
Indeed, but for these tiny whirlpools and the soft moan of
foam at the bows of the ship, I should not have guessed
that we were moving, so imperceptible was the motion of
the dark hull and so deep the silence aloft.

There is nothing in the world that so heightens the mood
with which you survey it as the sea, be your mood what it
will. Had I been light-hearted, I should have doubtless
beheld in the spacious fields of ebony waters gleaming down
to the stars upon the horizon, a symbol to quicken my
pulse with its magnificent suggestion of liberty; I should
have thought of the fretful and feverish worries of life
ashore, the baiting of man by his fellow-man, the struggles

of poverty, the pains and fears of wealth, the unhallowed romance of

"Loose life, unruly passions and diseases pale ;"

and constrasted some such a vision of populous human existence with the broad and majestic amphitheatre upon whose dark liquid floor our vessel hung, watched by a sky of silver stars and fanned by an air fresh from heaven's own nostrils.

But my mood now found the deep a heavy shadow, haunted by corpses, a "thrilling region" that deepened fancy until I gazed spellbound upon the visionary space, dreaming the dreams which out of its prodigal sympathy it yielded to my imagination. All the men who had been stricken down this day swarmed in the void like the ghosts in Glover's ballad: and my material eye—sharpened no doubt into keen perception of fantasies by the loss of blood, and by the whack that had given my senses a little interval of rest—did, and I will swear it, behold their misty shapes visibly lined under the black surface whose distance from the bulwark rail—for there was no starlight in the sea alongside—would have been an unguessable thing but for the blue fires creeping past.

"Pish!" I cried, giving my cheek a slap in pure vexation of my maudlin mood, whereby I dislodged a shower of red sparks from the bowl of my pipe; "wake up, thou mutton-headed dreamer!" and I was going to take my own advice and wake up, when lo! the hand I had raised to remove the pipe from my lips stiffened and remained forked up as though blasted by a flash of lightning. I felt my eyes protrude from their sockets, I held my breath, and a clammy dew gathered upon the skin of my forehead. "What *is* that?" I muttered. An outline of pale blue smoke—like a small hill of illuminated foam—passed swiftly through the water toward the bow of the ship; my startled eye shaped it into the likeness of a human figure—another and another sped after it—they looked like a flight of spectres: and the puffs of blue vapor that marked their passage through the pitchy water were like the fires which kindle in your eyes when you close them after looking at a bright light. Presently, and about a ship's length ahead, the sea flashed up in foam that was radiant with the magical coloring of the phosphorus. One would have said a waterspout was foaming, or that a dying whale was lashing the sea in its agony. In a moment it was abreast of me; I looked at the luminous disturbance—there was a rush of blood to my head that was like to choke me. I shrieked out, and springing backward in an agony of horror, my foot struck against the fake of a rope, and over I went, fetching the deck a rousing thump with the back of my head.

"Hi, help here!" I heard the fellow at the wheel sing out; "the chief officer's wounded!"

Some men came tumbling aft; but before they reached me I had made shift to gain my feet, though I trembled from head to foot, and the blood tingled in my extremities with the sensation a man feels when restored from drowning.

"Get me some water, one of you; thanks! there—that has set me up again."

I wiped a trickling line of perspiration from my forehead; but when I brought the handkerchief away, there was a deep stain of blood upon it.

"Oh, confound this wound! Here—pour the contents of that pannikin over this handkerchief." I threw down my cap, placed the soaked handkerchief on the wound on my head, and walked to the skylight where I seated myself, feeling uncommonly feeble and bewildered. The men were moving forward, speaking in low tones one to another, when I called to them. They drew near again.

"Were any of you looking over the side just now?"

"I was," answered one of them, and another replied that he was too.

"What did you see?" I asked, bringing out the words with difficulty; for I was fool enough to be agitated by a misgiving that my eyes alone had witnessed the sight that affrighted me, and I feared their answer. I could see that the men were as much surprised by the question as by the voice in which I put it. One of them replied: "Do you mean the sharks, sir?"

"Sharks!—were they sharks?" I shouted.

"I saw a queer sort o' scrimmage betwixt three or four large sharks, sir, as if they were wrestling for some kind of food they'd come across, if that's what you mean, sir," said the man.

"Sharks!" I muttered, passing my hand across my eyes, as though by some such gesture I sought to cleanse my brain of the fog that thickened it, "why, when I come to consider, I suppose they *must* have been sharks. Ah, I see now! . . . get me another drink of water, will you? What a sight to flash before a man on a sudden—illuminated by the horrible light churned up by the monsters! God have mercy! people have been driven mad by smaller things!"

I took a long pull at the cool water that had been brought to me.

"Men, I was standing yonder—looking over the rail there, just abaft that shattered gunport, and there shone amid the gloom ahead, whither I had noticed some shapes of fire dashing at full speed—sharks, of course—a big circle of lashed waters, as big as this quarter-deck, men——"

"That would be about it, sir," interrupted the fellow who had answered my first question.

"I was thinking of our poor shipmates whom the bloody buccaneers sent to their account this day, and—as heaven is my witness—I saw a crowd of their bodies in the centre of this foaming circle, which, as you know—you, Jackson, who saw it—was all on fire, and gleaming like moonlight streaming through blue glass—wasn't it?"

"Yes, yes; that's right, sir."

"And they held up, ay, so as to hoist two-thirds of him out of the water, the figure—of whom, think you?—the figure of your second mate, Mr. Silas Chestree. Yes, by heaven! men, they held him as though they would drive me mad with the dreadful sight, and his head wagged and his arms waved, and there he was swaying in the arms of the dead bodies around him. I saw him as plainly as I do the outline of that topsail-yard there against the stars!"

The men looked first at me and then at one another, as though (small blame to them) they believed me clean daft. Suddenly the fellow named Jackson hooked the quid out of his cheek with his forefinger, flung it into his cap, and exclaimed with great emphasis:

"I understand it now, sir, though I'm blowed if I wasn't

pretty well scared myself when I first see it.   Wot we saw was sharks."

"Yes, I know that—I admit that!" I cried impatiently. "But what *I* saw was Mr. Chestree."

"Wot *you* saw, sir," continued the fellow, deferentially but firmly, "was a dead body newly hove overboard from the schooner, and we passed just in time to see a swarm of sharks, that had been collected by the scent, a-fighting over it."

A light broke in upon my brain.

"Jump forward one of you, and fire a musket over the bows."

This was one of the preconcerted signals to be used by either vessel wanting to speak the other, and down in Shelvocke's written instructions to me. The musket flashed, and a small sharp report rattled across the water. Presently the schooner loomed near, proving that she had shortened sail, and we forged abreast of her.

I had acted impulsively and without rational excuse to signal her, but a feverish curiosity had mastered every consideration. Yet now that she was abreast of us I felt ashamed of myself, and was at a loss to know how to make my action appear reasonable.

"Ship ahoy!" shouted the familiar voice of Shelvocke.

"Hallo, sir!"

"Why have you fired a musket?"

"To report that all's well aboard of us," I blurted out, taking the first idea that came, "and to ask how it is with you."

"Is *that* ALL?" he cried gruffly; and I could figure the sea-blessings invoked on my head by the watch on deck, who had been turned up to shorten sail.

"Did you fling a body overboard just now, captain?" I called, determined to satisfy my curiosity before the schooner forged ahead.

"Yes, Mr. Madison; and sorry enough I am to have to tell you," answered Shelvocke, in a softened voice. "Poor Chestree died this evening, and we dared not keep the body through the night."

"Did you throw him overboard as he was, sir?"

"Eh—what do you say?"

I repeated the question.

"Certainly not," he answered indignantly. "He had no hammock, as you know, so he was stitched up in a pair of his sheets and launched. But this is worse than idling, sir! Do you mean to tell me you fired that musket merely to ask these questions?"

"Just listen a moment, captain," I answered. "We passed his body just now, worried by half a dozen sharks. The weight must have slipped from his feet, and the infernal fish had stripped him naked. God help me! when I saw him, I believed I was mad, and I fired that musket in order that your replies might assure me I still had my senses."

I could hear him talking to some one alongside of him—probably Tapping: the two vessels were indeed not a biscuit's throw from each other, and the wind blew from the schooner. I knew this information would shock him, as he was always jealous of the honor due to his officers; and I was sure that nothing but the excessive closeness of the cabin, and the heat of the temperature on deck, could have induced him to sanction a hurried and unceremonious burial of poor Chestree's remains.

Presently he called out:

"I am much grieved, but it cannot be rectified. The men are tired, and the 'tween-decks full of wounded. The shot, I fear, was hastily made fast; but our hearts are with the dead, and God knows there is no man of the *Tigress'* crew who would willingly do dishonor to the body of our brave and regretted shipmate."

He waited to hear if I had anything more to say, and finding me silent, ordered sail to be made, and resumed his former station ahead.

"Chestree dead!" thought I. "Alas! alas! what a day this has been!" Yet, sharp as was the pang caused me by the news, it yielded a feeling of relief too; for I knew, at least, that my eyes had not deceived me; that the ghastly and ghostly sight that had slid past was no phantasm of the brain; and I drew the same sort of comfort from the discovery that Dr. Johnson may be supposed to have derived from the manufacture of Greek and Latin verses in bed to satisfy himself that his intellect was still sound.

# CHAPTER XVI.

## JONATHAN AGAIN.

BEFORE my watch terminated, my nerves had recovered something of their old tone, and a four hours' deep sleep completed the cure. Parell aroused me and I presently followed him on deck. I peered about for some moments before I caught sight of the schooner's light; indeed, this was the proverbial black hour of the night, the stars languishing: it was like staring into the bottom of a coal-pit to look over the ship's side. There was a steady breeze, but unhappily it was blowing the wrong way, having veered dead ahead during my watch below, and the *Namur* was slightly heeling under it with her yards braced hard up against the lee-rigging, and steering three points south of the course given me by Shelvocke.

The profound darkness was not very comfortable, and I was glad enough, on casting my eyes over the quarter, to behold the sky taking that indescribable sallow, slate-colored hue which a tropical sunrise casts before it. I have always thought the aspect of the sea just before the sun rises the most melancholy sight in the world. The universal cold gray, the stony, chilly ash-color of the dawn reflected in the uneasy deep, fills the eyes with a picture of desolation. On shore a hundred cheerful signs herald the breaking day: the twittering of birds, the blue smoke rising from the cottage chimney, the laborer's hearty voice, the cackling and crowing in the poultry-yard. But at sea the dawn awakens no life: the horizon becomes a hard dark line girdling a melancholy waste of waters. But soon the rising sun, resting a dazzling silver point upon the rosy sea-line, makes the scene joyous: the waters flash like a mighty prism, you behold the topmost sails of the ship gleaming like porcelain, while the shadow of the night still lurks along the decks;

anon the whole fabric is steeped in the white radiance, and star-shaped brilliancies are kindled in the brass-work, and the glass breaks into a hundred flashing tints, and the decks glitter like fine dry sand. Another day has begun, and the watch on deck uncoil themselves from the nooks in which they have been dozing through the darkness, and grumblingly rig the head-pump and get the scrubbing-brushes and buckets along.

My eyes turned toward the schooner as the sun rose, and there she lay about a mile and a half ahead of us, with a narrow wake streaming a short distance astern of her, and the green waters caressing her glossy sides as she pressed smoothly and softly over them. A spark winked at her side, and a white cloud broke away from her, and sailed slowly down over her quarter, and before the report reached us a small red flag was quivering at her main.

"Lay aft here, Ransom!" I sung out, "and hoist the answering pennant!"

They hauled down the flag aboard the schooner, and substituted a whole row of gaudy bunting, that made the vessel look "dressed" for a holiday. I worked away with the glass consulting the signal-book as I made the numbers: "*Get your topgallant-mast swayed up and the yards crossed.*"

"Sensible advice, Captain Shelvocke; but you *might* have waited till eight bells, so as to give the watch below a couple of hours more rest."

"All right, Ransom; hoist your answering pennant again."

The flags were hauled down and another string of them hoisted.

"*Will send help if required.*"

I answered by signalling that we should not require help.

"Never mind about washing the decks down," I said to the men. "Call all hands, one of you, and the rest turn to and clear away that topgallant-mast among the booms there ready for swaying aloft."

The thumping of a handspike on the forescuttle was followed by a gruff cry. Parell was up in a trice: the rest of the watch below followed, and in a few minutes the men were springing about like cats to the tune of Parell's pipe. A jack-block was sent aloft, and the mast-rope rove. I pulled off my coat to give the men a hand. Slowly we swayed the mast up, fitted the shrouds, stays and backstays, manned the mast-rope, unbent the trippling-line, fidded, and then set up the rigging.

In the midst of all this business Miss Palmer came on deck. I raised my hat to her, and went on with my work; but now and again I would take a squint at her out of the corners of my eyes, and noticed how sweetly pretty her face looked, with the varying expressions which entered it, as she watched our complicated labors, and followed with her glances the fellows aloft, who no doubt appeared to her to be astride of nothing and holding on by their eyelids.

By the time breakfast was piped the yards were crossed and the sails ready for bending. This, all things considered, was a very smartly rushed job, and I praised the men highly for their activity. Aloft the ship now looked as taut and handsome as she had appeared when we first sighted her; and feeling exceedingly rough, dishevelled, and hot, I slung my coat over my arm and walked aft to the companion. Miss Palmer stood near it, and as I approached she exclaimed:

"Perhaps you will find time now, Mr. Madison, to shake hands."

"I will shake hands with pleasure, but I am not in the trim to talk. You don't know how hard it is for a sailor to make himself agreeable to ladies when he is not what you call tidy."

"I hope I have not annoyed you by watching you at work," said she demurely; but with a movement of the eyelids that gave an odd, coquettish expression to her face.

"On the contrary; nor am I annoyed that you should see me in this rig," said I, casting a look on my bare arms, and recollecting that the collar of my shirt lay wide open, and feeling that my hair was over my forehead, and my hat on the back of my head. "Still, I hope you will not think me rude if I ask you to excuse me until I have made myself ship-shape. You wouldn't like to be caught in the state you find me in, would you?"

"No, indeed," she answered, laughing heartily, "so pray let me keep you no longer," and she struggled with another laugh as she walked away.

When I came on deck again I found her talking to Mrs. Solomons, who was dressed in rose-colored satin, and an immense cream-colored silk handkerchief over her head: at each ear there hung a solid gold earring, shaped like a marlinspike and pretty nearly as long; a massive gold chain was slung around her neck, and under her half-dozen chins was a huge brooch containing Solomons in oils, with his right eye partially closed, as though he had just completed a bargain when he sat for this portrait. Against such a figure, Miss Palmer in her white dress and sunny hair looked like a lily alongside a peony. Her hat—I mean Miss Palmer's hat, for I love to be particular—was a simple white chip with a lilac satin ribbon bow in front; small pearl earrings, pale lemon-colored kid shoes. What sort of taste would this be considered nowadays? I am old enough to think that well-dressed women wore prettier clothes when I was a youth, than well-dressed women do now. But, be this as it may, I never saw a dress, a color, a pair of gloves or shoes or a piece of jewelry on Madeline Palmer, that did not appear to have been invented for her particular face, figure, and character of beauty alone, and for nobody else, by an artist of high and impassioned judgment.

I see her in my mind's eye now, sitting on the skylight with Mrs. Solomons by her side, the sky as white as silver, with the morning sun beyond her, her beautiful winning gray eyes fixed upon me as I advanced, threads of bronze hair stirring under the chip hat to the soft wind blowing out of the hollow of the great spanker, mittens as fine as cobwebs upon her hands as high as the sparkling rings, the clasped white fingers gleaming like new ivory upon the folds of her dress, the shadows of the two women black upon the sand-white deck at their feet.

"I hope—speaking of you of course as a sailor, Mr. Madison—that you now feel yourself equal to the task of making yourself agreeable to ladies," says she, with a grave face, and running her eyes, with a laughing devil in them, over my clothes, as I salute Mrs. Solomons, and ask after Jonas.

"My dear, the gentleman knows how to make himself agreeable," observes Mrs. Solomons, nodding at me amiably and encouragingly. "Will breakfast soon be ready, sir?"

"By half-past eight, I hope, madam. Miss Palmer,"

said I, "as I feel qualified to talk now, let me ask what sort of a night you passed?"

" A very good night, indeed."

"No nightmares, I hope—no shadows of long-legged, yellow-faced Yankees flitting through your dreams?"

"No, I was too tired to dream."

"Mr. Solomons was rather uneasy, or I should have slept well too," said Mrs. Solomons. "He was snuffling all through the night like a charity boy. He is still abed, sir. I think he's took cold."

"Very likely," I remarked. "I routed him out of a pool of dew here last night."

"Now isn't that Jonas all over!" cried she. "What does he want to go and lie in a pool of doo for? do you think he told me what he'd been doing? when I asked him what made him snuffle so, he said it was his nose. That's the thanks I got for troubling myself. But all husbands are alike. They only get took ill in my opinion to worry their wives. You never hear of a man falling ill when he's a sweetheart—do you now? No, he waits till he's a husband. But as my father, Mr. Aarons, of the Minories— perhaps you may have heard of him, mister? he has a pic- ter shop just opposite Wolf's, the wholesale clothier's— as my father used to say when anybody came to him with a trouble: ' *What!* you think you're going to mend matters by making a fuss! Make a fuss and see what I'll do for you!' There's a great deal in that, sir!"

"A great deal, no doubt," I replied, taking her word for it, and exchanging a smile with Miss Palmer, as the fat old woman took a squint down the skylight, to observe what progress Ransom's preparations for breakfast were making.

"I have been admiring your schooner, Mr. Madison, as she slides along yonder with that line of foam against the band that looks like gold," exclaimed Miss Palmer. "What an exceedingly beautiful vessel she is! Do you notice the reflection of her sails in the green water, and how lovely her wake looks upon the sea, like a streak of hoar-frost slowly melting off a field? You can see her better from the bulwark."

She crossed the deck as an excuse, I think, to get away from Mrs. Solomons, whose vulgarity, I was beginning to discover, was of that unpleasantly candid sort that keeps the fastidious listener in a constant state of suspense.

I followed her; but, instead of looking at the schooner, I watched her large, wistful gray eyes, and her coral-like ears, and her small red-lipped mouth with the pearly teeth glancing like snow, and the beautiful curve of her dimpled chin terminating in a throat of white velvet with the blue veins faintly marked; her cheeks and forehead purely fine indeed, though beheld in the searching light of the sun— whose microscopic illumination what woman does not dread? Well, well; this is parish talk indeed! But a woman is a rare bird to Jack, as any man shall discover who will ship himself for a voyage; and when he meets with a girl like Madeline Palmer, he may surely be excused for pitching his quid overboard and sentimentalizing for a spell.

And a word in your ear, mate, while I am on this tack. Might I make so bold as to suggest that it is pretty nearly time you dropped those notions of the typical sailor which you have got from your 'longshore literature, and begin to examine the real man himself with your own eyes at first hand? in order that he may get a chance of convincing you that he is not the wretched swab, the theatrical tar, the dummy in flowing breeches he is represented to be by writers who are as ignorant of the sea as any ploughman, and whose receipt for the concoction of a British seaman is an hour's study of Dibdin's songs for such nautical terms as may there be read, a glazed hat and a junk of tobacco; but (merchant mate or naval officer) a man who can act as a gentleman and converse as a gentleman—who in a word is about as much like the theatrical, poetical, and novelistic fresh-water mountebank whom the credulous people of the greatest maritime country in the world accept as a real sample of the men who fight their naval battles and circumnavigate the globe for their markets, as Punch is like Edmund Kean. Because a man is a sailor, because his life is passed upon the greatest wonder of the world, because he is driven by stress of profession to behold by day and by night the majestic scenery of the heavens and the deep— their glory, their terror, their beauty—must we have a mind impatient of higher objects than salt pork and rum?—must his mouth be full of oaths, tobacco-juice, and professional terms?—must he accept as his likeness any vulgar wretch whom the theatrical dressers force into duck-trousers, low shoes, and tarpaulin hat? Accept this low caricature as his portrait, and surely you do the seaman an unmanly wrong and a mean dishonor. Yet by such caricatures, literary and dramatic, is Jack sung, acted, drawn (and quartered, shall I say?) to the British public, who, in spite of leagues of after-dinner speeches, of poetry, stage-plays, and rant about meteor-flags, wooden walls *versus* wooden shoes, wet sheets and flowing seas, and bunting that has braved the battle and the breeze—know less about you, O ye mariners of England! your character, habits, and conversation, than the very rudest of the savage tribes, at whose distant isles ye have sometimes touched for water!

" I wonder how our friends like their new quarters?" continued Miss Palmer, keeping her eyes fixed upon the *Tigress*. "I dare say they miss the looking-glasses and gilt of the *Namur*, but Captain Shelvocke's cannons and men will comfort them; at least I can answer for Colonel Bray."

" I guess by the smile that twinkles at the corners of your mouth, Miss Palmer, that the gallant colonel is not a hero in your eyes," said I.

" Indeed he is not," she answered. "Why, you can't imagine the cowardice that was shown on board this ship when the Americans boarded her. Not the least resistance was made; the men yielded like a flock of sheep. Colonel Bray from whom much was to have been expected after the numerous anecdotes he had favored us with during the voyage, of his exploits on various battlefields, turned as white as a sheet when the American vessel came alongside, and rushed into his cabin. The only person that showed the least spirit was Mr. Solomons, who cried out to Captain Salmon, 'Do you mean to say you aren't going to fight?' 'No,' answered Captain Salmon, with his knees knocking together. 'Then you're a disgrace to your profession,' said Mr. Solomons, snapping his fingers, 'and the sooner the Yankees dispatch you the more obleeged English sailors ought to be to them!' "

The contrast of her sweet face and her mimicry was very entertaining but very fascinating, too; she burst into a laugh like a song when she saw me laughing, exclaiming:

"One ought to be angry to be made to blush for one's countrymen, but Mr. Solomon's face when he snapped his fingers at Mr. Salmon was quite irresistible. I am sure the recollection of it will outlive the memory of my own feelings of horror and despair."

"I rather suspected the colonel's valiance by his eager acceptance of our offer of the schooner's accommodations," said I. "Yet he may be a braver man than we suppose— courageous ashore, perhaps: on the principle of an Irish major I once knew, who terrified a house full of people one night by the cries and yells he raised over a black beetle he had found in his bed. When twitted on his cowardice— 'What do ye mane?' said he. 'Had a regiment of Frenchmen entered me room I'd have cut them to pieces, sir: such is me spirit. *But whose going to face a black beetle?*'"

"Yes, that is always the excuse of the small-spirited men," she said, laughing. "'Confront me with any other danger than this, and you would see what a terrible fellow I am!' Yet the English must be a brave race, or they never could have won so many battles. But surely there are some dreadful cowards among them, Mr. Madison?"

"A few more than the country wants, I am afraid, though I am astonished that the number should be so small, considering the heaps of incompetent fellows who are poked into leading positions by private patronage. The best proof of the high standard of English courage is, that centuries, I may say, of departmental truckling, time-serving, neglect of conspicuous merit, and bestowal of place, power, and honors on men whose only significance lies among their relations, have not, down to the present year, unfitted us for opposing, and sometimes beating, the arms of the countries who bid us defiance. . . . All right, Ransom. Mrs. Solomons, breakfast is on the table. I cannot offer you my arm as the companion-steps are rather narrow."

"Thank you, mister, I can manage without you."

We bundled into the cabin, where I had the satisfaction of perceiving that Ransom had considerably improved upon his first notion of table-laying. The snowy damask tablecloth; the silver and crockery; the ferns around the skylight; the bright sunbeams slanting into a tall mirror that redistributed the light in warm ripples of radiance upon the glossy panelling—the whole topped by the fragrance of coffee and other good things—made the cabin appeal comfortably to the nose as well as the eyes; but the sweetest and fairest part of the whole arrangement, to my mind, was the presence of Madeline Palmer, who, after removing her hat, took a seat opposite me.

Mrs. Solomons came out of her cabin, and told us her husband was still abed, but felt better; so we sent him his breakfast by Ransom, who, at the old man's request, left the door of the berth wide open.

"For I can listen to you talking, if I can't join in myself!" Solomons shouted; "and Rachel can hear me if I want anything, for I can't get out of my cot without help!"

"That's the worst of them things," observed Mrs. Solomons. "They're the orkadist inventions, and I only wonder that Mr. Solomons has the courage to trust himself in 'em. He has to get upon a cheer to reach it, and I've known him to be a quarter of an hour dodging it when the ship rolls, like a horse at the end of a bridle. He was as nigh killed as ever a man was a fortnight ago, for he jumped at the wrong time, the cheer upset, and there he was left clinging to the side of the cot. 'Push, Rachel!' he says to me; and push I did until the perspiration flowed down my cheeks; but the more I pushed, the further the orked thing went toward the ceiling, until the vessel gave a heave the contrairy way, and his whole weight came against me, which obliged me to let go, or I should have been thrown down; and then he says: 'For the Lord's sake, Rachel, spread a mattress under me, to let me drop soft, or I shall break my neck—I know I shall!' and I had to pull my bed to pieces to let him fall soft, as he called it. I'd as lief sleep hung upon a hook as in one of them swinging beds."

"There she goes—giving all the family noose!" shouted Solomons, with his mouth full, which, added to the cold in his head, did not greatly improve the natural melody of his voice.

Mrs. Solomons made no answer, and I took advantage of the silence to ask Miss Palmer if she had written to her father to inform him of her intention to join him.

"No; I made up my mind to go out to him as soon as I learned the state of his health; therefore I supposed my

24

writing would have been to no purpose, as I counted on arriving at Jamaica as soon as, if not before, my letter could reach him."

"He will be greatly surprised to see you, I dare say."

"He will indeed, and a little angry too, I have no doubt," she answered, smiling; "but I think the unexpectedness of my appearance will produce the effect I want."

"Your devotion should make him feel very proud of you," said I, admiring the thoughtful beauty her eyes had taken at the mention of his name.

"I hope—if the movements of your vessel permit—to have the pleasure of introducing you to him," she said. "I am sure, after you have known him a little while, you will not wonder at my devotion."

"Rachel, another cup of coffee," shouted Solomons.

A footstep on the companion-ladder caused me to look around. Parell entered hurriedly.

"The schooner has made a signal, sir, and shortened sail. We are driving down upon her fast."

With an apology to the ladies, I left the table and ran on deck. My first glance was at the *Tigress*, at whose main was blowing a long blue-and-yellow pennant, her sails were shivering in the light breeze, and she was almost stationary upon the water; we were approaching her quickly, and already I could see Shelvocke's figure mounted upon the bulwark ready to hail when we were within earscope. My second glance was around, but the horizon was speckless; indeed, the air was marvellously transparent, and the water so brightly and beautifully clear down to the remotest reaches of it, that it was like looking at it through a lens.

As we neared the schooner they let her gather fresh way, and then gave her a sheer that brought the two vessels close. I immediately perceived that something unusual had happened or was about to happen; all the passengers who had been transferred to the *Namur* were on the schooner's quarterdeck, and the bulwarks were lined with the heads of the crew. Two men were aloft on the topgallant-yard staring into the west with their hands sheltering their eyes, and above them on the royal-yard was Tapping, with his eye glued to a telescope that he was pointing into the quarter whither the men were gazing. I lifted my hat and waited for Shelvocke's hail.

"The royals and topgallant sails of what is apparently a large ship heading directly for us have just been reported by the lookout men aloft," he sung out. "Should she prove an enemy, I will bother her with my shot, while you crack on every inch of sail you can spread and get away."

"Right, sir."

"I will haul the wind for her, and meanwhile you can check the weather main braces. If she prove an enemy I will hoist a small red square flag at the fore—if a friend, the ensign at the peak."

I held up my hand to betoken I heard him.

"The instant you see the red flag at the fore, square away and be off. I will worry the enemy until you are out of sight. Once clear, you will of course brace up sharp again, and make a course for Kingston."

I touched my hat. He then turned and addressed some words to the passengers, and by the manner he pointed toward us and then toward the horizon where the stranger had been descried, I presumed that he was offering them a chance of returning to their old quarters. Evidently they preferred to remain where they were, for looking my way again he exclaimed: "Keep a bright lookout for my signal, Mr. Madison, and try your craft on all points should I fail to draw the enemy off. God-speed!"

He waved his hand and sprang on to the deck; the boatswain's pipe chirruped—jibs, topsails, and staysails poised their swelling folds between the lofty masts, and the noble vessel hauled away from us like a great white cloud.

I watched her, as she clove the bright green water, with a strong feeling of melancholy. I cannot express how endeared was the beautiful vessel to my mind, and how this adieu saddened me.

"Captain Shelvocke ought to be very proud of his *Tigress*," said a sweet voice behind me. "Surely, Mr. Madison, I cannot be wrong in supposing her to be one of the most graceful vessels ever built."

"What a marvellously quiet footstep you have, Miss Palmer! Your tread is as soft as the fall of a leaf. Ay, indeed, as you say, the *Tigress* is a graceful vessel. Look how delicately her side curves as she heels over, and how richly her copper shines against the white foam; and see how lovely is the swell of the central cloths of her sails, while the leeches are as taut as harpstrings; and notice how the sun sparkles in the bright wood of her masts and in the glass of her portholes and the burnished brass of the binnacle-cover! Can you be surprised that a sailor should sometimes love his ship as a sweetheart, and think and speak of her with as deep a tenderness as if she were a woman?"

"Not at all surprised, though I am unable to do full justice to the beauties you have so glowingly pointed out, as I do not quite understand all the terms you used," she replied, looking at me with a grave face, but with an arch expression in her eyes: "I thoroughly sympathize with a sailor's love for his ship, and think him a very wise man indeed to pin his affection to an object so full of life, beauty, and fidelity."

"Yes, fidelity certainly, whether beautiful or not," said I, searching her eyes for a deeper meaning than lay in her words, and only getting puzzled for my pains.

"Fidelity, of course, so long as she keeps afloat. If she sinks and drowns her lover she may be said, I suppose, to have betrayed his confidence?"

"You push the allegory too far," said I, laughing.

"Will you tell me what the schooner wanted?"

I explained.

"Where is the ship?" she inquired, looking around her.

"Yonder," I replied, pointing; "she will heave in sight presently. Meanwhile I must watch the *Tigress* closely for her signal."

I fetched a telescope, and placed a chair alongside the gun upon which I had been leaning. Miss Palmer seated herself while I sighted the glass. Some hands were aloft bending the royal and topgallant sails to the yards which had been crossed before breakfast. I called to them to tell me if they could see anything of the vessel beyond the schooner.

"Ay, plainly, sir," replied one of them. "She's under a press of sail, but she rises slow."

"I am not sorry that Mr. Solomons is in bed, Miss Palmer; his wife will no doubt remain in his cabin, and I shall be spared a worrying cross-examination."

"Oh, they are very good-natured people," she answered, "though more vulgar than I should have thought possible in persons possessed of so much wealth as they are said to have. Pray don't suppose I mean that money refines, but one always *is* astonished to find the airs and graces of cooks and dustmen in people possessed of wealth. I did not greatly fancy the Solomons at first, but as I grew used to their talk and manners, I found them more endurable as acquaintances, until at last they have really made me like them."

"For that they must surely be more indebted to your kindness than to themselves."

"Mr. Madison, as a sailor you ought to be a liberal-minded man."

"I am," I interrupted.

"Prejudice is bad enough in a person like me, who has never travelled out of England and is acquainted only with people in my own sphere of life. But in men who have visited all sorts of countries, and beheld all sorts of persons, prejudice is incomprehensible; to call it intolerable would not express my opinion of it."

"Really, Miss Palmer, I hope——"

"I am not in the least personal in what I am saying!" she exclaimed, with her rich, hearty laugh. "When one meets people like Mr. and Mrs. Solomons, one ought to think of one's self as a traveller who has lighted on a new kind of flesh and blood, that may be very vulgar, glittering, tawdry, and uncomfortable, according to one's own ideas of correct behavior, but that *is* flesh and blood, for all that, like one's self, and that may be—*un*like one's self—full of kindness, generosity, and good feeling—even above the mark that one has been used to find in fine ladies and gentlemen."

"Quite so, and I am thankful for a good idea."

"People like Mr. and Mrs. Solomons can no more help being vulgar and tawdry than a negro can help being black, Mr. Madison. But if the negro be a good man, shall his black skin prevent you from acknowledging him to be what you gentlemen call a good fellow, and liking him for that goodness? Mr. and Mrs. Solomons drop their *h's*, I know, and call you *mister*, and say 'you was,' instead of 'you were,' and have a shocking bad taste in colors and jewelry. But if they are a kind and friendly disposed couple, willing to oblige you in any way you may suggest, do not they deserve from liberal-minded persons the esteem they would get from narrow-minded persons were they *polished,* and only polished?"

"You reason so well that, to answer you like an Irishman, you would persuade me to your way of thinking, whether I agreed with you or not. But I do agree with you, and that my sincerity may be proved, I will ask you to observe the reverence which the Solomonses will henceforth receive from me."

The effort of speaking had raised a charming flush on her cheeks, and her fine eyes sparkled as she laid her head back on the chair and looked, with a smile brightening her parted lips, at the men at work aloft.

"I have done with Mr. and Mrs. Solomons," said she. "Let us talk no more of them."

"Very well, Miss Palmer."

"If that strange ship for which you are watching should prove to be an enemy, will you be able to escape from her?"

"With the help of the *Tigress* I shall hope to do so."

"And if you fail?"

"We mustn't fail."

"How can you have the heart to coolly argue with me on prejudice, Mr. Madison, when, for all you know, a serious danger is at hand?" said she, turning her eyes fully and searchingly upon me.

"The danger—if danger there be—is as obvious to you as to me; yet you can argue on prejudice as coolly as I."

"Perhaps I am not afraid," she exclaimed. "You see we have a new captain and crew; and besides, Colonel Bray is not here to dishearten me with his white face. However, do not suppose I undervalue the risk we are going to run because I find nothing to disturb me in your manner. I quite understand from your explanation that the *Tigress* will endeavor to divert the strange ship, should she prove an enemy, from chasing us by firing at her; but if the *Tigress'* tactics fail, and the stranger sails faster than we—

and I may tell you, Mr. Madison, that the *Namur* is not a fast ship—we shall be captured!"

"If—if. But you know that where there's an 'if' there's a way. You have certainly construed my brief explanation with surprising precision; no sailor who had been to sea all his life could have put our possibilities in a more ship-shape manner before me. And now I will ask you to let us talk no more of the strange ship. You owe me that kindness for dropping the subject of the Solomonses."

"Very well, Mr. Madison; but you must allow me to help you to watch for the vessel. What part of the sea will she first appear in, did you say?"

"Yonder, to the left of the schooner."

She shifted the position of her chair, and we watched together for some time without speaking. But though I did not speak, I was full enough of thought—as the boy said of the parrot that wouldn't talk. In writing of this girl I can only set down, of her conversation, the few passages of it which I recall—commonplace enough they are, too, you think: and so I should think myself, did they not come back to me informed and illuminated by her rich melodious voice and laugh, the varying expressions of her face, beautiful in every change; her deep, sincere gray eyes, now smiling, now wistful, now searching, now inscrutable, as they looked inward or away beyond where my imagination could follow: and, above all, by the permanent and picturesque quality of refined frankness, sometimes warmly cordial, but always maidenly, that was as active and as essential a part of her delightful character as her heart was of her body.

"Sail ho!" she presently sung out, imitating the nautical cry, but in tones like the lower notes of a flute.

I looked at her, and laughed, then peered; but seeing nothing, levelled the glass, and immediately made out a quivering gleam of white, like a fragment of paper upon the water-line.

All this while the schooner, under a whole cloud of canvas, was drawing away from us fast, and by this time had stretched well toward the stranger, lying up so as to bring her about two points on the starboard bow. The winds had breezed up somewhat and deepened the green of the water, and was making it twinkle under the brilliant sunshine with glancing foam, and my crew were singing out as they sheeted home the newly-bent royal and topgallant sails, and tailed on to the halliards. The sails of the distant ship rose out of the sea like the disk of the moon, with the silvery whiteness of the planet, and with much of the effect of the beauty of her slow and mild enlargement. I watched cloth after cloth rise up, until the foot of her fore-course was an arch upon the horizon; but it was impossible to guess her character or even to form an opinion of her size at that distance.

"Parell," I called, keeping my eye all the time at the glass that covered the schooner, "turn all hands up to stand by to man the weather-braces, and see your stun'sail gear all clear!"

"Is it possible to tell what country a ship belongs to before she shows her flag, Mr. Madison?" asked Miss Palmer.

"Sometimes, but we never can be sure. The Americans mix so much cotton in their canvas, that their vessels may occasionally be known by their sails. Yonder fellow's are white enough."

"They are like snow."

"Yes, but the morning light streams broadly on her," said I, "and it must be old and soiled canvas indeed that will not gleam like swan's down at that distance, and in such brilliant sunshine."

I shifted the glass as I spoke from the schooner to the ship beyond. The upper portion of her hull was just visible, and as she had studding-sails set on both sides, she looked like the brow of a big white cloud projecting above the horizon.

I put the telescope down and glanced aloft, mentally calculating the extra sail it was in our power to make. Some minutes passed—the *Tigress* had fined down into a small but clearly marked shape upon the sea; she looked like a toy, and yet the atmosphere was so exquisitely transparent that even at that distance her standing rigging was visible to the naked eye. Beyond and ahead of her towered the form of the stranger, heading so straight for us that her three masts were in one.

All at once I noticed a small black ball soar against the

schooner's foresail, and as it sped like a bird to the fore-masthead, the canvas quivered as though viewed through a haze of heat.

"By Jupiter, she is going about!" I exclaimed—"look out now!" And I had scarcely said this, when the little dark pellet at the mast-head broke into a gleaming red flag, and there was the schooner edging away on the port-tack. I dashed down the glass, and sprang to my feet.

"Round in the weather main-braces!" I shouted: "let go to leeward—put your helm up there—cheerily now!"

For some minutes all was bustle; ropes flung down, men singing, yards creaking.

"Steady—so! keep her at that. Up aloft, some of you, and get the lower fore and topmast stun'sail booms rigged out!"

The men, comprehending the position, rushed actively as cats into the rigging. I ran aft to look at the compass. The shifting of the helm had brought both the schooner and —as I might now call her—the enemy a little abaft the beam, by which manœuvre I had got the wind into the quarter that rendered every cloth we could stretch upon the *Namur* serviceable. Tearing off my coat, I sprang into the waist to help the men to send the studding-sails aloft; this done, the main-topmast studding-sail boom was run out, and while we were setting this sail, the topgallant studding-sail was got ready. We toiled like madmen; and thirty men, working with ordinary smartness, could not have made greater despatch with the job of crackling on sail than we. The ship felt the increased pressure, and a belt of foam, like newly-drawn milk, hummed pleasantly alongside.

Nothing more could be done for the present; and, glass in hand, I posted myself abreast of the main-brace bumpkin, and watched the two vessels to windward. Miss Palmer came quietly along the deck, and stationed herself at my side.

"The race has fairly begun," said she; "of course the ship is an enemy?"

"Yes; that red flag on the schooner says so!"

"She looks a very large ship, Mr. Madison?"

"Apparently what sailors call a heavy corvette. I think there can be no doubt of her being an American."

I was watching the enemy steadfastly through the glass, and was a little more dismayed perhaps than I ought to have been by the formidable appearance she presented, now that her hull was hove up and the whole massive fabric, from the water-line to the main-truck, visible. Suddenly she braced up her yards, hauled the wind, and took in her lee studding-sails. The whole manœuvre was executed in a breath.

"After us, by heaven!—and see, she tries her range!"

A mass of white smoke sailed out of her lee-bow from a gun evidently aimed at the *Tigress*, who was in stays, having tacked the instant the enemy put her helm down. But before the report of the cannon rolled down to us, a red light flashed on the schooner, and there blew from her side a cloud that resembled a small ball of cotton-wool, which grew bigger and bigger as it drove along the water. The two reports reached us one after the other like a double-knock on a door.

"This won't do, Parell!" I sung out. "We must make a stern chase of it, or that fellow will be striking us at an angle. So square away fore and aft, and get your port stun'sail booms rigged out, and the sails hoisted!"

The ship was now put dead before the wind. But a few moments after our helm was shifted the enemy shifted his, and there he was, dead in our wake, though, to be sure, a long way astern, with studding-sails out on both sides. It was now evident that he twigged our tactics, and that the *Namur* was the particular game he aimed for. This indeed might have been anticipated, for our character would be guessed by many signs transparent enough to a nautical eye, and they would reckon by the trim of our hull that we were a well-freighted ship.

But they had yet to learn the sort of stuff the *Tigress* was made of.

Shortly after she had discharged her first shot at the enemy, she again tacked, and while in stays, dosed the corvette with a broadside. The salute was immediately answered by a furious discharge that, to, all appearance, did the schooner no injury whatever. I saw her white sails gleaming unscathed upon the towering withe-like masts as the noble little vessel shot into the wind; and as she luffed to meet the breeze, she fired single shots at the big enemy, one after another as fast as her guns could be loaded.

"They'll never be able to stand her if once they let her get to windward!" I exclaimed, thinking aloud in my excitement. "Look how magnificently she holds her luff and crawls upon the enemy's quarter, closing her with shot which I *know* must be heavily telling; and every foot of progress she makes weakens the enemy by a gun while she keeps her helm amidships! Bravo, Shelvocke! that was nobly managed!" I shouted, as a line of flame belched from the schooner's side, and shrouded her in a thick canopy of smoke. "Will the fools let him rake them? See, he tacks again! By heaven, he has the English ensign hoisted! Well done, little one! Load again smartly—but hold your shot a few moments longer, until you open his stern!"

In my excitement, and utterly unconscious of what I was doing, I had seized Miss Palmer's arm by the wrist, and was flourishing it as though I grasped a cutlass.

"Dear me! I most sincerely beg your pardon. I hope I have not hurt you Miss Palmer?"

"Not in the least—indeed, I did not feel your hand," she replied, laughing heartily, but with her eyes all aglow with the excitement of the scene. "Oh, Mr. Madison, what courage your people are showing! How splendidly your captain works his vessel! It makes one's heart leap to see such heroism! Constrast the sizes of the two ships—and see how manfully the *Tigress* fights her enemy!"

By this time the men had done their work aloft, and, forgetful of the etiquette of shipboard in the deep interest of the moment, had grouped themselves upon the quarter-deck to watch the vessels astern of us; and there we all stood, looking intently one way, while from time to time exclamations broke from the men as the cannonading between the schooner and the corvette grew heavier and heavier. It was not always easy, however, to see what the combatants were about, for the smoke of the guns rolled down between them and us, and floated like a dense fog upon the water, producing a very remarkable appearance with the effect of the seas brilliantly sparkling on either side of it; but now and again the folds would be rent asunder by the breeze and form a lane, through which sometimes the ship and sometimes the schooner, sometimes both vessels together, were visible, gleaming like spectral forms amid the snow-white convolutions of smoke which framed their shining-sails.

"She don't seem inclined to let us go, sir," said Parell, chewing his junk of tobacco in his excitement as earnestly as if he were eating his breakfast. "The little un' can't divart her."

"It certainly looks like it," I replied gloomily, as, through a break in the smoke, I noticed the towering form of the ship heading dead for us and overhauling us slowly, but most surely. Indeed, the *Namur* was one of those fat, stumpy ships which need a gale of wind to drive them. She was what old women would call a safe boat, high and dry, very roomy and very strong—a big, motherly, lubberly craft, but heavy to work and heavy to sail; and that the corvette gained but slowly upon her was pretty good proof that *she* was by no means a clipper either, and that if Shelvocke could only induce her to tackle him, the field would soon be clear for us.

"*Now* what's the matter?" wheezed a voice behind me. "What a wonderful thing it is people won't leave one another alone. More powder wasting, and for *what?*"

I turned and confronted Mr. Solomons, and behind him stood his wife.

"Good-morning, Mr. Solomons; I am glad to see you on deck. I hope your cold is better?"

"Good-morning, thir. Good-morning, Miss Palmer. No, my cold is *not* better, I'm obliged to you. Will you be good enough to tell me what's going on yonder?" said he, extending his shrivelled shining hand toward the two vessels.

"The big chap is in chase of us, and the *Tigress* is trying to claw him into turning upon her, so that we may escape. That's all, Mr. Solomons."

"That's *all*, indeed!" cried Mrs. Solomons. "A pretty big all it looks to me, Jonas. What might the ship be, mister?"

"An American, I suspect."

"What?" squealed the poor woman, with a wild toss of her hands, while her face turned to the color of a blancmange, and looked uncommonly like one, too, with her chins quivering one on top of the other. "Another American! Now, Jonas, what did I tell you? didn't I beg and pray of you to change into the schooner? Here's a pretty mess! no sooner out of one trouble than into another. Why didn't you accept the gentleman's offer to change your ship like the others did?"

"Don't bother *me!*" growled her husband. "Blarst the Americans!"

"You needn't alarm yourself, Mrs. Solomons," said I, noticing the crew grinning as they ran their eyes over her figure. "We shall be able to give that fellow the slip, I have no doubt."

"Come and stand by me, Mrs. Solomons, and watch the magnificent courage the little *Tigress* is showing: such a sight would give spirit to a mouse!" exclaimed Miss Palmer, turning her flushed face and flashing eyes toward the fat lady.

"No; thank you, miss; I take no interest in such shows. I only beg and pray that this gentleman will take us away from that ship as fast as iver he can," responded Mrs. Solomons.

"Here, sit down, Rachel, sit down!" shouted Solomons. "I'll not have the gentleman worried in the execootion of his duty. Will one of you please to bring that cheer—thank you. Now, Rachel, sit down and make yourself comfortable, for God's thake!"

The poor woman, convulsing her body in dumb-show, after the manner of her nation, seated herself. Solomons approached me close, and with a slight drop in his right eye, as he jerked his thumb over his shoulder in the direction of his wife, whispered:

"Joking apart, thir, what's the danger?"

"There is really no *joking* that I am aware of," said I, drawing away and answering in my usual voice, and by no means relishing the cunning air he put into his accost, as though he were a receiver addressing a pickpocket. "Yonder are the two vessels, and by looking at them you will know as much as I do."

And to escape him I crossed the deck.

The breeze was scarcely noticeable as we drove dead before it. The smoke of the guns was blowing in long, languidly-moving lines past us, and the taste of burnt gun-powder was strong in the mouth with every breath we drew. The *Tigress* had got to windward, or, in other words, right astern of the enemy, who was blazing away at the little vessel with her stern-chasers, and receiving in return the whole fire of the schooner's port and starboard broadsides alternately. I was so certain that the corvette could not much longer endure these fearful and repeated scarifications, that I lost the fear of her overhauling us in speculating upon the moment when she would drop her pursuit to turn upon the schooner.

"She's being raked every minute, sir!" exclaimed Parell, coming over to me. "One 'nd think such an iron drenching was more than flesh and blood could stand. And yet her spars seem all right, sir."

"Forward they are; Captain Shelvocke always aims low. If the corvette lets him rake her like this, she'll soon have no men to resist him. But it *can't* last! why, good heavens, Parell, the *Tigress* has it all her own way—look at her under jib and foresail, porting and starboarding her helm as she loads her guns—how fiercely she fires! what a burr for a ship's skirts! . . . Hillo! is that for us?"

A puff of smoke leaped as I spoke from the corvette's bow, and a spurt of white foam sparkled like a bar of bright silver about a hundred fathoms astern of us.

"Heavy metal, sir!" grumbled Parell; "a thirty-two-pound ball that, sir."

"There! I *knew* it could not last!—goaded at last into it, are you, you villain?" I shouted, as the corvette took in her studding-sails, and slowly swept round, bracing her yards sharp up as she hauled her wind, while she discharged her weather broadside at the schooner, who with splendid alertness had covered her spars with canvas and was creeping dead away to windward, peppering the corvette as she went with balls from her stern gun. "Was there ever a finer fellow than Shelvocke?" I cried, in a transport of admiration. "Look! he brings the enemy after him as though he had her tow-rope aboard."

And assuredly the courage, the agility, the dashing and audacious seamanship that had been shown by the *Tigress* in this brief but decisive bit of work would have kindled enthusiasm in a heart of stone. But these qualities were immeasurably deepened to us witnesses of Shelvocke's conduct by the heaviness of the stake that depended upon the issue of it. Had the enemy been suffered to approach us within range, one broadside would in all probability have crippled us, and left us at her mercy; instead, there was the corvette stretching away from us in pursuit of the schooner, whose heels gave her about as much chance as Mrs. Solomons would have had in a race with a boy.

"One 'ud need read a good bit of history to come across anything neater than that, sir, exclaimed Parell, biting out another piece of tobacco to replace the quid he had masticated and probably swallowed. "She *is* a Yankee, sir; you can see her flag now," he continued, handing me the glass, "and you may likewise observe that she's lost her mizzen-topgallant mast."

Yes; the stripes and stars hidden from us while she had been running could now be seen streaming from the mizzen-peak as the corvette stretched her long, low, black hull broadside on to us, leaning under the volume of sail she carried, with men swarming like bees upon her mizzen-rigging and a sharp throbbing and quivering of foam along her side.

"There goes the enemy, Mr. Solomons," said, I crossing the deck and addressing the old man as he stood staring with knitted brows at the vessels. "You may very safely return to your bed now, sir, and continue nursing your cold."

"Thank ye, I think a cigar on deck'll do me more good, mister," answered the old fellow, slapping his vest-pockets in search of a cheroot; and then taking a look at the compass, he bawled out, "I say! where are you taking us, mister?—this here's the road to Europe, do you know?" and as he stood pointing at the compass he sloped his back in such a way that the sleeve of his coat was drawn up his arm, and his hand and wrist forked out like a skeleton's.

"I am very well aware of it," said I, in a voice that stopped him from asking any further questions. He joined his wife, and they sat talking together and gesticulating.

I stood near Miss Palmer, watching the lessening vessels, whose increasing distance was denoted both to the eye and the ear by their dwindling shapes and by the lengthening intervals between the flashes of the guns and the sound of the detonations. They glided along the water that ran up to the beautiful clear and blue horizon like a large and small cloud sailing across the sky, the schooner keeping well ahead of the corvette so as to enable her to use only her bow-guns, and keeping her station with the utmost ease under her mainsail, staysail, and jibs.

"I was very much afraid, Mr. Madison," said Miss Palmer, in a low voice, "that you were going to reproach me for having spoken well of Mr .Solomons. His remark just now was certainly very offensive. But you are too kind to make him a topic of conversation—at all events for the present."

"I wish they would both take to their beds and stop there until we arrived at Kingston," said I.

"Pray talk of the schooner, not of Mr. Solomons!" she urged in a half-laughing manner, though the flush and sparkle which the watching of the vessels had kindled in her cheeks and eyes still lingered, and made her look so beautiful that it needed all the forces of my good taste or good sense to prevent me from staring her out of countenance. "How wonderfully Captain Shelvocke has drawn the ship away from us! Mr. Madison, the very first person you must introduce me to at Kingston, should fortune permit us all to meet there, is your captain. I should like to tell him with my own lips what I have thought of his conduct, his skill, his admirable conduct this day."

Hallo, my boy! whence this palpitation, you fool? does the lovely girl's praise of a brother sailor set your heart bounding with professional enthusiasm?

"Why, Miss Palmer, as you say, the *Tigress* has been admirably handled no doubt, and it is quite natural that you should give all the praise to her commander, although his judgment would not have been of much use had he not had a number of brave seamen under him to execute his orders without a single thought of the perilous game their skipper was playing. He will, I am sure, be immensely gratified by your praise, and I heartily hope I may have an opportunity of introducing him to you."

This was not my usual style, nor my usual voice either. She bent her clear searching eyes on my face, and a smile twinkled through them like a sunbeam sailing betwixt two clouds over a space of water. I suppose the conscience that makes cowards of us all caused me to color up under her quick, penetrating glance. She was merciful enough to take no further notice of my speech, in which I assuredly did my heart a wrong, for I protest no living being could have had a warmer admiration for Shelvocke than I, nor could have taken a more critical delight in the genius with which he had pestered and goaded into courting him the ugly *baste* whose horns, but for him, would by this time have been goring the *Namur*. But Lord! what a poor and twopenny affair the human heart must be after all, when a pretty woman's praising a man will fill his friend's mouth with pooh-poohs, meanly intended to qualify the acquiescence he is too cowardly and yet too honest to withhold!

My thoughts went in this strain as Miss Palmer and I stood looking across the sea, until at last I did feel so impatient with myself for my self-misrepresentation, and was so worried by the subacid significance taken by my words through Miss Palmer's silence, that I could stand it no longer.

"That was a mean speech of mine," said I, "and not true in spirit. What on earth could have made me want to shake half the leaves out of your wreath for Shelvocke when only just now I was shouting my applause of him, and when I knew him to be as intrepid and fine a seaman as ever swung along a ship's deck?"

And as I asked this question I looked at her steadily, being at this time, for reasons I am unable to account for, in as verdant and unsophisticated a humor as was my uncle Toby when he explored the lambent and delicious fires of Mrs. Wadman's eye for the bit of green that never yet lurked in the deflowered optic of a widow.

"By proceeding just as we now steer, what part of the earth should we now come to, Mr. Madison?" she inquired artlessly, sidling to the compass, and looking at it steadfastly.

Well, if I was stupid enough not to know the cause, it was not her business to hunt about for it.

"I will repeat my question another day, as they say in the House of Commons," said I, smiling at the sweet, grave

25

face she bent over the binnacle. "And now, Miss Palmer, let me conduct you to a seat in the shadow of the mast yonder, out of reach of the sun, where I shall be happy to answer every inquiry you wish to make touching the navigation of the *Namur*."

She put her fingers under my arm, and walked a few paces, but stopped to look back at the vessels.

"They will soon be out of sight," said she. "Already the schooner resembles the white wing of a seagull, with just the graceful curve of that bird's pinion when it sweeps suddenly around against the wind."

"I cannot help fancying, Miss Palmer, that you are fonder of the sea than you have yet deigned to admit."

"Deigned to admit! pray speak naturally; half the charm of sailors lies in the sincerity of their conversation," said she.

"I am glad you hear me so plainly," said I, piqued by her manner, and yet not displeased by it either. "When I asked you a question, a short time ago, you did not answer me, by which I was afraid that the cannonading yonder might have slightly affected the organ of hearing."

"Ah, you are very plain now—almost rude, indeed," said she, laughing under her breath, as though she rather enjoyed teasing me. "I *did* hear your question; but—unlike most women—when I have nothing to say I hold my tongue. As to being fond of the sea—I am *very* fond of it; not with a young lady's fondness, which you know, means reading and writing verses about the bounding, the melancholy, the raging main, in her bedroom, and screaming when on the water if the vessel rolls. I like the sea because when on it I am happy, and whatever makes me happy I love."

How richly and sweetly this last sentence rolled out of her mouth!—"*Whatever makes me happy I love.*"

"Now, I wonder if you are a coquette?" thought I. And, as if she divined my thoughts, she cast up her soft, luminous, spiritual, gentle, maidenly eyes, as though she would say, "Look here—look as deep as the short scope of your optical lead-line will let you sound these gray calm depths, and judge for yourself, master!"

I placed a chair for her, and left her comfortably seated

in the shadow of the mizzenmast and where the deck was cooled by the breeze that buzzed like a thousand bees among the folds of the crossjack which hung in festoons from the yard, and went aft to watch the corvette. But I had not been looking three minutes, when the sound of a voice humming a tune made me turn my head, and there was Miss Palmer close behind me.

"I want to see the last of the brave little *Tigress*," said she; "and will you tell me if there is the smallest probability of the American ship catching her?"

By way of answer, I poised the glass on my shoulder and bade her look at the schooner.

"Only her sails are visible," said she.

I shifted the glass, and asked if she saw the American.

"Yes, quite distinctly."

"You can judge of the distance between the two vessels?"

"I can."

I told her to take notice that the schooner had only half as much sail set as it was in her power to carry, and that her being able to hold her distance from the American under such conditions proved that were the whole of her canvas to be exposed she would be out of sight of her pursuer in four hours.

"And why does not Captain Shelvocke run out of sight?" she wanted to know, continuing to peer through the glass, and to maintain a posture I was very willing and indeed decidedly happy to endure in her so long as she chose to preserve it.

I replied that if the *Tigress* ran away, the American would immediately pay off in chase of us again.

"Shelvocke's object," said I, "is to put the widest distance he can make the Yankee sail over, between us and the enemy. Jonathan's quandary is this: he can't capture the *Tigress* because he can't catch her, and he can't pursue us because the *Tigress* won't let him."

"And how will it end as regards the schooner?" said she, with her eye at the glass, and her face, in consequence, so close to the hinder part of my shoulder that once or twice the fore part of her straw hat tickled the back of my neck.

"Why, Jonathan will follow Shelvocke as long as he remains in sight," I replied, "putting his hopes, as all men must who chase a vessel, in a slant of luck. But blow high or blow low, the ship that can overhaul the *Tigress* is not to be seen within the circumference of this horizon, and I shall be very much astonished if the first person who boards the *Namur* on her arrival at Kingston be not Massa Shelvocke."

She lifted the glass from my shoulder, and while she slowly closed the tubes, she said:

"And now may I ask, Mr. Madison, what *you* mean to do?"

"Certainly you may. I shall steer as we go until noon" —I pulled out my watch and observed that it wanted twenty five minutes to eleven—" by which hour the corvette, unless she alters her course, will be some miles away behind the sea. I shall then order the men to trim sail, the helm will be shifted, and the good ship *Namur* headed as the wind will best let her go for Jamaica."

"Thank you for your answers," said she, giving me the glass. "You have made my mind so easy that the very least I can do is to unreservedly forgive you for pretending to believe that my hearing had been affected."

She dropped me a low courtesy, wonderfully graceful, indeed, and so playful that the fellow who was steering turned his head to hide a grin. I acknowledged the salute with a regular ballroom flourish of the leg to let those it concerned know that I could bow as well as she; then she tripped on her noiseless little feet over to the Solomonses, flinging, as she went, a backward glance at me that said, "I am going to comfort these poor creatures," and forthwith repeated to them what I had said to her, for which I was exceedingly obliged, as she saved me a deal of trouble by doing so.

I stood watching the two vessels, not without anxiety, and saw the topmost point of the schooner's canvas vanish like a tiny wreath of steam. Although the corvette's hull had sunk and half her courses were invisible, I observed by means of the glass that she continued to fire at the chase, for every now and again a shadow like that of a cloud passing over some distant point blew athwart of and temporarily obscured her, but as it went clear it became white, and large, and quivering, and hung like a burst of vapor from a steam boiler upon the sea, that was as blue as the sky out there. Bit by bit the gleaming and tapering height of canvas sunk lower and lower, until at last nothing but a fluctuating brilliant shred, hove slightly above the water-line by refraction, could be seen trembling like a sparkling dew-drop; it disappeared, and the whole bright circle of the horizon was a blank.

# CHAPTER XVII.

## FIRE!

WHILE the schooner was in sight my mind, so to speak, had something to hold on by, and the sense of loneliness was not so sharply brought home to me; but when at midday (the two vessels having then been out of sight from our main-royal yard for over an hour) I ordered the studding-sails to be hauled down and the ship to be brought close to the wind, the responsibility of my position weighed heavily upon me. Here was I launched in charge of a large and apparently a richly freighted ship upon a sea that was infested with picaroons, Jamaica distant a good ten days' sail under favorable circumstances, and with only fifteen men and a boatswain's mate to work the vessel and to resist any attack that might be made upon us.

And yet Shelvocke was not to blame for the situation in which he had placed or left me. I did not know what his loss had been in killed and wounded through the engagement with the prize-crew of the *Namur*, but I easily guessed it so severe as to prohibit him from weakening the available force of his men by a larger draft than the sixteen seamen whom he had placed under my command. That no one was to blame, however, and that what had happened could not be helped, did not improve my case. I could only trust to chance, and live in the hope of being lucky enough to carry the *Namur* to Kingston without misadventure.

Although the breeze that was blowing was strong enough to have driven the schooner eight or nine knots an hour, this lumbering West Indiaman was barely doing four. Indeed, she was the slowest sailer I had ever dealt with; a regular sugar-box, built for carrying, with bows as round as the back view of a Dutchman, and of a most massive scantling.  She was about six hundred tons burden, but her immense beam made her look two hundred tons bigger than that; and being very heavily rigged, with immensely thick lower masts and shrouds, which appeared to have been shifted into her from a line-of-battle ship, she would have passed very well, viewed lengthwise, for a man-of-war, though her stern was a strong indication of her true character.  Her weight and stubbornness made my lookout about four times as formidable as it would have been had she been a fast boat, and rigged with greater regard to the laws of proportion.  Her yards swung heavily, her running-gear "hung," she was as hard to steer as a raft; and when I looked over her stern and observed her broad oily wake stretching away toward her weather-quarter, I easily guessed, as any sailor will suppose, what her quality of weathering would prove in a gale of wind.

However, it was my duty to put a good face on the matter, as much for the sake of the men, whom the least air of misgiving in me would speedily dishearten, as for the passengers who had intrusted themselves to my keeping.  I left Parell on deck, and employed myself for some time in overhauling the chart and working out the observations I had taken at noon, and then lay down on my bunk and endeavored to snatch an hour's rest before dinner; but I was too anxious to sleep, and so to kill the time I took a book —I well remember it was a copy of the *Edinburgh Review* —and tried to get interested.  But it would not do.  All the time I was thinking of our defenceless condition in case of an attack, and asking myself if I had done my duty to Miss Palmer to suffer her to remain in the *Namur* after Shelvocke had ranged alongside to report a strange sail in sight; and I recalled—not willingly, by any means; the abominable memories *would* intrude themselves—various stories I had heard of the barbarities practised by the pirates and privateersmen, toward whose haunts we were hourly drawing near, upon the women who fell into their hands.

In short, I suffered my fancies to make me very nearly as miserable as the calamities I lay speculating upon would themselves have done.  But it is sometimes possible for a man to go on thinking until he thinks himself clear of disturbing thoughts. I lay reasoning so morbidly, that at last my common sense found imagination insupportable, and I sprang out of my bunk damning myself for a fool as heartily as Jonathan Wild did his Tishy for being something else.

"Is dinner ready, Ransom?" I sung out as I entered the cabin.

He answered that he was waiting for my orders to fetch it from the galley; and in a few minutes it was smoking on the table, and the passengers and myself seated round it.

"Once more assembled, Mrs. Solomons," said I, rather boisterously, as men sometimes will be who determine to be jolly in spite of themselves; "a most united and—shall I say, Miss Palmer—a most picturesque family? A smooth sea around us, fine weather over us, and a stout ship under us!"

"A very stout ship indeed!" growled Solomons; "I wish she was a little thinner—maybe she'd sail quicker."

"You must find sailoring a very risky business, mister?" said Mrs. Solomons, trying to catch sight of her plate by peering over her bosom—and failing. "There's always something dangerous happening at sea; isn't there? Either it's a leak, or it's wind, or lightning, or else it's a ship a-chasing of one. If I had a son, he'd never go to sea with my leave."

"Thank you!" interrupted Jonas; "a son of mine go to sea! he'd wait upon yer."

"For when all's said and done," continued Mrs. Solomons, "there's little enough money to be airned at it, they say."

"All very true, Mrs. Solomons," said I, "give me a good business ashore, I'd soon quit the sea."

"Did you ever hear of a thoroughbred sailor settling down to *business*, Mr. Madison?" asked Miss Palmer demurely. "Sailors abuse the sea heartily enough, I know, *when* at sea; but once put them on shore, and, like geese, they immediately waddle to the water."

"Pray say ducks," said I. "Ducks, as a word, is very much prettier than geese, and, when applied to sailors, truer."

"What is your opinion of the sea, Mr. Solomons?" she inquired, evading my point.

"My opinion, miss?" answered the old man slowly. "If I was Prime Minister of England, I'd do away with jails and make all felons thailors"—you have already noticed that our friend sometimes lisped. "That would give the country plenty of seamen, and save the pockets of the taxpayers."

"A neat compliment to the profession that has hoisted our little island at the world's masthead!" I remarked.

Miss Palmer changed the topic by asking Mr. Solomons questions about the West Indies. Perhaps she knew that this was one of the subjects upon which the old man could talk well; and I suppose she had a personal interest in the exhibition of his best paces after having spoken up for him and his wife. He had lived in Jamaica thirty years, and might therefore be supposed to know the country pretty intimately. He spoke with great intelligence, told two or three stories which really had fine humorous points in them, and gave me the impression, in spite of his lisping and his *h*'s, that he could talk like a man of education if he pleased, and that he deliberately chose to be vulgar, either to keep his wife in countenance or that he might not forge ahead of the sympathies of his own sect.

There is always something interesting to me in an old man of this kind who, cunning as he may be, makes you see he is infinitely shrewder than he wants you to believe— whose eyes steal up and down from the table to your face, and whose conversation is picturesque with grammatical lapses, keen observation, misplaced *h*'s, and the illumination—the *lumen siccus*—of a mass of various, out-of-the-way, curious reading. He had much to say about slavery and the prospects of Jamaica, and although I had not the least interest in the subject, he kept me listening with steady attention.

I caught Miss Palmer watching me with a teasing expression in her eyes. "I'll make a large-minded man of you yet!" she seemed to say with those bright and eloquent telegraphs. "You are beginning to lose your prejudice against this harmless old creature, are you?" A woman's heart is shown in the victories she likes to win. Miss Madeline took as much pleasure in watching the favorable impression old Jonas was making on me as any Mrs. Candour would have taken in attending the funeral of a reputation.

The afternoon wore away; at six o'clock the breeze failed us, and the sea lay heaving like a surface of molten glass. A thin haze gathered round the horizon like the mist that rises from the earth on hot summer mornings, and the reflection of the burning sun was as dark as Indian gold in the spacious and polished folds of the water. Though it wanted but two hours to sunset, the heat had at no other period of the day been greater than now. A steam arose from the decks, through which the lower masts quivered like the reflection of a tree in a running stream: the smell of blistered paint and melting pitch made the stagnant air sickly with the taste of it; I placed my hand by accident on the brass hood of the binnacle, and drew it away with an exclamation—it was like touching the top of an oven. The languor of the heat crept into one's very marrow. The men lolled about the decks with their shirts open, feebly moving when called, and pulling off their caps, and shaking their heads, to rid themselves of the perspiration that fell in showers from their hair and foreheads.

I had caused an awning to be spread over the quarter-deck, and under it lay Mr. Solomons in his shirt-sleeves, flat on his back on the deck, with a rolled-up flag under his head, and a long cigar stuck out of his mouth; and Mrs. Solomons in an arm-chair, with her mouth open, and her arms hanging down her lap (her *lap*, do I call it?), and her face as scarlet as a powder-flag, nothing to show that she was alive but the brightening and fading of her rose-colored satin dress as her enormous shape swelled and subsided in it with her respirations; and Madeline Palmer, with her hat upon her knees, her slightly lifted dress exposing an exquisitely shaped foot, her head lying back, leaving the snow of her throat revealed from the chin to where the sparkling silver brooch connected the small white collar, sometimes languidly lifting her hand to stir the threads of hair upon her white forehead with a slow motion of the sandalwood fan, that wafted a perfume as fragrant as jasmine through the air to where I stood leaning against the skylight.

Happily the calm was but of short duration. Shortly

after one bell the haze in the northeast blew away, and a
light wind came down along the water like the shadow of a
cloud over the silver surface of a field of rye. The yards
were squared, the true course made, and with the light
canvas swelling and her courses softly lifting, the *Namur*
was again pushing through the calm sea, with her stem in
a line with the broad, deep-colored gold band of sunshine
that streamed from the horizon down, as it seemed to the
eye, to within a pistol-shot of the ship's bows.

The breeze was as good as a cordial; every faculty was
refreshed by the cool blowing, the bubbly tinkling of the
passing water, the diamond-like quivering of the whole sea.

"If you want to see a noble sight, look yonder, Miss
Palmer," said I, standing beside her, and pointing toward
the sun. "But you must make haste."

She instantly rose, and stood looking with me at the orb,
whose lower limb rested upon the water-line like a wheel.
There was not a fleck of cloud to tarnish it; the sky resembled a wall of resplendent brass, and the sun, by the unusually powerful refractive character of the atmosphere,
was swollen into gigantic proportions. I never saw the
like of it before; it was *startling* to behold; the men stood
in a group watching it, looking aft from time to time hurriedly, as though to mark the effect of this unusual appearance upon me.

"See, Miss Palmer!" I exclaimed: "the blazing circle
compasses the whole bow of the ship! Look how the magnificent circumference arches from one rail to the other on
either side the bowsprit like the glory around the head of a
saint. One would suppose that some star was on fire, and
was falling close past the earth! Did any one ever see the
sun so big before! How clean the circle is! not a single
ray shoots from it—do you notice? And observe the color
of the sea—one should be able to dip up gold enough to
purchase a kingdom."

"No wonder it's so hot, with such a sun as that to burn
one up!" cried Mrs. Solomons from her chair.

"Confound her!" I muttered. "Her voice destroys the
charm, like a cry of oranges in a tragedy."

"One never sees a sunset like that in England," said
Miss Palmer, almost in a whisper, so subdued was she by

the sublimity of the spectacle.   "How the golden splendor
runs up out of the sea as the sun sinks!"

The last glowing fragment throbbed and vanished! she
turned her eyes to the east, and looking up with her face
like alabaster in the brief pause of twilight, pointed toward
the sky.

"Do you remember the sweet old hymn?" she said:

> "' Soon as the evening shades prevail,
>    The moon takes up the wondrous tale.'"

And there was the new moon like a thread of silver in
the light blue sky over the mizzen topsail yardarm.

"I have wished," said I: "have you?"

"That our voyage may be speedy and safe, is my wish,"
she replied.

"Amen to that for your sake," said I.

At eight o'clock my watch came around.   I was not sorry
that it should be so, as I had not only no inclination for sleep,
but had no fancy for the sultry atmosphere of the cabin.

I was in anything but a cheerful mood.   Something of
the despondency that had bothered me during the morning
had again visited me; my nerves were irritable; I was restless, journeying here and there about the deck, staring into
the starlit distances, and vexed by the droning of old Solomons' voice as he sat reading to his wife by the light of a
little silver hand-lamp.

I attributed my mood, which was certainly an unusual
one, to the blow I had received on the top of my head, and
to the weakness caused by the effusion of blood; neither of
which things was calculated to rout out any remains which
yet lingered of the long illness that had prostrated me before
joining the *Tigress*.   But this by the way, though I like to
bear it in mind, as the confession of the temper that then
possessed me does not quite give me the figure that the hero
of a story should make.

Miss Palmer, who had been chatting with the Solomonses
since supper, that was served at half-past seven, drew away
when old Jonas began to read, and carried her chair right
aft, where she sat leaning with her arms on the grating
abaft the wheel.   I imagined, by her turning her back on
the deck, and by her thoughtful pose, that she wished to be

alone, so I did not go near her—though perhaps not more
for this reason than because of my own peevish indisposition to talk.

Presently I sung out: "Forward, there! who is that on
the lookout?"

"Saunders, sir," came back the answer.

"Is Anderson there?"

"Yes, sir," replied the man himself.

"Take this glass, Anderson, and jump aloft and let me
know if there is anything in sight."

I followed his dark figure as he ascended the shrouds.
He was remarkable for having the keenest eyes of any man
aboard the *Tigress*, and had been Shelvocke's favorite
lookout.

Miss Palmer turned her chair round when I ordered the
man aloft, and Solomons stopped his reading to listen.
After a while the man hailed the deck; the sound of his
voice floated down through the darkness, and he seemed
half a mile high in the air.

"There's nothing in sight, sir."

"All right, my lad; that will do. You can lay down."

Solomons resumed his reading—*mum, mum, mum*. I
went to the side to judge the speed of the ship by the passage of the bubbles which winked in the starlight as they
slid along. Heaven knows it was slow enough, although
there was sufficient weight in the breeze to tauten the staysail sheets.

"What makes you so restless, Mr. Madison?" said Miss
Palmer.

Her lips seemed at my very ear, so clear and bell-like
was her articulation.

"Upon my word, Miss Palmer, you have a famous knack
of taking me unawares. Do you carry a pair of invisible
wings, or have you the spirit-like quality of treading the
viewless winds that you make no sound when you walk?
Small wonder, with such a marvellously delicate tread, that
you are one of the finest dancers mortal man ever had the
honor of leading out. I can speak from experience, you
know—of your dancing, at all events!"

"I like your compliments very much," said she; "but I
should prefer to have my question answered.

"Unlike most men, Miss Palmer, when I have nothing to say I hold my tongue," I answered, quoting her.

She laughed, remembering her phrase; but immediately afterward said, very gravely, "Have you any cause to feel uneasy? You can answer me candidly, because you may trust me implicitly."

"See here, Miss Palmer. This is my first command. I am in charge of a ship manned by sixteen men, instead of the crew of four times that number which a vessel of this tonnage needs. I am answerable for the lives of three passengers; one of whom has a stronger claim upon my protection than I should know how to express in words were I asked to do so. Should I be fit for the post I occupy if the responsibilities of it did not make me anxious?"

"Then you are uneasy only because of your responsibilities, and there is nothing but the fear that something *may* happen to worry you?"

"Why, yes; that's about it," said I.

"I should like a walk, Mr. Madison. May I take your arm? Thanks—the vessel rolls a little now and then, and the dew makes the deck slippery."

She commanded me just as a helmsman governs his ship. There was never anything very remarkable in her words and yet they acted upon me like a tonic. But it was not what she said; it was her way of saying it—the beautiful song-like charms of her voice—the firm but womanly decision of character her manner expressed, that influenced me. Before we had taken half a dozen turns, she had made me as cheerful as I was before dull; reasoned me out of my forebodings, and artfully drawn me into talking of pleasant things. And then—what was a charming surprise—she had no sooner effected her purpose of heartening me, then she changed her character. A sweet, teasing, coquettish air replaced her grave demeanor; she had put herself in my place, so to speak, in order to advise and inspirit me. This done, she became the woman again; and having got me into a condition of mind fit to be played with, she played with me.

Heaven knows if she was conscious of what she was doing; I was inclined to think she was. Anyway, it pleased me better to imagine that her captivating posture-

making was no involuntary exercise, for I will say, at once
—I was in love with her.  Ay, the admiration she had
kindled in me in Lady Tempest's ballroom had proved a
rich soil; besides, here we were in latitudes proverbially
favorable to speedy and luxuriant growths.  But she was
the first girl I had ever fallen in love with in my life, and,
honest soul that I was—for my heart esteems that man who
is a greenhorn in his emotions—I was not only persuaded
that she had no suspicion of what was in my mind, but I
took, as I fancied, the utmost care, as we patrolled the
*Namur's* quarter-deck, that no words of mine should make
her reflective in that direction.  .

"It is much too early," said I to myself, "and perhaps
she may have left a sweetheart in England, or perhaps, in
spite of her professed admiration of the sea, she would
shudder at the notion of marrying a sailor, or perhaps"—
but my modesty had a score of reasons which need not be
catalogued for throwing a veil over my heart, and though I
believe I may have unconsciously pressed her hand under
my arm against my side, and snatched every excuse to peer
closely into her face, I flattered myself when I bade her
good-night that she had as little suspicion that I was deeply
in love with her, as I had that she had any more romantic
feeling for me than a kindly friendship.

She had lingered to a late hour on deck—it was past
eleven—Mrs. Solomons had withdrawn half an hour before;
and Miss Palmer would have stayed longer still, I believe,
had not Mr. Solomons gone below.  There was no prudery
in her, but her notions of propriety were English; and one
of those notions was that there was no harm in remaining
on deck with a young man so long as an old man sat near:
though the old man might have been asleep, or as good as
asleep, with his thoughts among his share of the ship's
freight, or upon the bills that would have matured before
his voyage was ended.  But every nation must have its
manners, and it is better to subject our girls to a foolish
than to a barbarous code of etiquette.

And yet it was annoying to hear Miss Palmer say, as she
stood upon the companion-steps:

"I am afraid I shall find it very hot in the cabin.  However, I don't feel at all sleepy, so I shall open the window

and get the air in that way, and watch the blue fires smouldering in the wake of the ship; there is nothing prettier and nothing that fills the mind with stranger fancies."

"As though she couldn't remain on deck to keep me company," thought I. But it would not do to suggest it, and for three-quarters of an hour I remained alone, thinking of her sweet figure sitting at the great stern window of her cabin, and wondering what form her musings took, and if I was as much in her thoughts as she was in mine.

Eight bells were struck—midnight: a hoarse voice bawled the hour down the fore-scuttle.

"Star-bowlines, ahoy! out with you, my hearties!"

Presently a man came along the deck to relieve the wheel; he was followed by Parell.

"Still very quiet, sir," said he, gaping around at the sea and taking an unpoetical squint at the stars. "The breeze holds, though, and it's a mercy to feel the air; for of all fok'sles as ever I slept in, I never knew the likes of this ship's for heat and cockroaches."

"You will keep her as she goes," said I, "and see that a bright lookout is kept. I heartily hope we may overhaul some British cruiser, or stumble upon some friendly ship. A crew composed of you and me and fifteen men is hardly numerous enough for a ship of this size to make a man sleep with an easy mind. However, there is nothing to be done but to shove the old wagon along as fast as she will sail, and to keep our weather-eye lifting as we go."

Saying which, and ordering him to arouse me should a sail heave in sight or the weather change, I wished him good-night, and withdrew to my berth.

I went on tiptoe through the cabin, and listened a moment or so at Miss Palmer's door to ascertain if she was still up: all was silent and I passed on. Roomy as my berth was, it was as hot as an oven. I threw open the window, and pulling off my shoes and coat, lay down in my bunk, leaving the candle alight in the lamp that was hooked to an eye in the bulkhead. My bunk faced the window, and I lay watching the dark sea swelling to the stars upon the horizon, and the dome of heaven that was covered with a glittering dust, amid which the larger stars floated in bland, yellow, clearly defined shapes. The vessel heaved slightly upon the ink-black invisible swell, and now and again the rudder drowsily jarred or a beam under the floor creaked faintly, and occasionally I could hear the flap of the mainsail against the shrouds, while the refreshing bubbling of water under the counter was like the tumbling of a fountain or the sound of rain among leaves.

What was that?

A loud cry and a sudden rush of feet, and then another shout and the splash as of a human body thrown overboard.

I was on my legs in an instant, my momentary impression being that we had been surprised by some enemy's boats, though another sense in me, so to speak, found this impossible, as, even supposing every man on deck to have been asleep, no boat could have approached the ship without my hearing her through the open window.

I threw open my cabin door and ran out. It was dark—to my eyes pitch-dark after the bright light in my own berth. I felt for the end of the table, and sculled along the edge of it as swiftly as the chairs in the road would permit me, and just as I reached the foot of the companion-ladder, the starlight above was blotted out by the interposition of a human body in the act of descending.

"Who's that!" I exclaimed in a loud whisper.

"Me—Parell! Is that you, Mr. Madison?"

"Yes, yes; what is the matter?"

"For God's sake, bear a hand and come on deck, sir. The fok'sle lamp's been capsized, the oil set flaming, and the ship's on fire!"

A man need not have been to sea to conceive the effect these words produced in me. Of all the perils which beset the sailor, fire is so incalculably the worst, that alongside of it the direst horror you can pick out of the maritime catalogue is mild as a benediction. The very word—"fire!" —curdled my blood. I drew a thick, half-suffocating breath, reached the deck with a bound, and rushed forward.

A dense volume of smoke was pouring out of the fore-scuttle, going up in a thick, black pillar, spangled here and there with sparks to half the height of the foremast, where the wind caught it and bent it into the shape of a bow, and, dark as the sea was, I could see this hideous coil pouring slowly along it

26

All the men were on deck, some of them only in their shirts; four or five of them were throwing buckets overboard, and hauling them up full, and dashing them down the scuttle; others had rigged the head-pump; others, again, at their wits' end darted here and there, hoarsely shouting out their notions of what should be done.

"Silence!" I roared. "Where's the hose? get it along, and keep that head-pump going. Some of you get that lower stun'sail clear, and souse it overboard. Parell, give me a hand here."

A spare flying-jib was lying on the forecastle. I bent a line on to it, and flung it into the sea; it was dragged up along with the studding-sail, streaming wet, and bundled down the scuttle. Instantly a fearful, suffocating volume of smoke belched up in hideous convolutions, driving away the men as though a giant's hand had pressed them back.

"Keep that head-pump going, men!" I shouted, "and form you into a line for the side buckets. Have no fear—keep cool. If the worst comes to the worst we have good boats, and our number is small. Stand to your duty, my brave fellows! Ransom, come you along with me to the main-hatch."

I rushed aft, followed by the boy, but instead of descending into the 'tween-decks, I scampered to the gig that was slung to the stern davits, jumped into her, handed out the breaker to Ransom, and ordered him immediately to fill it with water and replace it in the bows of the boat. I then ran below to my berth, unhooked the lamp, and flinging all thoughts of propriety to the wind at such a moment, threw open Miss Palmer's door.

She was standing by the side of her bunk, fully dressed —even to her hat: precisely as she had quitted the deck. Her eyes sparkled in the lamplight as she turned them upon me, but no exclamation escaped her, and I knew by her demeanor that she was conscious of what had happened, and was waiting for me to come to her.

"The ship has taken fire forward," said I. "Give me your hand—have no fear—it is fifty to one if we don't master the flames. Meanwhile my business is to place you in a safe place. Come!"

She ran to me; I grasped her wrist and hurried her through the cabin. As I passed the Solomonses' door I flung it open.

"Follow me on deck!" I cried. "We are in great danger! Ho, there! are you awake?"

I flashed the lamp upon the cabin, and saw Mrs. Solomons sitting up in her bunk, and Solomons' head over the side of his cot.

"I cannot stay!" I shouted. "If the men miss me they will think I have betrayed them, and abandon the ship. Follow me on deck, I say. The vessel is on fire."

A loud shriek broke from the poor woman, and the old man threw himself out of his cot. Knowing they would follow me, I hurried Miss Palmer on deck and ran with her to the gig.

"Jump into that boat," I said to her, "and we will lower you into the water. Ask no questions, and have no fear. Do as I say."

"I *have* no fear," she answered, in a steady voice, and slightly raising her dress, she sprang on to the taffrail, and seated herself in the boat.

I took a hurried glance forward: the fire was gaining upon the men fast; forks of flame like flashes of lightning glanced upon the ponderous column of smoke, and lighted up the half-naked figures toiling like demons round the mouth of the fiery cavern.

I got into the stern of the boat, and took a turn with the hauling end of the after-fall round a thwart.

"Get your end of the fall round a belaying-pin," I said to Ransom.

"Ready, sir."

"Then lower away."

The boat sank to the water. I unhooked both falls, and, making the painter fast round my waist, I clambered up the port fall, gained the deck, and hitched the end of the painter to the starboard vang. The very slow way the ship had, enabled me to perform this job without risk; and the whole business occupied very little more time than I have taken to write this account of it.

"You are perfectly safe there, Miss Palmer," I shouted out, peering over the taffrail at her as she sat in the boat, that was now towing astern, and whose stem broke the water into threads.

"I know I am safe," she replied. "Do not forget that there are others."

"I will see to them," I answered; and rushed forward again to let the men know I had not deserted them—marveling at the wonderful courage of this girl from whose lips not a sound had broken as the boat sank into the water, nor when she had seen me clamber on board again, and who still preserved her heroic fortitude as she sat in the deep shadow thrown upon the sea by the high stern of the ship, alone, with the black water within a few inches of her hand!

But her being where she was made my heart lighter. I had provided, at all events, for her safety—such as that provision was—against the terribly sudden and unexpected occurrences of a fire at sea, and, noticing that the Solomonses had not yet arrived on deck, I plunged among the men.

Hardly had I reached the fore-scuttle, when an immense body of flame soared up. The brilliance blasted the eyesight; the heat was scorching; the foresail caught, and spanged into a terrific blaze; the men at the head-pump, fearing to be cut off by the fire, darted aft, and there was a rush into the waist.

From the moment my eye had caught sight of the smoke, on my arrival on deck, I had no hope that my slender crew would be able to save the vessel; but I never could have imagined that the fire would have gained upon the ship so fast and furiously. Already she was in a blaze forward: a quantity of vapor was pouring out of the main-hatch, which we had not had time to close; her foremast was in flames; her canvas streamed in ruby-colored trails; the tar on the standing rigging burned swiftly and dropped in flaming lumps, which emitted a sooty smoke; and yellow fire flickered along her forestays, and worked its way among the jibs down to the bowsprit and jibboom; and masses of smoke overhung the sea like a huge thunder-cloud.

The men stood in the waist paralyzed. I saw their eyeballs rolling like redhot cinders in the crimson radiance of the flames, which darted up and coiled around the foremast with the hoarse and rushing sound of a sweeping wind. Their shadows lay like bronze effigies upon the dusky yellow sheen on the decks; their faces gleamed like quicksilver in the overpowering light—and who could describe the anguish and dismay expressed in some of their postures as they turned toward the fire after their rush from the forecastle, and stood—every one of them—motionless as images, as long as it would have taken a man to count twenty?

For the space of half a mile to leeward of the ship the heavens were hidden by the smoke, and the stars replaced by millions of fiery sparks, which sailed away in whole constellations, for among the other things I took notice of in this awful time was that the smoke from the fore-hatch did not go up steadily, but was vomited out in black, fat masses, like a succession of discharges from a gun, and with every belch of jetty vapor there rushed forth myriads of sparks, while between the puffs the flames soared in a column the circumference of whose base was the aperture through which the fire darted, but whose summit branched out like a palm-tree, slightly inclined over the ship's head by the light breeze.

I was in the act of shouting to the men to clear away the pinnace and get it overboard, when the wind was knocked out of my body and I was nearly thrown down by Mrs. Solomons flinging her whole weight upon me.

"Oh, Mr. Madison!" she shrieked, "for God Almighty's sake tell us what to do! Make 'em put the boats over: it'll be too late soon!"

And she recoiled from me with an ear-splitting yell, as the flames, reaching a large pivot-gun on the forecastle, exploded it with a violent concussion, while almost at the same instant the foretopmast fell—a huge glowing beam—sweeping the blazing yards and rigging through the air in its descent over the bows, amid a roaring like the breaking of a heavy surf.

"By God, she is right, Parell!" I shouted. "Get the pinnace over, man. The ship will be on fire from stem to stern in another five minutes. Take your wife's hand," I exclaimed to Mr. Solomons, who stood looking up at the blazing rigging so phlegmatically that I believed he was dazed by the sudden calamity; "and stand at this gangway while I haul the gig round. Keep your presence of mind, Mrs. Solomons; there are boats enough to save ten times our number."

I ran aft to loose the gig's painter from the vang to which I had hitched it. Where was it? I rubbed my eyes furiously, and looked again: *the hitch had slipped, and the rope had gone away overboard.* The blazing heights of mast and sail sent the red glare broadcast over the sea, and to my horror and despair I beheld the gig, with Madeline Palmer standing up in it and waving her arms, floating a quarter of a mile astern.

The misery of a lifetime wrenched my heart at the sight: I am sure it drove me mad for the moment. I whipped out my knife, cut the lanyards of a life-buoy that hung over the taffrail, slipped the thing under my arms, and threw myself overboard—a twenty-feet fall. It was all sputter, giddiness, froth, and splashing; I was then on the surface with the life-buoy under my armpits, and swimming with eager, feverish sweeping of my limbs toward the gig.

The cold water gave me back my mind, or at all events the capacity of understanding my actions. The life-buoy securely floated me, and I merely needed to move my hands and legs to propel myself toward the gig. My brain then became extraordinarily active; no drug could have produced so great and violent a passage of thought, though without confusion: for I was perfectly cool; I reasoned collectedly on the impression my jumping overboard would produce on the men, and assured myself that my action would immediately be justified to them when they saw that the boat was adrift with Madeline Palmer alone in her; I also knew that they would launch the pinnace, that there was room in her for twice their number, and that I could have done no more for Mr. and Mrs. Solomons than I could trust that intelligent seaman, Parell, to do. And then I thought of the agony of mind the girl I was making for must have suffered when she found the boat stationary, and the flaming ship leaving her.

And then I wondered if there were any sharks in the neighborhood!

At *this* thought the blood tingled in my system with the violence of the cramp, and, setting my teeth, I swam with all my might. The vision of Chestree's dead body in the midst of the foam lashed up by the bloody worrying of the sharks rose with horrid vividness to my mind's eye, and a dreadful expectation tortured every nerve in my body from the top of my head down to the soles of my feet. O God ! what agony was there in *this* thought! To this hour I marvel that I did not clamber out of the water into the gig a white-haired man. Do not call it cowardice, but rather consider the many surrounding horrors whose whole forces contributed to exasperate the poignant expectation that possessed me during my lonely swim : the sea was colored like sulphur by the blazing ship down to many fathoms ahead of the boat, but beyond it was stone black, and the short horizon I commanded with my head and shoulders above water brought the stars down to the very surface of the ebony space, and the mere unearthliness of the effect of the color of the water in which I swam against the black sky and the stars which reeled upon the sea within the distance of a few strokes of an oar, might have unstrung the nerves of the most robust man living; behind me I could hear the roaring of the flames, the crash of falling spars, the hissing of huge glowing fragments quenched by the sea as they plunged over the side, the occasional boom of ordnance as from time to time the loaded guns were exploded by the heat, and the permanent undertone of crackling and splitting wood, of huge timbers warping, of solid plates and bars and fastenings of iron torn out of their holdings by the blasting and withering hand of the fire-fiend, an uproar blended by distance into one dreadful sound that lurked among and ran through the explosions of the guns and the splintering of wood, as though it were the moaning of the ship herself in her agony.

These things my consciousness took note of, in spite of the pressing fear of having a shark in my wake, as I mowed through the water with my hands and made the life-buoy splash up the foam as though I were in tow of a boat.

I had but a quarter of a mile to swim—perhaps less, for at that time I had no eye for the calculation of distance— and already, in the clear yellowish radiance shed by the burning ship, I could distinguish Miss Palmer's face, and see that she was watching me. I continued swimming

with all my strength without once looking behind me until
I reached the side of the gig, and then telling Miss Palmer
to sit lest she should be thrown into the water by the swaying of the boat, I clambered over the gunwale, threw off
the life-buoy, and lay back, spent by my fierce exertions,
and incapable of speech.

The moment I was in the boat, Miss Palmer knelt down,
took my streaming hands in hers and held them without
speaking, looking eagerly into my face, which, as it was
turned toward the ship, was distinctly visible to her.  This
was her manner of showing her sympathy and the gladness
my presence gave her;  but how am I to convey to you the
tenderness, the compassion of her posture?  I raised her
hands to my lips, and then drew my own away to squeeze
the salt out of my eyes and to open the collar of my shirt,
that was half strangling me.  I drew a deep breath.

"Are the others safe?" was the first question she asked
me.

"Yes," I replied, having no doubt of it; "by this time
they will have launched the pinnace."

I stood up in the boat to see if I could make out any
signs of them.  I was surprised to observe the distance the
ship had travelled from the gig.  She had paid off dead
before the wind, and her helm being, as I might take it,
amidships, she was steering as straight as an arrow;  the
after-part of her from her main-hatch was free from fire,
but forward she was a mass of flames, upon which the
breeze acted as though they had been sails, and the pall of
smoke that was swept forward with her concealing the summits of the spikes and forks and lancings of the fire, she
resembled a sheet of flame as square as her foreyards and
as high as her tops driving along the sea.  A magnificent,
an awful sight, though distance robbed it of something of
its sublimity;  the sea was blood-red under her, and a wide
circumference of sky was illuminated by a ruddy glow that
was almost as vivid as a flush of sunset, but rendered un-
speakably impressive by the midnight gloom into which it
paled away on either hand.

I thought, indeed I was sure, that I could see the pinnace towing at the ship's quarter, and I pointed it out to
Miss Palmer, saying that they ought to make haste to get

into the boat and cast her adrift, as the ship might explode at any moment.

"If they allow themselves to be dragged much further, we shall lose sight of them," she exclaimed.

"Yes, I am thinking of that too," I answered. "What is Parell about? Is he taking in some stores while time remains? Pray God he is!" I cried, remembering that there was nothing in the gig but the small cask of water. "But, great heaven, let him be quick! should the after-guns explode, the pinnace may be knocked into staves."

I threw myself down on the thwart alongside of Miss Palmer. I was giddy, my legs trembled under me; my physical strength was lamentably betraying me, and swift feverish shudders were chasing through my body, to which my streaming clothes hung like plasters.

"What a frightful situation for you to be in," I said: "though, Heaven knows, you meet it with a most coura- geous heart." I clasped and held her hand as any child might have done, and said, "I hope the men will not be- lieve I deserted them. The sight of your drifting away alone in this boat drove me crazy! surely when they saw me making for you they would understand my action, and know that I was doing my duty in leaving them for you."

"Oh, they will not misjudge you," she answered, in a low but perfectly calm and sweet voice; and she was about to begin another sentence, but stopped with a little convul- sive breath that was like a sob, and her hand trembled in mine.

"See!" I cried. "The mainsail has caught fire! How the blaze seems to gash the sky with a bloody wound! Hark! that was a main-deck gun—another! why do not they shove off? the fire will be into the magazine in a few moments! The main-topsail catches now—heaven and earth! it is as though a volcano were blazing in the midst of the sea. Can you see anything of the boat? My eyes are dazzled with the light and sore with the salt water!"

She held her hand to her brow and looked.

"I see the same small black object near the stern," she answered. "But how fast the ship goes! She is no more than a ball of fire now. Oh, what madness to remain in her!"

"Madness, indeed!" I cried passionately. "Is it the cursed *drink* that keeps them? Once adrift, will Parell be able to find us amid the darkness?"

I now, for the first time, noticed that there was but one oar in the boat; and for the moment this discovery gave a new edge to the misery of our situation. "But what does it matter?" I thought. Had we a dozen oars, what would they profit us? Should the pinnace miss us, our only chance will lie in a passing ship.

However, I held my peace on this point; and we remained gazing at the burning ship, and watching the illuminated water astern of her for the black speck that would denote the liberation of the pinnace from the side of the vessel.

The wind blew softly; but my hot cheeks found no refreshment in it. From time to time a fit of terror that no exertion of my will could repress seized me when I turned my eyes from the scarlet glare ahead to the black water alongside, and noticed how close we lay to the surface of it. At other moments, I was sensible of an amazing lightness of my body; and this feeling possessed me with a violent inclination to laugh out, the vanquishing of which caused me an agonizing struggle.

"Why, how strangely things come about!" I exclaimed presently, in a voice so hoarse that, like Fear in Collins's ode, I started at the sound myself had made. "*Figurez-vous,*" as Johnny Crapeau says, a gentleman and a lady meeting in a ballroom—wax-candles sparkling over them—the polished floor reflecting their figures as clearly as a looking-glass—brilliantly dressed people around—the flash of epaulets, diamonds, glass-clear scabbards dancing upon the eye with the diamond-like playing of the waters of Plymouth Sound when the high sun stands over them! Now drop the curtain upon the glittering scene. Hey, presto, pass!—as the conjurors say—the curtain rises again. Father of mercy, what is here? Two figures in a lonely boat: the outline of their faces"—I dropped my head on one side to peer at my companion—"faintly touched up with the sulphur-colored radiance of their ship, that blazes like a burning mountain on the midnight sea. Who are they? Why—did not the curtain fall upon them a moment ago? O my God! spare one of them—spare one of them for the sake of her beautiful nature and her courageous heart!"

I raised my hands to the stars like a ranting tragedian, and then covered my face with them.

Phew!—it was like touching my cheeks with heated iron.

"How horribly hot these hands of mine are!" I exclaimed, looking at them. "And hark to the croak in my voice. Am I going mad? I would swear that there is a demon perched on each of my eyeballs, hammering my temples, here"—touching them—"with a calking mallet."

"Why not lie down, Mr. Madison?" she said, so calmly that I could clearly hear and feel the sympathy of the rich sweet tones. "You are exhausted and feverish. Take some rest, and I will keep watch. For my sake, lie down. If harm befalls you, what will become of me?"

"Harm shall not befall you, Madeline—why, what do I call you? Oh, I *cannot* say Miss Palmer——"

"Say Madeline."

"Madeline—what a tender name! Madeline——" and I lingered over the word, repeating it several times. "What was I saying? Ah, you wished me to lie down. But not while that vessel lies flashing like a brand against the stars. No, let me see her vanish, Madeline, and then we will consider what is best to be done."

I endeavored to rise, but reeled like a drunken man, and dropped heavily upon the thwart again, with my hand upon her shoulder. Alas! alas! that I, who would have died for this girl, should, in the insanity of the fever that was eating into my brain, have refined the torments of her situation by my language and conduct! I was like a half-drugged man, inspired by some devil that made me say and do a hundred extravagant things of the imbecility, ay, and even of the cruelty of which I was perfectly sensible, though I could no more control my tongue and gestures than I could have extinguished the burning ship by blowing through my lips at her.

From time to time I would look from the flaming vessel to Madeline, and by such feeble light as the distant glare and the stars threw upon her, I saw that her face, pale as marble, was as steady and tranquil as marble too. She let me take her hand and hold and even kiss it without even offering to withdraw it, and sometimes she would dip a silk handkerchief she had removed from her throat in the water alongside and press it to my burning forehead, and whenever she saw me rocking in my seat, she would pass her arm round my back to support me.

All this I noticed and tried in my delirious way to thank her for, but after a little while I found that speaking gave me pain, not because of the effort of it, but because my tongue seemed formed of molten lead, so heavy that the muscles of it had scarce power to move it, and so burning hot that every wag of it was like the red-hot end of a lighted cigar tossing in my mouth.

There was the half of a cocoanut shell lying in the bottom of the boat that had probably been used as a baler. Madeline's foot striking against it called her attention to it; she picked it up, and I gave a strange laugh as she examined it. It evidently put an idea into her head, for she rose and was moving forward. I clutched her dress.

"Madeline," I cried, "don't leave me! sit where you are! Where would you go?"

"To get you some water," she answered.

"Oh, that is what I want!" I exclaimed in my thick voice. "Ay, get me some water, Madeline; it will cool my red-hot tongue, and I shall be able to talk to you. Yes, to be sure, water is what I want," and I mumbled this over and over until she came out of the bows of the boat with the shell full of water.

She held it to my lips, and I drank with terrible eagerness. Strange as it will seem to you, I did not know—or shall I say I did not feel?—the craving of thirst until the water was at my lips, and then the sense of thirst became a madness. Oh, the deliciousness of that draught! the blessed though short-lived relief it yielded me!

"It has made a man of me, Madeline!" I exclaimed, covering her hand with kisses in my delirious gratitude. "Let God but give me strength and health to hold by you until you are rescued, and I shall be ready to die!"

I hid my face in my burning hands, and felt the boiling drops searing my face as they oozed like blood from my eyes.

"Julian," she whispered, putting her lips to my ear and passing her hand round my neck, and pronouncing my name with exquisite tenderness; and I knew as well as though my pulse beat moderately and my head were cool and my brain clear, that she called me by my Christian name for the greater sympathy it would express and for the happiness it would give me, speaking it out of her full tenderness and eagerness to soothe and comfort me.

I removed my hands from my face and looked at her.

"You are ill, Julian," she whispered, "but rest will make you well. Take that rest while you can. See how calm the water is, and how clear the sky! In such weather we are as safe in this little boat as we were in the *Namur*. Don't let us forebode until real danger threatens us. To-morrow a ship may come and rescue us. God is our Father: His eye is upon us; my faith in His mercy was never greater than it is now."

I grasped her hands, looking her steadily in the face.

"Madeline—dearest girl—this fever is killing my mind, and I shall die delirious. I love you, Madeline—kiss me before I lose consciousness."

"You *shall* not die!" she cried, with an outburst of passion; then, controlling herself, she bent close to me, that I might see she smiled, and pressed her lips to my forehead.

"You will do now as I ask you—you will lie down."

She took the light shawl from her shoulders and rolled it up to serve me as a pillow, and stood up: I rose too, but as I did so the ship, that had driven at least three and a half to four miles away from us, and rested upon the sea in what resembled a circular shape of fire—a huge red-hot globe—blew up. At that distance every glowing portion of the ill-fated vessel looked but a mere spark, and the effect was much as though a shipload of rockets had exploded. A large space of sky in the southwest was filled with brilliant spangles; their radiance glanced with a pale yellow glare upon the air and the water like a flash of lightning; then the whole was extinguished as though an impenetrable cloud had rolled between us and the flaming particles, and the crash of the explosion boomed past us along the smooth surface of the deep like a short peal of thunder.

I looked around me, and rubbed my burning eyes furiously, in the belief that I had lost the use of my sight. The heavens and the sea were black as pitch; I could see no stars, no swelling gleam upon the water.

Well do I remember the fit of horror that seized me now.

"Madeline!" I shrieked, "we are alone—give me your hand—where are you?—quick, your hand!"

I gasped for breath, and was suffocating: I felt her seize my arm, and recollect muttering, "This is death!" and feeling my legs give under me as though they had shifted and dissolved like pillars of sand, and falling in a heap in the bottom of the boat, and that is all I remember.

# CHAPTER XVIII.

## H. M. S. SPEEDWELL.

WHEN consciousness dawned on me again, the scene had changed; the night was past, the morning had come: but where was I?

I tried to move my head, but I might as well have endeavored to carry a sixty-four pound carronade on my back. As I had not the power to turn my head to *look*, I thought I would *touch*, and make discoveries with my fingers; but here I was balked again, for my arms lay by my side as dead as a pair of wooden legs. "Good heaven!" thought I, "what *is* the matter with me, and what has been done to me?" That my consciousness must have been tolerably active, however, I know by recollecting that I said to myself, "Gulliver must have felt like this when he awoke from his first sleep in Lilliput." I dwelt upon this comparison with a species of mild and foolish complacency, and then tried to make out the character of the place in which I lay. It might have very well passed for a coffin, and had it not been dark when my senses returned, and I had been able to use my hands, no doubt I should have believed I was between the boards, and either buried or ready to lower away.

I looked steadily at the sort of decked covering over me, which was all that I could see. "This must be a bunk." thought I, "and—yes, I am on board a vessel. I feel the movement of her, and hear the straining of bulkheads. What vessel?" and I fell into a vile quandary. Lord! the pitiable puzzlement that afflicted me! "Pooh, pooh!" I said to myself, "do you ask *what* vessel, you fool? What vessel but the *Tigress* can this be, think you, poor simpleton? Ay, to be sure—what vessel could I be aboard of but the *Tigress?*" Nevertheless, I was not such an ass as I thought. "This is *not* the *Tigress*, for all that," said I, and I tried to shake my head; it would have been easier to make a turtle laugh by tickling its shell.

Presently I was sensible that some one was looking at me. I wanted to apologize for not being able to turn my head: some disjointed words rumbled in my throat, but no nervous bridegroom, returning thanks, ever made a more terrible mess of a speech.

"Hush, pray! do not attempt to speak; endeavor if you can to sleep," said a male voice very gently, almost in a whisper.

Some breathless talk went on, and a door was closed. Almost immediately I either lost my reason again or fell into a profound sleep—which lasted, I was afterward told, twenty hours—and when I awoke, I discovered, to my great delight, that I could move my head.

I was lying in a bunk in a small cabin lighted by a middling-sized port-hole, that was wide open, and through which a strong tide of warm sweet air was pouring. A cot swung near the door, and I noticed not only the rude plainness of the interior, but the thickness of the bulkheads and the prodigious strength of the beams, and indeed of all the timbers and fittings my eyes rested upon. A large plain black chest stood in a corner, and after several attempts I made out the white marks upon the lid of it to signify the initials ".J. G. P." A military cloak, a military undress-jacket, and other wearing apparel were hung upon hooks against the bulkhead near the door, and a small pendant lamp was affixed to a stanchion in the centre of the cabin.

I lay dreamily watching these things as they swung with the roll of the vessel, languidly wondering where I was, but without, as yet, the faintest recollection of the experiences I had gone through before my senses quitted me.

I had been awake about ten minutes when the door was very stealthily opened; a precaution that rather amused me, considering that the straining sounds in the cabin were equal to the creaking of a hundred rusty hinges all worked at once; and a tall, handsome, soldierly looking man in a dark-blue braided tunic and white nankeen trousers entered very cautiously, stopping to peer at me, and holding on to the open door as he balanced himself to the movement of the ship.

On observing me to be lying with my eyes wide open, he carefully closed the door, advanced to the side of the bunk, and asked me in a very gentle voice how I felt.

"Very weak, but beyond that I hardly know," I answered feebly, looking at him very earnestly, however, for something in his face—something in the expression of his eyes—fixed my attention, and I stared at him like one fascinated.

He was, as I have said, an extremely handsome man, his features high-bred, his forehead lofty, and his eyes dark and thoughtful; but he had a worn and suffering look, his cheeks were hollow, his complexion an ashen gray, and his fingers as emaciated as those of a consumptive person.

"You have had a long sleep," said he, "and I was glad to find your repose so sound, for the surgeon informs me that sleep is the great remedy in illnesses of this description. I will go and tell him you are awake."

He was moving away.

"Pray, sir, forgive me," I exclaimed. "Your voice has broken a spell. I am recalling the past that was just now as blank as death. I had escaped with a young lady from a burning ship. Ah! I have it! I have been rescued—picked up, of course—and the lady? for God's sake tell me of her, sir!"

My eagerness to have his reply was so great that I succeeded in raising myself on my elbow, but I was too weak to maintain that posture, and fell back with a heavy sigh.

He looked at me doubtfully, as if debating whether he should answer my question; but I suppose the wistful expression in my eyes was too strong an appeal for him to resist, for he came back to my side, tenderly raised my hand in both his, and answered:

"The young lady is safe, Mr. Madison—safe, and, thank God, well; and I may inform you that she is on board this ship."

"Pray stay, sir," I exclaimed, thinking because he let fall my hand that he was going away. "Your answering a few questions will really do me good. How long was the young lady in the boat?"

27

" You and she were rescued the morning after the *Namur* was burnt," he replied, speaking as though reluctant to converse with me, and yet not liking to refuse.

"And I was ill through the night, I fear. Indeed, I know now that I must have been *very* ill—insane, perhaps with delirium! No doubt I was, and O my God! what sufferings must that noble girl have endured, alone—alone in a boat with a madman! She is well, do you say? That is welcome news to me. Had ill befallen her it would go desperately hard with me now, indeed it would, sir!" and I felt the hot tears swelling into my eyes, a melancholy proof of the weakness both of my mind and body.

He drew a chair to my side, being sagacious enough to perceive that his leaving my curiosity unsatisfied would do me more harm than talking.

" You will also be glad to hear," he said, "that the boat containing Mr. and Mrs. Solomons and the crew of the *Namur* was picked up by this ship. Indeed, we sighted her first, and it was owing to her report that our captain altered his course to seek for your boat."

" So no lives are lost?"

" None; all are safe in this ship."

" What ship is she, may I ask?"

" An English ship-rigged sloop-of-war—the *Speedwell*, homeward bound from Kingston, Jamaica, with invalided soldiers."

" From Kingston, Jamaica?" I muttered, looking from him to the initials on the black chest in the corner. " May I inquire your name, sir?"

He gazed at me curiously; then a slight smile played over his worn features.

" My name is Colonel Palmer," he answered.

" Yes—I might have thought so—she has your expression. This is a most wonderful meeting. How strange are Heaven's ways!" and I lay looking at him so bewildered by the discovery that I thought I was falling crazy again.

" If *you* are surprised," he said gently, "you may conceive what *my* feelings were when, on our coming up with the boat, I saw my daughter in her! It is an old story now, and I can talk of it calmly. You are aware that I had no idea she was coming out to join me, and even when I had her in my arms I could not credit the reality of our most astonishing, and, I may truly say, God-guided meeting."

" You speak of it as an old story. How old might it be?"

" It will be ten days to-morrow since we picked up the *Namur's* boats."

" And where have I been all this while?"

" Here, in my cabin, Mr. Madison, upon that bed in which you are now lying."

" God preserve us !" said I.

I had thought we had been rescued that morning.

" Ten days !" I went on : " is it possible that I have been without my mind all that time? This is knowing what death is, sir : and what fools men are to let it frighten them !"

I closed my eyes, for my brain was beginning to simmer again : and shutting my eyelids seemed like clapping rolling-tackles on to my wits.

He rose from his chair, and said he must go tell the surgeon I was awake. I had a thousand more questions to ask him, but he would not stay. However, he had left me enough, in all conscience, to chew upon; and bit by bit I got all the points together, until the whole story lay clear in my mind.

Astounded as I was by the coincidence of the meeting between Colonel Palmer and Madeline, I made a greater wonder of my long unconsciousness. It stirred the hair upon my head to consider that to all intents and purposes I had been *dead*—not even a ghost, but a corpse—for nine days. I tried to sit up to assure myself that my body was as much alive as my mind, but could not manage it, though the plunge I gave in the effort was tolerably reassuring.

About ten minutes after Colonel Palmer had left me, the door of the cabin was boisterously flung open, and in walked a short, thick-set, bow-legged, and wall-eyed man; his busy, bustling, bouncing movements, the hard, blunt expression on his face, the square, heavy hands, with red knuckles and red finger-points—bah! this sketching grows fantastic; besides, if the men were no better he was no worse than the average of the leather-headed butchers—

ill-paid, half-educated, and superlatively coarse-fibred—
who operated on the wounded lieges in his Britannic Majesty's cockpits in those times.

"Hallo!" he sung out; "awake at last, my man, are
you? After such a spell of rest, by Jupiter, you should
be able to keep late hours for the rest of your natural days!"

He broke into a loud laugh, that earned him an indig-
nant scowl from the colonel, who towered behind him.

"Well, how do you feel now?"

I told him, and then he felt my pulse, and put his great
hand, that felt like a warm beefsteak on my forehead, and
said to Colonel Palmer:

"He'll do, sir. He wants no physic—rest and time are
the only medicines for him. Are you hungry?"

"Yes," said I, "I am hungry."

He winked at the colonel, and broke into another guffaw.

"Ah!" said he, "we naval men pretty well know what
a privateersman's maw is. However, you must belay your
professional instincts until you are stronger. Hearty eating won't suit a stomach that's been empty nearly a fortnight. The steward shall bring you a basin of broth
presently."

He was going, but the colonel stopped him and whispered a question.

"Why, yes," answered the surgeon loudly, "It'll do him
good, sir. He's had his sleep, and promised well. But he
ought to get shaved first."

And with another noisy laugh he bounced out hurriedly,
leaving a dull flavor of rum in the air, though, mercifully
for me, it was quickly dispelled by the glorious rush of
wind through the port-hole.

"I hope you will not let that man's manner vex you,
Mr. Madison," said the colonel.

I smiled, and begged him to believe that, low as my
nerves were, they were strong enough to support the surgeon's voice, and even his face.

"I whispered to him to tell me," he continued, with a
fatherly kindness in his manner of addressing me, "whether
there would be any indiscretion in my daughter's seeing
you. He said—but of course you heard his answer. Madeline is anxious to thank you for your devoted conduct to

her when the fire broke out in the *Namur*. She has watched by your side very constantly during your illness," he added, with a smile, "and it is reasonable enough that she should wish to be one of the first to congratulate you on the happy turn your malady has taken."

There must have been a wonderful magic in the name of Madeline to stir the blood of a man so prostrated as I was, yet before the colonel had done speaking I felt my face uncomfortably hot.

"It will be a happiness I should not have liked to ask for," said I.

Without another word he left the cabin, and in a few minutes returned, and held open the door to let his daughter enter.

There was a little hesitation in her walk, but none in her manner when she took my hand. She may have rehearsed a speech, she may have schooled herself to meet me calmly; but our glance meeting, the greeting faded upon her lips, the tears gushed into her eyes—we looked at one another without speaking.

The colonel walked to the open port-hole and stood staring out of it with his back upon us.

She was the first to break the silence.

"I have been waiting a long while for this," she whispered. "You have been insensible ever since that dreadful night."

"Yes, your father told me so; but I am sensible enough now, thank God," said I, speaking feebly, but noting her well, and observing that she looked in good health, somewhat pale, indeed, and a trifle dark under the eyes, but cheerful, and gentle, and beautiful. "Next to my having been dead for all this while, the most astonishing part of our adventure, to me, is this meeting of yours with your father. I know by the amazement in my soul, that if I was stronger my demonstrations of wonder would be terrifying."

"We have much to talk about," said she, "but I promised papa that I would only say a few words and go. To-morrow you will be better able to converse."

"I can't let you leave me yet!" I exclaimed, holding her hand. "I know you have nursed me through this illness——" Here I tried to press her hand to my lips. I was too weak to raise it, but she helped me, and so I got the kiss; "and that you nursed me in the boat——"

"Do not speak of that now."

"And I dare not yet trust myself to think of the terrible night you must have passed alone with a raving madman——"

"I ask you not to speak of it now," she pleaded.

Between us I kissed her hand again.

"I should know better how to thank you, and even to talk to you, if, before we say another word, you will renew your permission to me to call you Madeline."

"Do you remember that?" she asked, with just the shadow of one of her coquettish smiles hovering on her lips.

"Indeed I do. I remember calling you Madeline; and telling you," I said, toying with her little hand, but keeping my eyes on her face, "that I loved you"—I said this, squeezing her fingers as tightly as my strength would permit, and speaking in a whisper that obliged her to stoop her head to my face to hear me.

Witness in this the power and the philosophy of impulse. A moment before she entered the room I had no more idea of making my first accost a love-address than I had of standing on my head. One glance of her bland and beautiful eyes awoke with its light the memory of my delirious love-speech in the boat and the kiss she had given me. I could not call her Miss Palmer after I had called her Madeline—I could not renew my claim to call her Madeline without recurring to my love-speech and her kiss. Out of my heart, like an owl out of a hole, flew the awakened memory with a clumsy flapping and a wild gyration.

"I remember calling you Madeline—I remember that and more. One precious word from you now—nay, why not *now?* I shall never be *saner*—and you alone can give me the happiness that makes strength and health. While your hand is in mine, one precious word! Madeline, may I call you by that name?—and say again, as I said when we were alone on the wide midnight sea, and when I believed the hand of death upon me—*I love you!*"

Heavens! when I look back and think of myself lying black-bearded and sallow and gaunt in that bunk, and

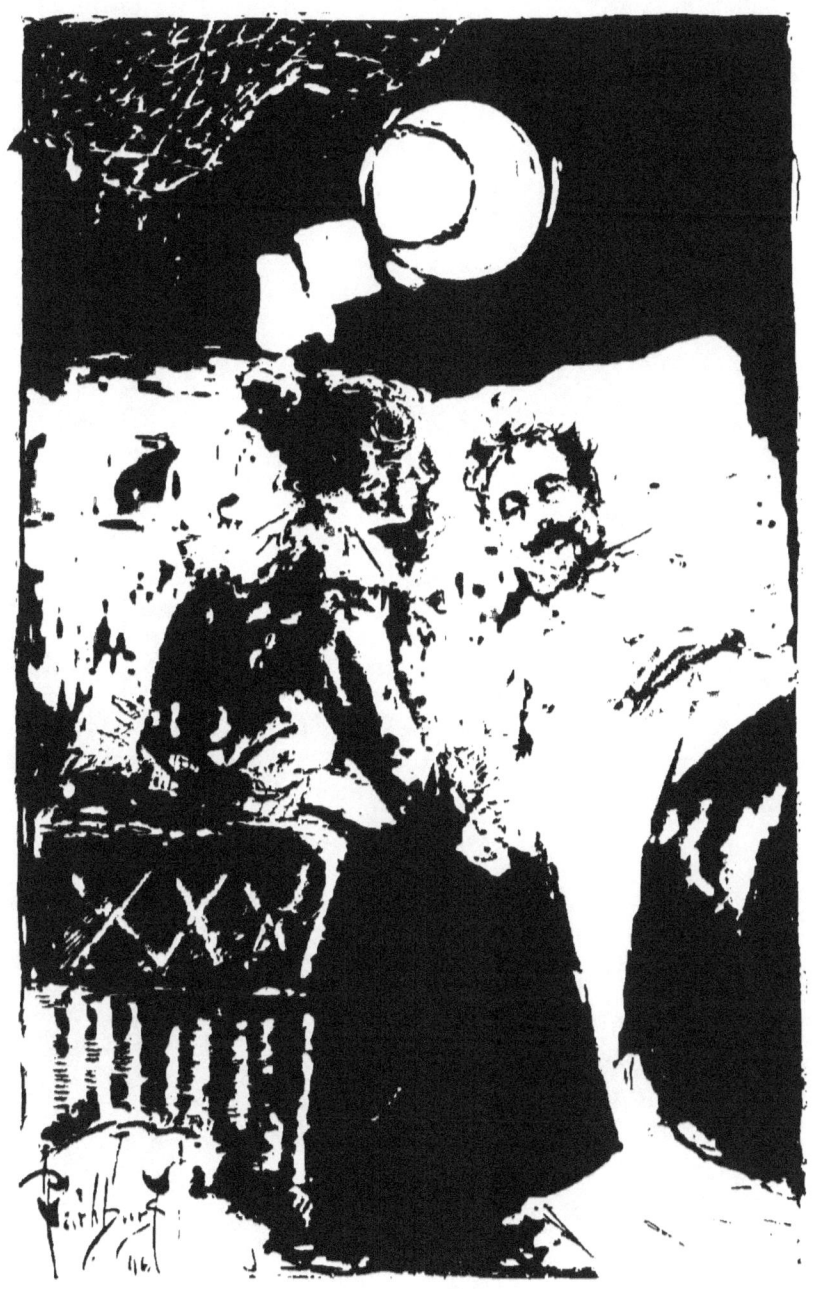

"I have been waiting a long while for this," she whispered.

--*Page 421.*

mouthing in anything but a melodious voice, God knows, the twopenny rant that passion will wag out of the most prosaic tongue, I can only wonder that she looked at me without laughing.

Instead, she drooped her sweet face over mine, and I saw a smile—not derisive, my friend—trembling among the tears which sparkled upon the long lashes.

"I wish to make you happy," said she.

A single word from me would have spoiled it.

The colonel looked around.

"Maddy, my love, this first visit was to be a short one, you know."

"Not for my sake, Colonel Palmer," said I. "You can judge by my voice what it is doing for me."

"It is certainly clearer. Who's there?"

The steward in a camlet jacket, and burlesquing Atlas by carrying his globe under his waistcoat instead of on his shoulders—in all my life I never beheld so orbicular a belly—his nose a fiery pimple, and his left cheek handsomely engraved with a broad scrofulous scar, rolled into the cabin, bearing a basin of broth and a jug of water, in which floated a small squadron of cut-up lemons.

Madeline took the tray from him, propped my head with a pillow, and fed me. No doubt by trying I might have made shift to feed myself; but it was pleasant to be fed by Madeline; and had I been a street artist, I could not have composed my arms in a more helpless attitude upon the coverlet.

"That will do you good, Mr. Madison," said the colonel, watching the operation with great interest.

I dodged the spoon to say, "I am overpowered by your daughter's goodness, sir."

"She is equally obliged to you. Your first thought was for her when the fire broke out, Mr. Madison."

"But nothing that I tried to do or could do," said I, again dodging the spoon that had grown suddenly jerky and sloppy, "could compensate her for the alarm and misery my delirium in the boat——"

But a dexterous pop of the spoon now closed my mouth.

A long night's rest greatly invigorated me: I slept from

eight in the evening until nine in the morning, and when I awoke I sat up in my bunk, and cast my eyes around for my clothes; had I seen them, I should have dressed myself.

My first visitor was the wall-eyed surgeon, who, after telling me I was very much better, prohibited me from rising, so I plumped my head into the pillow again, and lay quiet and full of thought for about half an hour, at the end of which time the steward entered with another dose of the broth I had swallowed on the previous day; and he was no sooner gone than Madeline came in.

I looked, suspecting her father was behind her; but she was alone.

There was a freshness and sweetness of complexion, manner, smile, in this girl that gave the same sort of pleasure to every sense in a man that the fragrance of a flower gives to the sense of smell. The brown, plain, sturdy solid cabin in which I lay took from her presence such a light and perfume as one could only imagine it receiving from the flash of sunshine upon white roses and gleaming lilies.

There are some women who waft a sweet and subtle odor through the air with every wave of the hand, with every movement of the head, with every sweep of the dress. It is not a perfumer's fragrance; it was never contained in a bottle or a powder-box. Whether it is peculiar to certain types of beauty—most auburn-haired girls have it. I have found—whether it is a blessing bestowed by Nature upon such of her creatures as delight her eyes; whether it is peculiar to certain complexions; whether it emanates from sweetness of disposition, or is purely a physical quality, I have never yet had the leisure to very carefully consider; perhaps the subject has been already treated. Anyway, no girl that ever I met had this gift of fragrance in greater perfection than Madeline Palmer. As she leaned her face forward to wish me good-morning, it was like holding a bouquet to my nose.

"I have seen Mr. Cutler" (the surgeon), said she, "and he says you are much better. But you are not to get up, and you will require nursing for some time longer."

So saying she put my broth before me.

"I shan't want to get up," said I, working at the broth,

"while you are within hail, Madeline. Does your father know that I am in love with you, dear?"

"Why, yes—he did not require to be told, but I did tell him," says she quite simply.

"But how could he guess what *my* feelings were when I was without my senses, Madeline?" said I, stirring the broth to cool it.

"Why, Julian, are you sure that all your wits have returned to their home, that you ask me such a silly question? Didn't he see me nursing you, you foolish child? And *do* you suppose that I attended to you like a hired nurse so that no trace of what was in my heart was visible in my face?" and her rich contralto laugh rang like a fine melody through the cabin.

"Deuce take this broth! I have burnt my mouth. Hand me that lemon-water, like a darling. Well, do you know I *am* a fool to ask such a question. But what does he think of it all?"

"He is quite satisfied; besides," said she, fixing her lustrous, honest eyes full on me, "he knows I would accept only the love of a man whom I could trust and be happy with, and when I told him I was silly enough to feel that it would make me unhappy to lose you—*why*, I'm sure I don't know" (a sigh), "he kissed me, and no more was said."

"Madeline," said I, looking over my spoon at her—three spoons in a line!—"I never thought it would come to this. I never dreamt that I should have the luck to win you. I am dreadfully happy, my precious one! Who the deuce am I that such a glorious gift as you should come to me?"

"Eat your broth, and don't disparage yourself. I am tolerably well satisfied with you, so don't try to weaken my good impressions," said she, with one of her sly glances.

"How are the Solomonses?"

"Quite well, and so are all the men. Parell has been very anxious about you, poor fellow, and begged leave to watch by your side; but I did not intend to give up my place. You will be sorry to hear, however, that the whole of the men have been impressed by the captain of this ship, and have become men-of-wars-men."

"Parell too?"

She nodded.

This did vex me very much; so much so that I could not hardly speak for some minutes. But there was no help for it, though I considered that impressment was a barbarous usage to give to shipwrecked men. She watched my face, and changed the subject by telling me that Mr. and Mrs. Solomons had been very kind in their inquiries after me; but it had cost her several long arguments to convince them that I was not actuated by any indifference to the value of their lives because I jumped overboard when I saw the gig adrift. She added that Mr. Solomons was exceedingly mortified and disgusted to find himself carried back to England after the arduous and tragical experiences he had passed through in his effort to reach Jamaica; and her description of the old man's rage with Captain Lomax (who commanded the sloop) when he, the captain, angrily refused to return to Kingston, made me laugh so heartily as to pretty well clear out of my mind the annoyance caused me by the impressment of my men.

She then spoke to me of her father, and, with much concern, of his health, that had at last compelled him to invalid himself and return to England; and gave me the full particulars of their meeting, *her* amazement when he rushed forward to receive her on her being handed over the side of the sloop, and *his* blank bewilderment at finding her—of all places in the world—in a small open boat at sea, when he had not the least doubt but that she was with her aunt in his house near Canterbury.

She also described the night she had passed with me in the boat: how she had had one dreadful struggle with me to prevent me from throwing myself overboard; how we had nearly upset the boat between us in the frantic wrestle; and how nothing saved me—"for you had the strength of a giant, Julian," said she—but my tumbling backward over a thwart and falling into the bottom of the boat; and how she had taken the boat's painter (of course she did not talk of "painters" and "thwarts," but I prefer to tell her story in my own tongue) and secured my arms and legs with it.

"May Heaven bless you for your noble pluck!" I cried, breaking into her story out of the fulness of my heart;

"and for your devotion to a man who has caused you so much misery."

She silenced me by clapping her hand over my mouth, and proceeded to relate how she sat watching all through that terrible night, praying for strength and courage and for the help that came at last.

"I never knew what the horror of loneliness was before," said she. "It is past, and I can speak of it calmly; yet I know that my whole life will be haunted by the memory of that dark sea and the frightful solitude of it, and of your moans and cries as you lay bound, and the burning ship whose image was in my eyes turn them where I would, so that the spectre of it, as it were, was constantly before me, until the sun rose and showed me this ship, like a tiny cloud, a long, long way off."

"It is past, as you say, Madeline; and having given us the love that we have exchanged, let the knowledge that it has left us happier than it found us make us think generously of that bitter time."

I drew her toward me in a passion of love and gratitude —as who will not understand in me that will but consider how I had made this girl suffer; how beautiful had been her courage; how faithful the affection it had been my unexampled fortune to excite in her pure, gentle and heroic heart?—and kissed her with my arm round her neck; and she had barely time to release herself, blushing and somewhat disconcerted by the ardency of my embrace, when her father walked in.

"Now," thought I. "I'll plump my thoughts into him at once. The sooner we clear up and coil down the better."

He shook my hand with great cordiality, and expressed himself heartily rejoiced to observe the marked improvement in my appearance ("Nothing like kissing to clear the complexion," said I to myself); and I glanced at Madeline, who immediately arose and left the cabin, mistaking the look I gave her, as she afterward admitted, as a hint that I wished to speak to her father alone.

I immediately opened upon him.

"Colonel Palmer," said I, "with your permission, I should be glad to have a few words with you on the subject of your daughter."

He smiled, and with much kindness in his voice, said:

"There is no occasion to approach the subject with formality, Madison. I find you and her attached to each other, and I am quite content that it should be so. You have been associated in a singular misfortune, and your devotion in making her the first object of your care, and hers in protecting you against your own violence in the boat, are fitly rewarded by your common affection. You will also see that her name, in consequence of the burning of the *Namur*, is particularly identified with yours—in such a way, indeed, that I will say your wish to make her your wife exactly accords with my desire."

"I am very glad to hear that, colonel, and thank you for your candor. As I have some reason to believe Madeline was not indifferent to me before she and I went adrift in the gig, no excuse can be made for supposing that my good fortune in winning the dear girl is entirely due to our having been alone in an open boat."

"Certainly not," he answered earnestly, and yet amused by my plainness, too; "her happiness is my chief consideration. I know she is attached to you; still it is fit and even honorable that I should give you one of my reasons for readily acquiescing in her engagement to a gentleman who, down to yesterday morning, had never set eyes on me, and whose character I could only admire in Madeline's stories about him."

"Well, we are not arrived in England yet, Colonel Palmer. I hope you'll get to know me better before the old home is hove up."

"Why, I may say I know you very well already," he answered; "but, as you suggest, we have four or five weeks before us in which to improve our knowledge of each other."

"With regard," said I, wishing to heaven I was dressed —for lying in a ship's bunk, habited I knew not in whose bedgown, my manly figure (the best part of me) concealed by the bedclothes, incapable of making a bow, and a little too weak to help out my words by the graces of my hands —I was, as you see, cruelly disadvantaged and made even more insignificant in my own esteem than was fair to my gift of the gab, by the towering, well-bred, well-dressed, dignified colonel—"with regard, colonel, to my position and prospects——"

"We will discuss these subjects another time," said he.

"Still, I should like to say——"

"My dear friend, there is no occasion whatever to discuss your prospects and position with me now, or at any other time, though I give you full permission to talk about them with Madeline as long as you choose. For myself, I will take advantage of this chat, that must be cut short for your health's sake, to tell you that I am a widower, which, however, I believe you know, and that Madeline is my only child. I am afraid, indeed I am sure, my health will oblige me to quit the army, and as you would not have me companionless during the rest of my days, I will merely stipulate, as a return for the gift of my child, that you and she live with me—that is, of course, if you abandon the sea, which I believe," said he with a smile, "she will insist upon your doing. My house at Canterbury would be uninhabitable to me without Madeline, and as I cannot be a mother-in-law, Madison, you will have nothing to fear from my interference in your domestic affairs."

"Your programme, my dear sir, is an overpoweringly liberal one; but such one-sided——"

He would not hear me.

"All that need be said at present has been said," he exclaimed. "We have several weeks before us to discuss any other points which may arise."

I was so far recovered on the fifth day, dating from restoration to consciousness, that the surgeon gave me leave to dress and take the air on deck for a couple of hours. As yet I had seen no other faces than Madeline's and her father's, and Cutler's, so that it was really like rising from the tomb to go upon the breezy brilliant deck of the sloop, and find myself among sailors again.

It was known among the officers that Madeline and I were betrothed—I knew afterward that the colonel had propagated the news—he was mighty sensitive on the subject of that open boat, and reported that his daughter and I were engaged before the *Namur* caught fire—and there·

fore nobody was surprised to find her busily preparing an arm-chair with cushions for my reception, in the shadow of the mizzenmast, round which the cool wind blew refreshingly. Captain Lomax, a stiff-backed old fellow, greeted me with a pompous shake of the hand and a gruff congratulation on my recovery, and I was very civilly received by the first lieutenant, a young and delicate-looking man, a thorough gentleman, between whom and myself there sprung up during the voyage a friendship that terminated only with his death a few years ago.

I had scarcely seated myself, and Madeline had got the pillow at the back of my head in a ship-shape posture, when Mr. and Mrs. Solomons came up to me. I know not from what part of the deck they emerged; I had not noticed them when I arrived.

Mr. Solomons shook my hand rather slowly, but his wife was somewhat demonstrative.

"Bless my heart!" cried she, "I thought to find you skin and bone. To hear Miss Palmer talk, one would have swore you had fallen into a mere skiliton. Well, and how are you, mister? You don't ask how I am after the fright of the fire and your leaving of us to swim to your lady, not caring, I dare say, if Mr. Solomons and me became cinders so long as the *sweets* was saved. But I bear no malice, sir, and now that it's all over, I'm not for saying you didn't show a proper feeling in jumping overboard after Miss Palmer. It's more than Jonas would have done for me."

"I'm glad to see you pretty middling," said Jonas. "I can't pretend *I'm* the thing, whatever my looks may thay. Fancy my being taken back to England again, after being almost within sight of Jamaica, and suffering from pirates and fire! And my goods! I suppose you know I was only insured for two-thirds."

"I am sorry to hear that," said I; "but two-thirds are better than nothing, and you'd have got nothing had the Yankees walked off with the *Namur*."

"There's Parell trying to catch your eye, Julian," whispered Madeline.

I looked, and saw the honest fellow upon the booms forward, figged out in man-of-wars-man's rig. He grinned and touched his hat, and pointed significantly to his garb, and would probably have expressed his feelings in further dumb-show, had not the captain slewed round in his walk along the quarter-deck, whereupon Parell toppled off the booms and vanished.

Finding me indisposed to talk, Mr. Solomons left me after a further bewailment of his misfortune in being forced back to England, and was followed by his wife; and with Madeline at my side, and her father within earshot behind us, reading a book, I lay back on my pillow, surveying with a sailor's delight, and with every sense in me exquisitely relishing, the sunshine and the breeze, the beautiful spectacle of the British sloop's decks holystoned unto the very complexion of snow, blackened at regular distances with the bronze-colored shadows of the heavy guns, with the brass-work flashing out red beams as the vessel rolled with a stately movement over the long swell that underran the blue and frothing surface of the windy, sparkling sea; while the forecastle was colored with the uniforms of groups of soldiers, and the heavy, wide-spread shrouds, soaring like bars of iron from the white line of the hammock-cloths, led the eye to the proud and swelling canvas, which floated like piles of vapor against the heavenly blue of the sky.

I turned my eyes from the soft white of the towering sails to Madeline. She was looking at me.

"Already there is a little color in your cheeks, Julian," said she. "Your heart is with ships, I fear—there is no room for me."

"My heart is full of you, Maddy. Don't question *that* truth, even in play. If my eyes are brightened by the sight of this ship, it is because she is showing by her pace that her instincts are sound, and that *we* have her sympathy. Every minute of this sailing carries us nearer home; and home means so much to me *now*, dearest, that this speeding vessel delights me with a significance no other ship ever yet yielded, and the very song of the foam as it rushes past has such a meaning in my ear as any man would think me moonstruck to find in it."

"I believe you, dear; but don't ever let your poetical fancies make you forget or regret your promise to me that you will give up the sea for good as a profession when we are married."

"Trust me," said I.   And will any bluejacket doubt that of all the promises a sailor could be warranted to keep, the promise of never going to sea again would be the very easiest?

THE END.

www.ingramcontent.com/pod-product-compliance
Lightning Source LLC
Chambersburg PA
CBHW030941110726
47900CB00004B/1076